Quintin
Jardine

THURSDAY
LEGENDS

headline

First published in 2000
by HEADLINE PUBLISHING GROUP

First published in paperback in 2001
by HEADLINE PUBLISHING GROUP

First published in this paperback edition in 2011
by HEADLINE PUBLISHING GROUP

4

Cataloguing in Publication Data is available from the British Library

ISBN 978 0 7553 5867 0

Typeset in Electra by Avon DataSet Ltd,
Bidford-on-Avon, Warwickshire

Printed and bound in Great Britain by Clays Ltd, St Ives plc

Headline's policy is to use papers that are natural, renewable and
recyclable products and made from wood grown in sustainable forests.
The logging and manufacturing processes are expected to conform
to the environmental regulations of the country of origin.

HEADLINE PUBLISHING GROUP
An Hachette UK Company
338 Euston Road
London NW1 3BH

www.headline.co.uk
www.hachette.co.uk

Quintin Jardine gave up the life of a political spin doctor for the more morally acceptable world of murder and mayhem. Happily married, he hides from critics and creditors in secret locations in Scotland and Spain, but can be tracked down through his website: www.quintinjardine.com.

Praise for Quintin Jardine's novels:

'Very engaging as well as ingenious, and the unravelling of the mystery is excellently done . . . Very enjoyable' Allan Massie, *Scotsman*

'Remarkably assured . . . a *tour de force*' *New York Times*

'Quintin Jardine . . . a magnificent crime writer' Michael Dobbs

'Jardine manages to combine the picturesque with the thrilling and the dreamlike with the coldly rational' *Glasgow Herald*

'Engrossing, believable characters . . . It all adds up to a very good read' *Edinburgh Evening News*

'[Quintin Jardine] sells more crime fiction in Scotland than John Grisham and people queue around the block to buy his latest book' *The Australian*

'There is a whole world here, the tense narratives all come to the boil at the same time in a spectacular climax' *Shots* magazine

'A triumph. I am first in the queue for the next one' *Scotland on Sunday*

'A complex story combined with robust characterisation; a murder/mystery novel of our time that will keep you hooked to the very last page' *The Scots Magazine*

My thanks go to:

Professor Sir James Armour
Scott Wilson and David Johnston, Radio Forth, Edinburgh
Jack Arrundale, for a flash of inspiration

One

'Dammit, Diddler, you were a bit late there!'

He glowered up from the floor for a second or two, then grasped the outstretched arm and pulled himself to his feet.

'Sorry, Neil,' the sweating man acknowledged, gasping for breath. 'I guess I'm just not as quick as I used to be, only my brain doesn't know it yet.'

'Hmph! From what I've heard you never were as quick as you used to be. Ah, 'scuse me.' McIlhenney shoved him to one side and lunged towards the yellow football as it flew towards him, trapping it close to the wall of the sports hall, and holding off the recovered Diddler easily, as he looked inside.

'Right, son!' The call came from Andrew John, surging towards goal at a rate just slightly above his normal walking pace. He rolled the ball into the path of the bearded banker, whose side-footed shot beat the token efforts of Mitchell Laidlaw, taking a breather in goal.

The sturdy lawyer restarted the game quickly, throwing the ball out to the halfway line. The hall was big enough to accommodate full-sized tennis and basketball courts – although it was rarely used for either of those sports – with a raised spectator gallery along one side and two glazed panels set in the other, allowing a view from the Centre's cafeteria.

'Pick him up, Neil,' John called out, as Benny Crossley cut towards the wing. As McIlhenney sprinted across the court, it occurred to him that his team-mate was at least five yards closer to their opponent, but he let it pass. Benny was no flying winger and was usually predictable, and so he knew that he would turn back on to his right foot for a strike. His block was timed almost perfectly; he won possession as he surged through the tackle, sending the other man spinning, and headed back towards Mitch Laidlaw.

As he moved past the wall panels, he was aware of his son, Spencer watching him, his face almost pressed to the glass.

'Get stuck in, man!' In spite of his exertion, he smiled at the bellow, knowing that it was directed at the unfortunate Crossley, rather than at him. Stewart Rees appointed himself captain of every team in which he played, laying down the law to his colleagues at a volume which rose steadily as the hour progressed; to be fair to him, he did his waning best to set an example. As Rees rushed towards him, Neil played the ball to himself off the wall, avoided his lunge, then set himself to shoot.

For a moment he thought that he had been hit by a car. As Benny Crossley had found a few moments earlier, so the fabric-covered ball seemed to become an immovable object as his right foot slammed against it. His momentum sent him flying forwards, off his feet, twisting instinctively in mid-air to land safely on the hard floor.

There was no apology from Bob Skinner, only the sight, for McIlhenney, of a retreating back, a long pass being rolled wide of Grant Rock into the path of a grateful Diddler, and an awkward mishit poke which eluded the flapping left hand of David McPhail, the duty goal-keeper.

He picked himself up, moved down, unmarked, to the halfway line and signalled to McPhail to throw the ball out quickly, but just as his team-mate saw his waving gesture, the heavy glazed door to the hall swung open; their equivalent of the referee's whistle. Full-time: the Diddler's goal had been the winner.

Bob Skinner came towards him, smiling, hand outstretched. Edinburgh's Deputy Chief Constable was wearing a Motherwell Football Club replica shirt; he was perspiring, but not as heavily as the others, and his breathing was steady. 'We did you at the end there, fella, did we not?' he chuckled, as McIlhenney accepted the handshake.

'Maybe, but what a goal to win by. A bloody toe-poke, and sclaffed at that.'

Skinner beamed at him. 'For the Diddler, that was the equivalent of a thirty-yarder into the top corner. All we can do here is our best – whatever that might be.'

Two

'Just one, as usual, then I'll need to get the kids home.' McIlhenney dropped a five-pound note into the kitty jar, a half-pint tumbler which sat on the bar. 'Make it a pint of lime and soda, please, Lesley, and a couple of Cokes for Lauren and Spence.'

'I don't remember ever seeing you have a beer in here,' the bar stewardess ventured as she filled a tumbler from the dispenser. 'Don't you drink at all?'

He shook his head. 'Not any more, other than the odd glass of wine with a meal. That's a luxury I can't afford, not with those two.' He carried the Cokes, and two packets of cheese and onion crisps across to a table in a big bay window, where his two children were seated, playing a board game.

'I won't be long,' he said.

Lauren looked up at him; her brown hair was still damp from her swim in the Sports Centre pool. 'No,' she agreed, severely. 'Spence mustn't be up too late.'

He was frowning as he joined his football friends. Bob Skinner had noticed the exchange. 'She giving you a hard time?' he asked; quietly, so that none of the others could overhear.

'Not really. She thinks of herself as a sort of surrogate mother sometimes, that's all.'

5

'Aye, well. She would, wouldn't she, the poor wee lass. She's cut out for the role though.'

Neil looked up at the ceiling and laughed. 'Indeed she is; but what a teacher she had.' And then the lump was in his throat again. Still, it came without warning; usually when he was alone, but sometimes, in the company of very close friends, people who had known them both. At first it had overwhelmed him; there had been a couple of occasions on which he, big, hard, Detective Sergeant McIlhenney, had shocked his companions, by dissolving, quietly, and without warning, into tears. Now though, he was able to master it, to control the sudden surge of grief before it got to the stage of public embarrassment.

Skinner, having been down that road himself, knew when to say nothing. Eventually his companion dragged his gaze away from the ceiling and looked around the bar of the small North Berwick hotel. The usual Thursday-night banter was picking up pace; the evening's game was being replayed, notably by the Diddler, who was well into the second talk-through of his winning goal.

'Bloody toe-poke!' McIlhenney grunted.

'Skilfully guided away from the keeper, I'd put it,' the scorer insisted.

'Aye, you would. Now move a couple of your bellies along that bench and give me a bit more space.'

More seat-room materialised for the big policeman; he leaned back and let the chat continue, listening as it widened out, from the Diddler's never-ending store of gossip about the lives of Edinburgh's elite to take in the week's televised sport, which had highlighted the closely fought conclusion of the battle for the English Premiership.

He looked around his new friends, realising again that he, still in his thirties, was the youngest member by several years:

Stewart Rees: as quiet and friendly in the bar as he was loud and hectoring during their game, a chemical engineer and head of production in one of Scotland's smaller breweries.

Andrew John: an assistant general manager with the Bank of Scotland, possessed of a laconic sense of humour, and excellent footballing skills, even if these had been a shade eroded by ageing joints and an expanding waistline.

Benny Crossley: one of four squad members from Gullane, a man of few words, but every one of them weighed and sensible, with the precision of someone who made his living as a builder of quality houses.

Mitchell Laidlaw: managing partner of Edinburgh's biggest legal firm, a legendarily successful litigator of formidable determination, which he brought with him on to the football courts.

Grant Rock: the man about town – in this case, North Berwick – of the group, local Government official, Rotarian, and like many of the group, a golf addict.

David McPhail: a successful advertising executive, his roots, like those of Skinner, were in the west of Scotland, but he had transplanted successfully to Gullane more than a quarter of a century earlier.

Spike Thomson: in a sense the odd man out, the senior disc

7

jockey on one of Edinburgh's commercial radio stations, the nearest thing North Berwick had to a resident celebrity.

Howard Shearer: the Diddler – McIlhenney had often wondered where the nickname had come from, but had still to ask – the most enthusiastic, if least skilful member of the squad. A high-ranking fund manager, whose secretary arranged his diary to ensure that he was always at home for the five-a-sides on Thursday evenings.

And on his right, Bob Skinner: boss, friend, benefactor, whatever . . . the man who had brought him into the squad, at a moment in his life when he had needed it most, killer squash player, karate maestro, golfing shark, but rough-and-ready footballer.

'The real high point of my night, though,' – the Diddler's high-pitched voice broke into his thoughts – 'was shifting big McIlhenney here off his feet.'

'Ye'd better bring some extra padding next Thursday night then,' Grant Rock told him. 'The sergeant's going to be looking for you.'

'No need for padding, Grock,' said Neil. 'Not with an arse like he's got.' He drained his glass and stood up, waving across to Lauren and Spencer. 'Got to get these two home, lads. See you next week, and thanks once again.'

'He's a good bloke, that,' said Andrew John, moving his seat closer to Skinner, as the door of the lounge bar closed on the father and his children. 'You did well bringing him along here. Hellish shame about his wife.'

'Aye, it was that.'

'How long's it been now?'

The big policeman scratched his chin. 'Let's see. He's been with us for five months, since January, and she died about six weeks before that. Yes, just over six months.'

'What was she like?'

'Olive? Simply the best, like the song goes. A tremendous woman.'

'Cancer, was it?'

'Aye, in the lung. She gave it her best – they both did – but it was too much for her.'

'And how's he settled down since? It must be difficult for him with the two kids.' The banker paused. 'Of course, you would know that, wouldn't you?'

'That was a long time ago, Andrew, and I was only left with one – wee Alexis. You could argue that having the kids will have helped ease the loss, in a way, but it's not true. It occupies you, but you never forget; not for a second.'

'This boys' club of ours must help him too.'

'It does. Gets him out of the house once a week at least.'

'He's not a bad footballer.'

'Better than that. He played Junior, for Armadale, before he joined the force.'

Andrew John's eyes lit up with a new respect. 'Why d'you not bring him before, then?'

Skinner grinned. 'Never thought to. Anyway, he'd gone to seed. Since Olive fell ill he's lost a couple of stone at least, and got himself back into training. His father died of a heart attack a few years back; it's all the more important to Neil now that he stays fit, for the kids' sake if nothing else.'

'Talking about kids,' John continued, 'how's your new one getting on?'

The grin turned into a beam of delight. 'Our wee Seonaid? She's absolutely great. Sleeps all the time, unlike her brother.'

'And Sarah? How's she?'

'Loving it. For the first time in her adult life, she isn't thinking about work at all. The day after Jazz was born she insisted on being picked up from the Simpson to go to a crime scene. Not this time, though. Motherhood's finally got to her . . . thank Christ for it too, with three on our hands.'

The banker nodded. 'Of course, your adopted lad. He's settled in.'

'Fine, thanks. He's an intense wee boy, very clever; to see Jazz and him together you'd never know that the two lads weren't natural brothers.'

'Your older daughter, how's she?' John grinned. 'Might as well ask about them all,' he added.

'You'd be better asking Mitch Laidlaw about our Alexis. He sees more of her than I do; ten hours a day in the office at least. She's living in Leith now; nice wee flat she has.'

'No romantic entanglements?'

Skinner looked at him and sighed. 'I never ask, my friend. I never ask.'

Three

Andy Martin stared at the wall. He had become familiar with it since moving into his town house in Dean Village. One or two friends and colleagues had asked him why he had bothered, since his new home was less than half a mile from his Haymarket flat; but those who really knew him needed no explanation.

Since his break-up with Alexis Skinner, the detective had been focused almost completely on his work. Sure, there had been the odd night out with his team. Sure, Bob Skinner and he remained as close as ever, and if Andy suspected that his friend was secretly pleased that the engagement was over, neither of them ever discussed the matter. Sure, on more than the odd occasion, he had dipped into his old address book for dates and the odd one-night stand, instant flings which more than anything else had served to show him that he had virtually no friends outside the job. And even they, or most of them, tended to be just that bit more distant now that he was high on the ladder, and on the fast track for Chief Officer rank.

He had never thought of himself as a lonely man; now he realised that, before Alex, he had been just that and, without her, he was once more. The Haymarket place had become intolerable for him. The part of him which mourned her loss saw her in every shadow; but the part of him, the stronger part, which

11

could never forgive her, could never forget either, never forget the shock of discovery or the choking, blinding, deafening rage which had overwhelmed him when she had told him, in that damned house, that she had aborted their child.

So he had sold it, to a young, upwardly mobile couple, as they had been once, and had moved into the modern three-storey end-terraced house with a living room on the first floor, a small balcony overlooking the Water of Leith, and with at least one bedroom more than he felt he would ever need. And the wall had become his companion.

Of itself, it was nondescript, without windows, painted in a pale pastel colour, a barrier between his solitude and the busy life of his neighbour, a pleasant, middle-aged woman with a senior job in the Scottish Government administration, two daughters and a Vauxhall. But since moving in he had hung it, and most of the others, with his collection of paintings by contemporary Scottish artists, acquired over the years from galleries and sale rooms in and around Edinburgh, and on one or two occasions, from exhibitions at the city's respected College of Art.

Each one had for him its own personality, and said different things to him. They were his friends, although they were still acclimatising, blending into their new surroundings as he moved them around, finding the arrangement within the room's differing patterns of light which showed all of them at their best. 'Maybe now they're right,' he said aloud as he sat in his armchair and gazed at them. It occurred to him that he had not felt as peaceful for months, not for more than a year, when all was serene with Alex and him, before their conflicts had arisen; yes, maybe now they were indeed right.

The ladies liked them too; he grinned at the recollection of his pleasure at showing his collection to someone for the first time. Sally, an old flame, had been bowled over by them – literally, as it had turned out – only a week before. So had Jane, a month or so back. Karen Neville had never seen them, though, and he doubted if she ever would. The others were . . . safe; Karen was trouble waiting to happen.

He and the spectacular sergeant had come together in the wake of violence and of two vastly different personal tragedies. They had both meant it to be a one-off, but there had been a repeat performance, then another, and another, until finally he had allowed the relationship simply to fade away, before it reached the point at which he would have been obliged to move her out of her job in his office. He liked Karen, and undoubtedly they were great together under the duvet, but the memory of Bob Skinner's indiscretion with a member of his personal staff was too strong for him to push away.

The paintings seemed to gaze back at him; he grinned as he wondered if they might be trying to tell him that they needed a wider audience. There was the girl next door for a start. Rhian Lewis, the older of the civil servant's two daughters, was a medical student at Edinburgh University; she was tall, blonde and athletic, and she had that look in her eye. He had seen her running at weekends; once, indeed, he had overtaken her on the Water of Leith Walkway, and they had jogged back to Dean Village together.

Yes, Rhian would like the collection, he was sure; and the paintings would like her. But . . . the girl next door? Fraught with problems, he told himself at once. And she was so young; younger even than Alex. He'd be a real idiot to make the same mistake twice, would he not?

'Yes,' he said aloud. 'A real idiot. No more twenty-anythings

13

for you, Martin. You'll play in your own age group from now on. Starting this weekend.' He pushed himself up from the chair, picked up his cordless phone from the coffee table, and dialled a number, plucked from his memory. 'Hi, Janey,' he began, as the call was answered. 'Andy. You doing anything tomorrow night?'

'Washing my hair,' the woman on the other end of the line said, tersely.

'On a Saturday night? That sounds like the bum's rush to me.'

'You could be right there, Mr Martin. Tell you what, why don't you ask that Sindy Doll I saw you with in George Street last weekend?' The line went dead.

'Ouch,' he said, staring at his handset. 'You get away with nothing in this bloody city, do you?' he complained to the paintings. He started to dial Sally's number, but paused. Two weeks on the trot could lead to a third, and so on; these things could come about almost by default. He and Sal had been live-ins a few years before and, nice as she was, he didn't fancy going there again.

'Bugger,' he swore, and began to whistle tunelessly, an old Sinatra song about lonely Saturday nights. And then he had a brainwave. He picked up his Filofax and flicked through its telephone listings, until he got to the 'Macs' section. He found the number at once; scrawled in over the one which it had replaced, and dialled it up.

The ringing tone sounded four times, before it was replaced by a honey voice. 'Yes?' she said, cautiously; the tone of a woman living alone. 'Ruthie?' he asked, although he knew that it was her. Ruth McConnell, Bob Skinner's secretary, a Kim Basinger lookalike with legs which went all the way up to her bum; gorgeous and currently single.

'Yes?'

'It's Andy Martin. Listen, this is a bit of a cheek, so don't worry about blowing me out, but I'm at a bit of a loose end tomorrow night. I wondered if you fancied dinner.'

Only three or four seconds, but seeming twice as much. 'Andy, I'd love to,' she answered. He could tell from her tone that she meant it; he could tell also what she would say next. 'But I can't. I'm going through to Ayr tomorrow to visit my Mum. She's just come out of hospital.'

This is not your day, son, he thought. 'Ahh, too bad,' he said. Still, there had been that hint. 'How about next weekend?'

'That would be great.'

'Okay then. I'll see you sometime and you can give me directions for picking you up.'

'In that new car of yours? Yes, please.' The anonymous Mondeo had gone as part of his personal make-over, to be replaced by a sleek red MGF.

He ended the call feeling vaguely uncomfortable, as if he had boxed himself into something, slipped the small telephone into the pocket of his shirt, picked up that afternoon's *Evening News* and wandered out on to his second-storey balcony. The summer sunshine hit the river side of the house in the late afternoon and evening; next door, in the garden below, Rhian, in tee-shirt and shorts, was sprawled in a chair, reading. His appearance through the patio door caught the corner of her eye. She looked up and smiled at him. 'Hello, Andy,' she called up. 'Nice night, isn't it.'

'Sure is.'

She put down her book and stood up, long tanned legs unfolding. 'Social life let you down?' she asked.

He laughed. 'That's perceptive of you.'

'Mine too. Take me for a pint then; a walk up to Rutland Place would be nice.'

15

Andy Martin was rarely caught off guard. 'I suppose it would,' he said, cagily. 'Ahh, what the hell, you're on. See you outside.'

The girl ran indoors and he was turning too, when a figure appeared on the next balcony. It was Juliet Lewis, Rhian's mother, dark-haired, shorter than her daughter, but trim nonetheless; he was quietly relieved to see that she was smiling. 'I should apologise for my forward daughter,' she said. 'She didn't give you much chance to say "no", did she?'

The burly, fair-haired policeman grinned back. 'She's right; it's a nice evening for a walk.'

'She's in safe hands, at least.'

That's all you know, lady, Martin thought.

'Let me be as forward as Rhian now,' she went on. 'It's Margot's eighteenth tomorrow, and I'm having a party for her. If the weather holds we're going to have a barbecue; if not, I'm cooking indoors. If you're free would you like to join us, rather than sit up there exposed to the cooking smells and annoyed by the music?'

Jesus, he thought once more, *when you least expect it . . .*

'That's very thoughtful of you, Juliet,' he said. 'Yes, thank you, I'd like that.'

'Good. Around seven, then.'

Rhian was waiting when he stepped outside into the street. She had changed from her shorts into black jeans, but was still in the loose-fitting tee-shirt which she had worn in the garden. 'Hi,' she said, brightly. 'We could always run to the pub, I suppose, but we'd hum a bit when we got there.'

'No,' he said, looking at her and reminding himself again just how young she was. 'Let's just stick to walking pace.' They set off out along the narrow street which led out of their part of Dean Village and on up towards the city's West End.

'You're a police officer, aren't you?' the girl asked, as they crested the rise into Belford Road.

'That's right.'

'So my mum was right. She thought that's what you were.'

'She's well informed. I try to keep home and work separated.'

'Mum's usually in the know about the police; it's part of her job. What do you do? You're not in Special Branch, are you?'

He laughed; her brightness was infectious, just like Alex. 'If I was, I couldn't tell you.'

'Or if you did, you'd have to kill me?'

'It's not that cloak and dagger, honest. But no, I'm not in SB; not any more.'

'So what are you? An Inspector, like that man in the TV series?'

'No. Actually I'm a Chief Superintendent. Detective.'

She looked at him, apparently impressed. 'God. You must be older than you look. That's next to Chief Constable, isn't it?'

It was his turn to laugh. 'Not quite. I'm Head of CID. There are three people between me and Sir James.'

'Sir James? I thought that man Skinner was the Chief Constable.'

'Bob? He hates even the notion that he might be one day. No, he's the Deputy Chief. I report to him.'

'I see.' She looked him in the eye. 'So how old are you, then?'

'What do you think?'

'Thirty-five.' She was only a year out.

'That's near enough. How about you?'

'What do you think?'

'Looking at your mother, you can't be much older than Margot.'

'Thank you, sir, on her behalf. I'm twenty-one; Mum's forty-four.'

'As if I'd ask you that.'

'You just did, Mr Detective, by implication.'

'So what about your father?' Martin asked.

'Gone to the other side,' she answered.

'Ahh, I'm sorry to hear that. What was it?'

'Latent homosexuality – he's living in Brighton with a chiropractor. He's a gynaecologist; I think it got to him eventually.'

Andy gasped, stopped in his tracks and looked at the girl. 'Christ,' he murmured, slowly. 'What age were you when you were born?'

'About fifteen, my mother says.'

Which makes us the same age, he thought.

'And you're going to be a doctor, like your father?'

'Yes, but not quite like him. I think I'll specialise in proctology. Better career prospects, I reckon; after all, everyone's got one of them.'

'You're quite a girl,' he said, once he had stopped laughing. 'Do you always go on like that to guys you've just met?'

'Only if I think they're up for it. Besides, we haven't just met. We've been neighbours for months, and we're jogging companions.'

'Running, my dear,' he corrected her. 'That might have been jogging for you, but it was running for me.'

'Don't kid me, Mr Andy. You might be a bit of a bufty, but you're as fit as a fiddle; you were scarcely breathing hard that day you caught me up. And I saw you out cutting your grass last week. There's not an ounce of fat on you.'

He tapped his head. 'It's accumulating up here, though. Come on, enough about me. How long till you graduate?'

Rhian's stories of Edinburgh University School of Medicine lasted the rest of the way up to their destination. As they approached the two-storey pub in Rutland Place, across the street from the Caledonian Hotel's grand main entrance, they could see that the usual Friday night throng had developed inside. There seemed to be space available, but the doors were guarded by squat men in dark blazers. 'Damn,' Rhian muttered. 'Do you think we're going to get in?'

'Stick with me, kid.' Martin led her towards the main door; one of the bouncers stepped across his path.

'Full up, pal,' said the man, with the air of one who did not expect debate.

Andy looked him in the eye. 'Police.'

The bouncer stood his ground. 'Aye, that'll be right.'

'Aye, it will,' the detective agreed, speaking barely above a whisper. 'I can see in there well enough. They can take two more, so do it the easy way. Believe me, you don't want to try the other.'

The man considered his options for a few seconds, then stepped aside.

'Can you talk your way in anywhere?' Rhian asked.

'Not the New Club. In the bomber jacket and the chinos that would be a bit difficult; but pubs, sure. The guy on the door just fancied himself a bit; on an authority trip, that was all. Now what'll you have?'

Indeed, the bar was not quite as busy as it had appeared from the street; they found a couple of high stools by a shelf along the back wall and perched themselves there. 'Right,' said the girl briskly, after a first sip at her pint of lager. 'You've had my story, now let's have the rest of yours. What happened to Mrs Martin?'

He wrinkled his nose. 'That role is currently vacant.'

'Indeed? Then you're holding regular auditions, from what I've seen on Sunday mornings. But you don't seem like the playboy type.'

'I like to think I am; don't shatter my illusions, please.'

She hesitated. 'Ahh, I see. "Shut up, Rhian, and mind your own business." Okay. Sorry.'

He shook his head. 'No, no. I didn't mean to cut you off. The fact is I lived with someone until about nine months ago. She was going to be Mrs Martin, but it didn't work out.'

'What happened?'

He shrugged his shoulders. 'She caught me screwing someone else,' he said, quickly.

Rhian gazed at him. 'If you'd looked me in the eye when you said that, I'd have believed you. It's just as well you're a copper, not a crook, for you're a really lousy liar. Let me guess. It was the other way around?'

His vivid green eyes fixed on hers. 'Nothing to do with it,' he murmured. 'There were things we couldn't reconcile, that's all.'

'And you've been blaming yourself ever since?'

His gaze did not waver. 'No. I'm not that much of a romantic. I've been blaming her ever since, and I always will.' He drank deeply from his beer. 'It's time to move on, though. I know that.'

She drained her glass and looked at him. 'Fine. Let's go to Mather's.'

'You're a bit of a girl, aren't you?' he chuckled.

'No,' she shot back. 'I'm a lot of a girl. Just what you need, officer; you've been brooding for long enough.'

They eased their way out of No 1 Rutland Place and crossed Shandwick Place to Mather's, different surroundings altogether, more of a traditional man's pub. Initially, he felt uneasy about taking her in there, but he had learned enough about his enticing neighbour to know that the alternative was to let her go in alone.

The two fair-haired newcomers drew a few looks as they stepped into the dull, high-ceilinged bar, and a few smirks too. As they walked up to the bar, Andy looked around slowly and deliberately, and recognised half a dozen faces; men-about-town of a certain sort whose paths had crossed his, over the years. Two of them nodded in his direction, the others looked away, arousing his suspicions at once. He made a mental note to pass their names on to Dan Pringle, the divisional CID Commander for the area.

'Eighty shilling?' Rhian's question reclaimed his attention. She had a five-pound note in her hand.

'Yes,' he answered, glancing across at the barman, 'but you can put that away. I don't accept drinks from members of the public . . . and certainly not from students.'

'Hey, I'm a liberated lady.'

'Maybe, among your generation; to me you're just a kid.' As he passed his own fiver across the bar, she frowned and looked away from him; the first crack in the shell of her self-confidence. 'Hey, I'm sorry,' he offered at once. 'I didn't mean to put you down.'

That look in her eye came back at once. 'Don't flatter yourself. You haven't picked me up yet.'

They stood at the bar in Mather's while they drank and talked. Rhian tried to prise police stories from him, but he steered her gently on to other topics. For all her assurance, she was too young for many of the tales that he could have told her. Fleetingly, the thought came to him that if he did, the temptation which she represented would go away at once, but he rejected it.

Instead he talked all the usual small-talk, music and movies, all the harmless stuff which he used to build a screen between his companion of that and other evenings, and the real Andy Martin. Only Alex knew him, and she had rejected him; it would be a long time before that man came back. Better casual affairs and loneliness than experience that pain again.

'Am I starting to bore you?'

He blinked and smiled at her. 'Far from it. I was somewhere else for a minute, that's all.'

'No, you weren't. You were in Bert's Bar all along, and my glass is empty . . . but it's okay, I think it's time to go. A pint and two halves is enough for me.'

He finished his third and last pint of the evening, and they left their third and last port of call, walking out into William Street, into the still, mild summer evening. She took his arm as they turned into Walker Street, quiet at ten-thirty, even on a Friday night. She was silent on the walk home, along Rothesay Terrace and down the hill towards the Village.

'Thanks, Andy,' she said at last, as they arrived at their neighbouring homes. 'This has been nice . . . even though you have been blocking me out all night.'

'I haven't,' he lied; she was perceptive, this girl-woman.

'Oh no? Ask me in for a coffee, then.'

He looked at her, temptation on legs, in the gloaming of the June Scottish night, lit by the blue glow of the northern sky. And then he thought of the paintings. 'Do it,' they seemed to whisper to him.

'Okay,' he said. 'Would you like a coffee?'

She seemed to twinkle at him. 'Well, just the one . . .'

He unlocked the door and stood aside for her; the houses in the terrace were identical in lay-out, so she headed straight upstairs to the first-floor living area, above the garage, laundry and store rooms. He flicked a light switch and watched her as she stopped, as soon as she reached the top and stepped into the living room.

She was gazing at the paintings as he stepped up beside her. 'How do you like my friends?' he asked.

'Andy, they're really lovely. Are they all originals?'

'Sshh,' he said. 'You'll offend them, just by asking that. Stay here and get to know them; I'll give you the guided tour once I've made the coffee.'

He stepped through to his kitchen and made a pot of filter coffee, then brought two mugs back to the living room. 'I guessed no sugar, okay?' She nodded as he set them on a low table. She was standing by the cabinet which held his hi-fi equipment, holding a CD case.

'Who's this?' she asked.

'Mary Coughlan. Irish; what you'd call a torch singer.' He picked up a remote, and pressed a button; a few seconds later a smoky voice sang out into the room. 'Right,' he said. 'Andy's art gallery.'

He walked her round the pictures one by one, explaining the history of each and of its artist. The collection was a blend of modern and traditional art, oils, acrylics and watercolours. 'They're all beautifully framed,' Rhian commented.

'Most of them have been reframed to my taste. I can't paint for toffee, so I sort of see that as my stamp on them. Many artists will put any old cheap crap around their work, so there's plenty of scope.'

She turned to face him. 'So this is the man you've been keeping back from me all night. A secret lover of art and very sexy music.' She put her arms around his neck, and kissed him.

'Hey, hey,' he whispered. 'Rhian, this isn't . . .'

She pressed herself against him, provocatively; he was rock hard, no disguising it. 'Mmm, like I said. Not an ounce of fat.'

'Come on kid,' he protested. 'Don't rush your fences.'

'Ahh,' she said, softly. 'So the fence is there to be cleared . . .'

'I didn't say that. Look, you're very attractive, and all that—'

'But I'm only a kid. Don't kid yourself. You wouldn't be the first man I've slept with . . .' She paused. '. . . or the oldest either.'

'No, but I'll be the first who lived next door.'

'What's that got to do with it?'

'Ask your mother.'

'It's got nothing to do with her. Andy, I'm past my twenty-first. I'm a grown woman . . . damn well-grown at that. Now shut up and kiss me again.'

Oh shit! said the voice in his head. His hands, which had been together loosely at the small of her back, slid up under her tee-shirt. Her skin felt silky and smooth, as he drew her close against him. Her lips were soft, her full breasts loose, her nipples hard, rubbing against him even through two layers of clothing.

He gave himself up to Trouble, and in that moment didn't give a damn.

Andy Martin had long held the irrational theory that telephones are a malevolent life form, one which chooses to interfere in its creators' business at pivotal moments, out of sheer cussedness. But when his cordless phone rang out, he thought that, for once, it might have decided to save him from himself.

He extricated himself from Rhian's embrace. 'That's probably your mother,' he muttered, as he picked up the handset.

The girl shook her head. 'Probably one of your Saturday night women,' she laughed.

'Martin,' he said into the receiver. It was a woman, but one of the Monday-to-Friday sort. 'Andy,' a familiar voice replied. 'It's Maggie.'

He looked back across the room and put a finger to his lips. 'Yes, Chief Inspector Rose. What can I do for you?'

'I'm at a crime scene: a suspicious death.' He heard her pause. 'No, let's forget police-speak, a murder. I'm sorry to bother you with it, but I guessed you'd want to know about it.'

'Why's that?'

'Because it's a right nasty one . . . and because the victim's an ex-copper.'

'Shit. Where are you?'

'North Berwick. A house called Shell Cottage, in Forth Street.'

'I'll be with you inside an hour. I've had a couple of beers so I'll need to round up a driver.'

He ended the call and looked at Rhian. 'Sorry, love. It's the job; I've got to go and look at a body. You see? You don't really want to be involved with me: this sort of thing happens all the time.'

'Don't worry. It happens to doctors too. Can I come with you?'

'No way,' he answered, firmly.

'Then I'll wait for you.'

'No.' He frowned at her. 'Seriously, you should go next door. If for no other reason than that this could take all night.'

'Ahh,' she sighed. 'In that case, I'll see you tomorrow. I could take all night too.'

Four

Once upon a time, North Berwick was known as 'the Biarritz of the North' – a term coined, or so Detective Chief Inspector Maggie Rose had always thought, by someone who had never been to Biarritz.

In fact the term came from the Victorian era, when the small East Lothian town had been the main weekend and holiday resort for the merchants and financiers of Edinburgh. Even at the dawn of the new millennium, its beach-front area was little changed from those days, although the modern community which unrolled from it had become a dormitory for the city and an internationally recognised golf resort.

Maggie Rose was standing at the front door of Shell Cottage, between two uniformed constables, when Karen Neville's Nova drew up behind the ambulance and police vehicles, and the Head of CID stepped out of the front passenger seat. It was forty minutes past midnight. 'Hi, Mags,' he said. 'Sorry I didn't get here sooner, but I decided to ask Karen to bring me out, rather than take a patrol car off duty. ACC Elder gets humpty about that sort of thing.'

He saw her eyes narrow slightly and guessed that the DCI thought that they had been together when she had called. 'It took her a few minutes to get down to pick me up,' he added, pointedly.

Maggie flushed slightly, embarrassed that her mind had been read. 'Hello, Karen,' she said, as the detective sergeant approached.

'The man inside,' Martin asked. 'Who is he?'

'His name's Smith, Alexander Smith, and he's the only elector registered at this address. There are some papers inside which told us that he was a police pensioner . . .' She paused as she saw the DCS's face change. 'You know him?'

'Of course I do. I succeeded him as Head of Special Branch. Don't you remember him? Alec Smith; he was a DCI when he chucked it, like you are now. Jesus, this puts a bit of a spin on it. Have you told the Boss?'

Red hair swung as she shook her head. 'No. I left that to your judgement.'

'Let's have a look at him first. Are Dorward's scene-of-crime team here yet?'

'No, but the MO's here. He's still inside. I came out for a breath of fresh air. I'd have opened the windows, but I didn't want to touch anything unnecessarily before Arthur's lot have been over the place.'

'Lead on then.' Rose nodded and turned to go back indoors. Before following, Martin paused for a moment to look at Shell Cottage. It was a two-storey house, built of locally quarried red stone, with a pan-tiled roof, and separated from the pavement by a narrow garden. Taller buildings stood on either side, their walls adjoining.

'I never knew Alec lived here,' he murmured, absent-mindedly, then stepped past the uniforms and into the house, into a narrow hall, Neville at his heels.

Maggie Rose was waiting for them at the foot of a flight of stairs. 'He's up there, in his living room, or study. Whatever you want to call it.' She looked at the Sergeant. 'Karen, it's bad,' she warned.

'I've seen death before,' the other woman replied.

'Not like this, you haven't.' Rose led the way upstairs. 'Trust Brian Mackie to be on holiday when we get one like this,' she murmured. Four doors opened off the upper landing, which was lit by a skylight. Three led to rooms overlooking Forth Street; a tall man in his early thirties stood outside the other.

'This is Dr Brown, the duty medical examiner,' said Maggie. 'Dr Brown; DCS Martin and Detective Sergeant Neville.'

The Head of CID shook hands with the doctor, noting that the fresh round face was a touch pale. 'Pleased to meet you. Been doing this job for long?'

'No,' the doctor replied. 'I've only just joined your panel.' Martin caught a light Irish accent. 'Right now, I'm having second thoughts.'

'Have you got a cause of death for us?'

'Heart failure, technically; it'll take a bloody good pathologist to tell you what the principal contributory cause was.'

'Fortunately,' muttered Martin, 'I know one . . . if I can persuade her to do it, that is. Let's have a look at poor old Alec, then.' He pointed to the fourth door. 'In here, yes?'

'Yes.'

He opened it, took a pace inside, then hesitated, as if he had been checked physically by the smell which greeted him, a mix of blood, faeces and something else. Experienced policemen will assert that terror leaves a stench of its own; Martin caught it as he looked at the man into whose shoes he had once stepped.

Alec Smith's study stretched the full width of the house. The wall facing the door seemed to be one big, north-facing window. Although its slatted, vertical blinds were closed, Andy could still see in his mind's eye the view outside; the wide beach, the harbour, the old granary, now converted into desirable apartments, Craigleith, the Bass Rock, and in the distance the outline of the East Neuk of Fife.

The lights were off, but the glow of the northern sky in midsummer was strong enough to imbue the blinds with a pale blue pallor, and to let the Head of CID, and Karen Neville as she stepped in behind him, see the full horror of what was in the room. A beam split the high ceiling, from gable to gable. Into its side, at around the mid-way point a big hook was sunk. Alec Smith was suspended from it, on the tips of his toes; he hung by his wrists, which were lashed together with blue nylon rope, tied in turn to the hook. He was naked and his back was to the door, his head lolling forward on his chest.

'Outside, Karen.' Martin's voice was little more than a whisper, but she obeyed, without argument. As the door closed again, he crossed the room and adjusted one of the blinds, allowing a little more light in. Then he took a deep breath and turned to take his first close look.

For all his experience, for all that he had seen, his stomach heaved instinctively, and he felt a beery taste in his mouth; he was glad that he had not switched on the array of lights which were positioned along the beam. Smith had been disembowelled; his entrails had burst from a diagonal rip across his abdomen and hung down to the floor. Andy clenched his teeth and looked closer. Behind the exposed, tumbling intestine, he could see that the man's genitals were badly burned, as were his nipples, and large areas of his chest and lower torso. A blowlamp, he guessed. Steeling himself once more, he raised the man's heavy head and looked at his face. The mouth was gagged with several strips of broad, brown gaffer tape, and the eyes had been burned out.

Quickly he let go and stepped back; as he did so the body swung round on the hook, and more of its guts slipped out. His hands felt odd, he realised. He looked at them and saw that they were covered in blood. Of course, Alec Smith had been grey, yet the body's scalp was dark, soaked, and matted. Suddenly, he felt himself going; he turned to the blind, and closed it once more then stepped back out of the room.

Dr Brown looked at him, knowingly. He held up his hands. 'Bathroom?' he asked. DCI Rose pointed to the middle of the three doors on the other side of the landing.

A couple of minutes later he was back on the landing, knowing from the bathroom mirror that he was as pale as the medical examiner. 'Was he dead before all that stuff was done?' he asked.

'I very much doubt it,' the young doctor replied. 'There was a lot of bleeding from the abdominal tear, but less than you'd expect from the head wound. I'd say he was tortured, then battered about the head to finish him off . . . except he may actually have been dead by then.'

'Did you see any obvious weapons?' he asked Maggie.

'Not in there. I didn't look. I didn't spend any more time in there than I had to.'

'No more did I. Any signs of forced entry?'

'None at all that I could see.'

He turned back to Dr Brown. 'Time of death?'

The Irishman looked at his watch. 'Three to four hours ago.'

'When was he found?'

'Around a quarter to eleven,' Rose answered. 'A guy who knew him came out of the Auld Hoose along the road, and saw Smith's dog barking at the door, wanting in. The animal roams about North Berwick apparently. The bloke rang the bell, then tried the door and found that it was unlocked. There was a light on in the cellar; he called down there and upstairs, got no answer and went to investigate.

'When he found him he ran back to the Auld Hoose and raised the alarm. He also had a very large drink.'

'How did you get here so fast?'

'I was working late in Haddington, reviewing the paperwork on a real bugger of a retail fraud case. I'm proposing to start door-to-door enquiries first thing in the morning, and to try to track down everyone else who was in the Auld Hoose during the evening, to see if any of them saw someone arriving or leaving Shell Cottage.'

The Head of CID nodded assent. 'Do it; but you know already what we're likely to find. Sod all. This was savagery, yet it was cold and premeditated too; it was planned. Whoever set this up is unlikely to have arrived or to have stepped back out into Forth Street, right in front of a casual passer-by.'

'They wouldn't need to, sir,' said the DCI. 'There's a door to the front garden, and steps down to the beach.'

As she spoke, they heard footfalls on the staircase, and the red head of Detective Inspector Arthur Dorward appeared in view.

'You ready for us, sir?' he asked Martin.

'Aye, sure. I hope you're ready for this.' He nodded to Brown. 'Thanks, Doctor. Welcome to the force. Mags, about the Boss, I'll tell him in the morning.' He glanced at Neville.

'Sergeant, let's get back up town.'

He followed his assistant back into the street and into her car. He asked her to roll down the windows. 'I need to get the stench out of my nostrils,' he explained, although she understood. Without warning, he shuddered, violently. 'Jesus, Karen. I knew that man in there.'

'Let's get out of here,' she said, pressing buttons to lower the front windows and let the cool night air flood into the car.

He thought of home, and imagined how it would be if, after all, Rhian was looking out for his return, her mind on unfinished business. He looked across to the driver's seat, a question showing through the strain in his eyes.

She nodded. 'Yes. My place.'

Five

It did not occur to either of them that they might make love. They simply lay together in the king-size, pine-framed bed, Karen dozing on her side with an arm thrown across his chest, Martin, on his back, stared at the ceiling, seeing nothing but the gutted, tortured body of Alec Smith.

He tried to chase the vision, but it would not go away. He closed his eyes, but still he saw the shape swinging gently in the half-light as he touched it. The smell stayed in his nostrils, unforgettable for that time at least. The Chief Superintendent was renowned for his calmness – privately he prided himself on it – yet he feared that somewhere, a scream, his own, lurked close.

He looked at Karen, thankful for his instinctive refusal to allow her further into the room, guessing what Maggie Rose might make of it, but not caring. He reached out and traced his finger very softly round the line of her jaw, and was glad when she smiled, fitting his touch into whatever dream she was having.

Knowing that sleep was not an option for him, he fought the horror by becoming a policeman, rather than a terrified on-looker. As a rule, he tried at every crime scene to imagine it being committed; coldly, dispassionately, professionally. That skill, learned from Bob Skinner, had been beyond him in the house at North Berwick, but there, in the night, he used it as a weapon.

Alec Smith had been a big man and had been known, even in the no-nonsense world of the police, as a hard man, too. Yet he had been subdued, stripped, strung up and gutted like a fish. How many people had it taken to do that, for God's sake?

In his mind's eye he looked around the big room, developing the subconscious snapshot which his mind had taken at the scene, using his photographic memory to recall details. The first and strangest thing: there had been no signs of a struggle. The room, expensively furnished, everything in its place. Smith's clothes; not thrown about the room, but laid across an armchair, almost neatly. A bottle of whisky, on a table positioned against the wall on the right of the room. A telescope, on a stand in front of the window to the left. And another stand, a tripod, unadorned. Beside it on Smith's desk, which he had set under the window, a big, expensive-looking 35mm camera, and a video camera. Shit! The table, the table. Two glasses. For the killers? Or one for the victim and an expected guest? Or left from earlier – Smith and someone else altogether? *Prints will tell, Andy, prints will tell.* Back to the desk! The cameras. A hobby? Photographing, filming shipping moving in and out of the Firth of Forth? Or put to more recent use? No! No?

Martin lifted Karen's arm gently from his chest and laid it on the duvet, then slipped quietly out of bed. Naked, he crossed the hall to the living room of the small flat and picked up the phone, which lay on the sideboard. He dialled 192, asked for and was given Alec Smith's telephone number, then called Shell Cottage.

Detective Inspector Dorward answered. 'Arthur. DCS Martin here. There are two cameras on the victim's desk, yes? Still and video?'

'Yes, sir.'

'I want to see what's in them, if anything. If there's a film in the camera, have your photographer develop it. If there's a cassette in the camcorder, play it back. Just in case, you understand.'

'Of course, Boss.' Dorward sounded slightly wounded.

'Sorry, Arthur. I'm sure you'd have done that anyway.'

'It's the thought that counts, sir,' the mollified Inspector chuckled. 'Hang on and I'll look at the video camera now.' There was a pause; in the background, Martin heard mechanical sounds. 'There's a tape in it, sir.' said Dorward. 'I'll run a few frames back and replay it through the viewfinder.'

'Okay.' He waited, taking care to stand clear of the yellow light which flooded through the living room window from the street lamp outside. As he stood there, Karen's arms wound around his waist. He felt her heavy breasts press against his back as she hugged him.

'I'm cold,' she murmured. He gasped as her hands slid downwards, and reached down to stop her.

'Shh.' He waved the phone in the air, so that she could see he was on a call. As he did so, he heard a cry from the handset.

'Fuckin' hell!'

'What is it, Arthur?' he asked, although, instinctively, he knew.

'It's him, sir; Smith. The camera's right in his face. He's alive and he's got no eyes!'

'Oh Christ.' Karen was standing beside him now, looking at him anxiously. 'Maggie will have the mobile HQ unit on its way to the scene, if it isn't there yet. Lock that camera in there. I'll be back out in the morning, probably with the big man.' He glanced at his wrist, but his watch was on Karen's bedside table. 'What time is it?'

'Quarter past five.'

'Okay. I'll be there before nine.'

He hung up and ushered Karen back through towards the bedroom. 'They filmed him,' he told her. 'The bastards filmed him as they killed him.'

'God! Why?'

'Crazy people don't need reasons,' he answered as they slid back into bed. 'That's the only thing I know for sure about this enquiry; we're looking for a complete fucking lunatic.'

Not for the first time that night, he shuddered; he felt himself on the verge of losing it again. She held him, drawing him to her. 'Andy,' she whispered. 'Shut it out. Shut it out.'

He tried; they both tried, in the only way they could.

Six

The Head of CID slipped quietly out of his sergeant's flat, just off Nicolson Street, at five minutes before seven a.m., after a wholly sleepless night. He left a note on the kitchen table; 'Thanks for the safe haven. Call you later.'

He took a taxi back to Dean Village, where he shaved, showered, and changed clothes. The thought of breakfast did not cross his mind for an instant; instead, when he was ready, he stepped into his garage through the internal door, opened the up-and-over and backed his red MGF into the street. As he jumped out to close the garage, the front door of the house next door opened, and Rhian stepped out, in her running gear; sweatshirt, shorts and trainers.

'Morning,' she said, young and bright; making him feel just the opposite. 'Busy night?'

'God awful,' he grunted.

She looked genuinely concerned for him. 'Oh, poor love. Never mind, tonight will be better, I promise.'

From out of nowhere he was swamped by a pang of guilt. If that phone hadn't rung . . . If Alec Smith hadn't been . . .

'About tonight, Rhian. I've got a major investigation under way. If we get a quick result, I could be involved in interviews and so on. Say to Juliet that I might not make it, will you?'

She raised herself quickly up on her toes and kissed him, lightly. For an irrational moment he wondered if she would catch a scent of Karen lingering on him. 'Let's just hope you do. Okay?'

She was infectious; for the first time since midnight, he smiled.

'If I can, I will. Promise.' He slid back into the tight cockpit of the sports car, set his cellphone into the hands-free holder and drove off.

The streets of Edinburgh were relatively traffic-free at that time of a Saturday morning, an hour or more before the first of the shoppers would head for Princes Street. He waited until he had cleared Milton Link and turned on to the A1 before he dialled up Bob Skinner's number.

Sarah picked up the phone on the first ring; in the background he could hear a baby's cry. 'Morning,' he said, 'I'm sorry it's so early, but I've held off as long as I could. Hope I didn't wake Seonaid.'

'No,' the gentle American voice replied. 'She's hungry, that's all. Here, speak to Bob while I plug her in.'

There was a pause, then Skinner's voice sounded from the car-phone's tiny speaker. 'Andy, what's this I've just heard on the radio about a suspicious death in North Berwick?'

'Last night. I got the call at midnight; I've been to the scene already. I'm on my way back out now.'

'Eh? Can't the Division handle it?'

'The Division is handling it, but I have to be seen up front on this one.'

'What's so special then?'

'The victim: ex-Special Branch. It's Alec Smith.'

The DCC's gasp seemed to fill the car. 'You're joking. What does the "suspicious" mean?'

'He was tortured and, or, battered to death. I've seen them after a month in the water, or burned to a crisp, but this is the worst ever.'

'I'm glad you didn't call me out, then. I can live without that.'

Martin chuckled, grimly; he knew that Skinner had come to detest bloody crime scenes. 'Don't be so glad. The guys who did it made a movie of the event and left it behind for us.'

'Some Saturday morning viewing, that.'

'Aye. *Dead and Kicking*, you might call it. Listen, Bob, we'll need the best available pathologist for the post-mortem. Professor Hutchison's on holiday, so . . .'

Skinner anticipated his friend's question. 'Sarah,' he called across the room, 'Andy's got a hot one. He's asking if you'll do it.'

In the background, he heard her reply. 'For him, okay. I guess he means today.'

'When, Andy?'

'Soonest.'

'Okay,' Bob told him. 'Book it for midday. But call in for me on your way past. I'm coming along there with you. My Saturday foursome's just become a three-ball.'

Seven

Bob Skinner shook his head as he stood in front of the house in which Alec Smith had been butchered. A small group of journalists and photographers stood on the other side of Forth Street. 'You know, Andy,' he said to his friend, 'I must be losing my touch. I'm a copper, I should know things. On top of that, I like to think of myself as part of the East Lothian community.

'Yet Alec Smith, an old acquaintance and colleague, lived in the middle of it for . . . What? Three years, you say . . . and I hadn't a bloody clue.'

The Head of CID glanced at him, surprised. 'I didn't know that you and DCI Smith were pals.'

'Well, sort of. He played football with my Thursday night crowd for a few years, before his right knee gave out on him. He lived out Pencaitland way in those days, with his wife. She did a runner, though, a year or two before Alec packed it in. Went off with a plumber, or something. I guess he must have moved here in the aftermath of that.' Skinner paused. 'There were a couple of kids, son and daughter; they'll probably be well into their twenties by now. He lived here alone, you said?'

'That's what the voters' register says. We'll see if the door-to-door tells us anything about lady-friends – not that this murder was your run-of-the-mill domestic.'

'No indeed. Better let me see where it happened, then.'

Another uniformed constable, so new in the force that Skinner did not know his name, was stationed at Alec Smith's front door. He stood to attention as the unmistakable figure of the Deputy Chief Constable approached. 'Morning, son,' Skinner said. 'This is a bloody awful job you've got: doorkeeper at a slaughterhouse. But I've done it in my time and so has Mr Martin. Just don't let the gawpers gather at the gate. The same goes for the press over there, and for the television crews when they turn up . . . as they will. This is a narrow street and the traffic comes whizzing round that bend sometimes. We don't want another body here, if we can help it.'

'Very good, sir,' the young man replied, put at his ease by the DCC's friendly manner.

'Who's in there?' asked Martin.

'No one, sir. They're all round the corner at the mobile HQ.'

'Then why's the front door open?'

'Inspector Dorward said to leave it open, sir. To blow the smell out of the place, he said.' Skinner winced, as he stood aside to let Martin lead the way into the house.

Even after Dorward's crew of technicians had done their work, the room upstairs still seemed relatively tidy, considering what had happened there. The slatted blinds were closed once more, but the windows had been opened and they were blowing up and rattling on the through draught. In spite of it all, some of the stench from the night before crept back into the Head of CID's nostrils.

Smith's clothes still lay across the armchair, where the killers had left them. A blue velvet drape still lay across the back of the sofa. The whisky bottle and glasses were still on the table, and the telescope was still on its stand, although they had all been dusted with white fingerprint powder. The cameras were gone from the desk, though, taken away by Dorward as ordered. The only other thing missing from the room since Martin's first visit was the body itself.

Its presence lingered nonetheless. Directly below the hook in the roof beam from which it had hung, a dark stain disfigured the beige carpet.

'The room was like this when you were here last night?' Skinner asked.

'Yes. No signs of a struggle, as you can see. I guess that Alec must have known the guys.'

'Guys?'

'There must have been more than one, surely, to handle a big, rough bloke like him with no obvious effort.'

'Aye, but you said that he was battered about the head. Couldn't a single bloke have slugged him from behind, knocked him unconscious, then strung him up?'

Martin frowned. 'He could have, but if it had happened that way, then almost certainly there would have been blood spattered around. I don't see any. I reckon he must have been overpowered, and that would have taken more than one guy.'

The older man grunted. 'Knowing Alec Smith, age fifty plus or not, I can promise you that it would have taken a small fucking army to overpower him, strip him, tie him and hoist him up on that hook. No, somehow or other he must have been knocked unconscious.'

'That's something else Sarah will have to tell us, then,' the DCS murmured.

Skinner looked around the room: at the expensive, carefully-placed furniture, television and video; the tall lamp in the far corner; the lap-top computer on the desk; the bookshelves built in to the back wall; the ornaments on the desk, table and wide window sills.

'Yes, very neat, very tidy was the late Mr Smith.'

'Was he like that as a copper too?'

'He sure was. A very capable detective. Of the last generation rather than ours, I'd say, but a meticulous, careful operator.'

'Why did he pack it in?'

'Money, he said. He took the pension and went to a bloody good private-sector job. I guess too that he knew he had peaked at DCI.'

'But if he was as capable as all that . . . .?'

'I wouldn't have promoted him, though, and that was that. Horses for courses, Andy.' He turned, separated two slats of the billowing blinds and peered out on to the beach. 'Come on. Let's see what's happening in the mobile HQ.'

They left the house, turned right and walked a few yards along the narrow pavement, to the point at which Forth Street opened out on to a broad green area which fringed the beach. The mobile operations centre, a high articulated vehicle, had been stationed on a narrow strip of roadway.

'The weekend sailors will love that,' said Skinner. 'The thing's blocking the launching ramp for dinghies.'

'Tough,' Martin grunted. 'For today they can use the other one, over by the harbour.'

A dozen police officers, some in uniform, some CID, were milling around on the street outside. 'What the hell's this?' the Head of CID asked a blue-jacketed sergeant. 'A crowd scene?'

'We're just waiting for Stevie Steele to allocate addresses for the house-to-house, sir,' the man answered.

'When did DCI Rose leave?'

'She's still here, sir.'

46

'Jesus, she's been here all night.' Martin climbed the three steps to the door of the mobile HQ and stepped inside.

The van had no windows; even at around nine on a summer morning, it was lit by neon tubes. The light they cast made Maggie Rose look chalk white and emphasised the dark circles under her eyes. She and Detective Sergeant Stevie Steele looked up as the two Commanders entered; they had been leaning over a small desk making up interview sheets into bundles, and attaching them to blue plastic clipboards.

In another corner of the mobile office, Inspector Arthur Dorward and his assistant, Detective Constable Sharma Ghosh, stopped work on their report and stood up.

'Relax, for God's sake,' said Skinner. 'Sit down, Arthur, sit down all of you. Mags, you look puggled. Finish what you and Stevie are doing, give me a run-down, then get off home.'

The DCI frowned. 'I was planning to grab a couple of hours' sleep in the North Berwick office, then get back to look at the results of the door-to-door interviews.'

'You can't drive yourself that hard, for God's sake. If Brian Mackie was here, you and he would be splitting rest periods.'

'But he isn't here, boss. Look, is this a divisional investigation or are you and the DCS taking over command?'

Skinner raised a hand. 'Hey, I'm little more than a spectator here.'

Beside him, Martin shook his head. 'You're in charge, Maggie. We're here to offer help and support, that's all.'

'Very good. Then I'll do it my way.' She smiled; a thin, half-grin. 'Besides, I've co-opted my husband. Mario says that since his weekend's buggered anyway, he might as well come out to help.'

'That's not inappropriate,' Skinner murmured. 'He's Head of

Special Branch, the job Alec Smith used to hold. We may need his input from that angle before we're done with this one. Okay, you two finish up, while we talk to Arthur.'

He and the Head of CID crossed the room to Dorward's table, which was larger than the other. It was piled with papers and notebooks, and in one corner sat a television monitor, connected by a cable to the dead man's video camcorder.

'What did you find in the house, Arthur, apart from that?' asked Martin.

'Nothing I didn't expect to find, sir. Loads of the victim's fingerprints . . . we lifted them for comparison before the body was taken away. There was another set too, all over the house, but I wouldn't get too excited about that. They were at their heaviest in the kitchen, and we found some on the Domestos and Flash bottles and on the Hoover, so my best guess is that he had a cleaning lady.

'The front door was unlocked, and there was a good palm print on the outside. I'm guessing that it might belong to the guy who found the body.'

'Whatever happened to Alec's dog?' The Head of CID murmured.

'It's at North Berwick nick,' Rose answered. 'When we arrived it wouldn't let anyone near the body, so a couple of the boys took it away.'

'I'm sure we'll find it a home,' said Skinner. 'What else, Arthur? No obvious weapon?'

'Only one, sir. There were plenty of objects that could have been used to inflict the head injuries – there's a whole range of tools down in the cellar – but they were all absolutely clean. We did find a blowlamp, down there, but there's no chance that it was the one used on Mr Smith. It was stone cold and it had a full gas-fuel cylinder. The cellar door was open too, sir. It was very slightly ajar and there were footprints leading to the ladder that goes down to the beach. It looks as if that was the perpetrators' exit route, right enough.'

'I take it we're—'

Rose read the DCC's mind. 'I had uniformed officers begin a search of the beach as soon as the light was good enough, Boss. The trouble is, though, there was a high tide last night, so if the killer did discard something, he probably threw it in the sea. It might be difficult to definitely tie anything we do find to Alec's house.'

Skinner grunted agreement, then looked at the scene-of-crime inspector. 'Write up a provisional report as quick as you can, Arthur, and let DCI Rose have it.'

Martin pointed to the camcorder. 'You played that back yet?'

'No fear, sir,' said the Inspector. 'That quick look through the viewfinder was bad enough; I've got no wish to see it blown up. I'll only watch that again if you order me to.' He paused. 'Oh, by the way, there was nothing on the still camera, other than pictures of wee boats sailing in the bay out there. I've told the lab to print them anyway, but there'll be bugger all in them for us.'

Skinner tapped the pile of papers on the desk. 'There may well turn out to be bugger all in these too, but we'll still have to go through them.' He turned back to Rose. 'This is something your old man could do, Mags. If Alec hung on to any of his old SB contacts, Mario might recognise the names.

'Arthur, you'd better go for a walk on the beach now. DC Ghosh, you're excused too. The front-line officers are going to have to look at that video now.' Dorward and his assistant looked at him gratefully and headed for the exit. For a moment, Skinner thought about following them; instead he switched on the monitor, picked up the camera, found the 'play' button and pressed it. Rose and Steele crossed the room to stand between him and Martin.

For around ten seconds a scrambled image appeared on the screen, until it turned to black. Then gradually a picture appeared; Alec Smith, hanging, naked, from his hook. His mouth was covered by the brown tape, but his eyes were blazing with fury. Skinner used the remote to turn up the volume, and the room filled with the sound of the trussed-up ex-detective cursing unintelligibly behind his gag.

'No blood,' said Martin. 'The head wounds aren't there at this stage. So how the hell did they get him up there?'

Suddenly, out of shot, they heard a click, followed by a soft hiss, which mutated into a husky roar. As they watched the look in Smith's eyes changed from belligerence to terror, as the nozzle of a blowtorch appeared in shot.

'The same person.' Rose's voice was almost matter-of-fact, but a slight tremor gave away her horror. 'It's the same person holding both the camera and the blowlamp.'

'Look for shadows,' Martin whispered. 'Anything, any sign of anyone else coming into shot.'

But all they saw was a hand in a red rubber glove, with a long cuff, gripping the roaring torch as it moved towards Smith. 'How tall do you think the person holding the . . .' Steele began, but his voice tailed into a gasp as the white flame seared against the helpless man's penis. The twisting victim's eyes bulged, threatening to come out of their sockets. His shouts became an awful, muffled scream. His back arched as he tried to pull away from his torturer, but he had been hauled so high up on his toes that he was completely helpless.

'Try not to look at him,' Skinner barked, urgently. 'Look for the killer instead, listen for him; any sights, any sounds that aren't Alec.'

He tried to follow his own instruction, but it was virtually impossible in the face of the most awful horror movie any of them had ever seen. The blowlamp did its work on the genitals, charring, scorching, blackening, then moved up to the nipples, the heat melting Smith's chest hair. Finally, Skinner looked away as the lance of flame aimed for the eyes. He tried to shut his ears against the awful noise. There was a scrambling beside him, Stevie Steele heading for the door, yet no other sound, only Smith's choking screams, rising to a crescendo, then gradually, weakening and fading. Then the roar of the flame dying away, replaced by another noise, a rending, tearing sound, and by one last muted howl from the doomed man on the hook.

At last, Andy Martin pressed the remote to switch off the monitor. 'My God,' Maggie Rose whispered, over and over again, until a sob forced its way out. Skinner leaned on the table, grasping it almost hard enough to splinter the wood, staring once again at the empty screen, listening to the hum as the camcorder continued to replay its tape.

'No other officer is to see that recording,' he ordered. 'Chief Inspector, I want you to take personal charge of it. Take it back to Haddington when next you go there, and lock it in your safe.' He turned to look at her with a gleam in his eyes that she would rather not have seen. Two people had; they were both dead.

'When we arrest this beast, Maggie,' he said, grinding the words through his teeth, 'you'll have to interview him. But not alone; with Brian, if he's back by then. If not, with someone other than one of us, someone who hasn't seen that. I don't know about you, but if I caught the people who did that right now, I'd have a hell of a job keeping my hands off them . . . I don't think I'd even try.'

Martin's voice broke the silence. 'There was nothing on it to help us catch them,' he muttered. 'Mags was right, the killer held the camera while he did that stuff to Alec. There's not a sign of anyone, not a sound . . . and no indication that there was more than one person in the room.'

'What a terrible person, though.' The DCC looked at his colleagues, as Stevie Steele came back into the van, sheepishly. 'What the hell could Alec Smith have done for someone to do that to him?'

'Like I said to Karen,' Andy Martin murmured, 'that sort of mind doesn't necessarily need to have a reason.'

'Don't say that, for fuck's sake!' said Skinner, urgently. 'If that's true, he might do it again!

'I don't need to say it, people, but I will. All the stops! Maggie, what are you doing about the press?'

The DCI glanced at her watch. 'Alan Royston's issuing a statement around now, up in Edinburgh. I'll take a press conference once we've done the initial door-to-door sweep.'

'Where?'

'Here, if can find a suitable room. I'll try the community centre.'

'Fine. You get that rest now; if you want me to see the press with you, you only have to ask. But first of all, I've got to tell the Chief Constable what's happened here.'

He caught her glance. 'Don't worry,' he reassured her. 'I'll tell him he's not seeing the video. Jimmy's made a good recovery from his heart attack, but I doubt if he's up to that.'

Eight

When Skinner and Martin arrived back at the DCC's house in Gullane, Alex's car was parked in the driveway. Sarah's was gone.

'Ah, my kid's here,' said Bob. 'I guess she's child-minding while her step-mother works on poor old Smith. Good, that means I can go and see Jimmy, rather than just phoning him.' As he opened the door of the sports car, Bob looked at his friend. 'I'll bet you haven't had any breakfast. Come on in and have something, a coffee at the very least.'

Andy shook his head. 'Thanks, but . . .'

'Listen, son. The two of you can't avoid each other for the rest of your lives. You'll be sad bastards if you try; now come in, and no "buts".'

Reluctantly, Martin climbed out of the MGF and followed Skinner into the house.

Alex was in the kitchen, emptying the dishwasher, with her back to the door. 'In you go,' said Bob, in a whisper, then turned towards the stairs, leaving him there.

For a second, he thought about turning to go, but instead he stepped into the kitchen.

She heard his footfall and straightened up, a plate in her hand. 'Hi, P—' she began, her voice tailing off as she glanced over her shoulder. If anything she was even more beautiful than he remembered her. He guessed that she had lost a little weight; her face seemed more angular, her eyes deeper.

'Hello, Alex,' he said. 'How are you doing?'

She turned to face him, with an awkward smile which eased the tension. 'Oh, fine. Still stuck in the bloody kitchen, as you can see. You?'

'Okay. Getting on with the job.'

'I heard you've moved house. Dean Village, eh? Going upmarket.'

He shrugged, self-consciously. 'It was just something I felt I had to do. It's better for the collection,' he added lamely.

'Collection?' She smiled, her eyes sparkling – a flash of the old Alex. 'Ah, you mean the paintings . . .'

'Call in and see them if you like.'

'What? As in "Come up and see my etchings?" We're a bit beyond that.'

A corner of his mouth flickered; more of a grimace than a grin. 'Maybe . . . But come up anyway. I've missed you.'

For a second, her eyebrows came together in a frown, a trademark gesture inherited from her father. 'I've missed you too. And I'm sorry for the way I behaved . . . for everything but one thing, that is,' she slipped in, quickly. 'But when we split up, Andy, we didn't just burn the bridges between us – we mined the bloody river.'

'Maybe, but we were friends before we were ever lovers. Can't we get back to that?'

'I didn't think you wanted that.'

'Come on, I hated what you did, but I couldn't hate you, not ever. Anyway, I was way in the wrong too, before then.'

She picked at her fingernails. 'Friends then?' she murmured.

'Okay. I'll come and see the paintings in your new house. I'll call first, of course, just in case you've got company. As a matter of fact, a colleague of mine called me last night to say she saw you muscling your way into One Rutland Place with a very tasty blonde.'

He flushed; there was no way of preventing it. 'The girl next door,' he protested.

'That'll be handy for you.' She smiled again, wickedly. 'Does Karen Neville know about her?' His mouth dropped open as he stared at her, as the smile became a laugh. 'Andy, this is a village. When will you realise that?'

'Hey, since when did you listen to gossip? Karen's an off-duty pal, that's all. Just like McGuire and Maggie.'

'Maybe, but my friend Liz's taxi-driver brother didn't pick you up from their house at ten o'clock on a Sunday morning a couple of months back.'

It was his turn to laugh. 'Jesus wept, woman, I'm supposed to be the detective in this relationship.' The last word hung awkwardly in the air for a few seconds, until he pressed on. 'But you tell your pal Liz to tell her brother to be a bit more discreet. One word from me to the traffic boys and he could find life becoming very sad. There are so many reasons for us to pull a black cab over, he could wind up spending more time in the garage than on the road.'

'Andy,' Skinner's voice boomed from the doorway. 'It looks as if you're making your own breakfast at this rate.' He was carrying the baby, carefully, in the crook of an arm. 'Alex, your sister was crying. I think she needs changing.'

'So change her. I'll do a couple of bacon sannies for my ex – just this once, mind.'

He helped Alex make his breakfast, then ate it with her

watching him across the kitchen table. 'I couldn't help noticing,' she said, as he sipped his coffee, 'that all that time I was ragging you about your sex life, you were gallant enough not to interrogate me about mine.'

He flashed a look across the table. 'None of my business – as you told me once, I seem to remember.'

'I remember; and I suppose I have to admit to having been wrong, since we were still engaged at the time. Anyway, for what it's worth, I don't have one right now. One thing that you and I did have in common – we were neither of us very good at celibacy. When we broke up, I decided that I should learn. You know, it's quite good for you, really.'

'What is?' asked her father walking back into the room, carrying a newly changed Seonaid.

'Bacon.' Alex looked up from the table. 'You staying for a bit, Pops?'

'No. I've got to go and see Jimmy.'

'Give me ten minutes before you leave. Come on, Andy; finish your coffee and take me for a spin in this new car I've heard about.'

He did as she asked, handing her the keys and allowing her to drive the two-seater out of Gullane, down the Luffness straight, around the Witches Hill Country Club, as far as Ballencrieff, then back through Drem towards the village. He watched her as she flicked the car through the gentle curves of the road as it ran alongside the railway line, nodding approval at the smooth way in which she took the tricky hairpin beyond Drem and accelerated away. She looked as if she had been driving an MGF all her life.

'I like this,' she said, as she cruised back into the driveway of the bungalow.

'Get yourself one then.'

'I'm still too young; the insurance would cripple me. Besides, Dad wouldn't like it. He has a thing about fast cars and me, after what happened to Mum.'

'Your mother's death wasn't her fault. We know that now.'

'She went like the wind all the same; Pops told me once that he was sure that if she hadn't bought it then, it would have happened another time. He never let her drive him if he could help it.'

'He doesn't have a problem with your driving,' Andy grinned. 'You're nearly as good as me.'

'How could I aspire to that?' She kissed him; for a second or two beyond friendship. 'I'll come to see the pictures soon,' she promised as she climbed out of the driver's seat. 'And don't worry, I'll phone first.'

He thought about Alex all the way back to North Berwick. Was she offering him a way back? Maybe, but on her terms . . . and he could never forget. It wasn't a matter of forgiveness any more, he knew that. No, he could never forget.

Detective Inspector Mario McGuire was in the mobile headquarters, alone, when Martin arrived back from Gullane. 'Maggie gone for a kip?' the Head of CID asked.

'Yeah. I told her she should go home, but you know her. She wants to co-ordinate the door-to-door results as soon as she's got enough in. Stevie's round at the local office too, getting catering organised for later.'

'What's Mags got you doing?'

McGuire frowned. 'It's not a matter of that, sir. I've got my own locus in this investigation. This guy used to do my Special Branch job. Unless we find out very quickly that he was shagging the woman next door and her husband took revenge . . .'

'Unlikely,' said Martin. 'She's about eighty-five.'

'Two doors along, then. Unless it's a local vendetta or a family thing, I'm going to have to look back through the stuff he was involved in as a copper, to see if there might be a connection. You've sat in my chair too. You know how sensitive it can be.'

'Aye, and how confidential. You're right; you do that. Report anything you find to Maggie privately, but keep me in touch as well.'

'Of course. There's one thing I did say I'd do for Maggie this morning, though.' He glanced at his watch. 'I have to see the owner of the pub along the road – or last night's bar staff – to get a list of all the people who were in there.'

'Sure. The alarm was raised by one of their punters; maybe another one saw someone going into Alec's house. The Auld Hoose isn't the only pub in town, though. We should check the others, starting with the Golfer's Rest round in the Main Street. I'll tell you what; you take that, I'll take the Auld Hoose.'

McGuire nodded, stood, and turned towards the door. Before he and Martin reached it, it opened, and a young woman constable, in uniform, appeared. The DCS recognised her at once. 'PC Cowan. What brings you here? Finished your door-to-doors?'

She brought her left arm round from behind her and raised it. She was clutching a plastic supermarket bag, wet and encrusted with dark sand. Martin took it from her and looked inside; it contained a blowtorch, a knife, and a heavy steel wrench, all still soaking. 'I was on the beach search team, sir. I went round to the harbour when the tide was low enough, and I saw that on the bottom.'

'Where?' asked Martin, urgently.

'Near the wall beside the car park, sir.'

'Good for you, PC Cowan. Did your sergeant tell you to do that or did you work it out for yourself?'

The woman looked diffident. 'I sort of worked it out, sir.'

'Well done, you. Is the beach search still going on?'

'Yes, sir. There are people out in the east bay.'

'Get on your radio, then, and tell them to chuck it. We won't find anything else. Call everyone back in here.' He pointed to the desk at which McGuire had been sitting. 'There are still streets to be allocated for door-to-door interviews. I want you to dish them out to the search teams as they get here, along with interview sheets and clipboards.

'Before that, though, I want you to tag those three items, put them in the evidence bags which you'll find in that cupboard over there, and call for a car to take them to DI Dorward in the forensic lab. Got all that?'

'Yes sir.'

'Good; get on with it, then. The Inspector and I have a couple of calls to make. You're in charge till Sergeant Steele gets back.'

The two detectives stepped out into the street. 'Bright girl, that,' said Martin. 'Ready for CID, if she wants it.'

'Don't they all want it?' McGuire suggested. 'I couldn't wait to get out of uniform.'

'Me neither; but they're not all like us. Besides, this force needs good people in every department. Cowan's divisional commander might kick up hell if I try to pinch her.'

'You can fix him, though.'

'Probably, if I brought the Big Man into it, but I'd rather not have to. Ask Maggie to have a look at the girl; if she'd like her on her strength, she can ask for her. It'll make it easier if it comes from within the division.'

They set off across Forth Street; on the other side they walked directly into a television cameraman, with a reporter by his side, microphone in hand. 'A quick word on camera, Andy?' asked Julian Finney, of Scottish Television.

'No way. This is Maggie Rose's investigation; ask her when she gets back.' He nodded towards McGuire, who was heading in the direction of the Golfer's Rest. 'Don't go pointing that bloody thing at Mario either; that ain't allowed, and you know it.'

'It's okay, we won't do that. I know the SB people are off limits. Alec Smith wasn't though, was he? I've just spoken to the guy who found the body. The way he described it, this was a torture killing. But, don't tell me, that's not for quoting, is that right?'

Martin looked at the journalist. 'Yeah, I guess that having your balls burned off with a blowlamp could be described as torture.'

'Ahhh!' Finney winced.

'That was only the start. It could happen to you too, if you cross-examine our key witnesses.'

'Point taken, Andy, but the guy approached me, honest. Have you got a precise cause of death yet?'

'I honestly don't know. It could have been head injuries, but we'll need to wait for the post-mortem. Sarah should be starting it soon.'

'D'you expect a quick result?'

'We'll let Maggie answer that one; at the moment we're doing the usual, asking lots of people lots of questions and hoping that at least one of them saw something that'll help us.'

'What's your gut feeling, though? Still off the record.'

'My gut feeling is that there's a very dangerous man walking about. If he lives in North Berwick we'll catch him easy, but I doubt if he does. After he killed Alec he walked round to the harbour and dropped the murder weapons into the sea, right beside the car park. My guess is that after he did that he got into a motor and drove off.

'This guy's long gone; and I'll tell you something else, Julian – very much off the record – he hasn't left a ghost of a trail.'

Nine

They did it all: all the routine slogging that is part of every murder enquiry. By the end of the afternoon every one of Alec Smith's neighbours in Forth Street had been interviewed by CID officers. Most of the other houses in North Berwick had been canvassed by senior officers. All of the Friday evening customers listed by publicans had been located and questioned.

With DCI Maggie Rose back in command in the van, the Head of CID had taken on foot-soldier duties. He and McGuire had visited every resident of the converted Granary flats, and of every other house clustered around the small tidal harbour. No-one could recall seeing anyone drop anything into the water late in the evening. No-one could recall anyone being parked there, or driving away.

Andy Martin was dog-tired when he arrived back in Dean Village, just before seven. It had been a blazing day, and there was still real heat in the sun. He slid the MGF into his garage and was about to pull down the up-and-over door, when Rhian stepped inside.

'Hi,' she murmured. 'I was beginning to think you wouldn't make it.'

'So was I.'

She slid her arms around him as he pulled down the door.

'That would have disappointed me. I hate disappointments. I don't think I could stand two in two days; you're not going to disappoint me again, are you?'

He grinned down at her. She really was very attractive, in a bikini top and shorts, her tan dark and shiny; very much a woman, not a girl at all. 'I think there's every chance of that,' he chuckled, as she reached back to flick the catch of her top. 'But I'll do my best.'

He picked her up and carried her, through the garage exit and into the house, up the first flight of stairs, then up the second, and into his bedroom.

Yes, you surely are mad, Martin, he said to himself, but right at that moment he cared not a bit.

Rhian was a screamer and the window was open; at first he hoped like hell that the music next door was loud enough to cover her cries, but after a while he stopped caring. 'You have definitely done this before,' he said, afterwards, as the air seemed to sizzle round them.

'I did tell you that. You're not too shabby yourself, officer, definitely not a disappointment.' She nestled into the crook of his arm. 'There. Feeling better now?'

'And how.'

'Has it been a bad day?'

'Yes, but don't let's talk about it.'

'Have you caught anyone yet?'

'Nah. Fact is, we haven't got a bloody clue. All those folk in North Berwick, but no-one saw a damn thing. They don't, you see; most of the time, people just don't notice other people. They only register them as part of the background, and that can make life very difficult for us.' He glanced at the bedside clock. 'Here, we'd better get ready.'

She chuckled; deep and wicked. 'You don't think I'm finished with you yet, do you?'

If Juliet Lewis had noticed her daughter's absence, or marked the fact that Andy was over an hour late for the barbecue, she said not a word about it, only, 'Welcome,' and 'You shouldn't have,' as he handed over two thick fillet steaks, bought in Struth's of North Berwick and wrapped in greaseproof paper, and a bottle of reserve claret from the delicatessen in Gullane. She was beautifully dressed, in a close-fitting skirt and a long-sleeved blouse, in stark contrast to many of her younger guests.

Rhian had gone upstairs after showing him through to the garden. Just as her mother was handing Martin a goblet of red wine she reappeared, dressed in jeans and a tee-shirt, and with her hair tied back in a pony-tail. She picked up a bottle of Belgian beer from the serving table, took his hand and drew him towards his fellow guests, who were gathered on the lawn.

'Come on, let me introduce you around.' As he had expected, most of them were young, around Margot's age. She pointed to a group gathered around the younger Lewis daughter, a tall dark girl, in a light blue dress. 'You know the guest of honour, of course.' Actually, he had never exchanged a word with her. From what he had seen she was a serious type, who looked, as did Rhian, a year or two older than she really was. He gave her a smile and a wave. She responded, almost shyly, sneaking a quick look at her sister. For an instant, he detected a hint of a smirk on her face, and wondered.

'These are the serious people, though.' She led him over to a group of half a dozen men and women, older than the rest and standing a little apart. 'Hi everybody,' she called out.

One of the men, who had been looking down on to the dark, slow-moving Water of Leith, glanced over his shoulder. 'Ah, it's herself,' he said, turning. 'I wondered where the hell you'd got to.' He grinned at Martin. 'Can I guess?'

'I've been changing,' Rhian answered.

'That'll be the day, honey. You'll never bloody change.' There was a familiarity in the exchange; two people comfortable with each other. Andy eyed the other man appraisingly, remembering Rhian's remark about older lovers, trying to guess his age. He was small but trim, with dark, grey-flecked hair which was thinning on top; well-preserved, but probably in his early forties.

She brought him back by squeezing his hand. 'Don't listen to this so-and-so. Have you two met before? Andy, this is Spike Thomson, Edinburgh's oldest teenager and a legend in his own mind. Spike, this is Andy Martin; he lives next door.'

The man's eyebrows rose. 'Ah. I've heard of you. You're Bob Skinner's pal, aren't you?'

The detective looked at the other man warily, although he was not certain why. 'You know Bob?'

'Of course. I'm one of the Thursday mob.'

Spike Thomson. *Get the brain in gear, Andy boy. How many Spike Thomsons can there be?* 'The disc jockey? Fair footballer too, according to Bob.'

'That's kind of him. How come we've never seen you on a Thursday night?'

The detective grinned down at his new acquaintance. 'I've been asked, but football's definitely not my game. I used to play rugby.'

'Me too. I played scrum-half for North Berwick High, then for the rugby club for a while. What was your position?' He took a pace backwards and looked Martin up and down, noting the thickness of his neck, the breadth of his shoulder. 'Prop?'

'For a while, at school, but I played all my senior stuff as a flanker.'

'Ah. That explains why you're not a football man. Bloody lethal on the football field are flankers, to a man. Who'd you play for?'

'West of Scotland.'

'Any good?'

The policeman smiled at the directness of the question, sportsman to sportsman. 'Some folk thought so. I played for Glasgow District a few times; got as far as an international trial, but that was it. I joined the force and packed it in.'

'Why, for God's sake? Couldn't you have carried on playing as a policeman? Others do.'

'Maybe, but working shifts in Edinburgh meant that I couldn't guarantee to make training in Glasgow. I could have played for Edinburgh Accie Firsts at one point, but I decided against it. I took the view that, since the force was going to be my career, I'd better devote myself to it full-time if I was going to make a success of it.'

'You've done all right so far, haven't you?'

'I'm more than pleased with where I am now, yes.'

'Where do you want to wind up?'

'In a Chief Constable's chair.'

Thomson looked up at him. 'Won't that mean leap-frogging Bob?'

Martin shook his head. 'No, it doesn't mean that at all . . . although there is a hell of a lot of leap-frogging in the police. No, there are other forces. I'll have to leave Edinburgh sometime if I want to carry on up the ladder, I know that.'

He might have said also that he would have to leave to move out of the Deputy Chief Constable's shadow, but that was a thought which he had voiced to only one man, Bob Skinner himself.

He looked over his shoulder at Rhian, but she had moved away to join another group. Turning back to Spike Thomson, he realised that he had been quizzed gently by a professional interviewer. He had his own skills in that department.

'How about you?' he asked. 'What was your career path?'

The little man smiled. 'A lot less conventional than yours. I went to Heriot-Watt University and did a Chemistry degree, then went to work in a path lab. On the way through Uni, I did discos at weekends to make a few extra quid; eventually I realised that I was far more interested in that than in my day job. This was back in the seventies, when commercial radio was in its infancy – the pirates had just come on shore, so to speak – so I sent in a tape to the managing director of Radio Forth, just for fun.

'To my great surprise, he liked it . . . no taste, that man. He gave me an audition and hired me on a short contract, to present the weekend breakfast programme. Twenty years or so on, I'm still there.'

'You've been at Forth all that time?'

'More or less. About fifteen years ago, I was lured away to the flesh-pots – Glasgow – but it didn't feel right so, after a year, when Forth asked me to come back and be the station's Head of Music, I haggled for about half a minute, then agreed.'

'Have you never fancied the BBC?' Martin asked.

Spike Thomson drained the last of his red wine. 'I was approached, a while back, by Radio One. They offered me a bigger salary and the chance to increase my ancillary earnings about ten-fold. But I'd have had no control over anything, I'd have had to start by doing a through-the-night show for six months, and it would have been another short-term contract.

'Didn't fancy it. I like my local audience, I like the instant feedback we get from our listeners, and I like the feel of what I do. This might sound pompous, but I believe that local radio is socially important. We talk to a lot of people, and we have the ability to change the way they think.'

'Why don't you work more closely with my Drugs Squad then?'

'Because as soon as we start to sound like a mouthpiece for the police – or anyone else for that matter – we're dead. We're *independent* local radio, remember; the word means something. Don't worry, Andy, we get the drugs message across, all of us, but through the attitude of our presenters, not through propaganda.'

The disc-jockey paused. 'Come in and watch us at work sometime. You can sit in with me in the studio.' He grinned. 'You can bring Rhian if you like, although she's been already.'

He caught Martin's look. 'Some girl, that. Twenty-one going on forty; you watch yourself there. She can be a real heart-breaker.'

'You speak from experience?' the detective asked. There was an edge to his tone.

Spike Thomson held up a hand, as if to keep the big policeman at bay. 'Not guilty, honest, officer,' he protested. 'The truth is that my interest is in her mother. Juliet and I have been seeing each other for a while.'

He broke off. 'You eaten yet?'

'No,' Martin replied, hunger biting at once.

'Come on then, let's get some grub and a refill.'

They were halfway to the barbecue when the detective's mobile phone sounded in his shirt pocket. He stopped and took it out. 'Yes?'

'Andy, it's Maggie.'

'Hi, Mags. How's it going out there?'

'A town full of brick walls so far. I do have Sarah's post-mortem report though: it answers a couple of questions. I'm having a team briefing tomorrow morning, at ten in the mobile. Want to come?'

'Sure, I'll be there.' He ended the call and put the handphone away. 'Work,' he said to Thomson.

'Not that thing our newsroom was on about today, was it? Out in my home town.'

'I'm afraid so.'

The little man shook his head. 'Poor old Smithy. He was one of us, you know; one of the Thursday Legends. Something come back to haunt him, did it?'

Martin frowned at the shrewdness of the question. 'Maybe, maybe not. Too early to tell. Come on, there's been enough shop all round. Let's get to the grub.'

They were almost there when the scream rang out behind them; short, sharp piercing, then dying into a gasp. The detective turned on his heel. Margot, the birthday girl, was standing to the left of the garden with her back to her guests, leaning over the boundary fence and gripping its rail tightly. She was staring down, back along the river towards the Belford Bridge.

The rest of the gathering seemed to turn in slow motion towards her, but Andy Martin was by her side in three strides. 'What's up, Margot?' he asked urgently.

The girl said nothing, did not move, as he put a protective arm around her shoulders. She could only gaze at the greenish-tinged water, her mouth hanging open slightly. At last she raised a hand and pointed. 'There,' she whispered. 'What's that thing along there? Is it what I think it is?'

The detective followed the direction of her outstretched finger, leaning outwards, just as she did. At last he saw it, just under the far parapet of the bridge which carries the road above across Edinburgh's little river. It was a large green, puffy object, swollen by the water, not going with the flow but snagged on something. He might have thought that it was no more than a roll of carpet – but for the thing, the pale white thing, which floated on the surface.

'Oh no,' he muttered. 'Just what I need to round off a perfect day.'

He felt a strong hand tug at his elbow and turned to face Rhian. Juliet, Spike and the others had gathered behind her, one or two of them leaning out over the fence. 'Back,' he called out, sharply. 'Everyone get back towards the house, please.

'There's something in the river and it's given Margot a fright. It's probably nothing –' He knew as he spoke that his urgency made his lie sound unconvincing. '– but I'm going along to check it out, just in case. Come on now, back, please.'

Frowning, Juliet Lewis took her younger daughter, who had begun to tremble, by the hand and drew her away from the fence, while Rhian began to usher the rest of the gathering towards the back of the garden as Martin had asked. As she did, he glanced down at his clothes, then eased out of his sandals to stand barefoot on the grass. He stripped off his Hugo Boss shirt and hung it over the top rail then, deciding that his cotton slacks were expendable, vaulted over the fence on to the sloping embankment which ran along the other side.

The arch of the bridge was about fifty yards away; he made his way crabwise along the grass banking until he reached it, then stepped out into the murky waters. Almost at once he was more than waist deep, wading through ooze and slime, pausing to balance himself as he stepped on the occasional slippery stone. The river was no more than a few yards wide, but under the bridge it was so gloomy that he could not see the object clearly until he was almost upon it.

Close to, the pale thing had a bluish tinge. It was a hand, on the end of a shirt-sleeved right arm which seemed to have worked its way awkwardly from the dark-coloured rug which had enclosed it. The head was almost clear too; a man's head, face down in the water, sparse hair floating on the surface.

The detective allowed his eyes a few more seconds to become accustomed to the gloom. Gradually he saw that the rug had been tied with thick twine, top, middle and bottom. It was hooked on the branch of a tree, which had fallen somewhere upstream and become snagged itself on the riverbed.

Something made him look again at the hand, closely this time. The thumb and little finger were missing; bones showed where they had been snipped or sawed off. He switched his attention to the other end of the rug. Two bare feet protruded: the big and little toes had been severed on each.

'Fuck,' he swore quietly, feeling his stomach prickling. He decided to touch nothing. The rug was stuck fast to the branch which was itself solidly based in the river: there was no chance of anything floating away. Taking care not to slip, he turned and waded back across the river, scrambling, with some difficulty since his feet were slippy with mud, back up the embankment.

Rhian was standing by the fence. Everyone else was standing around the barbecue, but no-one was eating.

'What is it?' she asked.

'Male, human and very dead,' he answered, grimly. 'What we in the business call a stiff. It had to happen tonight, too, and here. Just great for poor wee Margot's birthday. Do me a favour.

Fish my cell-phone from my shirt pocket. It was a bit pricey so I don't want to muck it up.'

She did as he asked. He switched it on and pressed buttons in sequence to call a short-coded number. 'Aye?' came a gruff voice as his call was answered.

'Dan, it's Andy Martin; glad I caught you. I'm at home, or rather next door, at a birthday party. We've just had an unwelcome extra guest.'

'Why's he unwelcome?' asked Detective Superintendent Dan Pringle, commander of CID in Edinburgh's city centre.

'Because he's fucking dead, and floating face down in the Water of Leith.'

'Suicide?'

'Would I be calling you if it was? No, this is definitely not suicide. We'll need photographers, and suited divers to get him out. He's stuck under the Belford Bridge. It's not very deep, but it's mucky down there. Even as I speak I've got half a hundred weight of slime clinging to me.'

'You'll be lucky if that's all it is,' Pringle chuckled, darkly. 'Okay, I'll get things moving. Should I have Belford Road closed off?'

'I reckon you should, for a while at least. I'll put an end to the party; it'll get hellish busy down here very soon.'

'Won't we need statements from everyone?'

'Only one, I reckon, and she lives here. You get on with it and I'll see you shortly.'

'Fine, but do me a favour, Andy.'

'What's that?'

'Wash the shit off before I get there.'

Ten

Bob Skinner looked at his sons as they played on the grass, on the lawn which overlooked the sea. It had been a hot day and it was still warm inside the house. Normally, young Jazz would have been in bed at a few minutes after nine, but that evening he had been even more full of energy than usual, by no means ready for sleep.

Bob had given up all thoughts of Saturday golf; instead he had visited Chief Constable Sir James Proud, to brief him on the facts – all the brutal, bloody facts – of Alec Smith's death. Proud Jimmy had been desperate for a role in the aftermath, and had been insistent at first on going to North Berwick to see for himself. However Skinner had persuaded him that Maggie Rose had had enough top-level presence at her headquarters; he had made the point also that if the head of the force were to visit this murder scene when he did not routinely turn up at others, then he might be accused of implying that the killing of an ex-policeman warranted special treatment.

Instead, the Chief had decided that he would visit Alec Smith's estranged wife, whom he had met once at a formal police event. Content with that, Skinner had run the former Mrs Smith to ground through the Police Pensions Office records and, after making sure that she would be home, had called up a car to drive Sir James to Penicuik, where she and her new lover had settled.

'Just remember, Jimmy,' he had warned, as the patrol vehicle had been about to leave. 'Keep it a bit formal.'

'Come on, this is a sympathy visit, Bob. Why should I do that?'

'Because the woman hasn't been eliminated as a suspect. You'd better ask her when you see her whether she and Alec were on reasonable terms . . . and just find out quietly where she and her boyfriend were last night.'

Proud Jimmy had driven off, secretly pleased by the opportunity to be a detective, a job he had never done during his long and distinguished police career. As the car turned and disappeared from his sight, it was Skinner who had been left feeling useless. He would have liked nothing more than to go back to North Berwick and take part in the house-to-house canvass, or to beat Mario McGuire to the punch by beginning the trawl through Smith's Special Branch career, but he knew that he had to take the advice he had given the Chief about interference in the investigation.

So he had gone home, switching himself off from the murder hunt as best he could by taking Mark and James Andrew to the busy beach, swimming with them in the incoming tide, and towing them along in their yellow inflatable dinghy.

He had expected to find Sarah at home when they returned but, instead, Alex was in the kitchen, feeding her baby half-sister from a carefully prepared bottle. 'Any word from your stepmother?'

'Yes, she called from her car. She was on her way to catch Maggie at North Berwick with the p.m. report.'

Now, in the evening, he waved to the boys from the doorway. 'Time's up, lads.' Jazz looked at him, angrily; for a moment he thought that they were in for a crying match. But Mark spoke quietly in his adoptive brother's ear as he helped him down from the top level of the colourful climbing frame, and the toddler nodded, breaking into a smile as he ran towards his father.

Different boys in many ways, Bob mused, *yet they couldn't be closer. Blood brothers, you might say, without the blood link.*

Sarah was in the nursery, settling Seonaid down for the night, as he ushered the pair towards the shower. She had come home, just after seven, and had gone straight into the bath – her routine after a post-mortem examination – after seeing Alex off to Edinburgh, and her Saturday night date with a couple of girlfriends.

'Our older daughter seemed pretty bubbly tonight,' she remarked. 'I think seeing Andy again may have had something to do with it. You don't suppose there's a chance . . . ?'

He shook his head, firmly. 'Not a prayer. It's good that they can be friends, but what happened will always prevent them from being as they were. I know Andy almost as well as I know her; he thought she was perfect, and it nearly broke him when he found out that she wasn't.

'Twice now, that's happened to him with women. No wonder he's back to playing the safety in numbers game.'

'Is he?' Sarah asked, surprised.

Her husband chuckled, quietly, careful not to disturb the baby. 'Is he ever! Christ, this morning, I tried phoning him just after seven, after I heard mention of an incident at North Berwick on the headlines. He wasn't in. But last night he turned up at the crime scene with Karen Neville driving him, and they left together.'

'That doesn't mean anything.'

Bob tapped the side of his nose, knowingly. 'Trust me, I'm a detective. Those two are of the same spirit; both determined not to be tied down in case they get hurt again. I tell you, my love, Andy's black book is legendary. I even know someone who's keen to get in it.'

'Who's that?'

'Ms Ruth McConnell, no less. Just lately, since her big romance split up, I've caught her giving Andy the odd thoughtful glance.'

'If that's right, will you warn her off?'

'Do you think she'd thank me? Do you think it's any of my business?'

'She is your secretary.'

'So? Does that give me seigneur rights, or what?'

'It had better not!' She was smiling, but he changed the subject nonetheless: dangerous ground, still, for them.

'What about Alec Smith then?' he said. 'You still haven't told me about the autopsy. Christ, autopsy indeed . . . listen to me, picking up your Americanisms.'

Sarah stepped out of the nursery, switching on the baby alarm, but leaving the door ajar also. Bob glanced into the bathroom, where Mark and Jazz were both in the shower, covered in foam.

'It was a difficult one,' she said. 'The man was so badly brutalised. The head injuries didn't kill him though; they were inflicted post-mortem. No, Mr Smith died of shock; his heart just packed in. I took a very careful look at the video the sicko made of the killing, and I could see the moment when it happened. If you take another look you'll see it too.'

He winced. 'I promise you this, my darling girl, I will *never* look at that video again.'

'By the way, I discovered how he was overpowered. He was—'

The telephone rang out, interrupting her. Bob stepped quickly into their bedroom and answered, before Seonaid could be disturbed. 'Skinner.'

'Bob, it's Andy. Sorry to disturb you yet again, but what a bloody day I've had! As if the late call last night about Alec Smith wasn't enough, tonight I'm at a party next door and someone spots a floater in the Water of bloody Leith! I had to go in there and check it; I've only just dried off.'

'Murder?' the DCC asked. 'Aye I suppose it must be. Not suicide, anyway. You'd have to be trying really hard to drown yourself in that stream.'

'You could manage it if you were able to tie yourself up in a carpet then hop in. But this one didn't. Someone had some fun with him before he put him in the water. Pringle's on his way with a team and we've closed the road around the area. I've had to empty the downstairs bar of the Hilton Hotel too; it's not far from the scene, and we don't want an audience.'

'What does it look like?'

'A gang thing, maybe. Time will tell.'

'Let Pringle get on with it then. I'll give him a call tomorrow.' Skinner chuckled. 'Buggered up your Saturday night, eh? Still, it'll have kept you out of mischief.' In the silence that followed, he heard a female voice say, 'Andy, are these the jeans you meant?'

He laughed again, loud enough to make Sarah throw him a warning frown from the bedroom doorway. 'Ah, Jeez. I should have known better.'

Eleven

Andy took the tailored Lacoste jeans from Rhian, slid them on, then found a blue crew-necked sweater in a chest of drawers opposite his bed.

'I'm sorry about breaking up the party, or at least about sending everyone off to the pub,' he told her. 'But I don't think your pals would have appreciated watching our diver team haul a very dead guy out of the water.'

'You're kidding. Some of Margot's friends would have loved that.'

'In that case, they're well off out of it.'

'Can I watch them? I'm a medical student and would really like to do scene-of-crime stuff after I qualify.'

'I thought you were going to specialise in proctology. Or do you see working with the police as falling within that field?' She frowned at him for a second, then grinned as she caught up with his sense of humour. 'Seriously though, the answer's no. We have a panel of appointed medical examiners and they're not encouraged to bring students with them.'

'But you're Head of CID, aren't you? You could fix it, surely.'

'I could,' he agreed as he slipped a pair of walking sandals on to bare feet, 'but I'm not going to. I'll tell you what I will do though. Sarah Skinner – Bob's wife – is a pathologist. If she does the post-mortem on this one, I'll ask her if you can sit in.'

'I've seen a dissection before.'

'Maybe, but you haven't seen Sarah at work on someone fresh from the river. Come on now, we have to go. Dan Pringle will be here any second.' He ushered her out of the bedroom, towards the stairs.

'Can't I stay here?' she asked. 'You won't be all night, will you?'

'No, but . . .'

'Just this once, please, Andy.'

He relented. 'Okay, but tomorrow morning we've got to have a talk about things.'

She smiled. 'Who says I'll fancy you tomorrow?'

In some ways that might be a relief, he thought.

'How could you not?' he said.

He left the house and jogged out of the village, then up and round into Belford Road towards the bridge. Uniformed officers were on duty on either side, stopping and diverting traffic and pedestrians. The forecourt and foyer of the Hilton Hotel was thronged with guests, intrigued by the sudden Saturday night action and eyeing up a big dark blue van which was parked a few yards away.

As Martin approached, its rear doors opened and two men jumped out. They were wearing wet-suits. They spotted the Head of CID at once, and walked towards him, a little stiff-legged.

'Will we need tanks, sir?' one of them asked.

'Not at first, Sergeant Hayward. Later on Mr Pringle might want you to have a look at the river bed, but it's shallow enough for you to get the guy out without them. You've got a waterproof camera in the van, I take it.'

'Yes, sir. And a video.'

'Good. On you go then; get down under the bridge; take plenty of still and video shots of the body . . . and focus on the way it's been trapped. Once you've got enough, bring him out and lay him on the walkway.'

He looked around and saw a uniformed Inspector on the other side of the street. 'Bert!' he called across. 'Have you got screens here yet?' The man nodded. 'Good. Set them up down there, to block off the view from the houses opposite.' He smiled briefly as he thought of Rhian, stood in his garden for sure waiting for the excitement to begin.

The two-man diver team, cameras fetched from their van, flopped awkwardly down the steps which led from the bridge to the Water of Leith Walkway, and as they did, a dark blue Vauxhall Vectra pulled up beside Martin. Dan Pringle heaved himself laboriously from the front passenger seat and walked round behind the car. Martin grinned; the Superintendent enjoyed his Saturday nights. He guessed that he had called him just in time.

'Where is he then, sir?' he asked, through his thick moustache.

'About twenty feet below where you're standing right now. I've just sent the recovery team down. I didn't want him in the water any longer than necessary.'

'Any idea how long he's been in there already?'

'I didn't look at him that closely, only at the bits that were sticking out of the carpet he's wrapped in; they didn't look especially puffy, but maybe the constraint of the binding restrains the bloating process. We'll get an idea in a minute, once the guys get him out.'

Pringle and his driver, Detective Constable Ray Wilding

followed Martin down the steep steps to the walkway. It was approaching ten o'clock, but summer nights in Scotland seem to last for ever, and so there was enough light for them all to see the divers working under the bridge.

They waited while they finished their task of filming and photographing the corpse *in situ*, then, with the cameras secure on the shore, they watched the two men free the dark bundle from its entrapping branch and carry it, like pallbearers, from under the bridge. Martin and Wilding, both younger and fitter than the middle-aged Pringle, took it from them as they passed it up, grasping the burden by the cords which secured the carpet, carrying it behind the screens which the Inspector had erected and laying it gently, face down, on the ground. As they did, the smell of it reached them for the first time. The Head of CID found himself hoping that it would carry all the way up to the gawpers outside the Hilton.

'Any more film in the still camera?' Pringle asked the divers.

'A few shots,' the older of the two replied.

'You'd better take some as we do this.' He bent and rolled the shrouded body on to its back. 'Fuck,' he whispered as he looked at the face – or at the place where a face should have been. The man had been battered beyond recognition. His nose had been pounded flat, his eyes smashed in their sockets, his lips torn to ribbons by broken teeth as they had been ground to fragments.

'Someone definitely had it in for you, mister,' Pringle murmured. He seized one of the cords which tied the carpet. 'Bugger. How are we going to get this undone?'

'No problem,' said Martin. He took a big clasp knife from the pocket of his jeans, knelt beside the body and cut the twine with single strokes, then stood to watch as Wilding unrolled the carpet.

The dead man looked to have been in his forties, with a roll of fat around the waist but not completely gone to seed. He had been of no more than medium height. The body was naked from the waist down. The legs were twisted and grotesque; they had been battered as badly as the face and head. Two big crosses had been carved into his torso with a knife, through his blue shirt. Martin glanced down at the genitals; the penis was tiny and shrivelled from its immersion, but the area seemed intact.

'I don't think he can have been in the water for more than a day,' he said. As he spoke, one of the divers leaned over the body and took a close-up shot of the smashed face.

'That's not going to be much bloody use to us,' grunted Pringle.

'What do you mean?' asked Martin.

'I mean we can hardly stick that in the *Evening News* with a "Do you know this man?" caption. His mammy wouldna' know him now. I tell you, sir, we could have a job even identifying this one, let alone finding the bloke who did this to him. We don't even know where he was put in the Water. Even supposing it was only half a mile upstream, that takes in a lot of territory.'

'You should check the missing persons list, first off,' said the Head of CID. 'As for a picture, if we need one, I'll ask the pathologist to brief an artist, or put together a photo fit. Too bad Joe Hutchison's away; he's done a lot of work on facial reconstruction. 'You'd better consult the Drugs Squad and Criminal Intelligence. See if there are any turf wars going on that we don't know about.'

'Whereabouts?'

'Any-fucking-whereabouts. For all we know this guy could

have been killed in another city and dumped here. Let's hope we get lucky, and soon; otherwise – I agree with you, Dan; we might never put a name to this bloke.'

Twelve

The key players in the Alec Smith investigation team were gathered in the command vehicle when the Head of CID entered, five minutes after ten on Sunday morning, with Karen Neville following behind: DCI Maggie Rose, standing nearest to the door, studying a report; Mario McGuire, Steve Steele, three detective constables . . . and Sarah Grace Skinner.

Martin glanced around the group and knew at once that they had been waiting for him. It had taken him longer than he would have liked to extricate himself from Rhian, even though he had postponed their promised discussion until the evening. He had called Karen, on a whim, reasoning that she had been in at the start of the investigation and therefore that she should be kept in touch with its progress.

There had been another consideration too. If he were to become heavily involved in the unpredictable affair of the Water of Leith floater, he might need her as liaison in both investigations.

'Sorry we're late, Mags . . .' he began.

'I know,' the DCI answered. 'Traffic. The Sunday drivers start early when the weather's good.' For a second he thought that there might have been a touch of sarcasm in her comment, but he rejected it at once. Maggie just wasn't made that way.

'I'm a bit surprised you're here at all, actually. I heard about last night's business on the radio. Has Dan made any progress?'

'He won't, until he gets an identification; and he's a long way off that. Missing persons drew a blank and so far we've had nothing from the fingerprints. Sarah's booked to do the post-mortem this afternoon.' He glanced across at her, while still speaking to Rose. 'I'm going to ask her if she can draw us a picture of the guy.'

'Eh?' The woman detective looked puzzled.

'His face was smashed in – and I mean smashed in. You'd have thought his head had been run over by a car.'

'What makes you think it wasn't?' asked Sarah, walking towards them.

'I don't know that it wasn't,' he conceded. 'You'll have to tell us for sure. But my guess is that if it had been, the whole skull would have been crushed. In fact, all the head injuries seemed to be facial.'

'We'll see about that. It's for later, though.'

'Sure,' he agreed. 'Maggie, this is your briefing. Do you want to begin?'

She nodded, sending a ripple through her glossy red hair. 'Yes, let's do that. Okay, everyone,' she called. 'Attention please. I've called this meeting to update everyone with progress in the investigation into the death of DCI Alec Smith. On the face of it, we haven't achieved a great deal over the last thirty-six hours, but everyone's worked hard to eliminate certain possibilities, if nothing else. We've also found out more about the way in which Mr Smith was killed.

'As you know, the person who killed Mr Smith fancied himself as an amateur film-maker. He used the victim's camcorder to make a very explicit movie, then left it for us to find at the scene.

Some of you have viewed it . . . those who needed to. Those who haven't, but feel the need, may do so, but believe me, it won't add anything to your lives.

'The video didn't answer all our questions. Alec Smith was a very neat man. Everything in his house was carefully arranged; everything had a purpose, and when we found him, everything was in its place. So the first thing we wondered was how he was overpowered.

'DCI Smith was a big man, yet he was trussed up like a turkey and hung up on a hook, ready to be butchered, and this was achieved without any sign of a struggle. A mystery, yes, but thankfully no longer. Dr Skinner has come up with the answer. Sarah, if you would.'

The pathologist pushed herself from the desk on which she had been sitting. 'Thank you, DCI Rose.' She looked around the group. 'Yes, a real puzzle, huh? Like the DCI said, the victim was a big man; in his fifties, but physically very fit. His legs were very powerful, indicating that he did a lot of walking, or cycling, or both. In addition to that, those of you who saw him at the scene will have observed that – apart from the injuries which were inflicted while he was being tortured to death – there were no other marks on the body.'

Detective Sergeant Steele raised a hand. 'What about the head injuries, Doctor? Couldn't he have been knocked out by a blow to the head, then strung up?'

'No. Don't believe the movies, Stevie. You don't just hit someone on the chin and knock them out. Even in professional boxing it's unusual for someone to be rendered completely unconscious for more than a few seconds. It takes a hell of a blow to do that, a severe concussion, and generally speaking the bigger the person, the more force would be needed.

'If Mr Smith had been hit hard enough to allow his attacker to strip him naked, tie him, then haul his limp body up on that hook, I'd have been expecting to find a skull fracture and probably a significant injury to the brain. I would not have expected him to be as alert and aware as the man we saw at the start of that video.'

'No. The head injuries were inflicted after death.'

Karen Neville raised a hand. 'Need there have been a struggle? Need he have been stripped? Couldn't this have been a sex game that turned into something else.'

'Wouldnae mind a game with her.' In the lull, Detective Constable Faxon's aside to Detective Constable Morrow was no more than a whisper but, as Sarah paused, it carried to the Head of CID. He shot DC Faxon a look that threatened to strip the flesh from his bones, but Karen cooled the moment with a laugh. 'You're not built for it, Constable,' she murmured.

'Shut up, Faxon,' snapped DCI Rose. 'Sorry, Sarah.'

'That's okay, boys will be boys.' She looked across at Neville. 'As a matter of fact, Sergeant, when I began my examination I considered that the likeliest possibility. It might even have explained why the genital area was burned to a crisp; to destroy the possibility of DNA traces remaining from a sexual encounter.

'But that wasn't the case. Mr Smith was subdued, and he was stripped. When I turned the body over, before beginning dissection, I found a puncture wound in the middle of the back. I examined this minutely and found fibres compressed into it. I sent them to Arthur Dorward at the lab and he confirmed very quickly that they came from the shirt which was found at the scene.

'Subsequent analysis of the blood and tissue samples showed that the victim was shot in the back with a tranquilliser dart. The substance used was Immobilon; it's commonly used in zoos and other places to sedate large animals. Whoever did it got the dose right; it would have knocked him down instantly and rendered him helpless for a few minutes, long enough for him to be made ready for what was to happen to him. If they'd used too much it could have killed him. Vets have been known to commit suicide with that stuff.'

'Does that mean that we're looking for James Herriot?' asked Steele, without a flicker of a smile.

'Detection is your field, Steve, but I'd have said that, at the very least, you should interview the local veterinarians to find out whether they have any stock discrepancies.'

'Would the local vets need stuff like that, Doctor? I mean, most of them just look after dogs and cats and hamsters and such.'

'And cattle and sheep, too,' Sarah responded, 'and horses, especially in a rural area like this.'

'I suppose so,' the young Sergeant conceded. He paused. 'All the things that were done to him; how much of that would he have been aware of?'

'You saw the video, remember; he was aware of all of it. No, we're talking about a tranquilliser, not an anaesthetic; he wouldn't have been numbed by the drug. This man must have suffered unimaginably. He died, eventually, from heart failure caused by the shock of disembowelment. Like I said, the head injuries came after that.' Sarah looked around the van, at eight shocked faces.

'A word about them. They would not have been fatal in any event. They were furious, angry blows, inflicted as a final act of, of . . . I don't know . . . savagery, that's all I can say. I do not always agree with my husband or with DCS Martin, but they're both right on this one. Whoever did this is a very dangerous person.'

Andy gazed at her. 'Singular, Sarah?'

'As far as I know. I've seen the video and the still photos taken at the scene. Now that we know how it was done, there is absolutely no evidence to indicate that there was more than one person involved. This was carefully planned and brutally executed; it didn't even require a great deal of strength: pure physics tells you that it would have been easy to haul Smith up on that hook, the way it was done.'

She stepped out of the centre of the group and sat once more on the edge of the desk.

'Thank you, Sarah,' said Maggie Rose. 'Are there any more questions for the doctor? If not, she has to leave us now.'

No-one spoke; Sarah waved a brief farewell, and stepped out of the van. Martin followed her outside. 'Before you go,' he said. 'About this afternoon's job; I know facial reconstruction's a science in itself, but if you could give me some idea of what this bloke might have looked like it might help us.'

She grinned at him. 'I'm not a complete ignoramus in that science. I did some studying while I was pregnant with Seonaid, and I've talked to Joe Hutchison about it. I couldn't build you a new head yet, but I'll give you some thoughts that are a little more than guesses . . . if only a little.'

As he turned to go back into the van, she laid a hand on his arm. 'Andy.' She was suddenly, untypically, tentative. 'Can I say something?'

'Always.'

'It's about you and Karen.'

He smiled gently. 'Bob's been filling you in on the office gossip. Or was it Alex?'

'No. You know Bob wouldn't do that. And what would Alex know? He mentioned something, that's all. I just wanted to say . . . and this is where it gets difficult . . . that if you like her . . . and I can tell you do . . . you shouldn't hold back from getting involved because of anything that's happened in the past . . . to Bob and me.'

He took her point at once. 'Listen, Sarah, one thing I like about Karen is that she *doesn't* want to get involved. We're good friends away from the office, and – I only say this because it's you – we've danced the occasional dance together, but it *is* a friendship rather than a relationship. Happily, that suits us both. It's a bit like Alex and I are now.'

She surprised him by frowning. 'As her step-mother, I have to tell you I'd be worried about you and her sleeping together just for old times' sake. Unless you were getting back together unconditionally, that wouldn't be good for either of you.'

He laid his big hands on her shoulders and looked her in the eye. 'We couldn't do that; we want different things from life and we both know it. As for the other, I hear what you're saying and I'll make sure that doesn't happen. Promise.' He laughed, suddenly. 'Christ, my love-life's chaotic enough as it is.'

'Then maybe Karen is what you need. Friendship should always come first, you know.'

'Ah, there's a slight impediment in the way of that at the moment.'

'Not Ruth McConnell, by any chance?'

He stared at her amazed, confused and guilty all at once. He had forgotten, completely, his date for the following Saturday night. 'No,' he said, 'not Ruth.' He paused. 'Well . . .'

She stood up on her toes and kissed him, gently, on the lips. 'Andy Martin, you are a one-off. Take a tip from Auntie Sarah.

Find a nice girl, one you like and respect, settle down, have lots of babies, and get on with becoming a Chief Constable.'

'That's all wonderful theory, Auntie, but when you find three at the same time it becomes completely buggered up.'

She shook her head, smiling, and pushed him back towards the mobile headquarters. 'I give up. Go on, get back in there.'

She was almost gone when he remembered. 'Hey, Sarah,' he called after her. She turned. 'The floater p.m. this afternoon: would it be all right if a girl I know sat in on it? Her name's Rhian, she lives next door and she's a final-year medical student.'

'If you're vouching for her and you tell her to keep her voice off the tape, that'll be okay.'

'Great. Thanks. I'll tell her to ask for you at the Royal.'

Maggie Rose had continued the briefing in his absence. 'I've just been summarising the door-to-door results, sir. Nothing, I'm afraid.'

'. . . but you're not surprised.'

'No. Not really. It fits the man.'

'What do you mean?' he asked

'I mean that no-one knew who he was. Alec Smith is the most private man I've ever encountered. It's as if he was born to do the SB job.

'Everything we've been able to find out about him bears that out. We've interviewed all his neighbours in North Berwick; not one of them, not even the man who saw the dog and found the body could tell us anything about him. The woman two doors along didn't even know what he looked like.

'I've spoken to former colleagues of his. They all said the same thing. "Oh aye, Alec." But they couldn't recall any stories about his career, or even any anecdotes. You know what I mean; Dan Pringle got pissed at a CID dance a few years back and folk still talk about it. But Alec Smith never even went to the CID dance . . . not ever.

'The Chief's even been to see his ex-wife . . . his widow, I should say. They were never divorced. She told him that he was courteous, a good provider, not mean in any way; but she said that he was a remote man, quiet to the point of coldness, and that no-one – not even she, not even his children – ever really got to know him. Eventually she decided that she didn't like living alone, so she found someone else.'

'Someone knew him, though,' Martin countered. 'Someone got to know him well enough to want to burn his eyes out and spill his guts out on to his living-room carpet. We're going to have to find the real Alec for ourselves. I'm pretty sure that's the only way we're going to find out who killed him.'

'I agree with you. That'll have to be Mario's job. There are places he can go and things he can look at that are closed to us ordinary coppers. He's asked for Stevie as back-up.

'As for the rest of us; we'll follow up the only lead we've had so far; Sarah's post-mortem report. The DCs, Faxon, Morrow and Braid, have been told to get round all the vets in East Lothian.'

'We should check out Edinburgh too,' said the Head of CID. 'I'll have Sergeant Neville and DC Pye from my staff get that done and report back to you.'

He called across the room. 'You hear that, Karen? You and Sammy do the Herriot round in the city. See if you can find out what sort of weapon might have been used to shoot Smith.'

Thirteen

'Calling Andy! Calling Andy! Where are you?'

He blinked and looked up, across the dinner table. 'I'm sorry, Rhian,' he said, sincerely. 'You're right, I was off somewhere . . . although I couldn't say for sure where it was. This has been an absolutely surreal weekend, in all sorts of ways. What a mixture; I've seen pure bloody horror . . . yet in the midst of it all there's been you. An island of beauty in a sea of ugliness, you might say.'

She grinned, dispersing the gloom which had begun to gather around him. 'I might indeed,' she murmured, 'but I prefer it when you say it.' She angled her head looking through the glass wall of Daniel's Bistro at the big modern Scottish Office building.

'My mum works in there,' she said, idly. 'She's quite important; a Grade-something-or-other . . . Damn! I always forget the number . . . they used to call it Assistant Secretary. Her division has something to do with Home Affairs . . . a family speciality, you might say.'

A smile flicked his mouth in acknowledgement of her small joke. 'Everyone's important, Rhian. From the foot-soldiers through to the field officers like me to the generals on horseback like Big Bob and Proud Jimmy, we've all got our part to play in

97

the service we give the public. If one link breaks the chain's goosed, and it doesn't matter where it happens.

'That's true of every organisation . . . including the Health Service. You'll be a better doctor if you remember it.'

'I'll be a better doctor for watching Sarah do that post-mortem this afternoon. She's terrific. Thanks for fixing it for me. Talking to her afterwards, listening to her talk about the way her career developed, has given me a different perspective on medicine.'

'Think long and carefully before making any decisions,' he warned her. 'There aren't many Sarahs about. You have to play to your own strengths, not those you see in others.'

'Andy: about that chain of yours. What do you do if you find a weak link?'

'You mean me? Personally?'

'Yes.'

'I cut it out.'

'Isn't that a bit brutal?'

His vivid green eyes fixed on her. 'It's necessary. I'll do anything that's necessary. I learned that from Bob.'

'What's he like, that man Skinner?' she asked him.

'Different. Inspiring, intimidating when he has to be. He has a tremendous analytical mind. Sum it all up, he's a great detective and a great leader.'

'But wasn't he all over the Sundays a while back?'

'I don't like to talk about that. It's true, but that's all behind him now, behind both him and Sarah. He's got over his obsessive period, now he's focused equally on his job and his family, as he should be. There's nothing he likes more than taking his kids for a walk of a Sunday afternoon; that's his greatest pleasure in life these days.'

A silence hung over the table as Rhian sipped her coffee. 'So what about this talk that we were going to have tonight?' she murmured, eventually.

'Let's make it tomorrow, honey. My head's wasted right now. How about if we just went home to bed?'

'I'll settle for that.' She smiled again, a big gloom-brightening grin which lifted his spirits in an instant. 'As long as it doesn't become a habit. I'm a lively young thing, you know.'

Two hours later, they lay entwined in each other's arms, in the dying light from the open bedroom window. The duvet was on the floor and they were slicked with sweat.

'Hey,' she whispered in his ear. 'Remember what I said earlier about not making a habit of this?'

'Mmhh.' His tongue flicked out, licking her neck gently, making her shudder.

'In case you were in any doubt, I was joking.'

'That's good. Handling rejection's never been my strong suit.'

'What do you mean?'

'I mean I don't like being chucked.'

'What happened with your fiancée? Who really chucked whom?'

'Let's say that we agreed it wouldn't work.'

'Sure you did. And that's why you have her photograph on the sideboard downstairs. All these girlfriends of yours, yet she's the only person on display, other than your mother. Something big happened. What was it?'

'Don't push it.'

'Ah, you did catch her, then.'

Sharp, way too sharp. 'Actually, she got pregnant, then had our child aborted without telling me about it.'

'So you broke off the engagement?'

'Yes. Immature, eh?'

'No. Principled, I'd say. I can tell how much it hurt you to finish with her, yet you had to.'

'Oh yeah? And why did I have to? Why couldn't I have gone along with it?'

'Because if you had, you'd never have been your own man again, not completely. And someone like you has to be, doesn't he?'

He looked at her, so close that it was an effort to focus his eyes on her. She was right; he had searched for months for an answer to the riddle of himself. Now Rhian had come up with it, on their second night together. And of course, Alex, her father's daughter, was exactly the same; she had his *no compromise* gene. That was why it could never work again, because neither of them was physically capable of doing the thing that would make it so; yielding to the other's will.

'So what about you?' he asked. 'What would you do in Alex's shoes?'

'I'd have the baby . . . but I'm not Alex. I mean, I'm not knocking her or condemning what she did. It was her right. But families are a two-way commitment, aren't they? Could you handle a family, properly, and your job at the same time?'

He rolled on to his back and stared at the ceiling. 'You were at that post-mortem this afternoon. Did it affect you?'

'I'm a doctor, or I'm going to be. I'm being trained not to form emotional attachments with live patients. Dead ones on a slab should be no problem for me.'

'Don't give me theory, give me fact.'

She thought about it for a few seconds. 'It wasn't the dissection,' she said finally. 'It was the commentary; the way Sarah described, for the tape, the things that had been done to that man. Did you know that he actually drowned in his own blood?'

'No, but it doesn't surprise me. I looked into the guy's face, or where his face should have been, as soon as we took him out of the water. I saw his hands and feet, his legs, his chest, everything that was done to him.

'I saw worse on Friday night; yes, worse than that. And you know what? Afterwards, I went home with Karen, my sergeant; she was there, she saw it too. We've got a history together, and right then we needed to help each other get over that hellish thing. We spent the night together because neither of us could face going home alone. I'm sorry if that hurts you, but it's the truth.' He looked into her eyes, and saw her flinch.

'Now, to bring it all back to your original question, could I handle family life? The fact is, Rhian, I don't know for how much longer I can live as I do, and carry on doing my job. I'm really envious of Bob, in that respect. I need stability, I need the normal home life that Alex and I had for a while. I suppose I've been looking for it since we split.

'Otherwise, things like Alec Smith's murder, or like looking at that bloke last night and realising that there's a fair chance we'll never even find out who he was . . . I have this fear that the job will either break me, or take me over to the point that there will be no room in me' – he tapped his chest – 'here, inside me, for anything else. When I can look at an ex-colleague with his–' He stopped himself. 'When I can look at that then go home as if it's just another day at the office, as a man, I'll be done.'

She gripped his fingers in hers, squeezed them and held them between her breasts. 'Then let's just make sure, that there's always someone there for you.'

She rubbed her forehead on his shoulder. 'Maybe I've been looking for something too,' she whispered. 'And maybe, just maybe, the first time I saw you, I knew I'd found it.'

Fourteen

Detective Inspector Mario McGuire wore a broad grin. 'Welcome to the shadowy, glamorous world of Special Branch, Sergeant,' he boomed. 'Welcome to the centre of this spider's web of intrigue. Exciting, isn't it?'

Stevie Steele leaned back in his hard chair and looked around the drab room, with its bare, magnolia-painted walls, and its single small window. 'Wow,' he said.

'This is the reality of the job, Steve. We're the true crime-prevention department; we keep an eye on potential trouble and even more important, on potential trouble-makers. That's the way it's always been. Back in the fifties and sixties we used to keep an eye on the local communists and fellow-travellers: trade-union guys, left-wing Labour Party guys and acknowledged CP members. Now terrorism, more than anything else, is the perceived enemy.

'Back in the old days we had help, of course – local journalists who'd go along to meetings and report back to us for a few quid. We could trust the local newspaper hacks, they were poorly paid and always needed the money. But there were journos on the other side too. The NUJ had a communist as its president back in the sixties: wherever he travelled, all over the country, he had a Special Branch escort.

'The boys in Glasgow, they had a permanent bug in the offices of the *Daily Worker*, but of course the hacks there knew it, so there was never anyone in their bloody office. They used to do all their business in pubs and send their copy to London from phone boxes. Everything we did, of course, was to ensure that guys like them couldn't deliver this great democracy of ours into the slavering Soviet maw.'

'It worked, then,' said Steele, dryly.

'Not really. Like I said, SB priorities changed in the early seventies when Ireland blew up. We had to stop playing with the wild-eyed Left to a great extent and concentrate on the real danger. It's been a different game since then, with a constant IRA and Loyalist threat for thirty years and, at the same time, the growth of international terrorism. We haven't always been successful in preventing attacks, but for every one that's succeeded there have been a right few others that we've headed off.'

'Isn't it quieter now than it was?'

'No it ain't, Sergeant. There will always be fanatics with a mission to destroy, quote, unquote, our decadent Judea/Christian Western society, and there will be idiots among us who admire and support them. The Special Branch task has never really altered; the enemy just changes every so often, that's all.'

'Have you always liked politics, Inspector?'

'It's Mario in here and in the pub – and I've never liked politics. That's why I'm in the job. In fact I hate politics. It doesn't matter whether they are the politics of state, religion, race, gender, or just wealth, they are inherently fucking dangerous and they can get you killed. There used to be a famous copper in the West of Scotland who argued that all crime was related to the theft of non-ferrous metals. I disagree; I believe that all crime is related to politics of one sort or another. They got me shot, for a start.

'I tell you, Stevie, politics can be hazardous to your health. Most of the people who practise them are well meaning, well-educated fools, but a minority of them, usually those who make it to the very top, are bloody dangerous.

'That's why we're the key players in the Alec Smith investigation. Alec moved in this world and he was good at it – the best, I'm told. He was an apolitical guy, just like me, like Brian Mackie, like Andy Martin, tasked with keeping an eye on politicians of all sorts.'

'Tasked by whom?'

McGuire's laugh was a bellow. 'By politicians, of course; to keep an eye on their enemies. But from the start, SB has taken the view that there can always be an enemy within.'

'So what are we looking for here?' Steele asked.

'We're looking for all the enemies Alec might have made in his time. We'll do it by sifting through the files for the period in which he was in my job, and through the private papers which I've brought here from his house.'

'And where do we begin?'

'We begin by interviewing the Deputy Chief Constable, who might be the only bloke here who can tell us anything about Alec Smith as a man, as well as a police officer.'

Steele gulped, involuntarily, as McGuire pushed himself up from his chair, and stepped out from behind his desk. 'Come on; he'll be waiting for us now.'

The Inspector led the way out of the Special Branch suite. They marched briskly out of the high-rise section of the Fettes headquarters complex and along the link which led to the

Command Corridor, above the main entrance, where the chief officers were based.

McGuire leaned into a small room, off to the right. Ruth McConnell smiled up at him. *Gorgeous as always*, he thought. 'The Boss in?' he asked.

'Yes. He said to send you along when you arrived. Go on, and I'll buzz him.'

'Thanks.' Beckoning Steele to follow, he walked a few yards to Skinner's door, knocked and led the way inside.

The Deputy Chief was in uniform, unusually. He caught McGuire's surprised glance as he rose from his swivel chair and stepped across towards the low seating in his reception area, where Neil McIlhenney was sitting. 'Visitors,' he explained. 'A delegation from the Mossos Esquadra, the Catalan national police force. Then tomorrow, I'm off to a three-day conference in London. Great week, eh?' he grumbled. He pointed to a coffee filter in the corner of the big, bright room with a wall-to-wall window which gave Skinner a view of everything going on outside. 'Help yourselves, if you want. I've had my ration for the morning.'

Steele poured coffee for McGuire and for himself and joined the senior officers around the low table.

'So, Mario,' the DCC began briskly. 'What do you want to know?'

'Everything you know about Alec Smith, sir. We've got nothing out of North Berwick, or out of his widow even. We were told that you and he used to mix socially as well as professionally. I was hoping you might help us get a handle on the man.'

'I thought you might say that. Yes, Alec and I had a common interest away from the office; he was one of the Legends for a while.'

Steele frowned, puzzled.

Skinner explained. 'A bunch of us play five-a-side football – or four, or six, depending on how many turn up – every Thursday night at North Berwick Sports Centre. We've been at it for twenty years and more; we call ourselves the Legends because these days we're all so fucking old.

'We had a vacancy, oh, maybe ten years ago. I knew Alec had played a bit in his youth, and he lived in East Lothian, so I asked him if he wanted to come along. He was one of us for about five years, till he chucked it. He decided his right knee wasn't up to it any more.

'But that was the extent of our social mixing. The Legends is as much about the get-together in the pub afterwards as it is about the game itself but Alec rarely mixed in with that. More often than not, he'd get dressed, pay his money, say goodnight and go home to Pencaitland. He never came to any of our Christmas Dinners, no matter what time of year we held them . . . they're never at Christmas.

'On the odd occasion he did come to the pub, he rarely had much to say. He was pleasant enough, you understand; I never heard Alec Smith say a hard or rude word in my life. He was just a very quiet man, that's all.'

He turned to McIlhenney. 'Neil, you worked with him in SB once. How did you find him?'

'I was just seconded there for a short time, Boss, but I thought he was a magician. He'd allocate jobs and when you reported back to him, it was as if he'd known what you were telling him all along.'

'Who were in his inner circle in SB at that time?' asked McGuire.

'He didn't have one, Mario. He treated everyone in the squad

107

in exactly the same way; told them what they needed to know and that was it.'

Skinner picked up a folder on the desk and gave it to the Inspector. 'I thought you'd want this, so I pulled it from Personnel. It's Alec's service record, from the day he joined up. I worked with him myself, way back, in a serious crimes set-up we had then. He was about ten years older than me; I was a DC and he was a DI so I was a couple of rungs down the ladder from him. But I remember his nickname; the lads called him 'Mysterious Mr X'. To his face, sometimes; he just laughed it off.'

McGuire held the folder up. 'Does this tell us why he chucked it?'

'No, but I can. He told me that he had got to the stage where his pension was so healthy that he would be working for half pay from then on, unless he got promoted, and he knew that wasn't going to happen. Alec's privacy was ideal in an SB boss, but a bar to higher command. So he took the pension and went to work for Guardian Security, as its Chief Operating Officer in Scotland – on the same salary as an ACC, plus a nice company Jag.'

'Yet he chucked it after less than a year,' the DI mused. 'I wonder why?'

'I asked the company that very question this morning, Mario,' McIlhenney answered. 'I called the Group Human Resources Director, a bloke called Rylance. He told me that a job came up in London and the Managing Director wanted Alec in it. But he refused, point-blank. The problem was that they had already promised his job in Scotland to one of the MD's protegés. So they gave him six months' pay and his car, and that was that.'

'Give me the guy's number, Neil. We'd better look into the work he did while he was there.'

'That's in hand. Mr Rylance is putting together a full report;

their courier division will get it to you by close of play tomorrow, at the latest.'

McGuire raised an eyebrow and smiled. 'You after my job, McIlhenney?'

The big Sergeant gazed at him, poker-faced. 'You're still in it, aren't you?'

The Special Branch Commander rose, clutching the folder, Steele following his lead. 'In that case you and the kids can come to us for lunch next Sunday.' He looked back at Skinner. 'I report to you on this, Boss?'

The DCC shook his head. 'No. This is Maggie's shout; she and Mr Martin will keep me up to speed, I'm sure. Mind you, if you were to turn up any real nasties . . .'

Fifteen

'Have you seen this, Andy?' The Superintendent pushed a folder across his desk, in the Divisional CID Commander's office in Torphichen Place. 'The floater in the Water of Leith.'

The Head of CID looked at the slim file. 'That's it?' he asked, with a faint, but discernible trace of scorn.

'There's your statement, your girlfriend's sister . . .'

Martin held up a hand. 'What do you mean my girlfriend?'

'One of the detective constables who took Margot's statement saw you and the older lass coming out of Bert's Bar on Friday night.'

'You better ask him if he likes the seaside,' the DCS growled.

'Aw Andy, the lad's good, and I've already lost Stevie Steele to the Eastern Division.'

'I wasn't thinking about sending him to Dunbar; I was thinking about sticking him back in a uniform and having him patrol Seafield!'

'No, really. I've had a word with him about gossip. Christ, you know what he said to me, the cheeky bastard? "But I thought that gossip was the CID's stock-in-trade, sir." He's dead right, of course.'

'You just teach him the meaning of the word "selective", then. Who was it anyway?'

'Jack McGurk.'

'You're right. He is a good lad. How many years has he been with you?'

'Three.'

'And one of your detective sergeants is just going off on maternity leave?'

'That's right.'

'Okay, I'll tell you what. We won't send him to patrol the sewage works, we'll promote him. You can tell him that the vengeful Head of CID was going to give him the shit-kicker job, but that you talked me out of it. That should make you a bloody hero in his eyes, and it should teach him something at the same time.'

He picked up the floater file. 'Two statements; that's all you've got, is it?'

'Them and the post-mortem report. Know what the cause of death was?'

'Drowning.'

'How did you know that?'

'The girl you say I know, she's a final-year medic. I arranged for her to sit in as an observer. She told me that the guy drowned in his own blood.'

'That's right,' said Pringle. 'Every bone in his face was smashed to pieces. His legs and his ribs were pulverised. The cuts across his chest were bone deep. The missing fingers and toes were nowhere to be found in the rug, but it looked as if they had been cut off with scissors or something similar. There were bruise marks around the wrists and ankles; the poor wee guy – he was about five seven, Sarah says – was tied up then slashed and beaten to death.'

'What was the time of death?'

'Sarah fixed it as early Saturday morning. She said that the body had been immersed for about eighteen hours, give one, take one.'

'Give me that again.'

'Time of death early Saturday morning, say three o'clock. Immersed for eighteen hours, give or take. What do we take from that?'

'It puts a limit on where he could have been killed. If he died at three, and was in the water for a minimum of seventeen hours until we took him out at ten, then wherever he was killed is less than two hours' travel time from where the body was dumped. If Sarah's spot on with her eighteen, that's one hour. Allowing time to tie the poor bugger up in that carpet, on that basis, he was killed pretty close to here. If the eighteen stretches towards nineteen, then he was killed very close to where he was found.'

'That's true; unfortunately, all of it's true. It still means that the guy could have been killed in Glasgow and dumped here, if it was nearer seventeen.'

'Come on, Dan. Get real on that; who would bring a stiff through here and drop it in something that's not much more than a stream in places when he's got the Clyde on his doorstep?'

'All right,' said the Superintendent. 'I'll have Jack McGurk and a team begin interviews with people living in the vicinity of the Water of Leith, from Roseburn down to Dean Village. Mind you there's a lot more of them now, since all those flats were built.'

'Nonetheless. It'll keep the investigation moving, and you know how important that is.'

Pringle nodded and leaned back in his chair. 'You know, boy,' he whispered, under his breath, 'you're getting more like Bob Skinner every day.'

Martin gazed at the wall, oblivious to the Divisional Commander's scrutiny. 'Why was he wearing a shirt?' he asked, suddenly.

The burly veteran looked at him, puzzled. He tugged, unconsciously, at one end of his heavy moustache. 'Eh?'

'Why was he wearing a shirt and nothing else? They stripped off his trousers, socks and underwear, but they left him wearing a shirt.'

'Maybe they were going to make him eat his willie, but he died on them.'

'He died on them as an indirect result of having his teeth smashed into powder, Dan.'

'True. Tell you what, I'll have McGurk instigate a search for a missing pair of strides, thirty-six waist, twenty-nine inside leg. Maybe they'll give us a vital clue!'

The Head of CID grinned. 'Listen, it was just a thought. It strikes me as odd, that's all. Was there any sign of sexual interference?'

'You mean did they make him dance the Turkish two-step before they killed him? No, the report says that there were no genital or anal injuries. He did have sex at some point though. Sarah found a single pubic hair, not his, trapped under his foreskin.'

'That's something, at least,' Martin conceded. 'Maybe he was only wearing a shirt because he'd just been getting his end away . . . or maybe the rest of his clothes were traceable. What make was the shirt?'

'Marks and Spencer, collar size sixteen. It could have been bought any-bloody-where in Britain.'

'Could it, though?'

'Aye, I've checked. There is a tab on the inside of M&S shirts, near the foot, that has a garment number on it. But this one had been ripped off – although I suppose it could have come away in the wash.'

'Nothing new on the missing persons lists?'

'Aye, plenty as always. But no medium-sized males in their early to mid-forties.'

'How about the e-fit? Did Sarah give us any ideas on that?'

'She's dealing with that today. She gave priority to the post-mortem report, but she's going to take another look at the body and try to fit the facial bones back together. She said that if she could she'd give us something to release to the *Evening News* tomorrow.'

'Has there been much press interest?'

'Not in comparison to the Alec Smith case. Radio Forth picked it up first, at midnight on Saturday, too late for most of the Sundays.'

'That doesn't surprise me. Spike Thomson was at the party.'

'The disc jockey?'

'That's the boy. He's friendly with Juliet Lewis, Rhian and Margot's mother.'

'Lucky him. She looked quite tasty, from what I saw of her on Saturday while McGurk and Ray Wilding were interviewing the daughter.'

He beamed across the desk at the Head of CID. 'Tell me something, Andy. When you bought that house, did you check out the neighbours first?'

Sixteen

'I know, Stevie, this is a bloody dismal place to work. But face it, man; we all have to work our way up to the likes of Bob Skinner's office. It's in rooms like this that we do it. I've been asking for a spot of refurbishment for over a year now, but that Chris Whitlow, the force's civilian bean-counter, he's a real tight-fisted bastard.

'The Boss doesn't like to lean on him himself, but he's promised me that if I get no action within the next three months he'll bring the Chief down for a visit, to let him see the place, then wind him up to do some kicking himself.'

'Doesn't the Chief come down here normally, then?'

'Proud Jimmy? About once every three years, and then only when Bob invites him. I report to the Big Man direct, you see, and nobody interferes with his operations . . . nobody at all.'

'I can imagine. I've seen him in action. He saved my arse a while back . . .'

McGuire nodded. 'The Russians. I remember.'

'Fucking awesome, he was. You should have seen what he did to that big guy.'

'I'd rather not. We've all done things in our time that we wouldn't have wanted witnessed.' He laughed. 'I remember one night, when McIlhenney and I were in uniform, these gang lads thought they had him cornered in an alley; but they didn't know that I'd been checking out a shop down the street. I came in behind them and it was them that were cornered. What a fucking mess we left them in. But it was just as well no law-abiding member of the public wandered past. It'd have been "Police brutality" and no mistake – there were only four of them.'

He walked over towards the far wall of his office which was lined with cupboards, three of them, steel doors stretching to ceiling height, each with a combination lock.

'This is it, son,' he said. 'There's stuff in here that the *Sun* would die for. You're honoured, you know. You've been cleared to see all of it.' He smiled at Steele's surprise. 'You don't think we let any old plod walk in here, do you?'

Nonetheless, as he dialled up the first combination, he was careful to shield the lock with his body from the Sergeant's view.

He released the lock and swung the double doors open. The cupboard was full of side-racked files, row above row; the Inspector crouched beside them and flicked through the fourth row from the floor, then the third. 'This is where it begins,' he said. 'Alec Smith's reign as SB Commander. His files take up all the second cabinet and go on into the third.'

He straightened up. 'You're going to see things in here that will surprise you. Files on famous names, and I'm not just talking about the Bolsheviks. These cupboards are all about real or potential threats to national security; they cover, literally, a multitude of sins. For example, I've got files on three members of the Scottish Government. One of them's a closet lesbian, another's a thief, and the third was a once member of a group which was suspected of feeding information on potential targets to the IRA.'

'What do you do with information like that?'

'I pass it straight to Big Bob; I'm only a finder-out, he's the doer. In those cases I happen to know that he's shown the files to the First Minister and his Deputy. The three subjects are still in their jobs, but I'd expect two of them to disappear at the first reshuffle. Not the gay lady, though. Sex is nothing; in the fifties it was everything, but nowadays no-one cares how people get their rocks off . . . unless it involves children or farm animals, that is.

'Forty years ago, homosexuality was illegal, now it's almost bloody fashionable.'

'Why the file on her then?' Steele asked.

'Because it was there. SB was asked to vet her and it turned up in the process. There is a slight complication in the case which might make her vulnerable; she's married and has two children.'

'What will we find in Alec Smith's files?'

'Some right goodies. There's one on a former Lord Advocate who was into porking wee boys. Big Bob showed the file to Hughie Fulton, who was the Secretary of State's security adviser at the time. Fulton came back to him and ordered him to burn it. The DCC – he was a Chief Super then – went to see Proud Jimmy about it. The Chief called Fulton into his office and told him that if the guy wasn't removed, his file would be left accidentally in the *Scotsman* newsroom, and the Secretary of State's along with it. Exit Lord Advocate.'

'How do you know all that?'

'Because the file's still in that cupboard, with a note of Bob Skinner's conversations with Fulton, and a tape of the meeting in the Chief's office. Makes good listening, I tell you.'

'What happened to Fulton?'

McGuire frowned. 'That's not on file. No-one knows, but he vanished overnight, straight after the Syrian thing, and Big Bob took over his job. He did it for a while until he fell out with the Secretary of State.'

'What is the Secretary of State's security adviser anyway?' the young Sergeant asked.

'A superspook. MI5. Plays a whole different level of the security business, way above simple flatfeet like you and me.'

'And Mr Skinner used to do that?'

The Inspector gave him a long look. 'You're cleared to be in this room, so I'll tell you this. Sir John Govan, the retired Strathclyde Chief, does it now, but the Big Man's still connected. It comes in handy from time to time, like last year up in the Conference Centre.

'Come on,' he said briskly. 'Let's get started on taking Alec apart and looking for his machinery. I think the sensible thing to do would be to start at the end of his time in office and work back.' He opened the other two cupboards, identified a series of files in the top row of the third and took them out.

'This is going to be a long job, Stevie. We're going to have to check all these out and assess whether the subject was a potential threat to Alec, or whether there was an association between them that carried over beyond his police career.

. 'There's only one constraint on you.' He produced a list from his desk. 'There's a note of all the members of the current Police Board. If you come across old files on any of them, or on any serving officers, give them to me.'

Steele drew in his breath for a second. 'Have we got files on many of the councillors?'

'I've got current files on every fucking one of them. See that kind old uncle of a Chief Constable of ours? When he has to, he can be a right ruthless bastard, just like his Deputy. Sir James is more of a politician than all that lot put together. He had trouble with them once, just once. It took him about one minute to scare them back into line. He knows the power of information; so do I, and I learned about it in this room.'

He separated the files into two lots and handed one to the young Sergeant. 'Any questions?'

'Just one. Who's got your file?'

'Big Bob.'

'And who's got his?'

'I don't know, and I'm glad. Because I've got a feeling that there are things on it that I'd rather not know.'

Seventeen

As he rang the Lewis doorbell, Andy Martin was thinking about Sarah's advice, thinking hard. When Juliet Lewis opened the door he snapped back to the present.

'Good evening, Andy,' she said. There was nothing but welcome in her voice. 'You after my older daughter?'

'Yeah. I've got a couple of tickets waiting for us out at UCI.'

'You look as though you need a break. Come on in, Rhian's not quite ready.' She led the way up to the living room. He had never been upstairs before, but the house was built identically to his own, so the layout was familiar. He glanced around the room; it was expensively furnished, in modern style, with a large television set in the corner beside the patio doors. On the other side, a parrot, red the dominant colour among its plumage, sat on a swing in a big cage.

'Who are you then?' he asked. 'I'm Andy.'

'I'm Andy! I'm Andy!' the bird cawed.

'Clever bugger,' Martin chuckled.

'Clever bugger! Clever bugger!'

He turned to Rhian's mother, thinking as he did, that he could see what Spike Thomson saw in her. She was wearing cotton slacks and a sleeveless top which did her no disservice at all.

'Quite a mimic, isn't he?' she said. 'Say anything to him,

anything at all, and he'll copy it. His name's Hererro; some South American reference, I was told. I rescued him not long ago. His owner was leaving the country for good. I haven't had a quiet moment since.'

'I sympathise. You were right about me needing some time off.' He smiled. 'Normally, Edinburgh isn't a particularly dangerous place, but for the last few years, when things have happened, they've tended to come in clusters. Having two murder investigations running simultaneously isn't normal for us, but it isn't unprecedented either.'

'I know,' Juliet answered. 'My division at Victoria Dock deals with the incidence of crime, among other things. It's just so unpredictable, isn't it? I've actually been out into the field with serving officers; often I think to myself that we civil servants should know more about how the police work. Do you think it would be feasible for some of us to be seconded to forces?'

'I don't see why not. Why don't you float the idea with Ministers? If they give it the okay, I'm sure you could work something out with the Chief Constables.'

'Whose number you will be joining quite soon, I hear.' He looked at her in surprise. 'Come on,' she said, reading him. 'You're sleeping with my daughter; not only that, you're more than ten years older than she is. You think I wouldn't check you out?'

'Not at all. I'm just a bit disturbed that you could.'

'I have my sources . . . although, like you, I wouldn't dream of revealing them.'

'Sir John Govan,' he said. She flushed and he knew that he was right.

'I couldn't possibly say. Anyway, I was told that there will be an ACC job coming up in Strathclyde in round about a year and that you're favourite for it.'

He laughed. 'Jock was always a manipulator. I haven't even thought about it.'

'You don't have to. Everybody and his mother knows that Bob Skinner was offered the Strathclyde Chief's job and turned it down flat. So it's the logical place for you.'

'Why?'

'You know quite well why.'

He smiled at her, amused by the game, and in spite of himself a little flattered. 'And what about Bob?' he asked. 'What has Jock got planned for him?'

'I know, but I couldn't possibly tell you, I'd be fired if word got out to him before everything was ready.'

'Rubbish, mother,' said Rhian, appearing in the doorway. 'You're going to be head of your department inside two years, and Permanent Secretary before you're fifty. You're fireproof.'

'Jesus,' Andy cried out. 'Enough of the career planning. Let's go and hide out in another galaxy, a long time ago and far, far away. This one's getting too bloody crowded.'

She took his hand and followed him downstairs, waving goodnight to Juliet. The MGF was outside, top down in the warm evening. He drove slickly up Palmerston Place, along Morrison Street, and eventually down Holyrood Road, past Dynamic Earth and the rising Parliament complex. Soon they were heading out of town, for the UCI multiplex.

'What about that talk?' Rhian asked, suddenly, her voice raised above the rush of the wind. 'Are we having it later, finally?'

'No, let's have it now. Are you serious about this thing, or are you just a young girl having fun with an older guy?'

'I'm serious.'

'Fine. Let's see how it goes, then.'

'What about love 'n stuff?'

'I don't use that word any more. Too bloody dangerous.'

'My mother's ambitious for me as well as for herself, you know. She's trying to pair us off, if you haven't guessed.'

'Sure, I know. That's the norm in some cultures and it seems to work more often than not, too.'

She laughed, musically, like a chime in the wind. 'You're not exactly a great romantic, are you?'

'I've grown out of that too. I'm me and that's it; but I'm looking for someone. Maybe it's you.'

'So am I on trial?'

'No more than I am with you. So far all we know is that we're good in bed together. Now we have to find out what else there is.'

'Andy?' she asked, whispering in his ear as he drew into a parking space outside the cinema. 'Can you cook?'

'Yes.'

'Thank God for that.'

Eighteen

'That's it, then?' said Dan Pringle. He was gazing at a colour print of a computer-generated portrait. The subject was a man, in early middle age, with mousy receding hair. The pointed nose, small eyes and tight little mouth gave him a slightly rodent-like appearance.

'That's it, sir,' Detective Sergeant Jack McGurk confirmed. The Superintendent looked up and felt a pang of jealousy; the newly promoted McGurk was still in his twenties; almost a quarter of a century lay between them in age, fitness, enthusiasm and prospects.

Not that Pringle was dissatisfied with the way his career had gone; Divisional CID Commander was pretty good by most standards. But twenty-five years earlier, when he had stood in McGurk's shoes, his sights had been set higher, on Andy Martin's office at the very least, and beyond, on the loftier heights of the Command corridor. He had been wounded when young Martin, new in the superintendent rank, had been catapulted into the Head of CID post by Roy Old's death, but he had recognised that the man was on his way somewhere, fast, and more than that, that he was possessed of a level of energy and a quality of leadership far beyond his. So he had kept his disappointment to himself, and had been rewarded by Bob

Skinner with a recommendation for the award of the Queen's Police Medal.

Now here stood another young Turk in front of him. He looked up into McGurk's eyes – a long way up, since the lad was six feet five – and saw that they were bright, lit with more than enthusiasm. He shuddered, faintly, as he felt an army walk over his grave.

It's nearly time to hand on the torch, he thought. Rose, McGuire, Mackie, McIlhenney, Steele, even Neville, and now this boy; hand-picked, all of them, by Skinner and Martin. They're the future and, in a very short time, Dan, they'll be the present. The Chief, Jim Elder, John McGrigor, me . . . maybe even Big Bob himself; we're being lined up to march off into the sunset with our fat pensions and our gongs. Ah shit, it's been fun, though.

He forced himself to listen to McGurk as he continued. 'The pathologist said that she was confident of the general shape of the face and of the prominent features. The cheekbones were too badly smashed for her to be certain of their shape; she said that conceivably the face might have been longer, but that this is her best shot at it.'

Pringle grunted. 'Okay. Get it along to the *Evening News* office, as fast as you can; ask the desk sergeant to whistle up a bike. Then speak to Alan Royston at Fettes and tell him it's on its way. He can get on to his contacts at the paper and get it a good show; the front page, I hope.'

'I could call the *News* myself, sir. I've got a contact there too.'

The Superintendent's eyebrows rose. 'Is that so? Well, take some advice from your old Uncle Dan, and forget about it. Alan Royston's the force Media Manager. He's a civilian, a specialist, and he's our only contact with the press. The DCC and the Head of CID are red hot on that; they both believe in controlling the flow of information, and the best way to do that is to have it come through a single source. I see their point too; if every bloody DS was free to play his own games with the papers, it'd be bloody anarchy.'

McGurk nodded, making a mental note to make his relationship with his journalist brother-in-law purely social in the future. 'Understood.' He took back the portrait from Pringle and headed for the door.

As it closed behind him the Superintendent picked up his telephone and dialled the Head of CID's office. To his surprise, Andy Martin answered the call himself. 'Where are Karen and Sammy Pye?' Pringle asked

'They're checking vets in Edinburgh and West Lothian, to help Maggie with her investigation. Alec Smith was shot full of animal tranquilliser before his killer started to burn bits off him.'

'Jesus. Just like bloody Daktari, eh.'

'It wasn't Judy the fucking chimp that did that to him, I can tell you.' Martin paused; a grim silence. 'What have you got for me, Dan? An ID on the floater?'

'No, worse luck, but his likeness should be in the *News* this lunch time. Sarah's done us a picture. We'll give copies to the dailies as well, and television.'

'I've seen what she's done. I've been sent a copy. Mr Average, isn't he?'

'Aye, but he's someone's Mr Average.'

'So what are we doing about finding him?'

'Now we've got the e-fit, we're going to canvass houses from Roseburn up to your place, up to half a mile distant from the river, initially. I know that sounds a lot, but we'll use the Voters' Roll and eliminate households where there are no males registered.'

'A single woman might still know the man. Shouldn't you knock all the doors?'

'Give me Neville and Pye when they've finished the vets and I could. Otherwise I have to set priorities. It's holiday season, Andy; I've got my deputy, a DI, and two DCs on leave.'

'Okay,' Martin conceded. 'If you still need Karen and Sammy by then you've got them.'

Pringle beamed. 'Thanks, Andy. I was half-joking when I said that.'

'Why? It's a reasonable request. I don't want anyone ever to be able to say that your investigation is less important, or has a lower priority than the Alec Smith job. One's an ex-copper and the other's a nameless stiff who's been dead for three days without being missed, but we have the same duty to them both, and they have the same claim on my CID resources.'

Nineteen

'Ahh bugger it, I hate this sort of job!' Mario McGuire shouted in sudden frustration, leaning back in his chair, right fist punching upwards towards the ceiling. 'My wife can sit with piles of case folders, going through them for hour after hour like this, looking for linking factors. I don't have her sort of patience. I suppose that's why she's a DCI and I'm only a poor bloody Inspector.'

'With prospects,' said Stevie Steele.

'Aye, unless I get too good at this job and wind up stuck here like poor old Alec.' He stood up, walked to a small desk in the corner of the room, and switched on an electric kettle. 'Time for a caffeine fix.' The Sergeant watched as he mixed two mugs of Alta Rica coffee, added a dash of milk to each and brought them across to the table at which they had been working.

'Right,' he said. 'We're about a third of the way through working backwards; we've eliminated the obvious no users – which is most of them – and set aside our prospects. Let's see what we've got. You go first, Stevie.'

'Okay.' The Sergeant laid down his coffee and picked up a folder. 'In here are Angus Morrison, date of birth June 28, 1954, and Wendy Forrest, born April 4, 1959. He was a bus driver, she was a low-grade civil servant. They lived together at an address in

131

Lasswade. They were founder members – as far as I can see the only members – of something called the Scottish Republican movement. They were jailed in September 1991 for twelve years each after conviction at the High Court in Edinburgh for possession of gelignite and attempting to blow up an electricity pylon in Midlothian.

'According to Alec's file, they were observed every step of the way. SB officers watched them lay their explosives then lifted them before they could set them off.

'How about them?' he asked. 'They should be out by now, with remission.'

McGuire hunched his shoulders and took a sip of the strong coffee. 'Good trick if it was Wendy Forrest. She hanged herself in her cell in Cornton Vale in 1995. Gus Morrison's another matter, though. He was paroled in 1998. From what I remember of that file, she reads like a poor wee mouse, but he was a real nasty bastard.'

Steele nodded. 'That's what it says right enough. It says also Alec Smith and another SB officer gave evidence against them *in camera*; but DCI Smith notes on the file that Morrison got a good look at them all in the witness box. Where will Morrison be now, d'you think?'

'He's not under my eye yet, I can tell you that. He's out on parole, so the probation service will have him under supervision. We'll check with them. Who's next?'

'Lawrence Scotland. Date of Birth January 7, 1961, unmarried, lives in Gilmerton. Usually unemployed in the past, but a known associate of criminals, most notably one Tony Manson. According to this, Scotland was a known contact of the Ulster Volunteer Force, and was suspected of killing several Catholics in Northern Ireland during the 1980s. He was under

SB surveillance, but became aware of this. In 1990 he slipped his watchers and disappeared for several weeks. There were sightings of him in Ireland during this period, which coincided also with a spate of assassinations of senior Provisional IRA figures in Armagh.

'Scotland doesn't seem to have been convicted of anything. There's a note on the file by DCI Smith; all it says is "Interviewed, December 2, 1990," nothing else, but there are no reports of activity after that.'

McGuire grunted. 'I'm not surprised.'

'Why not?'

The Inspector looked at his colleague, unblinking. 'I've got a DC on my strength called Tommy Gavigan. He's been in SB for years, can't go anywhere else. I spoke to him on Sunday, just the two of us, asking for anything he knew about Alec that wasn't on the files. He told me about that "interview".

'He and Alec picked Scotland up at six in the morning; they drove him up into the Pentlands, to the part the army uses, where no-one else goes. They got the boy out of the car and walked him up the hill. Then Alec took out a revolver. He took out one bullet, showed it to him so he'd know it wasn't blank, loaded it, spun the chamber, put it to Scotland's head and pulled the trigger. The guy fainted.

'Alec kicked him in the ribs to bring him round and stood him up. He loaded another bullet, spun the chamber again, pointed the gun right at the middle of his forehead and pulled the trigger. Scotland shat himself and dropped to his knees, crying like a baby.

'Alec looked down at him and said, "Next time, Lawrence, there'll be six bullets in the fucking gun." Then he and Gavigan just walked off and left him there, squatting in his own shit.'

Steele's mouth hung open in amazement. 'How did Smith manage to make sure that the hammer hit an empty chamber?'

'He didn't.'

'You mean . . .'

'Five to one against first time, two to one the second; if Scotland had lost the bet, they'd have left him there and the Army would have buried him.'

'Just like that?'

'Just like that. The guy was believed to have killed at least ten people and he was thumbing his nose at us.'

'But . . .'

'Either way, he never did it again. Gavigan's been keeping an occasional eye on him. Does the file say where he is now?'

'Still in Pilton. He's got a job now; he's been with Guardian Security since 1995.'

'Guardian? Jesus! And that dopey old bastard Tommy never thought to tell me.'

'Maybe he didn't know that Smith had gone there.'

'Maybe not indeed,' the DI conceded. 'Alec never told him things; he just told him to do things.'

'What else have you got?'

'One more. Shakir Basra, date of birth not known, but believed to be around 1950, resided in Little France. An Iranian who wangled political asylum after the Shah fell; he was kept under surveillance here after he moved up from London. The main thing about him was that he was suspected of sexually abusing children, and of several child murders in London. He was never charged there but, according to the file, SB actually had a photo of him with an eight-year-old boy who was found raped and murdered near Craigmillar Castle in 1994. It's missing from the folder, though; the file stops just after that time with a handwritten note by Alec Smith, saying, "Left the District". Doesn't say where he went.'

'Forget him. Gavigan told me that story too. Basra's dead.'

Steele's face twisted with incredulity. 'He's not up the fucking Pentlands, is he?' he gasped.

'No, no, no, Alec wouldn't have dirtied his hands on that one. The fact is, there's a real Iranian dissident group in Edinburgh; they're just political activists mostly, but there are one or two real hard men among them. We know all about them, and they're smart enough to know about us. Alec went to see them; he gave them the photo, plus one of the kid's body, and he told them all about Basra.

'They took him away one night, executed him, Islamic-style, and let Alec know afterwards. They castrated him, then cut his head off with a sword and buried him, near where he killed the boy.'

'My God.' The young Sergeant looked distressed. 'What sort of a man was this Smith? Were there any more?'

'Not that Gavigan knew of. I sweated him a bit, but he swore blind that he was never involved in any other – what do we call it? – unofficial action. As to what sort of a man Alec was, he was a copper with the power to do what many others wish they could, and the strength of will to go through with it.'

'But he was a vigilante,' Steele protested.

'And an elder of his church when he lived in Pencaitland.' McGuire smiled at him, a dangerous, high-intensity grin. 'Have you never thumped anyone, Sergeant? Remember that guy who slashed Maggie's arm? She heard what you said to him when you had him on the floor, with your knee in the middle of his back. Something about cutting his fucking ears off, wasn't it?

'You were talking earlier on about what the Boss did to that big

Russian. I know what he did; Dan Pringle told me. I'd have done much the same in his shoes, except I might have given him an extra kick in the balls, just for luck. Between you and me, I think the way Smith handled the Basra business was just bloody wonderful. You've seen the file; you know what he did to that kiddie. The London murders were exactly the same. The man was an animal. Good for Alec on that one.'

'But still . . .'

'Aye, I know. You could argue that sometimes the real strength lies in not using your power. But that man Basra deserved to be in the ground. As for Lawrence Scotland, ask yourself this? How many lives did Alec save when he put the fear of God in that bloke?'

'Maybe, Mario. But maybe, too, the fear of God wore off and cost him his own life.'

'Let's find out. That's your lot, then?'

'Yes. What have you got?'

'Eff all . . . that I fancy at any rate. Let's work our way through the rest, although the further back in time we go, the less we'll get, I'm sure. We'll do it though, report progress to Maggie and then take a real close look at Gus Morrison, and Lawrence Scotland.'

Twenty

Dan Pringle sat behind his desk, like a bear in his lair, when there was a single sharp knock on the door. Before he could call out, 'Yes', it swung open and Alan Royston, the police force's Media Relations Manager burst into the room, clutching a newspaper. Royston was a mild-mannered man; the Superintendent had never seen him roused to anger before. Still, he reacted to being on the end of it.

'What the hell's this, Alan?' he demanded as the door closed. 'You might have fucking wakened me, bursting in like that.'

'I'm sorry about that, Dan,' the Press Officer retorted, 'but I do not like it when officers go behind my back, making unauthorised statements to the media. It undermines me and, frankly, it makes me look like a bloody Charlie.' He waved the tabloid in the air; Pringle could see from the mast-head that it was a copy of Edinburgh's 'other' daily, the *Evening News*.

He unrolled it and laid it on Pringle's desk. There, on the front page, was the e-fit likeness which the Superintendent had sent for publication a few hours before. 'They gave us a good show,' he grunted.

'Fine,' Royston snapped. 'But look at the heading, *Do you know him? Police fear they never will.* Look at the copy too, at this line in particular.' He picked up the paper. 'Listen! *Senior officers*

*investigating the case admitted privately that they are pessimistic
over their chances of ever identifying the mystery man, far less
finding his killers.'* And this. *The victim's face was battered to a
pulp, he had multiple fractures and several toes and fingers had
been cut off.* None of that stuff came from me, Dan, none of it. I
used only the statement that we agreed, saying that we were
confident of a speedy identification and of further progress
thereafter. I said that the man had died of serious head injuries,
and no more than that. I didn't give any details, far less all that
material. You've got a tip-off man on your team.'

Pringle nodded, his own anger simmering now. 'Aye,' he
growled. He stepped over to the door opened it and crossed the
corridor to the CID general office. He threw the door open.
'Sergeant McGurk,' he bellowed, 'My office!'

The tall young sergeant followed him, crossing the corridor in
a single stride. Pringle grasped the *News* and thrust it at him.
'Read that crap,' he barked, 'and tell me if any of it came from
you. Because if it did, the Head of CID and I have made a big
mistake and you're in for the fastest demotion in the history of
this fucking police force!'

McGurk went white as a sheet; he tore the paper from
Pringle's grasp and began to read. 'None of it, gaffer,' he
exclaimed when he had finished. 'Not a word of that came from
me. I swear on a stack of Bibles.'

The Superintendent stared up at him, eyes narrowed. 'A big
stack?' he growled.

'As big as you like.'

'Do you know the guy who wrote the story?'

McGurk nodded. 'Paul Blacklock. He's my brother-in-law.'

'Then get him to phone me and swear the same thing. Do it
right now, Jack: get going.'

The Sergeant nodded, and left the room on the double.

'Anyone else?' Royston asked.

'Only the divers and the ambulance crew, and they're hardly *senior officers investigating*. I'll check them all out though. Apart from them, as far as I can remember, the only people who got a close look at that body were the Head of CID and me. I'm really sorry about this, Alan.'

The Press Officer smiled. 'In that case, do something for me. Call Andy Martin and tell him about this; rather you than me.'

Twenty-one

The Head of CID looked around the outer room of his office suite. Detective Sergeant Karen Neville and Detective Constable Sammy Pye looked back towards the doorway in which he stood. 'What's odd about this picture?' he asked.

'Tell us, sir,' Sammy Pye replied.

'You two are both back behind your bloody desks.' He laughed. 'Even if it is only for a short time. Come on in here, both of you and tell me about the vets.' Neville and Pye stood and followed him into the inner office.

'We've just finished writing up a summary for DCI Rose,' the Sergeant began as they all took seats at the meeting table. 'We've spoken to every bloody vet in Edinburgh and West Lothian. Most of them, nearly all of them keep supplies of this stuff, but they hardly ever use it. Not one of them was aware of any being missing. We've checked out their College too – The Royal Dick Vet.'

'Where do they learn about the other bits of the animals, though?' Pye asked, drawing a frown from Martin.

'Shut up, Sammy.' Neville carried on, quashing the interruption. 'We spoke to a professor there. He told us that they only teach the theory, not the practice, so they don't keep stocks at all. He told us all about the theory, though – for example the

141

quantities you'd use to knock down a man would be the same as you'd use for a large chimpanzee.'

'As for administering it, that would depend on the animal,' said the DCS.

'Let's just assume that big Alec Smith would have been a pretty dangerous animal if you'd come at him with a hypodermic in your hand.'

'In that case, you'd have shot him with a tranquilliser dart, usually from a specially-adapted air rifle or air pistol. None of them was missing either, anywhere.'

'How about the zoo?'

Neville shot him a quick, private, chastening look. 'We checked that, of course – and the travelling circus that was pitched out in Livingston last weekend – and an ostrich farm down in the Borders. Nothing missing from any of them.'

'Only one other thing to do, then,' Martin muttered.

'We've just finished doing it. The names of all the vets, all the professional staff at the Royal Dick Vet, and all the zoo and circus people have been fed into the PNC, looking for anything that might connect them back to Alec Smith.

'A complete blank, I'm afraid, sir. Vets are straight-A people to the point of boredom. That really is as far as we can go. Like I've said, we've just finished our report for Ms Rose.'

The Head of CID nodded. 'Right; she's at the divisional HQ today, in Brian Mackie's office. Take it along to her, Karen, and run through what you've done, just in case there are any areas that you and her people might not have covered between you. After that, I want you both to report to Superintendent Pringle down at Torphichen Place. He's short-staffed and needs all the help he can get to put a name to the Saturday-night floater.'

'How about Tony Manero?' Pye suggested. Martin and Neville stared at him. 'You know, the guy in *Saturday Night Fever*?'

'Jesus, boy,' said the Head of CID, 'you need a spell as a Blue Meanie, out on the street persecuting motorists, to cure that sense of humour. For the record, this guy was not wearing a white suit when we fished him out, nor was he in any condition to go dancing.

'You get off to see Mr Pringle right now. Karen'll join you once she's been to St Leonard's.' Pye nodded and left the room with what looked like a quick disco shuffle. Neville turned to follow him, but Martin laid a hand on her sleeve. 'Hang on a minute, Karen.'

She sat down once more at the briefing table. 'You doing anything tomorrow night, after work?'

'Afraid so. I'm going down to Cockburnspath to see my mother; I'm staying over and driving back in the morning.'

'How about Thursday?'

She shook her head. 'Sorry again; I'm baby-sitting for Neil while he and the Boss kick each other around . . . not that I should be calling Lauren a baby. She's carrying the load amazingly well.' She paused. 'He'll be back before eleven, though. You could always come round to my place later.'

'Nah, that wouldn't do.'

'Andy,' she asked, 'what's up?'

He gave her a wry smile. 'My head, that's what's up. Completely fucked up. I need someone to talk to, someone close, someone who can help me get my priorities right.'

Karen looked back at him, not smiling; not at all. 'That's a coincidence. I need much the same myself. Yes, let's have a joint shoulder-soaking session. But not this week, eh?' She stood and kissed him, quickly. 'Sorry,' she said. 'Improper in the office and all that. Let's make a date for next week; if you still want to talk to me by then.'

'What d'you mean?'

'I mean that you're going out with Ruth McConnell on Saturday night. She let it slip in the girlies' room this afternoon.'

'Damn!' he swore. 'That's part of the problem; but only part.'

'And what about me?' she asked him, quietly. 'Am I part of it too?'

'I thought you and I were like-minded,' he said, eyes narrowing. 'I thought you wanted us to be the way we are.'

'You can't always get what you want . . . Am I?'

He sighed and walked towards the window. The view was not as panoramic as Bob Skinner's, but he could still see the front door. Sammy Pye was leaving the building, his light sports jacket slung over his shoulder. 'Yeah,' he murmured, at last. 'Yes, I think you are.'

'In that case,' she replied, 'don't be so crass as to think you can use me like that. In that case, I only want to talk to you when you've got something to tell me – or ask me. There's no point in having a sounding board who has an axe to grind – or plant in your head, as the case may be.'

He looked back at her, seeing things in her eyes that he had never seen before. No more steady, reliable, good buddy Karen; no more hot nights and hot breakfasts, with no complications. *Should have known better, Martin. It always gets complicated, sooner or later.*

'I'm off to St Leonard's, sir,' she said, suddenly businesslike. 'Then to Torphichen. When do you want me back here?'

'Whenever Dan gets a result,' he answered. 'Karen, I'm sorry. I know I'm a fucking idiot where my private life's concerned. I'll talk to you, soon.'

'Maybe; just don't promise what you can't deliver. I'll call you from Torphichen, when I've seen what Mr Pringle has lined up for us.' She left the room; he was relieved when she closed the door quietly behind her.

He turned and threw a punch at the wall; pulling it less than an inch short of making a fist-sized dent in the plaster. Swearing quietly to himself, he sat behind his desk, trying to restore some semblance of order to his mind. At once, he knew the first thing that he had to do. He picked up the telephone and punched in an internal number.

'Ruth,' he said, as the call was answered, 'it's Andy Martin. Listen, about Saturday night . . .'

'You want to call it off,' she replied, at once.

'I think I should.'

He heard her chuckle. 'Why am I not surprised? When I mentioned it to Karen, it was as if a freezer door had opened next to me. It's okay, really; I hadn't read anything into Saturday.'

'Of course not, but still . . . Look, this has got nothing to do with Karen . . .' He stopped at once, recognising his lie. 'Well yes, it has, but it isn't all about her.'

'Then God help her, Andy. She's a really nice girl and, if you'll pardon my French, she doesn't need to be fucked around. It might not look it, but I'm a lot tougher than she is. I could have a one-night stand with you and think no more of it. Karen might put on a front, but that's all it is. Be kind to her, please.'

'I will, Ruthie, I will. Honest.' He replaced the phone in its cradle, and stared at it for long, silent seconds, willing it to ring and distract him. It did.

'Andy, Dan Pringle. Sorry to bother you, but I've had Alan Royston here with his shirt-tail on fire. Someone's been talking to the papers about the Water of Leith investigation, giving away all sorts of stuff. Get hold of today's *News* and you'll see what I mean; it's right on the front page.

'I've had an on-the-spot investigation here, and I'm satisfied that the leak didn't come from this office. The guy who wrote the story was Jack McGurk's brother-in-law, but Jack's promised me it wasn't him, and the guy's called me to confirm that.'

Martin frowned. 'So are you suggesting that it came from my office?'

'No, no, no,' said the Superintendent, hurriedly. 'I'm just telling you, that's all.'

'Good, because my staff know bugger all about the detail of that case – so that would leave me as the source. And if you're suggesting—'

'I'm not, for fuck's sake,' Pringle protested. 'I'm just telling you this because Royston asked me to. Look it was probably one of the divers, okay. Or a paramedic. Or a porter at the Royal, even. I'll investigate it further and report back to you.' The veteran growled. 'Christ, another burning shirt-tail.'

The Head of CID was grateful for an opportunity to laugh. 'All right, Dan, I'll run some water on it,' he promised. 'Keep me in touch.'

He hung up and dialled Alan Royston's office, asking his assistant to bring him a copy of the *Evening News*. When it arrived he spotted the offending story at once. He read it, once, then again, then a third time.

When he put the newspaper down, his forehead was locked in a frown and his vivid green eyes, in their tinted contact lenses, were blazing like emeralds.

Twenty-two

'**D**o you ever think that our lifestyle might be bad for us?' Maggie Rose gazed at her husband across their small garden table. She was wearing a loose-fitting cotton shirt, bra-less, and denim shorts, an outfit as different from her business clothes as she could find, and the remnants of supper lay between them.

'What? Living off carry-out pizzas?' he said, with a disarming grin. 'We only do it once a week; that's hardly excessive.'

She raised an eyebrow. The evening sun shone on her rich, red hair as it fell across her forehead; it was dark, almost blood-like. Most people thought it was a tint, but Mario knew otherwise. Most people thought of Mags as serious and straight-laced, but he knew differently there too. She was deep, was Mrs McGuire, a bottomless sea in whom the big, tough Irish-Italian detective had swum lovingly since first they had met.

'Don't be flip,' she said. 'You know what I mean. I'm talking about our jobs; you in Special Branch, me in CID. Aren't you ever afraid that they might take us over?'

He laughed. He was in shorts also; tailored, with big pockets on each side. Strands of thick, black, curly chest hair had forced their way through his white tee-shirt. 'If you're suggesting I get a transfer to traffic, you're not on.'

147

She laid her glass on the table, smiling inside of herself. 'Mario!'

He reached over and took her hand; as he drew it towards him, he saw the scar. It was fainter than it had been, but it was still there. For all the surgeon's reassurances, he knew that it always would be, just as he would always carry a mark of his own on his chest, beneath the mat of hair. 'Maggie,' he answered. 'I love my job. It's fascinating and at times it's exciting. But I love you a hell of a lot more. If I ever thought it was any sort of a threat to you and me, I'd chuck it in a second . . . or I really would get a transfer to traffic.

'You feel the same way about yours too; so instead of seeing it as a potential problem, look at it from another perspective. Look at the commonality of interest it gives us.'

She nodded; more of her hair fell forward, throwing her face into shadow. 'I suppose so. Just promise me one thing, though: promise me that you won't stay too long in Special Branch.'

He released her hand and reached for his glass. 'Why do you say that?'

'What else? Alec Smith: the way he ended up. Mario, what if that was related in some way to the job he did? Your job now.'

'Hey, kid. The day I find myself turning into Alec, I transfer out. And that takes us back to the subject of this conversation. Alec never talked to anyone, other than Bob Skinner and his predecessor, and then only when he had to. He didn't go home to Mrs Alec and unburden himself; he was so remote, so wrapped up in it that it made her leave him.' He paused, and shivered in the evening sun. 'And it made him into what?' he mused, in a whisper.

'What do you mean?' she asked.

'I don't know, love. I don't know.' He picked up the Chianti, topped up Maggie's glass, and poured the last of the bottle into his own.

'See that lass Cowan?'

'Alice? Yes. I've been asked if I'd like her in CID. I'd take her in a minute, but I'll leave the decision for Brian when he gets back from holiday. I'd rather he had the argument with her line commander.'

'You rate her then?'

'Very much. She's very sharp'.

'She thinks for herself, and doesn't say any more than she needs to?'

'Yes, I'd say that.'

'I might save Superintendent Mackie from that Barney, then.'

'What? You mean you might pinch her?'

'If she comes through vetting okay, yes. There's someone I've got to move out.'

'Who's that?'

'Tommy Gavigan: the old DC. He's blown out and he's got to go now; I've sent him on leave already and I won't have him back. He's forty-seven with just over two years to go to retirement, so we'll give him the extra time on his pension rights and let him leave early. I told Big Bob this as soon as I'd interviewed Gavigan, so it's as good as done. If Whitlow the bean-counter moans about the cost, he'll get told.

'Something else too, that should please you. In future nobody does more than five years in Special Branch . . . ever. That comes from the Gaffer himself.'

Maggie looked at him carefully. 'I'm glad to hear that; but Gavigan's an old soldier. You sure you want to replace him with a youngster like Alice? She's only twenty-four.'

'I'm absolutely sure, because she *is* a youngster, she's uncorrupted, a breath of fresh air, and I need that in SB.'

'What's brought this on? Am I allowed to know?'

'I don't suppose you are but I'll tell you, because you couldn't do anything about it afterwards even if you wanted to. The Boss wouldn't let you.'

He told her the stories of Lawrence Scotland and Shakir Basra. When he was finished, she let out a long, low whistle. 'You were asked to get a handle on Alec Smith, Inspector. You've surely done it, haven't you? I can see why you want Gavigan out.'

Mario nodded. 'Aye, it'll make it easier to use him as bait.'

'Uh?'

'Think about it. If Lawrence Scotland has finally plucked up the courage to get even with Smith, isn't there a chance that he might go for Gavigan as well, especially if he's off the job? Even as we speak, the man's under surveillance.'

'And this Lawrence Scotland is one of the two possibilities you mentioned earlier. Who's the other?'

'One Gus Morrison; a would-be tartan terrorist.'

'Do you like either of them for it?'

'Couldn't say yet, any more than you could. I'll know when I've had a look at them.'

'What are you going to do?'

'Pick them both up; interrogation plus psychiatric evaluation. It takes a special man to burn off someone's balls with a blowlamp and make a movie while he's doing it. If it was either of them, we'll know.'

'And what if it wasn't?'

'Then the SB files have come up blank. There's no-one else.'

'And we're back where we started.'

He grinned, as Maggie's face fell. 'Not quite. There's still

Alec's personal papers; all the things that were taken from the house. They have to be gone through.'

'Where are they now? I haven't seen them in the van.'

'Too right you haven't; Christ knows what could be in there. No, I've got them.' He jerked a thumb back towards the house. 'In there, in my big briefcase.'

'You took them way from the investigation?' she exclaimed, indignantly.

'Special Branch prerogative, my dear. Our man, our files.'

'Time you shared them then. Come on, Mario, I'm supposed to be in charge of this investigation, but it seems as if it's you who's running it, really.' She stood and pushed back her plastic chair. 'Go on; get into the house and fetch that briefcase.'

'Okay,' he agreed. 'DCI or not, I may have to kill you once you've seen it, but we'll discuss that later.'

He led the way through the patio doors, into the small sitting room of their Miller villa, and fetched the briefcase from the hall. He opened it and took out a thick sheaf of material, which he laid on the long low coffee table which was set in front of their sofa.

'Have you looked at this yourself yet?' she asked.

'No, I gave priority to the SB file check.'

He picked a folder from the top of the pile, opened it and began to flick through its contents. 'Household bills. Gas, leccy, and rates. All in sequence.' A second folder. 'Telephone bills; BT and Orange. As far as I can see none of them are very big, but I'll check them out tomorrow – the itemised ones at any rate – and see if any numbers jump out at us.'

He picked up the next folder; it was lever-arched, and split into sections. 'Pension papers,' he said, after a few seconds perusal. 'Police stuff, and interest and dividend notices from other investments. Then bank statements and correspondence.'

Maggie looked at the coffee table, at the last thick brown folder which lay there. She reached across and opened it. 'Photographs,' she murmured. 'Just dozens of bloody photographs.'

Mario picked up the collection and looked through it, print by print. They were all seven-by-five colour photographs, and their content varied. Some were beach shots, some rural, some of Edinburgh scenes, one or two indoors. They were all clear and sharp, as if they had been taken on high-quality equipment, by an expert. And each print was numbered and dated; not an automatic camera feature on the picture itself, but hand-written annotations on the reverse side.

He frowned as he looked through them again. 'Funny,' he murmured. 'No two dates are the same. They're in number and date order, but there's no other sequence to them. He seems to have taken his camera out on a whim, then he seems to have picked the best of his shots on each day for this file.'

'Or as a record,' Maggie suggested, quietly. 'What if he just picked one innocuous shot from a wider selection? What if this folder is a sort of index?'

'Then where are the rest? And the negatives, too? But hold on a minute, maybe that's all he did: pick the best and junk the rest.'

'Maybe, but . . . Mario, there's something else about these photographs. They've all got people in them; every one, even the landscapes and beach scenes. It's as if . . .'

Her husband frowned as he nodded. 'By God, Mags; you're on to something; these are surveillance photographs. Most of the faces are obscure, but if you knew who they were . . .' He turned the pile upside down and flicked through the dates. 'Some of these go back to when Alec was still in the job and they continue right up to the present. What was the man doing?'

'I'll bet someone knows,' she fired at him. 'It could be that someone topped him because of it. How much did they take away with them, d'you think? The rest of the photos and the negs? His address book? Don't tell me Smith didn't have one . . . The camcorder: were there any tapes, other than the one we were meant to find?'

'Maybe,' he said. 'Maybe the murderer cleaned the place out, but . . .

'Remember, Alec Smith was a ten-year SB commander. If he was running a private surveillance operation, for whatever purpose, he'd have kept detailed files and he'd have kept them secure. But there were no secure cabinets in Shell Cottage, at least none that we found.

'That means that either we missed something in that house, or Alec Smith had a second site, where he kept those records.'

Maggie's eyes flashed with excitement. 'Tomorrow morning, Inspector, you're going back to Forth Street, and you're going to tear that place apart. While you're doing that, I'm going to have people identifying the tenants of every small office in East Lothian . . .' She stopped. 'Ahh, but you've got Morrison and Scotland to deal with . . .'

'No. You're right, we have to follow this up now; I'll have someone handle those two, very discreetly. Mags, we've got to share this, now.'

'Tell the Boss, you mean?'

'No, he's away at a conference. You have to tell your boss. Let's go and see Andy Martin, now, the pair of us.' He glanced at his watch. 'A good part of that Chianti's still in our glasses out there; we can drive. Let's get along to his place now.'

'Okay, but phone him. Make sure he's in.'

Mario nodded. He dialled the Head of CID's home number, but a machine answered. He dialled his mobile, but it was not receiving. He dialled Karen Neville who told him, curtly, that she had no idea where the DCS was. Finally he left a message on his pager, saying, 'Your place, urgent. On our way, M&M.'

Twenty-three

Something made Andy switch off his cellphone as he rang the Lewis doorbell. He was still uncertain of how he was going to play it; home game or away game, gentle quizzing or balls-out interrogation.

He had hoped that Rhian would come to the door herself. Neither Juliet's car nor the elderly Fiesta which the girls shared were in the driveway. But it was Margot who answered the summons of the bell.

'Oh, hello,' said the girl. 'Rhian isn't in.' There was something in her tone and as he tried to fathom it, he realised that he had never had a conversation of more than two words on either side with his lover's younger sister.

'Will she be gone long?'

'She shouldn't be. I'll tell her you came for her.'

'Don't put it that way, Margot. It makes her sound like a commodity. Just ask her if she'd come next door when she gets back. There's something I want to talk to her about.'

'Will I tell her to bring a toothbrush?' There was no doubt this time about the coldness, or about the sneer in her voice. He took a look at her, properly, for the first time. She was an inch or so taller than her older sister, and even from the way she stood, he could tell that she was an athlete. She was not unattractive, and her beautifully cut dark hair shone with natural highlights, yet there was something about her, the set of her mouth perhaps, the remoteness of her eyes, maybe both, which was instantly forbidding. Where Rhian's whole demeanour asked a gentle question, Margot's shouted an answer.

'Look,' he said. 'I'm sorry we had to pull the plug on your party.'

She shrugged. 'No problem; my guests all went to the pub anyway . . . after I made a hysterical fool of myself and your doctor put me to bed.' Her stare was unbroken; she was barely more than a child, almost twenty years his junior, yet there was something contemptuous about it. His head told him to leave it alone; normally, he would have listened.

'Have you got a problem with me?' he demanded.

'Happily, no,' she replied.

'Do you resent Rhian and me in some way?'

She gave a short, cold laugh. 'Why should I? I certainly don't fancy you . . . which makes me unique in this household.'

He frowned, checking an angry retort on his lips.

'That surprises you, does it?' she asked. 'That Mum should find you attractive? She's only forty-four, you know, and she's pretty damned attractive herself. Spike thinks so, even if you don't.'

'I never said that I don't; but you just destroyed your argument. Spike Thomson: Juliet's involved with him. What makes you think she'd have the slightest interest in me?'

'She told me; and she told Rhian. Look, Spike's nice, but he's more of a good reliable friend than anything else. Stable jockey, that's all; they're not engaged or anything. My mother took a shine to you from the moment you moved in next door. But she's not sexually aggressive in the way my tarty sister is. She doesn't flaunt herself like Rhian.'

156

'That's enough, Margot. I don't need to hear this.'

'Yes, you do,' the girl snapped. 'Not long after Dad . . . left, Mum invited a man to dinner. He was a civil servant too, single, and quite dishy. Two weeks later she called at his place unexpectedly and found him and Rhian in bed. When she let slip that she liked you, I knew what would happen, even if she didn't.'

'You're making all this up.'

'Am I? She offered me a bet about you! When Mum told us . . . We were just talking over supper, about men in general, you know, a "Who do you fancy?" game. Rhian said "Sean Connery," and Mum said, "The man next door, actually." I could see the look in my sister's eye as soon as she said it. When Mum went through to the kitchen, I said to her, "You wouldn't," and she said to me "Bet?" Just like that.' She glanced along to the end of the road. 'Here she comes. Ask her yourself.'

He looked at her. For one of the very few times in his life, his mouth ran ahead of his brain. 'Who did you fancy in the game, kid? Madonna?' At once, he wished he had bitten his tongue, but it was too late: he knew that he had hit the mark. For the first time, Margot looked like a hurt child as she flinched and slammed the door.

'What was all that about?' Rhian asked as she climbed out of the Fiesta. 'What's that brat been saying to you?'

'Nothing. Come on in next door, there's something I have to ask you.'

She flashed her eyes at him. 'The answer's "yes",' she joked.

'It had better not be.' The smile left her face as she saw his; she followed him inside and upstairs. As he stepped into the living room he saw his TAM flashing to indicate a waiting message. His pager was showing a light too, as it lay on the sideboard beside a copy of the *Evening News*.

He picked up the newspaper and showed it to Rhian. 'See that? It's a story about our investigation into the murder of the man in the Water of Leith. My Press Officer gave the media a statement when we issued our photo fit. It was very carefully drafted and cleared with Superintendent Pringle, who's in charge of the investigation. We have to be very careful what we say to the press, for all sorts of reasons, but most of all for fear of prejudicing a future trial.

'Now listen to this bit. *Senior officers investigating the case admitted privately that they are pessimistic over their chances of ever identifying the mystery man, far less finding his killers.*

'No senior officer has ever admitted any such fucking thing to a journo, privately or otherwise. But I seem to remember saying something like that to you the other night, in bed. Now let me read you this: *The victim's face was battered to a pulp, he had multiple fractures and several toes and fingers had been cut off.*

'The only people who would know that were those who saw the body: police, paramedics, and those who were at the post-mortem examination, like you.' She made to turn, as if to walk across towards the double doors to the balcony. 'No,' he said, firmly but not shouting. 'Don't turn your back on me. Look me in the eye.' She did as she was told and he fixed his gaze on her.

'Now I want you to tell me straight out, and no lies . . . I'm an experienced detective; only a real pro could hope to get away with lying to me. Are you the source of that information?'

She said nothing. 'Come on, Rhian, out with it. Did you feed our pillow-talk, and the things you saw at the p.m., to the bloody press? And don't think you can hide behind the notion that journalists always protect their sources; not from me, they don't. Now out with it.'

She looked as young and vulnerable as had her sister, a few minutes earlier, as she nodded. He knew that he was giving the Lewis girls a hard night. He felt many things, sorrow and sympathy among them, but betrayal overcame them all; he pressed on.

'Who was your contact? The guy whose by-line's on the story?'

'Yes,' she whispered.

'Fucking marvellous; his brother-in-law's a detective sergeant and Pringle's already given him the third degree. What's your relationship with this Paul Blacklock?'

'He's an ex.'

'Ex?'

'Yes. It's over, Andy, really.'

'Really. So when did you see him to give him this information?'

'Yesterday afternoon.'

'Where?'

'At his flat.'

'His flat? But he's married to Jack McGurk's sister.'

'Yes, but he has a place in Cockburn Street. He uses it when he's on really early shifts.'

'And what took you to his flat . . . or did you just go there to give him that information.'

'I went there to break it off with him – for good.'

'And how did you break it off with him? Vertically or horizontally?' She answered him, by biting her lip, unconsciously. 'Jesus,' he whispered, 'you gave him one for the road.'

He drew her eyes back to his. 'Why the hell did you tell him all that stuff?' he demanded.

'I don't know. I just started talking about you, and I told him about what happened on Saturday, and how you handled it and what you'd said about the man, and what I'd seen at the post-mortem . . .'

'Andy,' she insisted, 'I never thought for a second that he'd use it.'

'Why not? He's used you, hasn't he? Now did you tell the bastard anything else under his gentle interrogation?'

'No, nothing.'

'Nothing I may have said about the Alec Smith case, for example?'

'No, really, no.'

'That's some consolation.' He moved towards her and took her arm. 'Come on, you'd better go next door.'

She looked at him. 'Andy, I'm sorry. I was stupid. I promise I won't . . .'

He looked at her, and saw that her eyes were glistening. He thought of Friday night and of himself with Karen, and he almost melted. Perhaps he could have changed the course of his life, right there, by leaving one question unasked. But his character, as well as his training, forbade that. He knew that secrets make rotten foundations.

'One more thing. Margot told me you bet her that you could pull me. Is that true?'

She nodded.

'Well, you'd better not take her money. I guess you've lost.'

She came to him and put her head on his shoulder. 'Give me a chance, Andy, please.'

'I did, but you fucked it up. With me you only get one shot.' She pushed him away and ran down the staircase, ran out of the house. He heard his door slam, then hers. He thought about the two sisters together, at each other's throats. Something made him pick up the phone and dial their number. Margot answered.

'Give me Rhian,' he said coldly. He waited for a few seconds, until he heard a mumbled 'Yes?'

'It's me. Listen, I'm sorry I was so rough. Will you be okay?'

'Yes. I'll be fine. My sister may not, but I will.'

'Don't blame Margot. You know that wouldn't be fair.'

'Okay, I promise.' She hesitated, then spoke again, tentatively, almost pleading. 'Andy, can I come back in? Can we talk it through again?'

He hesitated. 'Rhian, I . . .' A bell rang, near him. 'Shit, that's someone at the front door. No, please leave it for now. Let's give each other some breathing space.' He put the phone down and jogged downstairs.

When he opened the door, Maggie Rose and Mario McGuire were standing on the step. The Inspector was carrying a large briefcase. He stared at them. 'Hello you two,' he said. 'What the hell brings you here?'

'Didn't you get any of our messages?' Rose asked.

'I'm sorry. I've been busy with some personal stuff. Come on in; straight up those stairs and into the living room.' He followed them and pointed them at his sofa. 'Where's the fire, then?'

McGuire tapped his briefcase and began to open it. 'In here, sir. You'd better sit down yourself.'

Wife and husband took the Head of CID slowly, meticulously, through the Alec Smith papers, pointing out the gaps, and explaining their theory, that the numbered, dated photographs were in fact an index for an undiscovered stockpile of material. When they were finished, he leaned back in his chair and looked at them.

'Okay,' he said. 'You were right to come here. I buy your

theory too. Now that you've told me, what do you need from me?'

McGuire replied. 'I have two possible enemies of Alec from the SB files; their names are Gus Morrison and Lawrence Scotland. They need to be lifted quickly, interrogated and, if necessary, given psych. tests. But I have to get after finding these other photographs and papers, if they exist.

'I need you to give me someone solid to take care of Morrison and Scotland, while I do that.'

'I can fix that for you, no problem.' Martin chuckled, but to neither Maggie nor Mario did he seem to be laughing. 'I've got the very man for that job; someone who's really good at sweating hard cases like these. Have your files sent along to me in the morning. Once I've got rid of some other business, I'll take care of them both myself.'

Twenty-four

Martin glanced into the Torphichen Place CID room. He was pleased to see that it was empty: it meant that everyone was where they should have been, out on enquiries, trying to put a definite name to the man with a provisional face.

Everyone, that was, but Dan Pringle and Jack McGurk; they were waiting for him in the Superintendent's office, where he had told them to be.

'Hi guys,' he said, as he walked into the room. 'How's it going?'

'Imagine, if you will, an old lizard's dick,' Pringle said. 'Imagine how dry and wrinkled it must get, after long years of being dragged around deserts, hot rocks and such, with not so much as a sniff of a lady lizard. Then take that concept and transfer it to the fruits of this investigation. That's how we've come out so far in terms of results . . . dry as an old lizard's bone.'

'You should know about that, right enough,' Martin chuckled. 'The door-to-door's given you nothing, then?'

'Well, it did turn up a boy in the new flats opposite the Roseburn pub who acted shifty when Sammy Pye knocked his door. Without any pressure at all, he confessed to growing cannabis plants in his back window box. Apart from him though, it hasn't given us a fucking thing. We've still got a lot to do mind, but . . .'

'Did Sammy lift the guy?'

'Aye, but there were only a few plants. I gave him a warning and let him go.'

'You both did right. What about empty properties? Have you checked them out?'

'There are none; not in the area we're looking at. Every flat and house is occupied, or at least there's Council Tax being paid on every one; there are registered voters at almost every address. They're still looking for possibles in Glasgow too, but so far all their gangsters are present and correct. I could have told you all this on the phone, you know. You've had a wasted journey.'

'That's not why I'm here,' said the Head of CID. 'I wanted to tell you personally, you and Jack here, that I've tracked down the leak to the *News*.'

'Who was it?' asked Pringle, eagerly.

'Me.'

He looked up at McGurk. 'Your brother-in-law and I have someone in common. Her name's Rhian Lewis. She's a final-year medical student. I let something slip the other night; I also fixed it for her to sit in with Sarah on Mr Nobody's autopsy. She, in turn, passed it on, in similar circumstances, to your man Blacklock.

'I've spoken to Alan Royston already. Now I want to apologise to you both; to you, Dan, for compromising your investigation and to you Jack, for getting you implicated.'

'Not your fault, sir,' said Pringle, tactfully. 'We all talk in the dark.' He paused. 'The Margot girl's older sister, right?'

'Right.'

McGurk said nothing; Martin glanced at him again. 'I want him sorted, Jack.

'I don't want you to ruin your sister's life, necessarily; whether you tell her or not, that's down to your judgement. But I want you to let that brother-in-law of yours know from me that if he ever goes near Rhian again, far less tries to use her to get sensitive information out of me, then he is fucking dog-meat.

'Understood?'

The giant Sergeant looked down at him, his face thunderous. 'Don't you worry, sir. After I've finished with him he won't be touching anything female for a long time, especially not my sister or your friend.'

Twenty-five

'Where do we start?' Stevie Steele looked round the big living room of Shell Cottage. The blinds were open; outside the untypical spell of early summer sunshine continued unbroken. The tide was out and people were walking, in ones and twos, on the wet sands, some of them giving their dogs a chance to run off the leash.

'The most obvious place,' said McGuire, beside him in the doorway. 'With that desk over there.' He looked around the rest of the room. Smith's clothes were gone, bagged as evidence and sent to the lab; the whisky glass was gone too. All of the ornaments which he had seen on the previous Saturday, each one carefully positioned, now stood together on the table.

The room seemed soulless; Mario thought of a house which he and Maggie had looked at before their marriage – the home of a dead person, being sold by her executor. It had given them the same chill that came now from Alec Smith's cottage.

'That's an antique, that thing. There may be a panel in it, a secret drawer, that Arthur Dorward's lot missed.'

'It couldn't be big enough to hold much in the way of papers,' Steele pointed out.

'No, but there could be something inside it that tells us where they are.'

167

'True.' The Sergeant crossed the room and examined the heavy desk. He slid out every drawer in the two pedestals, pulling each one free from its runners and turning it over, looking for anything that might have been taped underneath. He looked inside the empty space which they had left, then examined the panel above the kneehole, pressing it but finding it unyielding.

Finally, he and McGuire lifted the empty carcass of the desk from its position beneath the window and examined its front. The Inspector leaned over, peering at the section which mirrored the central panel on the other side. He looked at it, at the line of its inlay to the rest of the woodwork, then he blew, gently, at the joints, sending motes of dust flying, and rapped on it with his knuckles, quickly and firmly as if he was knocking on a door.

With a click, the panel sprung two inches clear of its surround, revealing a shallow drawer. 'How about that then?' he said, beaming with undisguised pride.

'Papa Viareggio – my mother's father – had a desk like this with a secret drawer; and no-one knew about it but him . . . and me. When I was ten, he told me about it, and showed me how to open it. When he died, six years later, he left it to me in his will. He was a well-off man, my Italian grandfather; owned a chain of fish-and-chip shops. My uncle inherited the business, my mother got a big bequest, and he left ten grand each to my two girl cousins. I was his only grandson and yet all he left me was his bloody desk.

'My mother was bloody livid; she said he had always been a crazy man. She was going to ask my granny to keep the desk and give me ten grand like the girls, but I told her to wind her neck in. "That's what Papa wanted," I said, "that's what's going to happen." So they brought the desk to our house and I made space for it in my room.

'The first time my folks were out, I tapped the panel, just like Papa Viareggio told me, and the drawer popped out, just like that one. There was a key inside to a safe deposit box and a letter from Papa giving me the address of the bank where it was kept, and another addressed to the manager. My letter said, "*When you turn twenty-one you can open this. Meantime, sell the bloody desk; it's a cumbersome thing but it's worth a few quid.*" Some man, my Papa.'

'What did you do?' Steele asked, fascinated.

'I did as he told me. The desk was far better quality than this one. I got ten grand clear for it at auction, the same as he left the girls . . . he never liked them. When I was twenty-one, I opened the safe deposit box and found all the paperwork related to a trust fund in the Cayman Islands. Papa had set it up with fifty grand when I was ten and it had been growing big-time ever since: it still is. I won't tell you how much it's worth, but the income – all legal, tax paid and everything – will pay off our mortgage by the time I'm forty.'

'What happened to the business?'

McGuire laughed. 'Ah, Stevie son, that's another story. Just before he died, Papa put together this plan to float it as Viareggio plc and develop it, nationally and internationally, on a franchise basis. A week before he was due to push the button on it, he took a heart attack in his office and dropped down dead. My uncle didn't think it was such a good idea, so he cancelled everything.

'Every time I drive past a Harry Ramsden, I think of my Uncle Beppe, and I marvel at what a stupid fucker he is.'

He looked at the desk again. 'Alec's estate might get a couple of grand for this thing, but that's all. Still, let's be careful with it.' Gently, he drew out the hidden drawer. Inside, the two detectives saw a small cloth pouch, secured by a red drawstring, a box, and three keys on a ring. McGuire picked up the bag, loosened the binding cord, and slid back the cloth to reveal the muzzle of a small, black, oiled automatic pistol.

'Nine millimetre something or other, I'd say . . .' He looked closely at the barrel. 'Beretta, I think.'

Steele opened the box. 'Ammo,' he said.

'Aye, and just as illegal as this gun.' McGuire took the weapon out, checked that it was unloaded, then secured it in its pouch once more and slipped it into his pocket. 'Whatever Alec was up to, he must have perceived a threat, to have taken the risk of keeping this. Even for an ex-SB guy, possession of a firearm and ammunition would have meant prison for sure.'

He picked up the keys and tossed them in his hand. 'I wonder what these are for?' He looked at them closely. 'This one's for a Chubb mortise lock and this one's a McLaren; both top quality. All the locks in this place are either Era or Yale, so these are for somewhere else. I wonder where? And the third key; see how thin it is? Odd-looking; not for a door, I'd say.'

'For a safe-deposit box, maybe?'

'Maybe.' McGuire scowled suddenly. 'The fact that there's nothing else in the bloody drawer makes me fear that we ain't going to find anything in the whole bloody house. If there was a pointer to a stash of photos and records, this is where we'd have found it, I'm sure. On the other hand, these keys might be a pointer of a sort; maybe he did have an office somewhere and maybe Maggie's search will turn it up.'

He dropped the keys into his pocket beside the gun, then took off his jacket and laid it across the desk-top. 'Let's get on with taking the place apart, anyway. I've been wrong before, so you never know.'

Steele nodded. Carefully, he replaced the empty drawers in the desk, then helped McGuire to turn over the heavy sofa. They checked underneath it and under the rest of the furniture in the room but found nothing.

They continued the search through the rest of the upper floor of the house, turning over mattresses, rifling through drawers, turning out the pockets of every garment hanging in Alec Smith's wardrobe, even checking inside the pill and plaster boxes in the bathroom cabinet. They moved downstairs through the dining room and into the kitchen, finding nothing but a large supply of Baxter's soup, a fridge well stocked with soft drinks and small bottles of Belgian beer, breakfast cereal, tins of nuts and a large box of sunflower seeds.

'Liked his nuts,' Steele commented.

'Had them burned off,' McGuire countered, dryly.

Finally they made their way down into the cellar; apart from a bulk supply of dog food, stored on a high shelf, there was nothing there but tools, as Arthur Dorward had reported earlier. There were no windows, only a door; McGuire opened it and found half a dozen steps leading back up to the level of a small lawn. As he stepped back inside, he found Steele examining a white line which ran round the wall, about four feet above the level of the stone floor.

'What do you think this is, Mario?'

'Looks like a tide-mark.'

'Yes. I reckon this place must be susceptible to flooding, maybe when there are high tides and bad weather combined. No way he's going to store anything down here.' The Sergeant looked up. 'That's us then. What's left to do?'

'We go up into the attic. Then we go back to every room that doesn't have a fitted carpet and lift the floorboards. I promised you a long hard day, Stevie, and I meant it.'

Twenty-six

The elderly Probation Officer stared across her desk at the Detective Chief Superintendent. 'I don't know if I like this, Mr Martin,' said Roberta Nelson. 'Ever since he's been under my supervision, Angus Morrison has been a model parolee.'

'I'm sure he has,' the policeman replied, evenly. 'Gus was pretty stupid as a would-be terrorist, but even he would know that the first rule of the turf, if the Parole Board gets soft with you, is that you're nice to your supervising officer.'

'That's a very cynical attitude.'

Martin sighed wearily. 'No, it's a universal truth. You see people like him at their best; all too often I see them at their worst.'

'I know Angus,' the woman insisted. 'He has a good job – I arranged it for him myself – as a van driver with Scottish Power.'

The Head of CID laughed. 'That's ironic; he was nicked trying to blow up one of their pylons.'

'He's paid for that mistake. He's a model employee; never a day's sick leave, never late for work. He never misses a meeting with me. No, no, no. I will not have you treat him as "one of the usual suspects". I refuse to co-operate with you, point-blank.'

'Ms Nelson, it isn't a matter of you co-operating with me.

I don't even want to co-operate with you. I'm not asking you, I require you, to give me the present address of Gus Morrison, so that I can eliminate him from police enquiries into the murder of the man who arrested him and who gave evidence against him at his trial.'

She snorted. 'Hmm! I know how the police work. You'll arrest him, you'll intimidate him, and you'll leave him believing that there is no such thing as a reformed offender in your eyes. And we know where that leads, don't we? Straight back to prison.'

The detective leaned forward in his chair. 'Lady, you know damn well that a significant proportion of people convicted of crimes and offences in Scotland are under probation orders at the time, or re-offend shortly after completing a period on probation. I promise you I'm not going to railroad Morrison; I'm simply going to find out whether or not he killed Alec Smith.' He stood. 'Now: unless you'll swear under oath that he was with you all last Friday evening, I'll have his home address, please, and that of the depot where he works.'

The woman shot him a last look. She had said her piece, but they both knew that she was not in a position to deny him what he wanted. She went to a filing cabinet, took out some papers, and copied some details from them on to a note pad.

'There.'

Martin took the note from her, with slightly exaggerated thanks – no point in rubbing it in – and left her office.

Gus Morrison's work address was a Scottish Power depot in Portobello. Andy drove straight there from Roberta Nelson's Haymarket office, not in his MGF but in a white Mondeo which he had taken from the police pool. Detective Constable Sammy Pye was by his side, borrowed back from Dan Pringle's team for the occasion, and grateful to be relieved of door-knocking duty.

They found the Depot Manager's office without difficulty, just after midday. 'Angus Morrison?' said Walter Gough. 'Oh aye, Gus. He's out with an emergency crew just now. Due back in half-an-hour, though. He might be early, ye never know.

'What d' yis want him for? He's no' in bother again is he?'

'No. This is just part of the parole supervision process,' Martin lied. 'How's he doing, anyway?'

'Gus? He's fine. He's only been with us a few months, since he got out, but he's never been a problem. Quiet bloke, like, and there's something a bit sad about him. The probation woman said his girlfriend hanged herself in the jail. Is that right?'

'Yes, I'm afraid so. Some people just can't do the time; men as often as women for all that the papers would have you think.'

'Aye well, no wonder Gus is a bit odd then.'

'What do you mean?'

Gough hesitated. 'Ach. It's just that the rest of the lads are a bit wary of him. They catch him talking to himself every so often.'

'About anything in particular?'

'Nah, nothing they can make out.'

They heard the sound of an approaching vehicle, a noise of wheels on gravel. Gough glanced out of the window of his small office. 'That's his van now. How long will yis want him?' he asked as the two policemen stood.

Martin shrugged. 'Give him the rest of the day off?'

'Aye, that's no problem. One of the other lads can drive if we get another emergency call-out.'

The Head of CID glanced at his file photograph of Morrison and showed it to Pye as they strode towards the big van. They flanked him as he stepped out of the driver's door. He was big, over six feet and bulky. His nose had been badly broken once, and blue stubble showed on his chin. *Real hard case*, thought Pye.

Martin showed his warrant card, briefly, so that none of the other workmen could see. 'Gus,' he said in a friendly voice. 'We need to talk. Come on along with us.'

'What for?' Morrison growled.

'We want to buy you lunch, that's all.' One to each arm, gently but securely, they walked him across to the Mondeo.

Twenty-seven

'I think I should close down the headquarters van, Mario,' said Maggie Rose, 'and base the investigation out of Haddington from now on.'

Her husband nodded across the table at which he and Stevie Steele were sitting. Their faces were streaked with dirt and their clothes were dusty. Each was in the process of emptying a can of lager; four more lay in a bag at their feet.

'You might as well, Chief Inspector. I've dug up as much of North Berwick as I'm about to. What a wasted day!'

'Not exactly,' the Sergeant ventured. 'That desk might have gone for auction with a gun in it, and those keys too if you hadn't known about that drawer.'

'No,' said McGuire. 'Absolutely not. The furniture specialist in any sale-room would have looked for that drawer right away. I'd rather it was us found the gun than him, though; that could have been embarrassing. We might have had a struggle keeping it out of the papers.'

'Aye,' laughed Steele. 'The *Evening News* is getting everywhere just now. Did you see their story yesterday on that other investigation. There was some very specific stuff in that. The guy who wrote that story, Blacklock: he's big Jack McGurk's brother-in-law. Did you know that?'

'I did not. I do know that big Jack better not have been talking to him, though. There are only three guys in this organisation allowed to speak to the press, and he's not one of them.' He considered his point for a moment. 'No, make that four; I suppose the Chief Constable can, too.'

McGuire drained his can, tore another open, then glanced at his wife once more. 'Did you get anything on the serial number of the pistol?'

'Drew a blank,' she said. 'Or should that be fired a blank? It isn't one of ours – it would have been posted missing if it was anyway – and it isn't registered to anyone in the UK. I suppose Alec must have acquired it on his travels and neglected to hand it in.'

'One more for us, then. We'll register it and keep it in our armoury.'

Maggie frowned at him. 'Not necessarily. We'll have to test fire a bullet from it; who knows, it might be a match for one in another open investigation somewhere, one with an untraced firearm.'

'We'll do no such bloody thing . . . Ma'am,' he retorted.

'But we have to! It's standard procedure.'

'It is not standard procedure to find an illegal hand-gun in the possession of a deceased former Special Branch commander. Suppose your test firing did come up with a match, in another force's area? What a can of fucking worms that would open!' He tapped the table. 'Tell you something, among the three of us. From what I've learned about Alec Smith, finding a match is not one hundred per cent impossible. No-one's testing that gun.'

Steele looked from one to the other, not wishing to be caught in the middle of a marital row between two senior officers.

'You can't take that decision,' Maggie protested.

'I just did. And if Brian Mackie was sitting in that chair, instead of sunning himself on the Costa de la bloody Luz, he'd agree with me all the way. So will Big Bob, when I tell him.'

She scowled at him. 'Secret bloody policemen,' she muttered; but she had been Bob Skinner's exec., and she knew at once that her husband was right.

'Talking about the Boss,' she said, changing the subject. 'I heard something on the grapevine today. You know there's been a small round of promotions?'

'Aye, Jack McGurk, for one.'

'Well, Neil's come through too. He's been made up to DI.'

Mario's face lit up. 'Hey, that's great. Does that mean he's moving on?'

'No, the Boss wants to keep him in his office for as long as he can, so he's promoted him in post.'

'That's smashin'.' He frowned for a second. 'No consolation, but smashin' nonetheless. Olive would have been dead chuffed for him.'

'So will Lauren and Spence be.'

'Yeah.'

For a while they sat in silence, until Steele broke it. 'Those keys,' he said. 'Has the check on tenants of small office premises thrown up anything?'

'No,' answered Rose. 'There are one or two vacant around the county, but the rest are all accounted for. Whatever those keys are for, I'm sure that they are not for an office around here.

'The bank statements gave us nothing either; it was nearly all domestic stuff, the routine standing orders and bills, money going out to his daughter through a university branch of Lloyds TSB in Birmingham – she must still be a student. The only thing we couldn't nail down completely was an annual payment of twelve hundred pounds to a firm of solicitors in Dundee, but Alec told the bank manager when he set up the debit that it was money for his wife.'

She looked at Mario. 'I think we should talk to the wife, don't you?'

'Aye. All due deference to the Chief, but when he saw her he didn't know the questions to ask. We should see her again, right enough.'

'Okay. You two do that tomorrow then; go to Penicuik or wherever and see her.'

McGuire shook his head. 'Hold on a minute there, Chief Inspector. This is becoming a threat to national security. I'm only involved in this investigation because it's Alec. I'm Special Branch Commander, so I have to spend some time commanding the bloody thing; plus I've asked for Alice Cowan as from tomorrow morning. I've already got the Head of CID picking up two suspects for me; I cannot go tear-arsing out on what is probably just a follow-up interview.'

'I suppose not,' she conceded. 'You do it alone then, Stevie. Just confirm that standing order was a token maintenance payment for her, and see if she knows about those photographs – and if she has any idea what they're about.'

'Aye,' said her husband, 'and ask her if he knows where he walked his dog. At the moment it looks as if Alec just buried his stuff. Maybe he got it to do the digging!'

'If that's right,' said Maggie, flashing one of her rare on-duty smiles, 'that dog'll be the first bloody witness we've found in this case!'

Twenty-eight

'I wasn't kidding about lunch,' said Martin. He laid a tray on the table; two large filled rolls, a Mars bar and a mug of coffee with two sugar lumps and a spoon beside it. 'Corned beef and pickle all right?' he asked. 'I wasn't sure about the sugar.'

Gus Morrison glared up at him, then at the food, suspiciously. 'It's all right,' Sammy Pye assured him. 'I've just got the rolls myself from a place across the street.'

'Don't worry,' the Head of CID continued, cheerfully, 'they're not laced with a truth drug or anything like that. We're not that subtle: we'll just batter the truth out of you if we have to, won't we, Sammy?' He held his hands up, quickly. 'Only joking, only joking. Now go on, dig in.'

Morrison reached out and picked up a flour-dusted roll, squinted at it, then took a bite. 'Ah want a lawyer,' he mumbled through a mouthful of corned beef and pickle. They were the first words he had spoken, from the moment they had left the depot to their arrival at the St Leonard's divisional HQ, chosen because of its link to the Smith case.

'I'm sure you do, Gus, and if it comes to the bit you'll have one; but you don't need one yet, you see. We just want to ask you a few things.' He sat back and waited, watching in silence as the blue-chinned man munched his way through the rolls, added

181

the sugar lumps to his coffee, stirred it, then tore off the Mars bar wrapping.

'Fuckn' bastards. Fuckn' bastards,' he muttered under his breath, shoulders hunched, staring down at the table top. 'Aye after us, fuckn' bastards.'

'What was that, Gus?' Pye asked. The man shot him a sideways glance. 'Nothin'.' He looked back at Martin. 'What's this about then?' he asked, his eyes clear suddenly, his voice lucid.

'Do you remember a man called Smith?' the Head of CID asked.

'Do I remember a man called Smith? I remember a hundred men called Smith, Officer. There was Tam Smith, who had the corner shop when I was a boy. There was Dandy Smith, who was in my class at primary school and got run over by a bus. There was Mary Smith, in the jail . . . his real name was Michael, but he was called that because he bent over in the showers. There was . . .'

'Did he bend over for you?' Martin asked suddenly, still smiling. 'Did you go queer in the nick?'

Morrison blinked. 'No,' he boomed. 'Certainly not. It was the wee hard men who did that. The mentality you see. They had to show who the top dogs were, in every way they could; so they buggered the likes of Mary to do it.'

'Did they bugger you?'

The laugh was so sudden, so sharp, so dismissive, that the detective almost reacted to it. 'Bugger me? Bugger big Gus? Did they buggery!' He laughed again, at his own sad humour.

'Ah. Sorry, it was just that I thought, with Wendy topping herself . . .'

Something seemed to swim behind Morrison's eyes; another creature, in there.

'Wendy never thought . . . Wendy? Wendy! It was the other way around!' His voice rose. 'I know what happened! All those fucking bull dykes in that bloody place, never leaving her alone and the screws – aye, know why they call them screws? – and wee Wendy. She was soft and weak and a gentle lassie and very private. Kept herself to herself you know what I mean, women's things; and it all got too much for her, and they killed her up there, the fucking bastards . . .' He broke off, his chest heaving, gasping for breath.

Martin rose and put two strong hands on the man's shoulders, holding him down in his chair. 'Fuckn' bastards. Fuckn' bastards,' he mumbled.

'Gus, that is pure fantasy,' said the Head of CID. 'It never happened; none of it. Wendy wasn't abused in prison; she became depressed. She saw counsellors there; she told them that what you had got her into, all that Free Scotland nonsense, had ruined her life. She was put on medication, but she didn't take it; they found it afterwards, after she hanged herself with her sheets, leaving a letter to you blaming you for everything.'

Morrison writhed in his grip; trying to stand, but Martin held him down. 'Balls,' he snarled. 'Fuckn' bastards bent her mind.' The voice, rising again, grating. 'Wendy was a good wee soldier, a good wee Scottish soldier. She and I, we did it; others talked, others marched up and fuckn' down but we did it. And those fuckn' traitorous bastards watchin' us all the time, watchin' us, watchin' us! Chief fuckn' bastard Chief fuckn' Inspector Alec fuckn' Smith . . .'

Martin slapped him across the face, hard, to stop the flow of spit-flecked vitriol. 'How did you know that Smith?' he snapped. 'He was never named in court. He never interviewed you after your arrest. How did you know that man called Smith among the hundred?'

As the man's hysteria subsided, he released his grip and sat down, facing his subject across the table once more, watching the eyes as they cleared. 'He wasn't as clever as he thought,' Morrison said, evenly, lucid once more. 'They followed us, sure, him and Gavigan; only Gavigan wasn't too hot at it.' He smiled, boastfully. 'So we turned the tables, Wendy and I. We followed him; and he led us to his boss, and we followed him too. Found out where he lived, who he was, what schools his kids went to, everything.'

'You couldn't have been that smart. Smith caught you trying to blow up that pylon.'

This time the laugh was a pure animal snarl. 'Caught us? Caught us? Framed us! Framed us! We told the papers about Smith and Gavigan; sent an anonymous letter to the *Sunday Post* telling them what they were. Never published it. Next thing Smith and Gavigan picked us up, with a gun. Took us up Sutra, with the gun. Made us handle gelignite, with the gun. Made us stand beside this pylon and took photos as if they had been watching us. Then they took us to the police station and charged us.

'We never blew up any pylon, Wendy and me. We were crucified. Chief fuckn' Inspector bastard Smith hammered home the nails.'

Martin stared at the man, unblinking, in the long silence which followed. 'When did you see him again?' he asked at last. 'After you got out, I mean.'

Morrison's mood was fragile once more. 'In the Ford garage next to the depot,' he said, quietly. 'Saw him looking at a car. I was going off shift so I followed him again; out to North Berwick. Wee house there, on the beach.'

'And did you crucify him?'

'Crucify? Crucify?'

'DCI Smith was killed, Gus,' said Martin, quietly. 'He was murdered in his home last Friday evening. It's been all over the papers.'

'Don't read the papers. Hate the papers. The papers betrayed Wendy and me. Sold us to Chief fuckn' Inspector bastard Smith.'

'Did you kill him, Gus?'

The eyes flashed again; the creature back, swimming inside.

'No.' A mumble. 'But I wish I had. Fuckn' bastard. Fuckn' bastards you all.'

Martin gazed at him as he sat there, big shoulders hunched round. Then he stood and patted him on the arm, gently.

'Why didn't you tell the story in your defence at your trial?' he asked.

'Lawyer wouldn't believe me.'

'No,' the detective sighed. 'I don't suppose he would. I do, though. Wait here for a bit, Gus. We'll look after you.'

Signalling Pye to follow, he left the room. A uniformed constable stood outside. 'Get in there,' he ordered, 'and sit with him.' As the door closed, he led the way along the corridor to Brian Mackie's empty office.

'What are you going to do, sir?' his young assistant asked.

As Martin looked at him, Pye saw the anger burning in him. 'I'm going to get that poor bastard a solicitor, and then I'm going to have Kevin O'Malley talk to him.'

'Who's Kevin O'Malley?'

'He's the best head doctor I know. Morrison needs his help.'

'D'you think he did kill DCI Smith, sir?'

'I don't know. If he did, Kevin will find out for us.' His eyes locked on to Pye. 'While he's doing that, I want you to find

Tommy Gavigan and bring him to me. Morrison might have been fantasising all that stuff about the gun and the frame-up; but it rang true to me.

'If it was, then there will be some crucifying done . . . and I've got the hammer and nails ready.'

Twenty-nine

'Yes, my name is still Bridget Smith, Sergeant. Alec and I were never divorced.' The widow was not dressed for the part; she wore light blue cotton slacks and a diaphanous, flowery top which showed more than a suggestion of a white Broderie Anglais bra. She was tall, with only a slight thickening at the waist, only a slight hint of a pot below, a strong firm chin and blonde hair, cut short; well cut too.

Edging thirty himself, Steele always found it difficult to assess the age of an older woman, but he guessed, from Alec Smith's age and from her reported twenty-something offspring, that she could not be far short of the fifty mark. *Well-preserved fifty, though. Working at it; proud of it.* Looking at her, he wondered what the late DCI Smith could have done to drive her away.

He glanced around the living room of the little house, a Wimpey semi-detached, 1970s vintage. It felt comfortable, lived-in, and looked as if she had made only a token effort to tidy up for his visit.

Mrs Smith laid a mug of coffee on a small table, one of a set, beside his chair. It was well used but looked like solid teak; she did not use a coaster, he noticed.

'I'm glad you could see me so quickly,' he began, as an ice-breaker.

'Not a problem,' she replied, in a light, cultured Edinburgh accent, not a cut-glass Morningside job. 'I work from home. I run a little market-research business, working for advertising agencies mainly, but retail groups too, and sometimes public bodies; I have a project for LEEL at the moment. Occasionally we do face-to-face interviews, but mostly it's telephone work.

'Have you heard of LEEL?' she asked suddenly.

'Vaguely.'

She laughed. 'That's what most respondents say. Maybe I can interview you after you've interviewed me. Ahh, but you're not a small businessman, are you?'

'No,' Steele grinned, put at ease by her style, 'I'm a large policeman.'

'And you're here to talk to me about another one. I thought the Chief Constable's visit was purely of the condolence variety; so I've been half-expecting someone else. What do you want to ask me? Whether I killed him or not?'

'I was assuming that you didn't; according to the Chief you and your partner were out with friends last Friday evening. We've checked that already.'

Bridget Smith raised her eyebrows. 'Did he indeed? His interview technique must be better than I thought. I don't even remember him asking me that, far less telling him.'

'That's how he got to be Chief Constable.' Steele took a sip from his mug. 'There are a few things about your husband, Mrs Smith, that we're still trying to get a grip of. Although he was a police officer for over thirty years, there's still a lot about him that we don't know. He was a very private man in the office – an asset, maybe, given the job he did . . .'

'He was a very private man at home too, Sergeant. What job did he do?'

'You mean he never talked to you about it?'

'Never. I knew what rank he was, that he was a detective and where he worked, but he never talked about his work. I was never allowed to phone him at the office either. When his father died, nine years ago, I had to go through the main switchboard to find him, and they had him call me back.'

Her voice lowered, and suddenly she seemed less vibrant, more vulnerable. 'Alec never talked to me at all, Mr Steele . . . well, hardly ever. It wasn't so bad in the early years, when we were going out together, when the kids were young, but as his career progressed he became more and more remote. He didn't speak about the house; to me, or John, or Susan even . . . and if he had a favourite, it was her. He didn't want to do things; for five years before I left we did not do a single thing together, go out for dinner, go to the theatre, go to parties. I used to get invitations; Alec always turned them down. As for him . . . I've heard that policemen do have balls, but I never heard about them from Alec. Never once did he offer to take me to a police social function; we were at a formal event once, but that was all.' She looked down quickly into her lap, her voice faltering for the first time. 'For the last six years of our marriage we didn't have sex: not at all.'

'The only thing he ever did that wasn't work-related was his Thursday night football thing . . . a group of ageing men having a kick-about. He said that that man Skinner invited him along. Alec probably interpreted that as an order. He did that for a while, then stopped. When I asked him why, he told me that he had knee trouble.'

'Wasn't he interested in photography, Mrs Smith?'

The woman frowned in surprise. 'Not that I was aware of. Of the few family snapshots I have, Alec is in every one. I don't remember him ever taking a single picture himself.'

'Oh he did,' said Steele, 'he did. We found a pile of photographs among his effects, and we believe there may be more; possibly records too, that we haven't found. We found some keys that we can't account for. I don't suppose you know if he had anywhere he might have kept stuff . . . a small office maybe?'

'Not a clue. There was nothing extraordinary around the house, that's for sure, or I'd have found it. I do clean occasionally. As for an office, I never knew of one, but then there was so much I didn't know.'

'Did you know about the secret drawer in his desk?'

'What secret drawer? In that big old desk of his, you mean? No, I didn't know – and Alec, being Alec, never mentioned it.'

'He never mentioned people, did he? For example did he ever let slip any hint that he might have been afraid of someone?'

'Alec was afraid of no-one . . .' She frowned. '. . . except. I remember once, about ten years ago. The television news was on, and Bob Skinner appeared, being interviewed about some crime or other. He wasn't as high-ranking then obviously, or as well known, but I remember Alec saying, not to me, really, more a whisper to himself, "There's something about that man that scares me shitless." That was all; it surprised me at the time, but I'd forgotten about it until now. But Bob Skinner hardly killed him, did he?'

'Hardly,' Steele agreed. 'What made you leave him, finally?'

'I just couldn't take being a non-person any more. After John died . . .' She stopped as she saw the Sergeant's reaction. 'You didn't know?'

'No. Not at all.'

'Our son, John,' she continued, her voice very small at that moment, 'died five years ago. I never really needed Alec before, but I needed him then, only he withdrew completely into himself. He wouldn't talk to me at all after it happened. I just couldn't go on like that; I started to go out with girlfriends, and with a couple of the women who work for me.

'One night I met Stan Greenwood: he was fun, he was friendly, he was free, and he fancied me. He didn't give a damn that I'm ten years older than him, or posh, as he calls me. He didn't give a damn that my son died of AIDS. He asked me to come and live with him, and I said, "Yes." I didn't even think about it.'

The young sergeant took a deep breath; he felt his pulse hammering. The extent to which Alec Smith, even as a serving policeman, had guarded his privacy, had kept his two lives from touching each other . . . it was astounding.

'Your son died of AIDS,' he repeated, slowly.

'Yes. John was gay, Sergeant. He knew it from an early age. He had sexual partners when he was still at school. Eventually as a student he formed a solid relationship – with a nice man, a lawyer, a few years older than him, but still in his twenties. Some might have said that John was promiscuous until then, but I prefer to see it as experimentation.

'Unfortunately, somewhere along the line one of those experiments went wrong. When my son was twenty-one, he found that he was HIV positive. Three years later, in spite of being on viro-suppressant drugs, he developed full-blown AIDS. It attacked his brain directly and he died very quickly.'

'When did Alec learn about him?'

'I told him when John was twenty.'

'And how did he react? Was he supportive?'

Bridget Smith let out a short, snorting, bitter laugh. 'Support-ive? He never spoke to John again; literally. When he was dying,

I told Alec. Yet even in that very short time he had left, he refused to see him. He didn't even go to his son's funeral. I almost left him there and then.'

'What about your daughter? How did he feel about her?'

'She cut Alec off because of his behaviour towards John. By condemning one of his children he lost both.'

'He still sent her money, though.'

'Did he? I wonder if she spent it. I didn't detect any tears when I told her he was dead. She didn't even ask when the funeral was. When will it be, by the way? Since Alec and I were still married . . . There'll be no-one else to organise it, will there?' She paused. 'You haven't found a girlfriend, have you?'

'No. No girlfriends. If you're prepared to make those arrangements, I'll have the Fiscal's office contact you as soon as they're ready to release the body. They may specify burial only, but I don't imagine that they'll take too long now.'

She sighed. 'I don't suppose that there'll be many people there, other than colleagues. Will there be many of them, do you think?'

'I shouldn't think so, Mrs Smith,' he answered, honestly, 'not many.'

'Surprise.' She glanced across at the young Sergeant. 'What job did he do anyway?'

Steele grimaced. 'One that I'm not supposed to talk about.'

'Oh my! He must have been really good at it, then. Even his wife didn't know.'

The detective smiled at the humour in her tone. 'There is something you can confirm for me,' he said. 'Your husband made an annual payment to a solicitor of twelve hundred pounds. He told his bank manager it was money for you. Is that correct?'

'No. I never asked him for a penny after I left. He gave me my share of the house in Pencaitland when he sold it, and I was happy with that.' She laughed again. 'That's typical Alec, I suppose, to leave you with one last mystery.'

Steele rose to go. 'More than one,' he answered. 'More than one.'

She walked him to the door. 'That's everything then?'

'Yes. Except . . .' he stopped, remembering. 'There was one more thing I was told to ask. Do you know where Alec walked his dog?'

'That's a good one. You'd be better asking the dog.' She opened the front door . . . and stopped halfway. 'Wait a minute,' she murmured. 'There was one time: I had made up my mind to leave, and I insisted on talking to him. But he wouldn't sit down with me. Instead he said, "You'd better come with me, then." I got in the car with him, and the dog, and he drove us to Yellowcraigs, just past Dirleton.

'He told me to sit on the beach while he walked the dog. He was away for a while, but he came back eventually and sat down beside me. I told him about Stan, and why it had come about. D'you know all he said? He just looked at me, after more than a quarter of a bloody century and he said, "Aye, right then."

'Nothing else, just that. Then he stood up, called to the dog, and we all drove back to Pencaitland. Do you know, that was the last time I ever spoke to my husband.'

Thirty

'He was a great believer in natural justice, was Alec Smith,' Andy Martin declared. 'But he went way over the top with Gus Morrison and Wendy Forrest.'

'And did Morrison kill him?' Skinner asked.

'Kevin O'Malley says absolutely not. He says that he has a persecution complex – which is not surprising since the poor bastard has been persecuted, wrongfully imprisoned and had his girlfriend driven to suicide – and that he is schizophrenic, but he says that he is a talker and not a doer. He says that if he's charged, he'll give evidence for the defence and he'll do it for nothing.'

The DCC whistled. 'That's it, then. Let Kevin section him and treat him for a while, but let's make sure that he gets his job back when he's fit for it.' He paused. 'And Gavigan?' There was an edge of savagery in the question.

'Like I said; I had him in last night and put the thumbscrews on him. He confirmed Gus's story. He said that the *Sunday Post* sent that anonymous letter straight to Alec. As soon as he saw it he knew who had done it. He didn't go apeshit – he never did, apparently – he just said "Better sort this, Tommy", then told Gavigan how they were going to sort it.

'Everything that Gus Morrison described to me was exactly as it happened. He and his girlfriend were no terrorists, just a couple of harmless fools with big patriotic dreams and big mouths.'

'Poor guy,' Skinner murmured. 'He sure didn't deserve that. And that lass, to die as she did, miserable and alone, locked up for nothing.' His eyes narrowed as he spoke.

'Alec must have known they were no threat,' Martin continued, 'but their big mistake was to embarrass him, by penetrating what he liked to think of as his own special world. From the moment he went into that SB job he was the wrong man for it, because he was a fanatic who had a narrow, unbending vision of right and wrong, as it applied to everyone, it seemed, except him.

'What he did to Gus and Forrest was hellish. Yet the way he dealt with Basra and Lawrence Scotland . . . it was effective, at least. Basra never raped and murdered another kid, and Scotland's been a model citizen ever since.'

'Maybe,' said the DCC. 'When are you going for him?'

'Later on this afternoon. When it's quieter at the St Leonard's' office.'

'Well, just watch it, eh.'

'Sure, as always.'

Skinner pushed himself up from his low seat and walked across to the big window of his office. 'Now, about Gavigan. Where is he now?'

'In a cell up at St Leonard's. I was so angry last night, I just locked him up.'

'Good for you. Mario had got rid of him, effectively; we were going to give him early retirement and send him on his way.'

'Not any more, I hope.'

'Ah, it's not as easy as that. As President Johnson said of

J. Edgar Hoover, the last thing I want is a guy like him outside the tent pissing in. It's always more comfortable the other way around.

'Ask yourself. What can we do with him? We could charge him with perverting the course of justice, perjury and all the rest. But this is all undercover stuff. Christ, his perjured evidence was *in camera*. On top of that, Alec Smith's dead, Wendy Forrest is dead, Angus Morrison is unbalanced and that anonymous letter to the *Sunday Post* will have been burned to ashes and crushed up long ago.

'Even if it was politically acceptable to try him, it would be legally impossible to get a conviction. Gavigan corroborates Morrison's story, but interview him formally with a lawyer present and he'd clam up, and all we've got is the unsupported allegation of a schizophrenic.

'Gus Morrison will be pardoned and compensated; it'll have to be done very quietly, but I'll see to it. As for our man, he's going to have to walk, Andy . . . but not before I've had a chat with him. Have Pye bring him down here.'

The Head of CID nodded. 'Will do.' He rose and headed for the door. 'I'll let you know how it goes with the other fella.'

Thirty-one

'What's she like, this Mrs Smith?'

'She's a really nice woman, and very attractive for her age.'

Maggie Rose looked severely at her Sergeant across her Haddington office. 'The menopause doesn't make you ugly, Stevie. I can think of any number of women who became even more attractive the older they got . . . my own mother among them.

'I meant did she strike you as completely frank, or might she have been holding something back from us? Do you think she was telling the truth about Alec's apparent lack of interest in photography?'

'Why should she lie?' Steele asked.

'What if he had some photographs of her that she doesn't want found?'

'I don't believe that for a second. Everything she told me bears out everything else I've learned about Alec Smith; that he was obsessively secretive. In their case, it turned the two of them into virtual strangers to each other.'

'So what does it leave us to go on, apart from the keys? What did you get from her?'

The Sergeant grinned. 'He walked his dog at Yellowcraigs.'

'Once, that we know of . . . and we can hardly dig up the

whole place. Anyway, if Smith did have a secret set of photographs and files, he was hardly the sort of guy to keep them in a knot-hole in a tree, was he? Whatever my daft husband or I may have said, the dog is not going to turn out to be our star witness.'

'Okay, there's the gay son.'

'Whom his father shunned. He's been dead for five years; how could he tie in?'

'Like you say, his father shunned him. Maybe John Smith had a partner who hated him for it.'

'A nice respectable lawyer, his mother told you. Maybe. Not. You can check it out if you like, but I don't see it as a runner.'

'Mrs Smith said that he let slip once, about ten years ago, that he was afraid of Mr Skinner. She said it was just a casual comment, but should we ask him if there was a reason around that time why he should have been?'

Rose chuckled, quietly. 'Nothing sinister in that, Stevie. All the villains in Edinburgh, and most of the coppers, are afraid of Bob Skinner. I'll ask him; but even if he and Smith did have a falling-out, way back, I don't see how it could connect to this investigation.'

'In that case, we're just left with that standing order as our only unanswered question. Mrs Smith didn't know anything about it.'

'Are you one hundred per cent on that? Maybe she hasn't been declaring it to the Inland Revenue and didn't like to admit it.'

'I'm certain, ma'am. If that money was for her then it was invested somewhere that she didn't know about.'

'Best tidy it up anyway. The Dundee solicitor firm was called Biggins and McCart. Give them a call and see what he was paying them for. Use my phone; ask the switchboard to get the number for you and put you through.'

Steele gave the instruction to the constable who answered the Haddington switchboard, replaced the phone and waited. Eventually it rang; he picked it up. 'Miss Malone, of Biggins and McCart, Sergeant,' the constable announced.

'Hello, Miss Malone,' said the detective.

'Hello,' a young female voice answered in an unmistakable Dundonian accent. 'Fit can ah do for you?'

'I'm Detective Sergeant Steele,' he began. 'I'm involved in an investigation here . . . a murder investigation,' he added to capture her interest, as well as her attention. 'We've discovered that the victim, a Mr Alexander Smith, of Shell Cottage, North Berwick, maintained a standing order in favour of your firm, paying you one thousand two hundred pounds, annually.

'We'd like to know what it was for.'

'Ah'll need tae check, like. Can ah ca' you back?'

'Sure, but as soon as possible.' He gave her the Haddington number then hung up once more.

This time, they had to wait for ten minutes before the phone rang again. 'Miss Malone,' the constable repeated.

'Yes?' asked Steele as the girl came on the line. 'What have you got for me?'

'I've found that payment,' she said, brightly. 'But Ah'm no allowed to talk tae yis about it. It's one o' Mr McCart's files; and only he's allowed tae talk about it. Ah'm no.'

'Okay. Can I speak to him then?'

'He's no here. He's away till Monday.'

'Monday. Is there no-one else?'

'Well, there was Mr Biggins . . . but he's died.'

'Miss Malone,' said Steele heavily. 'This is an important investigation.'

'Ma job's important to me. Mr McCart said Ah was never to give information off his files tae anybody.'

The Sergeant looked across at DCI Rose. She shook her head. 'Leave it. Alec's not going to be any deader, or any less dead, by Monday; this can wait till then. The chances are it's nothing anyway.'

'Okay,' Steele conceded, finally, to Miss Malone. 'But you tell Mr McCart to be there. I'm coming up to see him myself.'

Thirty-two

Dc Tommy Gavigan was thin-faced, weasely. *The desiccated shell of a man*, Skinner thought as he looked at him across the table of the small room. He was wearing a brown suit that was overdue a trip to the dry cleaners, he needed a shave, his grey hair looked lank and oily and he smelled of sweat. A night in the cells had done him no favours . . . or did he always look like that?

Gavigan, a Detective Constable, was older than the Deputy Chief Constable himself. He had been around for all of Skinner's career, and yet not around, since for almost half of that time he had been buried in Special Branch, doing the bidding of Alec Smith and his successors, Martin, Mackie and McGuire. Too convenient to transfer, too stolid to promote, he had stayed there, anonymously.

The big DCC took off his jacket and hung it over the back of the empty chair opposite the prisoner policeman. The room was hot; it was in the basement of the headquarters building and he had chosen it deliberately, knowing that Gavigan would have conducted more than a few interviews there himself, in his time.

He made as if to sit, but instead leaned across the table. A big hand flashed out and slapped the other man, powerfully, on the side of the head, sending him tumbling from his chair on to the floor.

'That wasn't just from me, Tommy,' he said, as the Detective Constable stared up at him, earlier apprehensiveness turned to sheer terror. 'That was from the Chief, ACC Elder, DCS Martin, Inspector McGuire, and everybody else whose work, whose very lives, you've soiled.

'Get up man!' he snapped. 'I'm not going to hit you again; you'll walk out of here . . . for now.' He waited as Gavigan, hair dishevelled, tie askew, clambered back on to his chair. Finally, Skinner sat himself.

'I know that I'm rarely accused of sentimentality,' he went on, 'but the fact is I love this force. I have done from the moment I joined, from the first day I put on its ill-fitting, uncomfortable uniform. I'm intensely proud of the job we do; I mean, in essence, that we protect the innocent and pursue the guilty.

'It makes me want to chuck my breakfast to learn of a case where the innocent have been persecuted. And it compounds it to know that in this case, I'm going to have to protect the guilty . . . by which I mean you, you little toe-rag, and if you show me even a glimmer of a smile of relief, I will break my word and put you back on the deck again.'

All the time he spoke, he stared across the desk at Gavigan, cold, deep and unblinking, mesmerising the man, holding him as securely as a hand on his throat.

'I've never gone into a murder investigation with mixed feelings before, but in the case of Alec Smith, I do. I dread the thought of what else we're going to find out about the man; I am gripped by a sort of certainty that whoever it was tortured him to death had a bloody good reason for doing so.

'DCS Martin has just interviewed a man who was driven mad by what Alec Smith and you did to him. Gus Morrison, poor sad bastard that he is, was a prime suspect, but we're certain that he didn't do it. If he had I'd have been really sorry about locking him up. I hate it when one of mine goes rotten. The only other time it happened I wanted to kill the bastard, and I was glad when he hanged himself in his cell. His widow got a pension and will be able to tell her kids, for a few years at least, that their daddy died in the service. On top of that the force wasn't embarrassed by a trial.

'I'm glad Alec's dead too, but I need to know who the other madman is, the one with the strength to do what Morrison wanted to, but couldn't.'

'How many others are there, Tommy? How many others like him, framed and persecuted by Smith because they upset him, or found out too much about him? You had better tell me now, because if you don't and I find out later that you've kept something from me, I promise you it will change altogether the way I think about you.'

He kept his gaze on Gavigan, reading the fright on the thin face. 'None that I know of, Mr Skinner, honest,' the man exclaimed. 'There was Lawrence Scotland, there was that Iranian, Basra, and there was Morrison and Forrest . . . that's all.'

'Did you ever give perjured evidence against anyone else?'

'No . . . sir.'

'Or combine with Smith to force a confession out of anyone?'

'No, sir.'

'Or turn a blind eye to anything that Smith was doing?'

'Sir, I never knew what DCI Smith was doing, unless he told me about it.'

'Scotland and Basra . . . you sure they were guilty?'

'Dead certain, sir.'

Skinner paused for a few moments. 'Remind me,' he continued, eventually. 'When you and Smith played your game with

Scotland, what did he tell you would have happened if Scotland had lost?'

'Mr Smith had a contact in the army, in military intelligence. He'd told him what he was going to do; he didn't care whether he killed Scotland or not. He wanted . . . and the army guy wanted . . . a scare thrown into the bloke so bad that word would get to the guys he associated with in Ireland. He told me that if it had gone wrong, his army pal would have buried Scotland up there, and that's what I told Mr McGuire. But thinking back on it, I'm not sure that he didn't palm the real bullets after he showed them to Scotland and load up with blanks, just in case.

'Whatever he did, Lawrence Scotland believed there were real bullets in the gun. His bowels emptied on him the second time he pulled the trigger.'

The DCC frowned. 'Funny. Alec Smith's bowels were emptied when he died.' He made a cutting movement across his lower abdomen. 'Only they were emptied right out.' Tommy Gavigan gasped and shuddered.

'So what about you, mister?' Skinner murmured. 'Let me tell you something. I have a friend in Military Intelligence; not the pal Smith had . . . if he ever existed. He really does have the power to bury you up on the Pentlands or something like that. Normally you'd be too small for him to bother with, but he owes me a couple of favours, so . . .' He paused, watching Gavigan turn even paler.

'For now, though, you can have your early retirement, Tommy. I don't want any scandal. You can have your full pension.' He locked on the stare again. 'But if ever I find out that you've breathed a word, a single word about any of this outside this room, or if ever I find out that you've been holding something back from us . . .

'You think about me, that's all. Remember me, because I won't forget you. And remember my army friend, and the favours he owes me. You look me in the eye and you know I'm not kidding.'

He put both palms on the table and pushed himself to his feet. 'Now get out of here. You're stinking the place out. Basement exit please; I'm not having you mixing with my people again, not even on the way out.'

Gavigan almost ran to the door; as he was about to open it, Skinner called to him. 'Hey, Tommy. You just remember now; we'll be watching you. You're not an SB officer any more, you're a target.'

Thirty-three

Martin read the report as carefully as all the others even though it was the last of the pile. It had been submitted by Detective Superintendent John McGrigor, CID Commander in the big, sprawling division which stretched into the hilly Borders country, summarising an investigation into stock thefts from sheep farmers in his area.

McGrigor was a big, bluff, ex-lock forward, who respected the young Head of CID as much for his success on the rugby field as for his achievements as a detective . . . maybe more, Martin thought on occasion.

The report was solid and workmanlike too, ending with the arrest of a gang of rustlers from South Shields and their initial appearance in the Sheriff Court. 'Sheep-stealers in Selkirk,' Martin chuckled. 'Right up big John's street.'

He had just initialled the report and placed it in his out-tray when his telephone rang. It was Sammy Pye. 'Sir, I've got Spike Thomson, the disc jockey, on for you.'

He frowned, surprised. 'Put him through.'

There was music in the background as the presenter came on line. 'Hello, Andy,' he began in a bright, friendly tone. 'Listen, I'm on air so this can't take long. A thought occurred to me this morning. Remember I invited you to sit in on the show sometime, to see how we do it?'

'Sure.'

'How would you like to come in on Monday as a guest, a bit of on-air chat? I promise I won't ask you anything about current investigations, or stuff you don't want to talk about. Just about police work in general. Good PR for the force.'

Martin's first instinct was to say, 'No, thank you', but he gave the offer a second thought. 'Yes, why not,' he replied. 'I'll have to clear it with Bob, but in principle, okay.'

'I'm seeing Bob tonight,' said Thomson, 'at the football. I'll mention it to him. Cheers, got to go, CD's finishing.'

Martin grinned as he hung up, until his direct line rang, a few seconds later.

'Afternoon, sir,' said Mario McGuire. 'I've had young Alice check with Guardian Security on Lawrence Scotland, like you asked. He works out of their South Gyle depot, but he's been on the sick all week. He called in on Monday with a stomach bug. He's at home. He lives in a flat up in Gilmerton, near the Drum: number seven Falcon Street.'

'How do we know he's actually there?'

'His office called him this morning,' McGuire replied. 'Just to see how he was . . . and to check that he was there. He was in.'

'What do they think of him as an employee?'

'Quiet and reliable, was how they described him. If they only knew, eh? I wonder why Alec Smith let him stay on at Guardian after he arrived there.'

'The Hoover Principle again, I guess.'

'Eh?'

'Have them where you can see them. Right,' Martin glanced at his watch: four-forty. 'I'll pick him up now.'

'Look, sir, I could do that,' the Inspector said. 'My feet are clear of North Berwick now; I could lift Scotland.'

'Nah. I said I would do it and I will. I want a look at this guy, anyway; you don't get to meet too many retired terrorist hit-men in the course of a working day.'

He put down the phone and walked into his outer office and called to DC Pye. 'Sammy, have we still got that Mondeo in the car park?'

'Yes, sir. I've got the keys.'

'Let's have them then.'

The Detective Constable looked surprised. 'D'you not want me to come?'

'I'd rather you got those performance-appraisal forms out to Divisions. I'll see to Scotland on my own. I don't think for a minute that he killed Smith. If he was going to do that he'd have done it before now . . . and he'd have shot him too, I'll bet.

'I might not even bring him in, I just want to talk to him; to find out what he knew about Alec, as much as anything else.' He picked up the car keys and walked out of the office.

The white Mondeo was in the Fettes park, where Pye had parked it the night before after bringing it back from St Leonard's. He drove out into the late afternoon traffic.

The drive to Gilmerton was tedious at the best of times. He switched on the radio, and selected Forth AM. '. . . and this is for Margot,' said Spike Thomson. 'I know it's a few days late, but it only came up on our play-list today.' His voice faded and the sound of Stevie Wonder singing, 'Happy Birthday' filled the car. Andy grinned to himself as he thought of his Monday appearance.

Falcon Street was hard to find. It was a cul-de-sac and it only had a few houses, built in two small terraces looking across an open field on the other side. Number seven was one from the end. He parked, stepped out, and walked over to it and rang the bell.

He was about to ring again, when a thin man of medium height opened the door.

'Lawrence Scotland?' he asked. 'I'm Detective Chief Superintendent Martin, I'd like a chat.'

'Yes,' the man replied, quietly, 'I've been expecting you, or someone like you.' He took his right hand from behind his back. It was holding a large pistol, which he pointed at the detective's stomach. 'You'd better come in.'

Thirty-four

Mcllhenney trapped the ball, fired a pass wide to Grant Rock and moved forward into position to take the return. He felt as fit as in the playing days of his twenties and, maybe, even fitter since he trained harder now than then, and drank less.

Grock's one-two pass was tantalisingly short; Bob Skinner had a fifty-fifty chance of getting there first. No bailing out now: quicken the stride, right foot in, sole-first, big Bob off balance for once, spinning off to the side, clear shot at goal, on weaker foot – so what – drive! Rocket, top-left-hand corner, Spike Thomson in goal, nowhere. Stick that on your turntable, sunshine.

He turned and flashed a quick thumbs-up to Rock, acknowledging the pass, perfect now that it had worked. 'Lucky bastard,' Skinner grunted as he ran past him, back into his own half. 'Used to be,' he replied.

And then the door opened, signalling the arrival of the nine o'clock crowd; another gathering of the Legends was over. As usual everyone knew which side had won, although no-one had any idea of the final score.

Upstairs they showered, dressed and paid their money for the hall, then McIlhenney drove Skinner, David McPhail and Benny Crossley, whom he had collected in Gullane on the way through, back to the Golf Hotel in Dirleton Avenue, their post-

213

match pub. 'I think I'll arrange to be on your side next week, young man,' said Skinner, as he drove up the slope into the small car park. 'You're coming on to something of a game; four don't usually beat five.'

'Yes,' muttered McPhail. 'Bloody Diddler not turning up.'

'Why do they call him the Diddler, anyway?' McIlhenney asked, as they stepped into the hotel's small bar.

Skinner laughed. 'That's down to Grant Rock; the man of a thousand nicknames. When he was younger Howard fancied himself as a great ladies' man. He was always going on about diddling this one, diddling that one. One night in the middle of the game, he's got the ball, dwelling on it as usual, and Grock shouts across to him, "For fuck's sake, Diddler, over here!"

'We all fell about laughing and the name stuck. He's never been called anything else from then on. Even Edith, his wife, calls him Diddler now, although she thinks the name refers to his alleged skills with the ball, rather than with his cock.'

Skinner picked up the pint of lager which Lesley, the barmaid, had poured for him unasked, and eased his way into a window seat, well away from the bar so that it would not be he who went up for the next round. Spike Thomson sat opposite him, then leaned across the table. 'Bob,' he said, quietly. 'I was speaking to Andy Martin today; met him at a disastrous party last weekend. I put forward the idea that he might come on the show next Monday as a guest. I've got more scope for chat on this new AM format, and I want to have more people in.

'I promised him that I'd steer clear of current stuff and just talk about the generality of his work. He said he'd do it if it was okay with you.'

The DCC took a bite from his pint, and shrugged. 'Sure, I

don't mind. You never bloody invite me, though,' he added, with a grin.

'I have done and you know it,' the presenter protested. 'You've always turned me down.'

'Aye, well. More Andy's style than mine. Even if you started playing games on air you'd never wind him up; stick an awkward question at me and I'm liable to put you off air . . . not that you would do that, of course!'

'I promise, I promise.'

'Make way, lads, make way,' came a call from above, as Neil McIlhenney leaned over the table looking for clear space for a tray, on which he was carrying a bottle of port and nine glasses.

'What's this?' asked Mitchell Laidlaw, his eyes lighting up at the sight of the W&J Graham's vintage. 'You had a birthday two months ago, Neil.'

The big policeman's only reply was a quiet smile.

'This is something else,' said Skinner, as his exec filled the glasses. 'As of this week, Detective Sergeant McIlhenney is now Detective Inspector McIlhenney. From now on, you lot'll be getting kicked by two line commanders, not just one.'

'Congratulations, Inspector,' Andrew John called out, triggering off a chorus of congratulation as he raised his glass in a toast. 'Can I sell you an ISA?'

'Not a chance,' the new inspector replied. 'But the Diddler's been trying to flog me one that his firm operates.'

'You won't go wrong there,' the banker conceded. 'The wee fella might be an eccentric on the football field, and a grade one chromium-plated gossip, but he's one shit-hot investment manager.'

He leaned back, allowing Lesley room to clear away some pint glasses; as he did he spotted a newspaper left on the floor by an earlier customer; he bent and picked it up. It was a copy of the *Evening News*, two days old. 'Have you put a name to this bloke yet?' John asked, pointing to the likeness on the front page.

'I don't think so,' Skinner replied, 'but I've been away; I don't know the whole story.'

'Let's have a look,' said McIlhenney. 'I haven't seen that e-fit yet.' He took the newspaper from John and studied it.

After a few seconds he started to laugh . . . and then the laugh tailed off and was replaced by a frown, as he thought of the man who treated Thursday as if his life depended on it, who never missed a game, yet who, without warning, had failed to appear that evening.

He passed the crumpled *News* to the DCC. 'Here, Boss,' he said. 'Look at this picture, this unidentified floater. Could that or could that not be the Diddler?'

Thirty-five

'This is very stupid, Lawrence. I'm the Head of CID, for God's sake; my staff and various other people knew I was going to talk to you. It's a matter of time before they come looking for me.'

Martin had been sitting on the wooden kitchen chair for almost five hours, his hands tied behind his back. In that time neither he nor his captor had said a word. Scotland had simply sat there, gazing at him, levelling the gun at him. He knew that he had been playing a game with him, a game of growing tension, growing terror. Okay, the guy had won.

'You better start praying that they don't then. For the first time that doorbell rings I'm just going to blow your fucking brains out.'

The detective looked at him and knew that he meant it; cold terror gripped him inside, but he made a conscious effort to keep it from showing. 'They won't ring the doorbell until there's an armed response team in position outside. How are you going to get out?'

'I'm not. Once I've shot you, I'll just give myself up. When they try me I'll tell them the whole story of what Alec Smith did to me. That Gavigan bloke; he's still around. I'll call him as a witness.'

'You've never met Bob Skinner, have you?' Martin asked.

'No, but I'd like to. I'd like to have him sitting in that chair next to you.'

'You wouldn't, believe me. There's a flaw in your plan; Bob's not going to let you walk away from here. You kill me and he's going to kill you, not just because he's my best pal, but because of the story you could tell in the witness box. He's a crack shot, incidentally, and he's a very patient man. I'd keep well away from that window if I was you.'

'I don't care about being dead, mister; I've been dead before. But thanks for that advice.' Scotland walked round behind Martin, to the window, out of any line of sight from outside. The kitchen went dark, suddenly. The detective glanced over his shoulder and made out the shape of Venetian blinds, now admitting only the narrowest strips of daylight.

'Is this your standard practice, pre-execution?' he asked. *Keep him talking, Andy. He's got a lot to say.*

'Was, Mr Martin, was. I'm retired now, remember. Alec Smith retired me about ten years ago: or he thought he did. But as it happens, you're right. I always used to do this in Ireland; the Provos, and the Ulster-based Loyalist guys, they would just kill quick and off. There's the target, bang, another couple in the head to be sure, job done.

'I didn't like that approach. That was much too impersonal for my taste. The way I saw it, the people I was sent to kill were human beings just like me; they had the right to know who was going to kill them, and why. Plus, they had a right to prepare themselves for the end of their lives.

'So I would pick them up, take them to a safe house and sit up all night with them, talking to them about the conflict, listening to their threats often enough, but very rarely listening to them beg for their lives. They were real soldiers, most of those boys, I'll give them that.

'Are you going to beg?' he asked suddenly.

'Fuck off.'

'We'll see, when the time comes. Anyway, we'd have our death watch, my customers and I, then at dawn I'd give them the Last Rites . . .'

'You'd what?' Martin interrupted.

'I'd give them the Last Rites. They were all Catholics, the people I killed over there, and I knew the words, sort of, so I gave them the Last Rites. It meant something to them, believe me.'

'Sure, the final insult.'

'Ah, you're a Catholic then. But you don't deserve the Last Rites, you're a copper.'

He leaned over and tapped Martin in the middle of the forehead with the barrel of the big pistol. 'I used to shoot them right there, so they could see it coming. I always wondered whether they did . . . see the bullet, I mean. Think about it: if someone shoots you right in the middle of the scone at close range, do you see the bullet just before impact? Do you die before you see the flash? I'm pretty sure you don't hear the bang. I used to time that; when I heard the bang the guy's brains were usually on the way out the back of his head. One or two of them flinched though, looked away just as I was pulling the trigger. Fucking brains everywhere then, even on me; top of the head comes right off with a heavy-calibre gun.'

'You're going to make a hell of a mess of your kitchen,' the detective growled.

'Ahh, a hard boy,' said Scotland, knowingly. 'We'll see that too, when the time comes, just how hard you really are. Anyway, I'm not going to shoot you here . . . not unless somebody rings the bell, that is.' Martin began to think, frantically. Who expected him that night, or might call on him, find him missing? Rhian? No, no more. Karen? No, baby-sitting for Neil. Alex? Unlikely. Pye? No. Mario? *Christ, I hope not. Change the subject, change the subject.*

'Earlier on, Lawrence,' he kept his tone even; no panic, no fear, 'you said that Alec Smith only thought he'd retired you. Are you saying you've been active since then?'

'No. I'm saying that the likes of big Smith couldn't retire me. I withdrew, because it was too dangerous for the people I worked with for me to be around them. I could never be completely sure that I had evaded surveillance.'

Scotland looked at his prisoner and let out a sort of snort. 'Hhghh. You realise you haven't even asked me how Smith thought he had retired me? That means you know. Probably always bloody known. I imagine that big bastard was really proud of himself, talking it all over Special Branch. Not so fucking cocky now, though.'

'I know what he did,' Martin acknowledged, 'but I only found out this week. I took over Alec Smith's job, but I never knew about it then. Alec never told anybody anything they didn't need to know, not even his family. He was the world's most secretive man and all of his secrets may have died with him.

'We only found out what he did to you because Tommy Gavigan was leaned on after his death. He told us all about it. He's out now, by the way; retired early, sent on down the road.'

'You mean he's got a fucking pension for that?' Another flash of anger.

'Which he'll never enjoy spending for looking over his shoulder. Unless . . . maybe we'll get him your job at Guardian.'

Scotland smiled, a cruel grin of power. 'You forget, Detective

Chief Superintendent . . . . you won't be getting anything for anyone after tomorrow.'

'As you say, we'll see about that.' *Move on, quickly*. 'How did you know who Smith was? What he was?'

'Come on, Mr Martin. Our intelligence wasn't that bad: I don't mean my Irish friends, I mean Tony Manson's intelligence. He always knew who all the coppers were, including the Special Branch people. Tony got me involved in Ireland, you know. Some contacts of his needed an outside worker to take on a special job; somebody very big in Sinn Fein, someone they couldn't get near. He could have sent big Lenny Plenderleith, only he didn't want to risk losing him; so, since I had done a few things for him by that time, he volunteered me. The job got done, and I got asked back for the tricky ones. I got paid, of course; I was strictly a mercenary.'

'So why the straight job now? What took you to Guardian?'

'I am straight . . . or at least I was. Tony's dead, big Lenny's in the nick for ever, Jackie Charles is banged up and his wife's a gingerbread woman, Dougie the Comedian's dead; all of it, or most of it, thanks to Skinner and you. I was a hired gun; now there's no-one left to hire me.

'So I took a job at Guardian. The money was good, the work was easy enough – on-site night-security work mainly, offices, the university, the zoo, even. Then, bugger me, what happens but big Smith gets appointed General Manager. I thought I was for the off right away, but no, he kept me on. He told me that he liked having me where he could see me. But then, after a year, he left. They wanted to make him a star down south, so the story went, but he wouldn't have it.'

'It wouldn't have suited his plans.'

'What do you mean?'

'I don't know, but he was up to something. Until last Friday night, that is,' Martin added, quietly.

Lawrence Scotland laughed. 'So you're finally getting round to what you came to talk to me about, are you? I knew somebody would, after that. I hoped it would be Tommy Gavigan, but you'll do. Oh aye, you'll do. A Detective Chief Superintendent, indeed.'

'How did you find out where Alec lived? Did you look at the personnel records at Guardian?'

'Don't be daft. I'm a shooter, not a safecracker. No, I just followed him home; back to his lair, the fucking animal, there on the beach with just him and his fucking dog. I thought about grabbing it off the street, you know, throttling it and dumping it on his doorstep . . . just so he'd know.'

'He'd probably have killed you, if he thought you were threatening him.'

'I worked that one out for myself, pal. Anyway, what harm had the poor bloody dog done?'

'So ten years on, you decided to kill Alec himself. The thing that surprises me is that I never really fancied you for it. That's why I was stupid enough to come to see you alone; just for a chat about Alec, to find out what you knew about him back then.'

'You mean you didn't come to apologise,' said Scotland, scornfully. 'No, I never thought you would. You don't really mind what Smith did to me, do you? Come on, be honest, admit it.'

'No, I don't really mind; I can't approve of it, but I can see why he did it. There were no cries of outrage when we found out.'

'Naw, I didn't imagine there would be. I can see why myself, truth be told. I made big Alec angry by slipping his surveillance that last time I went to Ireland, to Armagh. I don't think he was a man who liked to get angry. He was all about control, and anger signifies a loss of control.

'He must have planned it very carefully, and looked at all the reports of the jobs I did. All of them shot in the head, standing up, facing the gun, no blindfold, no bag over the head, nothing like that. He did the same thing to me; exactly the same, on purpose.

'There's an added element to being on the other end of it, you know, when you've done it yourself. I realised right then that of all the people I'd dealt with, the people who were the most terrified – they all were at the end, but I mean the most of all, crying, begging, pissing themselves, all that stuff – were the ones who'd actually killed people themselves. They'd seen the brains coming out too, and when you've seen that the last thing you want is that it should be your brains flying all over the place. No, you don't want that.

'Big Alec knew that; so he did what he did to me, and in a strange way I respected him for that. But it was way over the top. I hurt his pride, but he terrified me, almost to death, and he humiliated me in the worst possible way. Being left sat in your own shite miles from nowhere is worse than being dead. You might say that you have no sympathy for me, but you couldn't have done what he did, could you? Load the gun, spin the chamber, pull the trigger. Then do it again.'

He frowned at Martin. 'No, you couldn't have done that, not you.' Then he laughed.

'I saw your guy in the papers, saying that you were looking for a seriously disturbed individual over Alec Smith's death. Fucking hell, that's ironic; big Alec was a seriously disturbed individual himself.

'I looked into his eyes, behind that big gun that he pointed at me, just like this one . . .' He waved the big pistol in the air, '. . . and I could see something in there that was plain fucking crazy. That scared me as much as the thought of my brains flying out the back of my head.

'I will tell you one thing . . . just one thing. I could not think of anything worse in the world than being that man's enemy.'

'I can.'

'What's that?'

Martin gazed straight at the other man. 'Being mine,' he said quietly, '. . . as you will find out.'

'Big talk,' Scotland sneered. 'But no more talk now, no more till morning. We sit the Death Watch in silence; you with your thoughts, me just watching you. There's something incredible about studying a man who knows he's going to die in a few hours.

'I haven't done it for a long time.'

Thirty-six

'Sure,' said Sarah. 'I keep copies of all my autopsy reports here, on my lap-top computer and in hard copy.' She looked at her husband and at Neil McIlhenney standing in the conservatory, where she had been reading when they arrived.

'What's the panic anyway?'

'No panic,' said Bob. 'It's a thousand-to-one chance, but it's something we have to check. Will you get us a copy of the report on the second post-mortem you did at the weekend?'

He turned to McIlhenney. 'Neil, you'd better get home for your baby-sitter.'

'No, it's Karen. I'll call her; she'll understand.'

'Okay, but first let's try to knock this thing on the head. Let's just phone the Diddler just in case he's been at home all the time, let's not look any dafter than we have to.' He picked up the local telephone directory, a commercially-produced listing of village numbers, found the entry for 'Shearer, H', and dialled it.

The phone rang four times, before the Diddler answered. 'Hello,' he said. 'Howard and Edith are away from home right now, but if you'd like to leave us a message, or even send us a fax, we'll get back to you.'

'Bugger,' Skinner swore. 'Come on, Neil,' he said. 'He lives just up the hill; let's check out his house for signs of recent occupation.'

Sarah met them in the hall; she had a document pouch in her hand, and looked in surprise at the torch Bob held in his. 'We'll be back in a minute, love,' he told her. 'We're just going up to the Shearers' place.'

He led McIlhenney out into the bright night, down his long driveway and into Hill Road. Halfway up the steeply-rising street he stopped at a gateway; it led to a big bungalow, modern, like his own, in contrast to the great stone houses which climbed the hillside and which were silhouetted all around against the shining blue sky . . . until the glare of a security light obliterated everything else.

Diddler's outer door was locked, and the house was in darkness. The door was solid, with no glass panels. Skinner pushed the letter-box open and shone his torch through it. 'Fuck,' he swore quietly. 'There are newspapers all over the place; and one of them's the *Sunday Times*. Nobody's been here since the weekend.

'I don't like this. The Diddler might be a fucking wee sweetiewife at times, but he's a good bloke and I am worried about him.'

'Where else could he be?' his assistant asked.

'He and Edith have a place in the south of France; conceivably they could be there. But what isn't conceivable is that none of us knew about it. The Diddler has never missed a Thursday night without letting Benny Crossley, or Davie McPhail, or me know in advance . . . and I mean never.

'We'd better have a look at that report.'

They ran back down the hill to Skinner's house. This time, Sarah was waiting in the kitchen, making a pot of coffee, simply to have something to do. The Floater file was lying on the work surface; Bob picked it up and took out the report. 'Does this mention old scars and other distinguishing marks?' he asked.

'Yes. Right there on the first page. The body had an append-ectomy scar, and that's it, apart from a fairly unusual blood type.'

'Any sign of a healed fracture of the right big toe, about seven years old?'

'The right big toe was missing. Severed. Look, you two, what is this? You've just been to Shearer's place. You don't think that man could be the Diddler, do you?'

McIlhenney took a folded newspaper from his back pocket and handed it to her. She stared at the image on the front page; slowly her eyes seemed to widen. 'My God,' she whispered. 'I see what you mean. And I helped prepare this picture, too. Yet it never occurred to me.'

'Where's the body now?' Bob asked.

'It'll still be in the mortuary at the Royal Infirmary, I imagine. But Bob, you will not be able to identify it; take a look at the photographs in there if you don't believe me.'

He did as she suggested, taking the big colour prints from the pouch, and wincing as he looked through them. 'I believe you,' he muttered, at last. 'We'll need DNA testing, Neil. The trouble is we'll need something from the Diddler to make the comparison. That means we'll need to get into the house, to look for hairs off pillows and the like.'

'And Edith's in St Tropez with Victoria, their daughter,' said Sarah. 'I met her in the village last week and she told me they were going, now that the Highers are over.'

'Shit. We'll need her approval to get into the house: last thing I want is to scare the woman before we're certain that the wee bugger isn't shacked up somewhere, up to his old tricks.'

He took the coffee which Sarah handed him. 'Look, we're not

going to catch any killers tonight. You get back to the kids, Neil, I'll phone Dan Pringle and tell him to meet me in his office at eight sharp tomorrow.'

McIlhenney grinned. 'That should be an interesting phone call. Where we have the football on a Thursday night, Superintendent Pringle has the Masons: and Superintendent Pringle likes a drink.'

Thirty-seven

Karen Neville drove quietly along the narrow street. She took a deep breath as she saw the red MGF parked in the driveway. It was after midnight; she had thought it over several times, indeed she was still thinking it over, but she was there.

To hell with what he might have to tell her, or ask her. There were things that she needed to say to him, and she couldn't hold them inside over another long, lonely weekend.

Things like the way he had misread her, and how it wasn't his fault since she had misread herself. Things about stability and the need to stop being a human mayfly, before June came along and there were few options left, and even less future. Things about this bloody office situation and how untenable it was becoming for her, calling him 'Sir', or 'Boss', or 'Mr Martin' in front of other people. Christ, it was a wonder she had never said 'Thank you, sir,' as he had come inside her, 'Thank you for the part of yourself you've given me, the only part you ever give.'

That was at the heart of it: most of all she had to tell him outright that theirs was a taking relationship on both sides, with little or no giving at all, and that she could not go on that way. She couldn't go on being his safe house away from the demons, even if that meant that he could no longer provide the self-same comfort for her.

She didn't know what she was going to say to him after that, other than 'I quit: everything, as of now. Goodbye.'

Or maybe she would simply speak the truth and say, 'I'm sorry, Andy, but I love you.'

She took another deep breath as she parked in front of his car, blocking his driveway. The house was in darkness, but she knew that his bedroom and living room were on the far side. She pressed the door buzzer, hearing it sound inside. She waited; and she waited. She rang again, longer this time, in case he was asleep, although she knew he never slept all that deeply. Still she waited until the picture began to form in her head.

Why was his car in the driveway and not in the garage? Was there another car in there?

Andy, not asleep. Andy, not alone. Andy, with this week's blonde. Or maybe Ruth McConnell . . . or maybe Alex. Was he really over her? Would he ever be?

Yes, she got the picture.

Her nerve failed her. She walked away from his front door, climbed back into her car, turned on the engine and then, as quietly as she could, Karen Neville drove away.

Thirty-eight

He tried, but he couldn't; he couldn't think about his life. Only about his death, only about that bloody great gun and the cold, thin man who had been pointing it at him all night. It looked pretty old, a Webley service revolver maybe, or an American Colt, the sort of wartime souvenir that had been handed in by the thousands at firearms amnesties over the last fifty years.

It may have been a museum piece, but Martin was in no doubt that it was in working order. Lawrence Scotland knew his firearms; he'd had plenty of practice during his years as a consultant to the Irish Loyalists and to the late and infrequently lamented Tony Manson. A heavy calibre job; point four five, probably. For a second too long he found himself imagining what one of those would do to his head, how much of it would be left.

He had seen a murder victim once, years back, where a heavy weapon like that one had been pressed to the victim's temple. Contact wound; explosive, hardly anything left in the cranium. He thought of JFK and the apparent mystery of what had happened to his brain, when his body had arrived at the Dallas hospital. *Where was the mystery? It was all over Jackie!*

I wonder who'll identify me. Bob maybe, poor bugger. Not my

*dad though, please not him. Altogether too old for that; it would
kill him.* He pictured a funeral; solemn people in black suits. His
parents supported by his younger brother, David, and his wife
Caitlin. Bob, Jim Elder, Proud Jimmy in uniform . . . *Don't wear
uniform, Bob, not for me. I know how much you hate it* . . . Sarah,
and Alex, near the front. Karen, a row further back with Sammy
and Neil. Mario and Maggie . . .

Stop it, Martin, he shouted at himself, inside his head. *This
man only has your body captive. Let him take your mind and you
really are dead. If he does what you think he's going to do, you
have some sort of a chance. He's your enemy, he's the other team,
and what do you do to them? That's right: you smash them into the
fucking ground, ruck the bastards till they howl for their mothers.
You're going to get this guy with whatever you have and you're
going to hear his last pathetic gasp.*

*Anger, Andy, anger. No point in staying cool now; Mr Cool will
get his fucking head blown off. Be Mr Angry; anger is your only
weapon. Anger kills, cool is vulnerable. Yes, let Lawrence fucking
Scotland be Mr Cool.*

'Okay.' The man spoke quietly but the word was like a
shout, knifing its way into his thoughts in the gloom of the
kitchen. 'It's time to go. Time to meet your maker, Mr Martin.
Come along quiet now; be a good lad and I'll give you the Last
Rites.'

'Fuck you and your rites, you blasphemous bastard,' the
detective snarled.

'Ahh,' said Scotland, 'that's what you're going to be is it?
Defiant to the end. I had one of those once, in Armagh; only he
wasn't, not to the end. He was one of them who had seen the
brains flying out. At the end he was blubbering like a baby, not
facing the gun, turning away and getting his head blown all over

the place. I pissed on him afterwards; it was the only time I've ever done that. Before today, that is.'

'You'll piss yourself before the morning's out.'

'That's it. Keep it up, keep it up. Now, listen, this is what's going to happen. We're going outside, and we're getting into your car. I've got the keys from your jacket. If you think about making a noise when we get outside, then I'll shoot you in the back of the head. After that I'll drive to the *Scotsman* office and give myself up to them; that way your man Skinner can't kill me. That way it all comes out in Court.'

'What if they're outside now, waiting?'

'Then you'll be dead; me too probably. But we both know they're not, or we'd have heard by now. Come on.'

With surprising strength he hauled Martin to his feet, and pushed him towards the door. In the hall, the detective stumbled.

Do it now! a voice said. *Go for him!*

No; no room, gun cocked. No chance.

He picked himself up, and stepped outside, into Falcon Street.

'See?' said Scotland. 'No bastard here.' He opened the front passenger door of the white Mondeo, and jammed the gun into the middle of Martin's back, forcing him forward, awkwardly, his hands still tied, numb, behind his back, and on to the seat. Lightning fast, Scotland ran round to the driver's side and climbed in. Then, holding the gun to his captive's head with his left hand, he reached over and pulled the seat belt around him, fastening it, rendering him virtually immobile.

He started the car and grinned at the policeman wickedly. 'You know where we're going, don't you?'

'I can guess. I promise you one thing, bastard; I won't shit myself like you did.'

'You will, you know. They all do.'

Scotland put the car into gear and drove off, unhurried and steadily, out of Falcon Street and on to Gilmerton Road, turning left, heading for the City by-pass. He picked it up at Sheriffhall and headed west. Martin glanced at the car clock; it was six-twenty. Even on a Friday morning, the traffic at that time was minimal; no rescue vehicles, that was for sure.

They turned off at the Lothianburn Junction, then took the fork which led to Biggar, and eventually to the M74 and Carlisle. They would not be going that far, though, Martin knew. Still driving steadily, Scotland took the first turning to the right off the Biggar Road, a narrower country track, which climbed upwards into the Pentland Hills. After two, maybe three miles, they came to a car park, small but secluded, a clearing in a dark woodland area. They turned in and came to a halt.

'We walk from here,' said the man with the gun.

'Good, you fucker,' Martin hissed. 'I want to see how big your balls really are.'

'I've got to hand it to you, Mr Policeman.' Click; and the seat belt came undone. 'So far you're talking a good game.' Scotland climbed out of the car then opened the passenger door, hauling his prisoner out. 'Go on, that way. Take that path through the woods. Remember though, I'm right behind and I'll shoot you in the back if you do anything daft. I won't kill you, not yet, I'll just knock a piece of you out, but it'll be fucking sore.'

Not in the woods, Martin found himself praying. *Don't let him do it in the woods. All wrong, not enough room.* But they walked on, until the forest came to an end, giving way abruptly to open hillside, behind a fence and a sign which read, 'Warning. MoD Property. No admission. Live firing possible.'

'Live firing fucking certain,' said Scotland, gleefully. 'Go on, through it.'

The fence was three wire strands; no obstacle. Even bound, Martin slipped through, easily, his executioner following. 'Up the hill.' They climbed carefully, for the hill grass was suddenly thick in places, up towards a summit which turned out to be merely a crest, hiding another steep trek. On they trudged for, Martin judged, more than half an hour, mostly upwards, sometimes round the hillside, but always with purpose. Scotland knew exactly where he was going.

At last, they climbed another short slope and came to a rough, rock-strewn clearing; looking at it, the policeman guessed that it might have been an old crater, from a shell, or even a bomb.

'I've been here many a time since,' Lawrence Scotland murmured. 'Thinking about Alec Smith, wishing I could get him up here, crying on his knees. But I knew I never could; guys like Smith, the fanatics, the crazies, are always on their guard. And then you came to me.'

'What if I hadn't been alone?' Martin asked. The thought had never occurred to him, not once.

'There wouldn't have been more than two of you. I'd have killed the one back there at the Drum and brought the other one straight here.' The detective felt a chill as he thought of Sammy Pye and those performance-review forms; they had saved a life.

'Well, big deal, arsehole. It's worked out for you. Now let's get on with it.'

'Hah. You can't be that keen to die, Detective Chief Superintendent.' Mocking now; it was beginning. *God, this bugger's hard to rattle. Got to, though; got to.* Martin aimed a clumsy kick at him.

'Watch it, pal,' the man called out, stepping back lightly, out of range, 'or I'll kneecap you. I saw that done once, you know, in Ireland. Fucking brutal it was; often they lose a leg after it. No, you just stand there, like a good polisman and it'll be less painful for you.'

A slow, exultant, smile. 'You know what we're going to do, don't you?'

Anger, Andy, Mr Angry. Anger is your weapon; your life depends on it.

'Of course, I fucking know,' he roared, forcing a laugh, which for an instant seemed to take the man by surprise. 'I've always wanted to play this game. Come on, show me some stuff.'

Scotland shook his head, and took a pace back.

Come closer you bastard. Need you closer.

He was much faster than Martin had expected, as he broke the breech of the pistol, emptied six bullets into his hand from their chambers, replaced just one, snapped the breech shut and spun the magazine.

Fuck. Too quick, not a chance to move.

Panic now as the gun came up: cold, clammy, terror. Pressure on bladder. *Don't let go whatever you do. Keep your eyes open, look down the barrel. Take the bullet in the forehead if you have to.* Inching closer, staring past the gun into Scotland's icy eyes, heart pounding, hammering, faces in the way. *Dad, Mum, David, Alex, Bob, Karen, Sarah, Rhian, Jazz, Karen . . . Heart bursting, head swimming, he's squeezing the trigger . . .*

Nothing; only a click, an incredibly loud, almost deafening click, then a rushing in his ears. Sudden numbness, sudden explosion of sweat, sudden relief. *Brains are still there, but they're not working. What to do? Stay Angry. Unsettle the bastard, if you can.*

'So!' A shout; a Mr Angry shout. 'Disappointed, you rat-fucker?'

'Oh no. I'd only have been disappointed if you'd begged me, or if the gun had gone off. You know something? They say you can see the soul leave the body. I never have; but maybe you have to have a soul yourself before you can.'

Gun still steady, held on me. Now? Knew I should . . . sweet Jesus I've got to, but my Goddamn bloody legs are shaking. When I need them most they won't work.

'Round two.' Scotland, cat quick again, loading another bullet, spinning the chamber.

Missed it, fuck it. Missed the moment. Oh, Mother of Christ, I'm really dead now. No, six chambers, two bullets; two to one my favour. Take the bet, Andy. Go for him and he could fire four times before you get there. Dead for sure. Take the bet. After that . . . next try he's yours.'

Harder to hold it together this time. *No more humour in his eyes; supposed to die or crap myself. Won't do either. Kill that rat-fucker. Kill, Kill!* Heart still pounding, faces again; no, just one face. *Karen, Karen, Karen, Karen. Oh fuck, Karen, he's pulling the trigger . . .*

Karen still there, me still there, no more chat now, third bullet. Dead for sure. Yell! Rush. Yes, the fucker's startled, dropped it, dropped the bullet. Hit him now, shoulder first in the chest, remember the time you flattened John Jeffrey . . . reverse of the usual. Knock this rat-fucker down; yes! Drive shoulder in again, crush him into the ground. In with the head, yes, in the face, hurt him, break whatever you can! Lie on his arm, pin that hand, don't let him close the breech on those two rounds. Christ, he's almost . . . Teeth, anything, yes, bite, go for trigger finger. Yes, got it now; bite, harder than that . . . Taste blood; bite harder . . . bite harder ... shake like a terrier ... loose in my mouth. Who's screaming? Him. Great. You taste lousy, rat-fucker, your finger tastes lousy! Spit. Roll over on him, on your back; grab for gun with your hands ... Grab ... Got it ... no. Yes, got it. Breech is closed. Stand up, knee in his chest again on the way ... Turn around, try to shoot the fucker? No, could shoot yourself, just empty the gun, then deal with him. Pull trigger empty chamber, pull trigger empty chamber. On his feet now, punching me with his good hand and the other, the one with the bloody stump. Nothing stuff. Girlie hits. Pull trigger, bang round gone, pull trigger empty chamber, pull trigger bang other round gone. Christ he's got a rock now, big one, holding it up to brain me, charge again, drive harder faster this time head up kill the fucker kill the fucker head under chin drive up teeth into throat bite hard kill bite harder kill bite hardest kill kill kill kill ... Got to see Karen tell Karen Karen Karen ... bite still, tear, rip, more blood, lots more blood, listen rat-fucker for your last pathetic gurgling gasp ...

Thirty-nine

'How certain are you that this Howard Shearer's our man, sir?' Skinner smiled inwardly as he looked at the bleary-eyed Pringle. Eight a.m. Friday mornings in the office were not of his choosing, not any more, not at his age, not now that he was a Right Worshipful Panjandrum or whatever the hell he was in his Lodge. He thought for a moment of pointing out that there could be no degrees of certainty, but he let it pass; *Nobody loves a smart-arse*, he reminded himself.

'I'm not saying he is, Dan; I'm still a way short of that. But everyone who knows him . . . and there were nine of us last night, ten counting Sarah . . . agrees that the e-fit is a damn good likeness. There's an appendectomy scar too, and on top of that he was missing from action last night. We've always joked that the Diddler would skip his own funeral to make the game.

'I've checked his house, without breaking in, and I know that no-one's been there since Sunday at the latest. Still it's not conclusive; there could be an explanation. He's a high-flyer in fund management; he makes occasional trips to the Far East. He could be there, or he could be at a conference.

'I hope to God he is, for his sake and for his wife's.'

Pringle grunted. 'There's something else, for her sake

239

too, sir. The man in the water had someone else's pubic hair trapped under the bell-end of his knob.'

'I know . . . and I just hope we don't wind up having to ask Edith for a sample for comparison.' He paused. 'I've read Sarah's report till I know it off by heart. The part of it which deals with how he was tied up . . . What did you make of that?'

The Superintendent looked at the DCC suspiciously, as if he was afraid he had been asked a trick question. 'It said that there were marks on the wrists and ankles, showing that he had been securely tied up.' He paused. 'And it noted that the marks went all the way round, indicating that the wrists and ankles may not have been bound together, although not ruling out the possibility that there might have been a final layer of rope or cord over the top.

'In other words,' he concluded, 'Sarah couldn't say whether they were tied together or not.'

'Right. Ten out of ten; damn near word perfect. Now; leave the question of identification to one side for the moment, add your alien pube to the situation and try this. A sex game: our victim was into bondage. He liked it upside down, the woman in control, not him. So he lets himself be tied to the bed posts and be fucked . . . and then it all goes very sadly wrong.'

Dan Pringle's expressive face wrinkled; he scratched his heavy moustache. 'So are you saying he was killed by a woman?'

'I'm saying he could have been, not that he was. I don't know how the other half lives; maybe the victim was gay. Or maybe he was straight and it was a set-up; she jumped off and in came a squad of guys with big hammers.'

'Not hammers, not according to the report.'

'Okay then, baton-like instruments, if you want me to quote verbatim. Terminal, whatever they were.'

'What's the time?' Skinner asked suddenly, glancing at his watch to answer his own question. 'Eight twenty-five. Late enough to try the Diddler's office. They do business in Europe, so the switchboard's always open at eight. His secretary could be in by now . . . and so, of course, could he.'

'What's his firm called?'

'Daybelge Fund Managers.' He picked up Yellow Pages from Pringle's desk. 'I can never remember the damn number. Ah here it is.' He picked up the direct line telephone, punched in seven digits, and waited.

'Daybelge; how can I help you?' The telephonist's voice had the tone of a bell.

'Is Mr Shearer in?'

'No sir.'

'Janine Bryant?'

'Yes, sir. Who shall I say is calling?'

'Mr Skinner, a friend of Mr Shearer.'

He waited again, until a new voice came on line. 'Good morning, Mr Skinner.'

The DCC had spoken to Janine Bryant many times, and had met her once when he had given the Diddler a lift home from his office on a Thursday evening. She was a clever, confident, assured woman in her late thirties. He had never heard her sound remotely apprehensive before, and so when she spoke, it was as if a cold fist had punched him in the stomach.

'Where's the Diddler, Janine?' he asked, quietly.

'I don't know, Mr Skinner. I was afraid that you did and that you were going to tell me. He hasn't been in the office since last Friday; but he didn't warn me he was going away or anything. I've had to ask other partners to take over his meetings all this week.'

'Have you called Mrs Shearer in France?'

'I didn't like to do that.'

'Why not?'

He sensed her hesitation. 'I hardly like to say this, even to you, but I have a feeling that he might be with a girlfriend.'

'What makes you think that?'

'I can't put my finger on it; it's just that last week there was a spring in his step, one that I've seen in the past, one that's usually been associated with a discreet adventure. With Mrs Shearer and Victoria leaving for France last Friday morning . . . well, I have a suspicion.'

'Is that why you didn't raise the alarm?'

'No,' said the secretary, 'not at all. Mr Skinner,' she continued, 'Daybelge is a partnership, but Mr Shearer is very much the senior partner. He takes all the strategic investment decisions; the others implement them and report to him. We have some extremely important clients and if word got around the market that he was missing, I hate to think of the consequences for the firm.

'I discussed the situation with the others on Wednesday, and we agreed that we would do nothing and say nothing, but wait for him to surface.'

Skinner sighed. 'I fear that he may have surfaced already, Janine. Have you read about the unidentified man who was fished out of the Water of Leith last Saturday?'

She gasped, 'Yes,' she replied in a trembling whisper.

'There were terrible facial injuries, but in the circumstances . . . it could be the Diddler. Do you know who his doctor is?'

'He never goes to one, Mr Skinner. He's in perfect health. He has an annual check-up at the Murrayfield, just to be sure . . .

242

his MOT, he calls it and he always passes with flying colours.'

'Would they have a note of his blood group?'

'They have better than that. They have some of his blood. Mr Shearer has a rare blood type, so he has the hospital take a pint every six months and store it, just in case they ever have to operate on him.'

Skinner nodded to Pringle, who was standing beside him, hanging on to one side of the conversation. 'That's good,' he told the secretary. 'We'll get an identification from that; one way or another.'

'Now,' he continued, 'do you know where Graham, the son, is?'

'He's in Australia. He's spending the university vacation in Sydney working with a firm with whom Daybelge has a link. Mr Shearer arranged it for him.'

'Damn. I'd have liked him here for his mother, if it comes to that.'

'I have a number where you can reach him. Hold on.' He waited while she looked it out, then noted it down as she read.

'One last thing, Janine. If the Diddler was up to his old tricks and was shacked up somewhere, do you have any idea at all where that might have been.'

'No,' she replied. 'Unless . . . unless he used Graham's place. That would have been empty.'

'What's that?'

'It's a cottage. Mr Shearer bought it but the mortgage is in Graham's name. It's down in Coltbridge. I don't have the address, but I know that it . . .' She stopped in mid-sentence.

'You don't need to tell me,' Skinner said. 'It backs right on to the Water of Leith.'

'Yes.'

'Ahh, that's it,' the DCC hissed. 'Thanks, Janine. I'm really sorry. Look this has got to stay secret, even from the partners, until we've confirmed the identification by DNA comparison, and until Edith has been told. My colleague Dan Pringle will keep you informed of what's happening.

'So Daybelge can arrange damage control, we'll tell you before we make any announcement. That will not happen before Edith and Victoria are back in Scotland, or before Edith has spoken to Graham and he's on his way back home.'

'I understand.' She sounded under control.

'Good. You'd better give me your home phone number.' Again, he noted as she dictated.

'Thanks. So long, and again . . . I'm sorry.'

He hung up the phone, and turned to Pringle. 'Okay, Dan. I want you to get McGurk up to the Murrayfield to collect a sample of the Diddler's stored blood. Then I want you to find an address in Coltbridge occupied by one Graham Shearer.'

The Superintendent picked up a copy of the electoral register from his desk and flicked through it. 'There's no Shearer listed anywhere about there,' he announced, after a few minutes.

'The boy's only twenty, Dan. His vote's probably still in Gullane, but he'll be paying Council Tax in Edinburgh. Check it out with the City.' He turned towards the door.

'Damn!' he shouted suddenly. 'Damn! Damn! Damn! Who the Hell would want to do that to the Diddler? And why, for God's sake? Alec Smith and him, on the same bloody night!'

'But no connection between them, Boss.'

'No, but . . .' He gasped. 'Wait a minute, of course there's a bloody connection. They both belonged to the Legends. They played together.'

Pringle stared at him. 'My Thursday football group,' he

explained, curtly. 'Alec was a member for a while, till his knee went; the Diddler's been a member almost from the start. And they're both murdered on the same night. One in North Berwick, one in Coltbridge. And what was the time gap between the two killings?' He thought for a moment. 'Four hours,' he snapped. 'It's possible; it could have been done.

'Dan. Get that blood; find that house. I'm off to talk to Sarah.'

Forty

'No, Bob, no. Those two murders could not have been committed by the same person.'

'Come on, can you say that for sure? The time-frame fits.'

'Maybe it does, but that's all. There are major differences between the two. Look at poor Diddler; let's go with the sex-crime scenario, I accept that it's the likeliest explanation for the nature of the binding. He's tied, has sex, or at least there's enough contact for him to acquire that single strand of hair, then he's battered to death.

'The Smith case was completely different. He was stripped and bound, yes, but that was for torture. There was nothing remotely sexual about it.'

'What about the burning of the genitalia?'

'That's an anti-sexual gesture, a classic.'

'This is only theory though.'

'Okay, you want fact, here it is. The blows to Smith's head and the blows which Diddler sustained were certainly not inflicted by the same person. Now that is a hard, under-oath statement. I wouldn't call Smith's wounds superficial, but they were not the cause of death, nor did they contribute.

'Howard Shearer, on the other hand was battered savagely to

death, with great force. Different people, Bob, different people. I'm sorry to blow your theory, but look at it from this angle. How many people have played football with your crowd over the years?'

'God knows,' he conceded. 'Dozens of regulars; if you count the guys, and one woman, who have played just once or twice, you could be into the hundreds.'

'And Alec Smith really wasn't there for all that long, was he? Three years or so?'

'True. Okay, I get your drift.'

'Exactly. Two members of your squad of hundreds being killed violently in completely different circumstances is, I grant you, something of a coincidence, but it's not like winning the pools. Whereas, the possibility of their having been killed by the same person does not exist.'

'Right, right, right, I'm beaten. I guess I got over-excited. Give my love to the kids; see you later.'

Skinner replaced the phone and looked across his desk at Neil McIlhenney. 'Sometimes it's just impossible to argue with my wife,' he said. 'Especially when she's right.' He paused. 'We don't have a sniff of a motive. The Diddler was a wealthy man, he could have been killed for money, or for his Rolex, even; that alone was worth a ton.

'Nonetheless, as soon as we have a positive ID on the body, as we will, I want you to organise a meeting of the Legends, the other seven and us, or as many as are available, in the Golf in North Berwick, six o'clock this evening. I want to tell them all before they read it in the papers. If Grock or Stewart Rees or Andy John are golfing, tell them to cancel it. The poor wee bugger deserves a wake.'

'I'll need to bring the kids,' said McIlhenney.

'Fine, Sarah will give them their dinner, and they can have a play on the beach with the lads.'

He recalled the night before. 'Here, was Karen okay about you being late?'

'Aye, she was fine,' his exec replied. 'She was a bit strange, I thought, but it was nowt to do with that, I'm sure. Lauren said this morning that she seemed sad, and she has her mother's eye for people's moods.'

'She's a capable woman, is Sergeant Neville; she'll sort it, whatever it is.'

The big Inspector stood and made to leave. 'Oh,' he said, as an afterthought. 'I tried to raise DCS Martin as you asked, but he isn't in yet. I left a message with Sammy for him to call you.'

'Fine,' the DCC acknowledged, just as the telephone furthest from his right hand sang into life . . . the phone which hardly ever rang. He picked it up, frowning, as the door closed behind McIlhenney.

'Skinner.'

'Morning, Bob,' said a gruff voice, in a bluff Derbyshire accent. 'This is Adam. I'm about to get on to a plane at Farnborough and fly up to Scotland. I want you and McGuire to meet me at the General Aviation Terminal at Edinburgh.

'There's something I've got to show you . . . something fooking messy.'

Forty-one

'What's the number?' Dan Pringle asked, gazing along Coltbridge Terrace.

'It doesn't have one, sir,' Detective Sergeant Jack McGurk replied as they walked along, between linked bungalows on one side of the road and a small tenement on the other. 'Only a name; River Cottage. I think it might be along there, on the right. I can see a couple of houses on their own.'

They strode on, their car parked at the entrance to the narrow *cul-de-sac*, past a modern building on their right to the first of the detached dwellings. McGurk read the name-plate. 'No, that's not it.' They moved on to the next. 'Not that either.'

And then, a slight curve in the road, and a single-storey house which until then had not been in their line of vision; it was set back from the street, unlike the others, and had a small rose garden, with a path leading to the front door. It seemed to stand out into the flowing water behind, and as they approached they could see the structure below, built into the river bank.

McGurk's keen eyes read the name-plate from yards away. 'This is it,' he announced. 'River Cottage.'

'Aye,' said Pringle. 'Like Shearer's secretary said, it backs right on to the water. Come on then.' He led the way up the path.

The house looked, even felt, deserted. There were drawn

blinds on the two front windows; the frosted glass panels set into the green-painted front door gave no hint of light or life inside. There was no bell, only a big, black knocker. McGurk grabbed it and rapped it hard; once, twice, a third time.

They waited for no more than thirty seconds, before Pringle said, 'Right that's enough. Let's get in there. Let's see what the back's like.' He disappeared round the side of the house, the big Sergeant on his heels, but saw at once that there was no back door. The building stood, quite literally, at the water's edge.

They returned to the front door; it appeared to be secured only by a cylinder lock. McGurk glanced around until he saw a brick in a corner of the garden. He picked it up and, with a single quick blow, smashed a hole in one of the glass panels, reached in and opened it with a single twist.

'Smells in here, sir,' he said, as he stepped into the house. They stood in a dusty hallway, not large, but wide enough to allow a narrow stairway, on the right, to run up into the attic.

Pringle opened a door at the foot of the steps. 'Kitchen.' McGurk opened the door opposite. 'Living room. Looks tidy and undisturbed.' They moved through the hall and past the stairway to the back of the house, where they found a small neat bedroom, and a bathroom.

'Look at this,' the Sergeant called out as he looked inside. 'There are towels lying all over the floor.' He stepped across to the bath; a shower curtain on a rail, hanging inside the tub had been pulled most of the way across. He yanked it back, and took a quick look around.

A pink face-cloth had been thrown over the shower's mixer tap; the sergeant picked it up and saw quickly that it had not always been that colour. He handed it to Pringle. 'No prizes for guessing what that is.' He leaned over and picked up a cake of Dove cream soap; it bore faint red streaks.

'Someone's been cleaning up in here,' he muttered, 'in a hurry, from the way those towels were chucked about.'

'Upstairs,' Pringle barked. He led the way back to the hall, and up the narrow stairs to the attic, to a small landing from which three doors opened. He made for the nearest, the one in the middle: a cupboard. 'Bugger.'

McGurk threw open the door to the left: and recoiled as the sudden stink wafted out. 'Jeez.' He switched on the light, and looked at a slaughterhouse.

There was a bed; a big metal-framed bed, against the far wall. A duvet lay in a corner of the wide spacious room, made larger by the curtained dormer window which the detectives knew must overlook the river. A white sheet and pillows in the far corner. In another, a man's jacket, underpants and trousers, over a chair, socks and shoes on the floor.

But the bed itself . . . The remaining sheet told a horror story; it was soaked with blood, apart from a patch in the middle, which corresponded roughly to the shape of a man's body, and was stained a different, yellowish colour. Four lengths of white rope, blood-streaked again, were secured to the four corner posts of the frame; at some point the man they had restrained had been cut loose. A number of small objects lay near each of the strands; McGurk bent over them, peering. 'Don't touch,' Pringle whispered, unnecessarily. Severed thumb, severed little fingers at the far end, severed big toe, severed little toe at each of the nearer corners; discoloured but not yet black. Discarded, between where the feet had been secured, lay a heavy pair of garden secateurs.

And laid against the frame, caked with thick, dark, dried

blood, a full-sized, metal baseball bat. 'The murder weapon, d'you think?' asked Pringle heavily.

He looked around the room, feeling queasy and regretting his last four whiskies of the evening before. There were blood spatters on the walls around the bed, on the curtains and even on the ceiling. A red trail led across the carpet from the frame to the door.

'I noticed two bolts in the hallway floor,' said McGurk. 'I bet they're for securing a trap door, covering steps down to a boat-landing on the river. There's no rug in the hall, but I'll bet that there used to be, until it was used as this guy's shroud, before he was rolled down those steps and dumped in the river.'

'I'm not taking either of those bets,' said Pringle. He stepped carefully across to a dressing table, in the window space. A black leather wallet lay on it. He picked it up, by a corner and held it up. It held no money, but there were six plastic cards in slots. He slid one out with a finger until he could read the holder's name; 'H. Shearer.'

He set it back down on the dressing table, took out his mobile and dialled Skinner's number. McIlhenney answered. 'The Boss there, Neil?'

'No. He's had to go out.'

'You got an ID on your pal from that blood yet?'

'No, not yet.'

'We have, at his son's cottage. Sorry, lad, but he was here all right. Some of him still is, in fact; all over the fucking place.

'You'd better tell the Boss when he comes in that it's all right for him to call Mrs Shearer now.'

Forty-two

'Karen, this is for you,' Jack McGurk shouted across the CID room at Torphichen Place. She frowned; who knew she was there? She picked up the call on another extension.

'Neville.'

'Karen. Good, you're still there.' The voice of Sammy Pye.

'Just. I've been stood down: I'm just tidying my desk, then I'll be on my way back to you, my dear. We seem to have put a name to the man at the centre of this investigation.'

'Yes, I know.'

'Who is it then? No-one's saying around here.'

'Can't tell you; not over the phone. Neil McIlhenney passed on an order from the Big Boss that if there's another leak to the press on this one before he's ready to make an announcement, then the leaker will be out of a job.'

The Sergeant whistled. 'Heavy stuff. So what did you want me for?'

'I was wondering if you knew where our boss is; the DCS. He hasn't turned up so far this morning; he hasn't called in and he isn't answering his home phone or his mobile.'

'Why ask me?' she said, coldly.

'Come on, Karen. Don't be naive; if Mr Martin's missing you're one of the first people anyone would talk to.'

'Well, I don't know, okay? All that's over with.' She was angry now, but hurting as well; on top of all that she felt a twinge of fear. 'What about the DCC? Have you asked him?'

'He's out of the office. DI McIlhenney doesn't know anything; he asked me to have the DCS call Mr Skinner when he got in.'

She thought of the red car in the driveway. 'Ahh, don't worry. He'll be across some new woman or other. Is Ruth McConnell in yet?'

'Of course. There's nothing going on between them. They had a date for tomorrow night, but the DCS called it off.'

'How do you know that?' she asked, surprised.

'I know because I'm going out with her now; she told me what happened.'

'Don't bother taking her to dinner; it would just be an appetiser. Ruth will eat you, Sam. Now, who else have you asked about Andy?'

'SB. And that's what's worrying me. When he left last night, the DCS was doing something related to them. He was going to lift a guy that the Special Branch trawl turned up in connection with the Alec Smith investigation.'

'On his own?'

'Yes. He told me to stay here and finish what I was doing, that he'd have no bother. I called DI McGuire; he was out too, and that new girl in there Alice Cowan, she wouldn't say a thing. It hasn't taken her long to go native. A couple of days ago she was in uniform, now she's a bloody SB zealot.'

Karen thought once more of the red MGF. 'Did he take his own car?'

'No. He walked to Fettes yesterday. He was in a pool Mondeo, and it's missing too.'

Her fear was more than a twinge now; it was chilling her,

sending her pulse rate soaring. 'This is what you do, then. Don't make a fuss, but order every panda car, every patrol car and every biker we have to find that car. Tell operations that it's an order from the Head of CID.

'I'm on my way back now.'

Forty-three

They beat the plane to the General Aviation terminal by ten minutes. They stood side by side outside the building which had once served all of Edinburgh's air traffic, looking at its impressive and ever-expanding replacement across the old north-south runway.

Skinner had no idea what type of aircraft to expect, but even he was impressed when an RAF Tornado streaked in to land.

'Every time Adam Arrow shows up,' he shouted to Mario McGuire over the noise of the engine roar as the pilot eased the plane back to taxi-ing speed, 'it means trouble. For him to arrive like this, it means BIG trouble.'

'What is he, exactly?' the Inspector asked.

'The fact that you're a Special Branch officer and yet are asking me that says a lot in itself.' Skinner could speak quietly again, as the plane approached.

'Adam is everything. He was SAS, but now he's in charge of all MoD security and intelligence gathering, with the power to do things you would never want to tell your grandchildren about.'

'Who's his boss?'

'God, I think, but maybe he's under surveillance too.'

'What rank is he?'

'At this moment? I'm not sure, but it doesn't matter. That little man climbing out of that aeroplane could, if necessary, make a Field Marshal, Air Marshal or an Admiral of the bloody Fleet disappear off the face the earth.' As he spoke, Arrow jumped down from the navigator's seat and came bustling across the runway towards them. He was small, but built like a spinning top; massive shoulders tapering down through a stocky waist to short legs with little feet. His hair was cropped close and he was wearing civilian clothes – dark trousers, white shirt, an MCC tie and a check jacket.

'Morning, Bob,' he said, with a cheeriness which made McGuire wonder how he could possibly be the figure Skinner had described.

'Morning, Captain, Major, or whatever it is now . . .'

'Major, it says on my door.'

'What's with the tie?'

'My one aspiration to fookin' toffness.'

'God, you've sold out.' Skinner looked back over his shoulder to the Inspector. 'You remember our Head of SB, Mario McGuire, don't you?'

'Sure, from way back.' Arrow reached across and shook hands; an astonishingly strong grip for a man of his size.

'What's the crisis then, Adam?'

'I'll show you when we get there; there should be a chopper about here somewhere.' He looked around the terminal until he spotted a big grey-green helicopter around a hundred yards away, a pilot standing beside it. 'Come on.'

The pilot saluted as they approached, speaking quietly to Arrow as he ushered them up the few built-in steps to the passenger space.

'He says we're flying back south over the City by-pass, and up into the Pentland Hills. There's Army ground up there . . .' He shouted suddenly as the helicopter's engine roared into life. '. . . as you probably know.'

Something bit at the back of McGuire's mind; something ominous.

There was no conversation as the chopper took off, or as they rose and flew over the Gyle Centre and the impressive, and growing, commercial township known as Edinburgh Park, towards the dominating hills to the south. Instead the three men wore big ear-protectors, against the noise.

They had been flying for less than fifteen minutes when the helicopter began to circle. Arrow pointed downwards, and shouted something. Skinner could not make out a word, but he guessed that the pilot was looking for a safe landing area on the rising hillside. Then he saw a flare, burning on the ground on what appeared to be a flat area. Sure enough, they began to descend.

As Skinner and McGuire jumped out, each ducking instinctively under the decelerating rotor arm, they saw two red-capped soldiers a distance away, where the hill began to slope, standing beside a green Land Rover.

One wore sergeant's stripes; the other approached. 'Mr Arrow,' he began. 'Colonel Fielding, Military Police.' McGuire noted the odd deference; from Colonel to Major. 'Glad you could get here so quickly; a real bloody mess this is.'

The soldier ignored the two policemen; Skinner bridled. 'Then maybe you'd tell us about it, Colonel. I'm Deputy Chief Constable Bob Skinner and this is Detective Inspector Mario McGuire. What is this and, since we're on military property, what the hell does it have to do with us?'

Fielding looked at him. 'I'll show you presently,' he said,

coldly. 'Get into the vehicle. Once I've briefed Mr Arrow, we'll take you to it.'

A large part of the DCC wanted to point out to the Colonel that in equivalent ranking terms he was addressing a general; he might have done it too, had Arrow not stepped in. 'Let's not fanny about, Colonel,' he said quietly. 'Just take us there, now.'

'Very good,' the man replied, as stiff as his uniform.

The Land Rover was even less comfortable than the helicopter, it bounced over the rough terrain as the sergeant driver made his way round the hillside, then down, then round once more until he drew carefully to a halt, on an upslope.

Skinner glanced up as he climbed out; two more military policemen stood at the top of the crest, carrying carbines, on guard.

'This way,' Fielding called out, briskly and led them up the slope. 'There,' he said, as he reached the top, with something like awe in his voice.

Arrow, Skinner and McGuire stood on the rim of a small clearing. In the centre, on its back, lay the body of a man. It, and the area around it, was soaked in blood; the head was thrown back, and the throat gaped open.

The trio gazed at the sight in silent horror, until McGuire let out a half-gasp, half-cry of relief.

'What is it, Mario?' Skinner asked.

'I thought they were going to show us Andy Martin, Boss.'

He stepped down into the clearing, leading the other two as they approached the corpse and walked around it in a wide circle.

'Christ,' Skinner murmured. 'Is that a finger, bitten off?' No-one answered; no need. 'His throat's been torn out. What the pluperfect fuck did that? Is there a circus animal on the loose up here? Or are you guys training vampires as soldiers now? And how does this relate to . . .'

'I can tell you what did it,' Fielding broke in, quietly. 'Just under three hours ago, a platoon of Scots Guards was on exercise not far from here, when they heard two gunshots. There was supposed to be no-one else on the hill, so they investigated.' He pointed to the blood-drenched body. 'They found this. On top of him, was a man. His hands were tied tight behind his back, and his face and torso were covered in blood. He was gripping a Colt pistol, and his teeth were locked tight into this thing's throat.

'He had killed him, gentlemen, not even with his bare hands; he had killed him like an animal.'

Skinner stared at him, numbly, trying to comprehend what he was being told.

'At first, the soldiers thought they were both dead. Then when they touched the man on top, he went berserk. He was incoherent, swearing, rambling. They had to take him forcibly from the body and restrain him a little away. Then they called for Military Police and medical assistance.

'While they were waiting, they searched him. He wasn't wearing a jacket, but on a chain around his neck, they found a police warrant card, identifying him as Detective Chief Super-intendent Andrew Martin.'

In spite of himself, the DCC felt his throat go dry and his knees go weak. Unseen by anyone else, Adam Arrow grabbed his elbow, supporting him. 'Where is he now?' he asked, hoarsely.

'He was put under heavy sedation by the medics and air-lifted to the Hospital Unit at Glencorse Barracks.'

'What else did you find here?' McGuire asked.

'Only that pistol. There were two discharged rounds in the

magazine and four live bullets scattered around, one of them at the dead man's feet, almost hidden from sight.

'Now,' the MP colonel continued, his tone conciliatory for the first time, 'can you gentlemen tell me who this is and what's happened here?'

'I can,' said the Head of Special Branch. 'This man here was one Lawrence Scotland, who's been under my department's surveillance for years. He was once a professional assassin, involved in Ireland on the Loyalist side, with several known kills to his name, but he had been inactive for some time.

'Last night Mr Martin went, alone, to pick him up for interview in relation to a current murder investigation. Scotland wasn't assessed as a real suspect, or as a risk, but he had had dealings in the past with the dead man.' He looked at the MP. 'Tell me something. The two spent cartridges in the gun; were they in successive chambers, side by side?'

Fielding walked across the clearing; none of them had noticed the gun lying there; he picked it up, and broke the breech. 'No. There's an empty chamber between them.'

'Aye, I thought so. This is what happened. I must have been wrong in my assessment of Scotland. He must have been involved in that murder after all. When DCS Martin turned up to interview him, he took him prisoner and brought him up here to kill him.

'Only he decided to have a bit of fun first; play a game of Russian Roulette. He underestimated his man though. While Andy Martin's breathing, he's dangerous. Scotland made a mistake somewhere along the line and DCS Martin, hands tied and all, just tore right through him.'

The MP frowned. 'But why would he bring him up here to kill him?'

'Sorry, Colonel,' Skinner intervened, his composure recovered. 'That part of the story's for Mr Arrow's ears only. Adam, I want you to take me to see Andy, right away.'

'Sure. We'll take the chopper there now.'

'But what about this?' Fielding protested, pointing at the ravaged body. 'What do I do with him?'

'Get a shovel,' the DCC snapped. 'I want him buried up here. Your people, and the soldiers who found them, I want them all told that they've been hallucinating. This never happened. Lawrence Scotland goes on our missing-persons list, only we won't be looking for him.'

The MP turned to Arrow. 'Do it,' said the little man, in a flat, clipped tone. 'I will speak personally to all the men involved. If they want to have army careers, indeed if they want to have futures at all, they will do what I tell them.'

The Colonel made a mistake. He frowned. 'I don't know . . .' he began.

Arrow stepped up close to him; very close. 'Listen,' he whispered. 'If that man there asked me to bury *you* up here, I'd start digging. So: do as you're told.'

Forty-four

'Look, are you guys going about this systematically?' Karen Neville asked the Operations Inspector.

'Of course we are, Sergeant. But have you any idea how many white Mondeos there are in our area, let alone how many white motor vehicles? I will find this car for you, but I won't give you any guarantee as to how long it will take me.

'Now, I don't care whose bloody office you're in, stop being so bloody pushy and back off. Or I will call my boss, and have him call ACC Elder, and have him lean on your boss . . . I think he still outranks him. Or am I wrong?'

'He doesn't outrank Bob Skinner though. Do you want to talk to him?'

The phone at the other end of the line was slammed down.

'Karen,' said Sammy Pye. 'I think you should calm down. You losing it is not going to help us find him.'

'Plodding so-and-sos like him aren't going to help us either,' she shot back.

Pye stood and walked across to her desk; he sat on the edge and took her hand. 'Listen, Sarge,' the young Detective Constable murmured gently. 'You're giving away too much here. At the moment only we know that Mr Martin's missing; but pretty soon others are going to twig, and here you are sending the message loud and clear to everyone you speak to that this thing goes way beyond the professional with you.

'If that gets back to the DCS when he does turn up, that could be very embarrassing for him – and problematical for you, because you know he won't like it.'

She gave his hand a quick squeeze. 'You're right, I'm sorry. I'll tell you what, you do all the talking from now on.'

The phone on her desk rang. Pye grinned and shook his head, as she picked it up automatically.

'Karen,' a steady voice said. 'This is Neil. Tell me why you are antagonising the entire ops room with this vehicle search of yours? I have just had a mate of mine on the blower yelling at me, insisting that I kick your shapely bottom.'

'You know why I'm doing it,' she answered.

She heard McIlhenney's light, sad, laugh. 'Yes, love, I know. I couldn't tell him that though. Anyway, you are to stop it; cease; desist. This doesn't come from Ops; this comes from the Big Man himself. The DCS has turned up and he's safe.'

She slumped back into her chair, vision blurred with sudden tears.

'But there is to be no discussion of it,' the Inspector went on. 'In fact, after the waves you've made, best that you and Sammy just get out of everyone's way. Go and interview pigeons in the Botanics for the rest of the day.

'You'll be told where Andy is, maybe even get to see him, when Mr Skinner is good and ready. Till then, just be patient . . . and be relieved.'

Forty-five

Glencorse Barracks and its hospital wing were probably Victorian, Skinner guessed, but the equipment was high-tech.

Andy Martin lay on a modern hospital bed, his upper body raised slightly and supported by pillows. He was either asleep or unconscious; the former, Skinner hoped. Sensors were stuck to his bare chest, leading to a cardiac monitor, on a shelf. The DCC was relieved to see that his heartbeat was strong, slow and regular.

'How is he?' he asked the young Army Medical Officer by his side. 'Was he hurt in any way?'

'Physically, very little. He has a split lip, some bruising to his face and his shoulder, but otherwise he's fine. Psychologically, I couldn't say. He was in shock when he was brought in here, rambling and delirious. I gave him a strong sedative, enough to knock him out for a few hours.

'I can't predict what he'll be like when he comes round. What happened to him? How did he get like this? I haven't been told, but he was in a hell of a mess. He reminded me of a soldier I saw once who was too close to a colleague when he stepped on a mine. But this man . . . God, his teeth . . . the time it took to clean them alone.'

'Don't ask, Doctor,' said the DCC quietly. 'I want to be here when he comes round, okay?'

'Of course. If you're a friend, seeing you should be good for him.'

The MO left the room. Skinner pulled a chair up to the bedside and sat, looking at his friend's sleeping face, and wondering what his dreams were like, hoping that he had none. He tried to imagine the scene in the Pentlands, and Andy's fight for his life. Jesus, what must Scotland have felt like having this mad, desperate, bull of a man coming at him. What a way to kill someone. He imagined being in the same situation himself, then remembered that he had been; that man was in an unmarked grave too. There are no rules in a fight for survival.

He sat for over an hour, waiting, not thinking of McGuire and Arrow in the corridor outside, thinking only of Andy, and of what he would say when he awoke.

At last he began to stir on the bed. He whispered something. One word, very softly, but Skinner caught it; 'Karen.'

His right shoulder twitched; his head made a butting movement, then began to roll from side to side. His jaws clamped tight working, working. His eyes flickered, closed again, flickered, then suddenly, opened wide. He sat bolt upright in bed with an expression on his face unlike any that Skinner had ever seen – a mixture of terror and sheer animal ferocity.

The big DCC jumped to his feet and held him, using all his own great strength to counter Andy's and press him back down on to the bed. 'Okay, son, it's okay.'

Martin's face cleared at last. 'Bob?' he said, in a dazed croak. 'Where am I? Have I been in an accident? Or shot, or something?

'Bloody hell, that was some nightmare I was having.' He

looked at Skinner, read his face, and fell silent again. That unnatural look came back, but this time it was pure terror, and that alone, as everything came flooding back.

'That was no nightmare, was it?' he asked, at last.

'No, Andy boy. No, it wasn't.'

'Scotland. How's he?'

'How do you think? He's dead; you ripped his throat open.'

'Good!' For a second, the DCC was shocked by the intensity of the malice in his best friend's eyes, but then he remembered his own emotions at a similar time.

'I told the rat-fucker I would kill him. He should have believed me.'

'It's just as well he didn't. He wouldn't have played his bloody game if he had; he'd have shot you straight off.'

'You worked it all out then?'

'Mario did. So it was Scotland after all, Scotland who did Alec?'

'I suppose so. Even though it took him years to pluck up the courage; but he had to play his game too. He had to get someone up there.'

'Why in Christ's name did you go for him on your own, Andy?' Skinner asked. 'A man with a history like that.'

'I guess I have to call it an error of judgement. Between you and me, I've got a few distractions in my private life right now. I've done smarter things in my time, right enough.'

He paused. 'On the other hand, if I had taken Sammy Pye with me, one of us would have been dead now. Probably both of us.'

'Aye, well. You can hold an inquiry into yourself, later. You're alive, so fuck the recriminations.'

'What happens now?' Martin asked. 'Report to the Fiscal?'

'Hell no. Nothing happens. It's all taken care of; you're in Army hands at the moment. Adam Arrow's involved and he's made everything go away, including what's left of Scotland.'

The younger man looked up at him. 'You've done that?'

'Too fucking right. Not just for you, for the force. I don't want any of the Alec Smith story to come out.'

'I told Scotland that too. But the guy was only into talking, not listening.' He pulled himself up into a sitting position.

'When can I get out of here?' he asked. 'There's someone I have to see.'

'You can get out of here now, but you're coming home with me. No arguments; you're either under Sarah's care, or I'll leave you here with the Army doctor. We'll see how you're feeling tomorrow. Meantime, I've told everyone who needs to know that you're all right.'

Bob stood, and moved towards the door. 'I don't think you're going to want to see your clothes again, but I'll have the Army fix you up with some uniform stuff. Then you and I are going for a nice helicopter ride out to Gullane.'

Forty-six

The nine Legends sat around the table in the Golf Hotel bar, stunned and subdued. As a group they were rarely lost for a word but, after the bombshell which Skinner had dropped, not one of them had anything to say.

It was David McPhail who broke the seance-like silence with a blunt question. 'How come it took so long to identify him, Bob? I mean, a whole week . . .'

The DCC was stung by the implied criticism of Dan Pringle's team. 'Look, nobody reported him missing. Edith and the family were away, and his colleagues didn't want to make their client base nervous.'

He looked across at McPhail and added tersely, 'The fact that he didn't have a fucking face wasn't a big help to us either. My wife did the post-mortem; she knew the Diddler well – he lived just up the road from us, remember – and she didn't know who it was.'

'What happened to him?' Grant Rock looked a wholly different man when he was being serious; this occurred so infrequently that the policeman felt almost as if he was facing a stranger.

'I don't like to talk about it, and I only tell you guys on the basis that it doesn't leave this room. He was tied to the bed at his son's place, then beaten to death with a baseball bat. We only made a positive identification from blood samples.'

'Tied to the bed,' Stewart Rees mused. 'Was the Diddler diddling again?'

'Let's not speculate about that.'

'Has Edith been told?'

Skinner held up his empty glass and nodded to the Friday barmaid, prompting a rush of refills.

'I called France this afternoon,' he said, when everyone was settled again. 'They have a friend down there, a Scots guy; I met him once. I called him and had him go along to break the news to Edith. Always better face to face; it's harder to believe a voice on the telephone.

'She called me just before we came along here. Poor woman. She's flying home tomorrow morning with Victoria, Air France from Nice through Charles de Gaulle; I've said I'll meet them at the airport.'

'What are you going to do about your car?' McIlhenney asked, casually. 'It's still up at Fettes, remember.'

'I'll pull rank. I'll have a patrol car pick me up in the morning and take me to collect it. Andy too, if Sarah says he can go home.'

The Inspector leaned back against the window and whispered, so that no-one else could hear. 'You going to tell me what happened today?'

Skinner shook his head.

'Never?'

Skinner nodded his head.

'Fair enough then,' McIlhenney murmured. 'I won't ask again.'

'Bob,' said Mitch Laidlaw from across the table, 'it can't have escaped anyone's attention that two of our number have met violent deaths very close to each other.' He seemed to send a shiver round the table.

'It hasn't escaped mine, Mitch, that's for bloody sure. That's the other reason I called us all together . . . I mean, apart from believing it appropriate to give you all the bad news in person. You can forget the idea that there is any sort of a vendetta against our honoured group. There's no-one out there who wants our Thursday time at the Sports Centre so badly that he's prepared to bump us off one by one to get it.

'To put the thing in perspective, two guys who played together among us, for a fairly short time, set against the years we've been at it, met violent deaths within hours of each other. But they were very different deaths.'

'How was Alec killed, then?' asked McPhail.

'You do not want to know, David,' Skinner frowned at the interruption. 'The point I was about to make was that I am assured by an eminent and highly skilled forensic pathologist – with whom I am currently sleeping – that Alec Smith and the Diddler were killed by two different people.

'I can tell you also, in police speak, although I cannot go into detail, that I have reason to believe that the Alec Smith investigation will be closed pretty soon.

'So relax, lads. We don't have a stalker.'

'Yeah,' said Grant Rock, returning rapidly to normal. 'But what if there's a whole crowd of them after our time?'

McIlhenney looked at him from beneath his heavy eyebrows. 'If there was, the smart thing to do would be to give it to them.'

'I'll never be hung for being smart,' said Rock.

Forty-seven

'Are you going to tell me what happened today?' Maggie Rose asked her husband.

Mario McGuire shook his head.

'Never?'

Mario McGuire nodded his head.

'Don't you think this is taking Special Branch secrecy a little too far?' his wife asked.

'Mags love, what happened today goes way beyond Special Branch secrecy. But that's not why I'm not going to tell you about it. I'm keeping it to myself because it was so fucking horrible that I cannot bear the thought of you knowing about it. I will never tell anyone about what I saw today, nor will anyone else who was there.'

'What was Andy Martin's involvement in it?'

'Who says he was involved?'

'No-one, but . . . I heard there was some sort of a panic this morning, involving him; that Karen Neville had the whole Ops Room stirred up trying to find a car he was driving.'

'If that happened, then that's all it was . . . a panic. Karen got her knickers in a knot unnecessarily, until she was told by Neil to go away and untie them. Andy Martin is okay. I know this; I've seen him.'

'What do you mean you've seen him? Where?'

'Never mind. The DCS is okay, and you can bet that he will be back in the office on Monday, gung-ho as ever was.'

'What about this man Lawrence Scotland? You haven't said anything about him for a while. You told me about Morrison, and what Alec Smith did to him. That was heavy enough, but now you're clamming up altogether about the other suspect.'

'Mags,' he said, testily, 'stop trying to interrogate me, will you? Lawrence Scotland is missing.'

'In that case, I have to find him. He's a potential suspect in my investigation.'

'For fuck's sake,' he shouted, suddenly. 'Leave it!'

She sat straight up on the sofa and stared at him, startled and hurt. His anger vanished in an instant; he took her hand and drew her to him. 'I'm sorry, Mags, I'm sorry.'

'That's the first time you've ever raised your voice to me.'

'And it'll be the last, I promise. Love, I keep having to countermand you these days and I don't like it; not just because of our respective ranks, but because you're my wife and I love you and not least because you're a brilliant detective and I admire you for that reason too.

'But through no fault of your own, you are way over your head in this. The Boss has told me to rein you in on Scotland, very quietly. He told me to tell you that you are still in charge of this investigation and, further, that he couldn't be more impressed by the way you've handled it. Now you have to hold your horses for a day or two.

'Lawrence Scotland is missing, like I said. However there will be no man-hunt. There will be the illusion of one, possibly, probably, but Lawrence Scotland will never be found. The way it's looking now, your investigation will not conclude with the conviction of Alec Smith's killer, but given what he was and did – far less what we know about him now – that was never likely anyway.

'I know this runs against all your training and your personal beliefs, but that's the reality of it and you have to accept it.

'Listen, Dan Pringle and John McGrigor will be going in the foreseeable future. Whichever of those divisional CID commands you want is yours for the asking. But do not shake this particular tree, otherwise what falls out might squash someone very important. If that happened, and you were in any way responsible, you wouldn't be forgiven.'

'What do you mean?' She frowned, drawing back from him again.

'Mags, when he was in my job, Alec Smith did certain things that he shouldn't have. No-one knew about them then, apart from his side-kick, and no-one outside our very small group must ever know about them; otherwise questions will be asked. Questions like, "Why was no-one aware of what Smith was doing?" and then, "Who should have known?"

'Alec's line commander at the time of these incidents was old Alf Stein, the Big Man's predecessor as Head of CID. Once Mr Skinner took over, Smith behaved himself; he knew better than to do otherwise. Stein's dead now, so if any of this shit hits the fan it can only splash on one man – Chief Constable Sir James Proud. If it became public he would be forced to resign; the Chiefs' Association wouldn't be able to protect him. Our zealous new Justice Minister would have him out.

'You know as well as I do that Proud Jimmy is like a father to Bob Skinner. The DCC would do anything to protect him from an ignominious end to his career.'

'Is that what he did today?' Maggie asked, quietly.

He put a finger to her lips. 'No more questions.'

'One more, Mario, one more. This thing you saw today; if it was so horrible you won't tell me about it, what will it do to you? How will you forget it?'

'Darlin',' he said. 'I won't. I will take it to my grave. But in the short term – I'm going to drink another bottle of Amarone, then you and I are going to do what we do best.'

Forty-eight

A great wall of mist, two hundred feet high, clung to the middle of the Firth of Forth, shrouding part of the main shipping lane. Onshore, the weather was as warm and sunny as it had been for over a week, yet incongruously, the sound of a foghorn boomed across the water.

Bob Skinner sat on a dune, on the beach, looking at the haar, trying to assess whether or not it would sweep in from the sea before it burned off in the morning sun.

'This time last Saturday, eh?'

'Yeah,' Andy Martin, murmured, lying on his back beside him in borrowed shorts and tee-shirt. 'Seems like a long time ago. Fuck, it was a long time ago; I've been dead since then.'

'Want to talk about it? Or not . . . it's up to you. You'll never have to if you don't want. Boy's in a hole up the Pentlands; story's over.'

'Best place for him.' Martin's voice; hollow, lifeless.

'Man held a gun on me once,' Skinner murmured. 'Bastard shot me, but he made a mistake; gave me a chance. I got the gun. Shot him fucking dead. Someone, not Adam Arrow but like him, cleaned it up because of who he was, what he was. Different circumstances though. That was national security stuff; Scotland had to vanish to keep a lid on our local can of worms.'

'I know, Bob. I know. Don't justify yourself to me; you don't have to. I know why you did it and you were right.'

'I'm glad you killed him, Andy. Glad.'

'He died the way he lived. Alec should have shot him ten years ago, or someone in Ireland should have taken him out.'

'If he'd been on the other side, someone would have. Not all his orders came from the Loyalists; most of them did, but not all. Adam told me that.'

'No great surprise.'

They lay in silence, watching the mist evaporate.

'He pulled the trigger, you know.'

'Jesus. I'd hoped not.'

'Twice. Two bullets second time.'

'Andy . . .'

'Third would have been curtains. I just bellowed and went for him; went through him like a fucking train.

'I remember it all, Bob, in slow motion. Every single bit of it; the bitter taste of his finger . . . I think that must have been bone marrow . . . the blood. I was fucking swimming in it, but I couldn't let go. Could still be dead if I let go, I thought, and I couldn't die. Not there, not then, the time wasn't right.

'So I hung on, till the soldiers arrived, after that even . . . You know, looking at Alec, I thought, *I'll never see anything worse than this* . . . far less that I'd do worse myself.

'What did Scotland look like, Bob? When you saw him?'

'Dead, Andy. Very fucking dead.'

Skinner sighed. 'I didn't know at first, that he'd had you up there. Mario worked it out. Knew at once when he saw the bullets lying around and in the gun.'

He took a can of Irn Bru from his knapsack, opened it and handed it to Martin, then opened another, for himself. 'So it was

Scotland, eh?' he murmured. 'A blast from Alec's past, come back as a nightmare.'

'Looks that way. He told me he really wanted to take him back up there, but knew he'd never manage it. I was second best. He knew someone would be for him eventually. Took him ten years to pluck up the courage, or to catch Smith off guard.'

'Where could he have got that animal tranquilliser?'

'He did night security at the zoo. He told me that . . . deliberately, I suppose.'

'Ahh.'

'He never actually said to me, "I killed Alec Smith" but . . .'

'Maybe not, but the overwhelming probability is that he did. If we keep the investigation going, more than likely we'll be chasing an answer we've found already. I've asked Mario to explain to Maggie, without telling her too much.'

'It just goes away then?'

'It dwindles; after a while I'll tell Royston that we have a prime suspect but that he's disappeared, believed out of the country. He can leak that to the press; I might even let him leak the real name. The guy isn't going to turn up anywhere.'

'Only in my dreams,' Martin whispered.

'They'll fade, son. You don't think so now, but they will. Your mind protects you after a while.'

Skinner took a slug from his Irn Bru. 'Just one small niggle . . .' he said.

'What's that?'

'Alec's room; where he was killed. There was something odd about that. It's probably of no significance, but it's wrong. It's just a feeling I have . . . only I can't figure out what it is.'

Forty-nine

Karen Neville rarely smoked; occasionally in the pub after a couple of drinks, but never at home. She slammed her fourth cigarette of the day into the ashtray, knowing that none of them had done her any good.

'Karen!' she cried aloud. 'It'll be the drink next.'

She could restrain herself no longer; she picked up the phone and called Neil McIlhenney. He sounded not in the least surprised to hear her voice.

'Hello, girl,' he said, kindly. 'Doing your head in, is it?'

'And how.'

'I wish I could help, really, but you've just got to be patient.'

'Neil, he really is all right isn't he? No-one's keeping anything back about him, are they?'

'No, love. I promise you they're not. Believe me, he's okay.' He hesitated. 'I saw him myself last night.'

'You did?' she exclaimed. 'Where?'

'Gullane. He's out at Bob's. But you must not – understand, must not – try to phone him there. Wait till he gets back to Edinburgh; that'll probably be some time today.'

She heard him hesitate. 'But when he does get back home, Karen. What are you going to say to him?'

She fell silent, realising. 'I don't know,' she murmured, at last.

He grunted. 'You don't? Well, it's bloody obvious to me. I don't know if it's going to make you any happier, girl, but I do know you've got to get it out.' And then he chuckled. 'But you never know. You might get a surprise . . . stranger things have happened.'

'What do you mean?'

'I mean there's always a chance he might beat you to the punch.'

Fifty

'So this is where it happened,' said Skinner as he looked around the attic room. 'This is where the Diddler got done.' Detective Inspector Arthur Dorward's team had finished their crime-scene work; the bedding and the binding ropes had been removed for examination, but the bloodstains remained, disfiguring walls and ceiling.

'Aye, this is it, sir,' Pringle replied, gruffly. 'Come on and I'll show you how they got rid of him.' He led the DCC back down the stairs to the hall where he found a brass handle, recessed into the floor, and lifted up a wide trap-door, revealing another flight of steps. The sound of lapping water came up from below.

'Down there is a wee jetty place. He was shoved in the water from there in the middle of the night. The Water of Leith was still high and flowing fast last Friday night, after all that rain the week before. They probably thought he'd be out to sea by the next morning.'

'They were hopeful, then,' said the DCC. 'If he hadn't snagged under that bridge, he'd probably have been bobbing along through Leith when the dawn came up.

'You said there was no money in his wallet?' he continued.

'No, it was cleaned out. They left his cards, but took his cash.'

'His watch?'

'Wasn't here, Boss, and there was no personal jewellery on the body when we found him.'

'You keep saying "They", Dan. What evidence is there that there was more than one killer?'

'Nothing hard, Boss, but . . . There's the hair, right; the one caught in his dick. We've got that. We found more hairs on the towels in the bathroom, and Dorward's preliminary report says that they match that one and that they're all female. So the woman took a shower after having sex with Mr Shearer.'

'. . . and possibly also to wash off his blood.'

Pringle looked at Skinner, doubtfully. 'I just don't fancy a woman as the murderer,' he said. 'The battering that Mr Shearer sustained was ferocious.'

'Okay, but I ask you again. What evidence for this male accomplice?'

'Other people used that shower too, sir; males other than the victim. Let's say the woman set him up and someone else did the butchery. Arthur found several different hair samples down there, trapped in the wastepipe. Some belong to Mr Shearer and some will be from his son, but there are others. There's a possibility that some of them came from the bloke who used that baseball bat.'

'They won't help us find him though; not unless they match with something on the DNA database.'

'No, but we do have something that will identify him. Arthur's got a print from the bar of soap . . . over one of the blood streaks. Whoever left it did so washing off Mr Shearer's blood.'

'We haven't matched it, though?'

'No, not yet.'

'Could he tell anything from it?'

'It came from quite a big hand; that's all he could say.'

'A great help,' the DCC grumbled. 'What have you got to take this thing forward, Dan? I'm just about to meet Edith Shearer at the airport and I would like to tell her we're making progress without lying in my teeth.'

'McGurk's been interviewing Mr Shearer's partners, sir. One of them seemed to know a bit about his private life. He told Jack that he used this organiser thing – a palm-top, he called it – and that it had a lot of Mr Shearer's personal information on it. It wasn't here, so the man's taken McGurk into the office to look for it.

'There's the missing watch too; the Rolex. Ms Bryant, the secretary, said that it was bought from Laing's a couple of years ago. We're going round all the known receivers and the licensed pawn shops with a description. If anyone tries to flog it, we'll get them.'

Skinner looked at the Superintendent, scathingly. 'Do you really believe that, Dan?' he asked. 'You don't batter somebody unrecognisable just to steal a few quid and a watch that you'll probably get nicked trying to sell. That Rolex was only taken to fool daft coppers like you and me.

'You get those divers back out and have them look at the river out there. I would not be astonished if they found it stuck in the mud. If we really get lucky we'll find a palm-top as well. I remember that thing; the Diddler even brought it to the football sometimes. He didn't leave it in the office; no bloody way.'

'Could this have been business-related, sir. D'you think that could have anything to do with it?'

'Now you're on my wavelength, Dan. The Diddler was a fund manager, one of the very best. His death will have an incredibly damaging effect on Daybelge, and a whole flock of their business rivals could be in a position to benefit from it.

'I think you should get involved yourself in the interviews with these partners; but first, I would have a long talk with Janine Bryant. If anyone in the financial community had a real down on the Diddler, she'd be the person most likely to know.'

'Do you want to sit in, sir? You know the woman.'

'Thank you for that kind offer. I've just had a couple of days the like of which a man would go to jail to avoid, I am about to collect off a plane the grieving widow and daughter of a good friend of twenty years standing, to get them home before Alan Royston tells the world that he was battered to death, and you ask me if I'd like some more.

'I've been accused, properly of being a dodgy delegator; but this time, Dan, I'm going home to the arms of my wife and kids.'

Fifty-one

She couldn't wait any longer; she picked up the phone and dialled his number. It rang, once, twice, three times... she hung up before the answer machine could pick up the call. She looked up his cellphone number and called that, but a programmed voice told her simply that it was not responding.

'No, he isn't, is he, you smug bitch,' she snapped back.

She switched on the television; anything to distract her. Athletes raced round a tartan track somewhere. She had no idea where, or who they were, or whether they were competing for gold medals or gold coin, but she watched anyway.

The door buzzer sounded; not the entry phone call from the street, someone at the door itself. That bloody girl from downstairs wanting to borrow her hair dryer again. Once was enough, twice was too much, three times was going to get a dusty answer. She stepped into the hall, and swung the door open, ready to do some serious telling off.

He lifted her up in his arms as he stepped inside and hugged her to him, so tight that it hurt, but she didn't care. She stroked the back of his head as he buried his face in her hair, kissing her neck.

'I have been so ... worried about you,' she whispered. 'I have had the most terrible feeling since yesterday morning. I've been imagining the most awful things.'

'Well, you can stop that right now,' he said, quietly, grinning as they looked at each other, as if for the first time, Karen frowning as she saw his swollen lip and the bruising on his face. 'I'm sorry, just turning up out of the blue, especially after the other day, but I had to see you; I needed very badly to see you.'

'Why?' she asked him.

'So that I could be absolutely certain, beyond the last shadow of a doubt, that I am still alive. And so that I could tell you something . . . and ask you something.'

'There's a coincidence,' she murmured.

'Pack a bag,' he said.

'Where are we going?'

'Somewhere I should have taken you a while ago.'

'How much should I pack? How long are we going away for?'

'That's up to you. Pack as much as you like. But do it now; this can't wait any longer.'

'All right, I'll pack office clothes for Monday.'

He followed her into her bedroom, watching as she made selections from her drawers and wardrobe, fitting them into a big soft hold-all, and folding her work suit carefully on top. He grinned as he saw her police uniform hanging on the rail, and her cap on a shelf above. On impulse he reached for it and sent it spinning into a corner of the room.

'Why do we dress our women officers like waitresses in Miss Cranston's tea room?' he chuckled.

'Careful,' she protested, 'I might need that next week.'

'Why should you?'

'Because I'm not going to work for you any more.'

'How did you know I was going to fire you?'

She closed the zipper on her hold-all, dropped it on to the floor and reached for him, taking hold of the top button of his crisp new white shirt. He caught her hand, gently.

'Not here. Let's go.'

She locked up and he led her outside, carrying the bag and squeezing it into the tiny boot of the MGF, which had already attracted the attention of a traffic warden. He showed the man his warrant card and shooed him away.

'Where are we going?' she asked him as he turned out into Nicolson Street. He gave her no answer, only a smile but she knew anyway. He drove urgently, as fast as he could through the Saturday afternoon traffic, cutting along Chambers Street, along King George IV Bridge to the Mound, down the hill and across Princes Street, along George Street and round Charlotte Square and finally down Belford Road and into Dean Village.

His garage door was open; he drove straight inside.

'I am so sorry, Karen,' he said, as he took her bag from the boot, 'that I have never brought you to this house before. It's typical of the blind, stupid and thoughtless way I've treated you.'

She shook her head. 'Not you alone. We've treated each other in exactly the same way.'

He took her hand and led her out of the garage, into the house and upstairs, to the living room. To his paintings. She had never seen them before. She gazed around his gallery. 'Andy,' she exclaimed, 'these are lovely.'

'This is the second part of my life-support system.'

'How long have you had them?'

'I've been collecting for years, on and off. It was only when I moved here that they came together for me like this. They create something; I don't know what it is, only that I feel more at home among them than anywhere I've ever been before.'

'Okay,' she said, asking the begged question. 'What's the first part of your life-support system?'

'You are.'

She felt warmth that was almost orgasmic flood through her whole body and struggled in vain to keep it from showing on her face.

'Oh yes? And when did this come to you?'

'I began to realise about three days ago, but it came to me as a great certainty when I knew I was going to die. You guessed right, Karen; I've been in trouble. Serious, life-threatening trouble of my own making. It was very bad, and then it got worse, until there came a point when all common sense told me that there was no way out. I felt Death descending upon me and, as it did, all that filled my mind was you.

'I saw your face, I felt you with me and I knew all at once that, whatever logic told me about my situation, I could not die. So I declined Death's kind offer – You know how Death is always depicted as a great robed skeleton with a scythe? Actually he's a thin bloke with a gun – and eventually Bob Skinner turned up and, as he does, made everything all right.'

'What happened to Death?' she whispered.

'He went away; for good. All that he's left me is a compulsion to brush my teeth every couple of hours. That'll pass, though.

'And you know what? You're still there, filling my mind, with your strength, and your warmth, and your goodness and your sheer bloody niceness.' He tapped his chest. 'You've been in here for a while now, but I was too stupid to figure it out, hell-bent on making a virtue out of loneliness. It took Sarah Skinner, who is my best friend after you and Bob, to tell it to me straight.

'Now it's just so bloody obvious.'

She looked at him. 'That's what you had to tell me?'

'Not all of it.'

'What else, then?'

'I had to tell you I love you, before I could die.'

'And what do you want to ask me?'

'Forswearing all others, I wanted, want, to ask you to marry me. You saved my life, now I'd like you to live the rest of it with me. What d' you say?'

She frowned at him and his heart sank. 'I have to choose my words carefully here,' she began. 'I love you too. Yes.'

They gave simultaneous gasps of exultation and relief. The space between them closed in a second as they locked in an embrace.

'When?' she murmured.

'Soon as we can.'

'Can I stay here from now on?'

'Too right. We'll find a new place though; one that's ours together. This place has picked up some bad memories already, just like the last one.'

'That's all they are, though, memories. I've got my own, remember. We can live with them, no problem.' She reached for the top button of his shirt once again; this time he made no move to stop her.

'What about the job?' she asked. '. . . Sir.'

'You're not going back to my office, that's for sure. Do you want to chuck it?'

She nodded. 'Yes. It might suit the McGuires – they're zealots – but one copper in the house will be enough for us. I trained as a teacher before I joined up. I'll do some supply work, maybe . . . until I get pregnant, that is.'

He put his forehead against hers as she pulled his shirt free. 'Let's attend to that right now, shall we?'

Fifty-two

'That was a bombshell, was it not?' Bob Skinner gazed after the little red car as it turned out of the driveway, half an hour after noon on Sunday. 'When he phoned I thought he was just coming to return the clothes I lent him.'

Sarah smiled. 'A bombshell maybe; but think of the man who left here yesterday, then look at the Andy who's just left now. When did you last see him as happy as that?'

'Maybe never,' Bob conceded. 'Maybe not even when he was engaged to our Alex. But still . . . don't you think that this could all be a hysterical reaction to what happened to him on Friday?'

'He didn't seem hysterical to me. Nor did she. No, I'm going to take it at face value; I'm going to be pleased for them both. I don't know Karen very well, but I've heard a few stories about her from you and others. Nobody has ever failed to make the point that she is a thoroughly nice woman. She will add a stability to his personal life that's never really been there before. You just watch him go from now on.'

He looked at her, a little doubtfully. 'Okay, Sarah. But he must have some recovery to get through still.'

'With which she can only help him,' she replied. 'Andy is a very strong man, both mentally and physically. The only worthwhile things you can do for him are to fix him up with some private counselling with Kevin O'Malley, to head off any possibility of post traumatic stress, and to wish him and Karen the best of luck.'

'He's got both of those. Christ, after seeing it, I think McGuire and I should have counselling too.'

'Hah! This from the man who swore he'd never again let O'Malley or anyone else inside his head. No, you take those two boys for a walk, as you said you would; that's the best form of counselling. While you're doing that, I will phone Alex, as Andy asked me to.'

Bob nodded. 'You're right.' He called back into the house. 'Mark, Jazz, come on.' He picked up his younger son's carry-frame, slipped his arms through the straps and fastened it across his chest.

The two boys came rushing through the hall: Mark, incredibly bright for a boy just verging on eight, cut out already for academia rather than athletics; James Andrew, still short of three but a toddler no more, a sturdy child with his mother's eyes and the promise of developing his father's physique.

'Where are we going, Uncle Bob?' asked Mark, the adopted son. 'The beach?'

'The beach will be mobbed today; no, we'll go for a long walk round by Luffness to West Fenton, then back up to the village. You can see the horses and the cattle, and look out for the different sorts of birds, then look them up in your book when we get home.'

He loaded Jazz into the carrier, up and over his head, then set off down the drive on the forced march. Beyond the gate, Hill Road was lined with parked cars; he saw a red Ford, a silver Toyota, a big black off-roader of some sort with impenetrable smoked glass windows, a Mercedes, and more lined all the way up the slope past the Diddler's house. It had been abandoned finally by the journalists who had kept vigil there the night before, hoping for a glimpse of the grieving Edith. The vehicles were parked all the way up to the golf course gate. Either the Bents car park was full, or drivers were avoiding the small charge. Whatever, Skinner noted mentally, there was trouble heading the way of the local traffic warden.

He forgot the nuisance almost at once as he walked the boys out, down Sandy Loan, right and across the main street then westward, out of the village. Mark chatted incessantly as they headed down and round the bend in the road, Jazz joining in as they reached the part where the walkway was wider and he could be lifted safely out of his carrier. Eventually, they passed Luffness New Golf Club with its commemorative cairn outside, passed the sweeping Luffness corner itself, and turned into the rarely used road which twisted through the farmland and up to West Fenton.

'This is where we saw the albino squirrel, Uncle Bob, remember?' Mark called out, walking with Jazz a few paces in front. Bob smiled as he remembered the odd little animal, with its pink eyes.

'Want to see it, Dad,' James Andrew shouted. 'Want to see it.'

'I doubt if it will still be here, son,' he answered. 'It was so white that it might as well have been wearing a sign saying "Eat me" on its back. There are hawks and owls around here, looking for small game like that.' Never in his life, had Bob Skinner told a 'cute furry animal' story to any of his children; he believed in teaching them about nature rather than cartoon characters.

They walked on, past the stream which ran on their left through a narrow stretch of woods, round a curve, past an isolated, white, art deco house, planted bizarrely on the edge of

the fertile farmland like a great iced cake, then out into a straight
stretch of road, between two flat fields, one ploughed, the other
sowed.

'What's that, Uncle Bob?' There was something subdued
about the boy's tone.

'Barley. It'll be harvested in August then sold to a brewer.'

They walked on until they reached the old railway bridge; the
railway itself had been gone for sixty years, but the bridge over
the ghost line still stood, fulfilling no function other than to offer
a better view of Gullane from its crest. Bob picked up Jazz and
reinstalled him in his carrier, for the climb at least.

They stopped at the top, and looked back up towards the
village, even though Mark could barely see over the iron parapet.
'Uncle Bob,' he asked as they walked on. Jazz was still in his
carrier, his brother a few yards in front, so Skinner strained to
hear. 'Will that albino squirrel really be dead?'

He cursed himself for a fool at his abruptness. The child's
parents had met violent ends; death was still a dangerous topic
with him.

'Maybe yes, maybe no,' he replied as they descended the far
slope of the bridge.

Change the subject. What? Anything. 'What do you want to be
when you grow up, Mark?'

'Alive.'

The maturity, the perception, the sadness of the boy's
response; all of them stunned him, left him staring speechless at
the back of his little bowed head.

'You will be, son, you will be,' he promised.

And then a sound broke in, the sudden revving of an engine,
a big powerful engine. Tyres screamed as they took a grip of the
rough, tarmac road, gathering pace. He swung round, looking

back over his shoulder, seeing nothing but the big, black vehicle and the sun reflecting off its dark, smoked windscreen, a quick blinding flash as it roared over the hump of the railway bridge and hurtled downwards, racing straight and unmistakably for him.

As fast as he could, yet feeling as if he was running on soft sand rather than tarmac, he turned back and raced towards Mark. He stretched out his right hand and scooped the boy up, throwing him up and over the roadside fence and the bush which was twined through it, into the field beyond. Then, in the same movement, with the roar of the car sounding ever louder in his ears he threw himself, and his burden, after him.

He was in mid-air when he felt the blow on his left leg, harder than a McIlhenney tackle; it spun him round in his flight, sending him even further through the air, even further into the sanctuary of the field.

He lay there for a second, aware of Mark crying beside him. He tried to stand, to catch a glimpse of the vehicle's number plate as it roared away, but his leg was numb, and gave way under him. And then he realised that the carrier on his back was empty. He looked around and saw Jazz, yards away, lying on his back in a ploughed rut, motionless, looking up at the sky.

Desperately, he crawled and scrambled across the field towards him, over the newly turned land, until he reached him. Ignoring the growing pain in his leg, he pushed himself to his knees.

There was a light smile on the little boy's lips as he gazed upwards. Bob's mouth twisted into the start of a scream . . .

Until James Andrew looked at him and chortled. 'That was good, Dad. Can we do it again?'

Fifty-three

Janine Bryant had insisted that Pringle meet her at the Daybelge offices in Melville Street. He assumed that she did not want a policeman, even one out of uniform, calling at her home on a Sunday, but when he arrived for their appointment, he found that the place was a hive of activity.

'All of the partners and the senior people are in,' the tall, trim woman told the Superintendent, as she carried two cups of coffee into the main meeting room, laying them on white coasters on the long table. 'Mr Johnston-White has been appointed acting head of the firm, and he's instructed everyone to call round their contacts and reassure them that our operations and strategies will be unaffected by Mr Shearer's death.'

She frowned. 'Whether or not they believe us; that's something else.'

'Won't Mrs Shearer have a say in what happens?' the detective asked. 'I've been assuming that her husband's share of the business will pass to her.'

'It's not as simple as that,' said Ms Bryant. 'The firm has a Keyman insurance policy in place which provides funds for the purchase of the interests of a deceased partner, and the partnership agreement incudes an undertaking to sell which is binding on the heirs.

'Not that Edith will be thinking about that right now, though. I spoke to her this morning before I came here. The poor woman; she's distraught. We all are, of course, but for her . . . Their son is catching a flight from Sydney around now, but it'll be the middle of tomorrow before he gets home.'

'Give me the flight time,' Pringle said. 'I'll have a car meet him and take him out to Gullane.'

He sipped his coffee, then picked up a chocolate digestive biscuit. 'So Mrs Shearer will be looked after by the firm?' he continued.

'Mmm.' The secretary nodded. 'That's the theory of it. There is one big practical difficulty, though. The Keyman policy pays out at various levels, depending upon who the deceased partner is, but there's a cap of five million pounds. That's the amount which will be available to Mrs Shearer.

'The problem is that when he died, Mr Shearer was about to conclude the sale of the partnership to the Golden Crescent Bank of Malaysia for eighty-five million pounds. Since he owned sixty per cent of the partnership equity, that rather makes a nonsense of the Keyman policy cap.

'The surviving partners are still keen that the sale should go ahead. In fact, Mr Johnston-White is flying to Kuala Lumpur tonight for a meeting with the Golden Crescent people. If it does, then Mr Shearer's estate will benefit accordingly. But if it doesn't . . . it can still be argued that the negotiations have established a valuation of his holding which is far in excess of the sum available from the Keyman policy.

'The business is cash-rich, but it couldn't afford an extra forty-five million pounds, not to buy back its own equity, at any rate.'

'I see what you mean,' murmured the detective, through his moustache.

'Who knew about this deal?' he asked.

'The industry has known for some time that Golden Crescent was in the market for an independent British fund manager, to kick-start a European expansion programme. There have been newspaper references, and, obviously, as the leading investment house in Scotland, Daybelge has been the subject of a lot of speculation.

'Other firms have been mentioned too, of course. Mr Shearer was aware that Golden Crescent had been talking seriously to another Edinburgh house, but he saw them off.'

'How important was Mr Shearer personally to this deal?'

Janine Bryant looked into her coffee cup as if it was tea, and she was trying to read the future in its leaves. 'We'll find that out when Mr Johnston-White gets to Kuala Lumpur. He's worried enough to be taking Mr Laidlaw, our solicitor, and one of his partners along. My feeling is that he was almost essential. Golden Crescent may well look elsewhere.'

'Where?'

'I'm afraid they may be tempted to go back to Paris Simons, the house they turned down in favour of us.'

'So Mr Shearer's death could turn out to be worth a hell of a lot of money to their partners?'

The woman gave him a knowing look. 'Oh yes, Mr Pringle, it could indeed.'

Fifty-four

'We've got to stop meeting like this, pal, or people will talk,' said Bob Skinner, grimly, as Andy Martin looked down at him on his hospital bed, in a small private room in Edinburgh Royal Infirmary. 'A couple of days ago and it was me doing the sick visiting.'

'What's the damage?' his friend asked, gesturing at his left leg, which lay outside the sheets, encased in plaster from the knee down.

'They're not sure yet, although they say there's nothing broken. It could be no more than severe bruising, but there's the possibility of ligament damage in my ankle. They've put this pot on for a week, to immobilise it and keep me from putting weight on it.'

'I wanted them to plaster the other leg too,' Sarah chuckled from the doorway, 'to make sure he stays off it. They wouldn't, though.'

Her husband looked at her, unsmiling. 'When I find the driver of that car,' he growled, 'I want at least one good leg to stand on . . . so I can kick his fucking head in with this stookey.'

'You're still sure it was deliberate?' Martin murmured, gently. 'Couldn't it have been just an accident? A learner driver out on a back road.'

307

Skinner glared at him. 'I'm as sure as you were on Friday morning,' he snapped. 'The bastard was aiming at me – aiming at us! Christ, when I think of it . . .' His eyes were chilling.

'How are the boys?' Andy asked.

'Mark got a hell of a fright. As for the wee fella, he thought it was the best game I'd ever invented; he wanted me to do it again.' He grinned at the memory, through his rage. 'He's like a big rubber ball, that one . . .' The smile vanished as quickly as it had come. 'But he flew right out of the carrier, Andy. He could have hit his head on a rock or anything; for a moment I thought that he had.'

'Where are they now?'

'Alex is with them, out at Gullane,' Sarah answered.

'Alex?'

'Yes. And yes, Andy, I told her. She sends her very best – to both of you – and she really means it. She was as surprised as we were at first, but when she'd thought about it, she reckoned that it was the best thing that could happen to you.'

Martin nodded. 'That's good. I was just a bit worried about how she would take it.'

'Me too. But maybe it's the best thing that could happen to her too. It'll finally allow her to get over you.'

'Sure, she will.' He assured her, then turned to Skinner once more. 'But back to this car. As soon as I heard, I put an "all vehicles" call out for anything answering that description. I dropped Karen at the office to wait for any response, but to be honest, Bob, I thought at the time that we were way too late.'

'Aye, I know, Andy, but there was no more I could have done. My mobile was buggered by the impact, and it took me Christ alone knows how long to get out of that field. I had to calm Mark down before I did anything else. Then I found that where we had landed up, we couldn't be seen easily from the road. I thought about asking Mark to go out on to the roadside and flag down a car, but he'd have been too frightened – and anyway, there was the outside chance that bastard might have come back.

'So I had to get Jazz back into the carrier, then get myself mobile. Ever tried hopping on one leg across a ploughed field with upwards of twenty kilos strapped to your back, laughing all the way because he thinks it's funny?

'Anyway, I made it to the fence, and then had to wait a quarter of an hour before the first car showed up. Hardly anybody uses that West Fenton road, not even the bloody Sunday drivers.

'I knew fine that the bastard would probably have been back in Edinburgh, or miles down the A1, or anywhere else by the time I got through to you.'

'About the car, Bob. You gave a description earlier, but has anything else occurred to you about it? You haven't remembered the registration number, have you?'

Skinner shook his head, looking almost guilty. 'I honestly never saw it, Andy. When I looked back at it, I was dazzled by the sun off the windscreen. After that, I was too busy trying to save the kids to notice anything else.'

'Did you see anything of the driver? Anything at all?'

'Not a thing. The glass was too dark. The car was black, or very dark blue, with colour coded bumpers; a big four-by-four, not a Range Rover but something similar. That's all I can tell you about it – apart from one thing.'

'What's that?'

'It was parked in Hill Road earlier on.'

Martin's eyebrows rose. 'You sure about that?'

'Abso-fucking-lutely. There were cars parked all the way up; I remember making a mental note to bollock the local traffic people about it. The vehicle that ran me down was fourth or fifth away from my gate, facing downhill. Its driver was waiting for me; waiting for the chance I gave him.'

He took Sarah's hand as she sat on his bed. 'Which means, my darling, that three members, active or otherwise, of the Thursday Legends have now been the subject of murderous attacks in little over a week.'

'I knew you were going to say that!' she retorted. 'Bob, how many enemies or potential enemies have you made over the years, aside from people you may have upset at your silly football? If you are still harbouring a theory that there's someone out there taking revenge on anyone who ever kicked him on a Thursday night, then let me remind you of what I've told you already.

'Alec Smith and the Diddler were *not* killed by the same person.'

'No,' said Martin. 'And Lawrence Scotland wasn't your hit-and-run driver either. Listen, Bob, Dan Pringle called me just before I got here, to tell me that he has a strong new lead on the Diddler enquiry, which is certainly not connected to Alec Smith. We've got less evidence than ever to support the notion of a link between these crimes.

'I'm certainly going to treat the attack on you as a separate incident. I'm putting your house under CID observation – and don't try to countermand me on that, or I'll have the Chief countermand you.'

'All right, all right,' Skinner agreed, grudgingly. 'Now here's an order for you; the Alec Smith investigation stays open, in the meantime at least.' He looked at his wife.

'I accept what you say, Sarah, that there were two different killers. However that does not contradict my gut feeling that there's a thread which ties together the two murders and the attack on me. And you are right about one thing, Andy; that thread is certainly not your man Scotland.

'If there is a team working here, mate, then while I'm laid up I want you to find them. Most especially, I want you to find the one who drove that vehicle at me and my boys, and lock him up far away from me. That's another interview I dare not do myself.'

Martin nodded, grimly. 'I'll steer clear of that one too, for the same reason; that'll be another one for Maggie, I think.'

He headed for the door. 'I'd better get back to Fettes to let Karen off the hook . . . and help her clear her desk.'

'She's not going back then?'

'No. I've told her she's on leave from Monday. I'll formalise her resignation with the Personnel people.'

Bob smiled. 'I should be mad with you for costing us a damn good officer, but in the circumstances . . .' He broke off.

'Oh, by the way, it's amazing the things that come to you as you're lying in an ambulance. Remember I had a niggle about Alec Smith's room?'

'Yes.'

'Well, I worked out what it was. That hook – the one Alec was strung up on.'

'What do you mean?'

'It was a big shiny, steel hook, driven into the beam, and fairly recently by the look of it. Let's assume that the killer didn't put it there himself, but saw it and used it.'

'Fair enough. So?'

'So Alec Smith was one of the most methodical men I ever knew. Everything I saw in that room had a purpose; even the ornaments were functional. That's what set me wondering. What the hell was that hook for?'

Fifty-five

Detective Sergeant Steve Steele had been to Dundee three times in his life; once to play football, twice to watch it in that strange place where two arch-rival clubs and their grounds glower at each other across the street.

'The city is looking up,' he said to himself as he drove across the silvery Tay, over the road bridge, glancing occasionally at its neighbour, successor to the notorious structure which had caused the great rail disaster of the nineteenth century. The modern, redeveloped Dundonian waterfront shone attractively in the midday sun as he drove to the toll booth and paid the anachronistic levy.

He glanced quickly at his road map, trying to plot a way to the offices of Biggins and McCart in Albert Street. Eventually he gave up, drove to the nearest off-street car park, then set out to walk.

It took him some time to find the solicitors' premises but, eventually, he spotted their brass plate; it looked badly in need of the sort of face-lift which the rest of the city had received. He walked up three flights of stairs and, it seemed to him, back a hundred years. As he opened the glass-panelled door with its legend 'Biggins and McCart' written in discoloured gold leaf, he stepped into Victoriana.

Every piece of furniture in the room, even the tall wooden filing cabinets, looked like a genuine antique. The only item which did not fit that description sat behind a high-fronted desk, chewing gum. She had dull eyes and a small mouth above an even smaller chin; her dyed blonde hair had a pinkish tinge and she wore a tight-fitting white Lycra sweater chosen, beyond doubt, to display her best features.

Hello, girls, the detective thought.

'Miss Malone,' he said. 'DS Steele, from Edinburgh. We spoke on Friday.'

'Oh aye,' said the girl, disinterested. 'Mr McCart's no' here.'

Steele glared at her. 'Now look . . .' he began. But just at that moment the door behind her opened.

'Sergeant,' a voice said. He turned to see a small, impish, elderly man dressed, regardless of the weather, in a three-piece brown tweed suit. A watch chain hung across his waistcoat; he seemed to fit the room perfectly. He waved a brown paper bag. 'So sorry, so sorry. Saw you going up the stair ahead of me. I just nipped out for doughnuts; must have something with the tea. Molly, put the kettle on.'

The sullen girl nodded and did as she was told, pulling back her shoulders slightly as she rose. The little man threw her the bag and offered his visitor a handshake.

'Gilbert McCart,' he introduced himself. 'Come through to my private office.'

Steele followed him into a second smaller room, furnished in the same way as the first. He glanced around at tall glass-fronted bookcases, low door-fronted cabinets and a big inlaid desk, finer, even to his inexpert eye, than the one in Alec Smith's house. 'Does that have a secret drawer?' he asked, intrigued.

Gilbert McCart's eyes twinkled. 'Can't tell you that,' he replied, 'it's a secret.

'You like my furniture? Geoffrey Biggins, my late partner, and I built up the collection over the years. When I snuff it, my practice won't be worth anything, but this lot will.'

'You're a one-partner firm?' Steele asked as he handed over his business card, a Bob Skinner innovation.

'For three years, I have been; since Geoff went to the Great Conveyancer in the sky. It's just me and the slattern Molly outside. Her real name is Gabrielle, but she suits the moniker I gave her better. I can just see her selling cockles and mussels.'

At that moment the girl came in with a tray holding a tea-pot, china cups and saucers, milk and sugar and a plate with four doughnuts. She laid it on McCart's desk, on top of a copy of the *Courier*. 'Yes,' said the solicitor. 'Cover that damn rag up.' He frowned at the policeman. 'That publication has never been the same since they put news on the front page rather than advertising.'

They waited as Molly, née Gabrielle, poured the tea then sashayed out of the room, her third-best feature moving in her tight skirt like two cats wrestling in a bag.

'Now, Sergeant Steele,' her little employer began. 'To business. I apologise for dragging you up here, but one of the main qualities which I offer my principal client is discretion, and I never discuss his business over the telephone.'

'Your principal client?'

'Kinture Estates. Biggins and McCart – Geoffrey and I and our fathers before us – have been factors to the Marquis of Kinture for the last sixty-three years. Geoffrey's old man, Gilbert, and mine, Geoffrey, were both at Strathallan School, and St Andrews University with the father of the present Marquis. He inherited the title when he was still a student and set his two friends up in this practice pretty well as soon as they qualified.

'Hector, the present Marquis, reappointed us when he succeeded a little over ten years ago. We've always done a little general practice conveyancing work, but the bulk of our income flows from Kinture.'

'What do you do for him?'

'I manage his tenanted properties, of which there are a considerable number. My duties include the preparation and execution of tenancy agreements, the collection of rents, supervision, inspection and maintenance, legal actions against rent defaulters and so on.'

'Where are these properties?'

'There are some in Perthshire and some in Clackmannan, but the bulk of the Marquis's estate is in East Lothian. It includes Bracklands, Lord Kinture's main residence, and the land on which the Witches Hill Golf and Country Club is built. I'm not involved in the running of the club, though . . . God forbid.'

'You collect rents, you said.'

'That's right. Which brings me to the matter of the payment about which you asked the slattern Molly on Friday. Can you explain the background to your request?'

'Certainly, sir,' said Steele. 'About ten days ago a man named Alec Smith was murdered in North Berwick. He was a former police officer and he lived alone. It was a very brutal killing; you probably read about it.'

McCart shook his head. 'No, Sergeant. If it didn't happen in Dundee, it didn't happen.'

The detective smiled, briefly. 'In any event,' he continued, 'in looking into the victim's affairs, we found a standing order payable to your firm: twelve hundred pounds, annually. His bank manager was under the impression that it was a payment intended for Smith's estranged wife.'

'If she is the occupant, then in a way that might be the case.'

'Occupant?'

The little lawyer wrinkled his nose. 'There is a small part of the Kinture Estates holding in East Lothian which lies apart from the rest. It is near the sea and it is woodland, mainly, but within it, there is a small, fairly run-down, one-bedroom cottage. About five years ago, Lord Kinture called me to Bracklands and instructed me to prepare a tenancy agreement in respect of that property, at a rent of one hundred pounds per month, payable annually in advance. The name of the tenant on the agreement was John Green, but I noticed at once that the first rent payment was drawn on the account of an Alexander Smith. There was no clause in the lease specifying personal occupancy, so it is entirely possible that a Mrs Smith does live there.'

'No, sir,' said Steele. 'She doesn't, I assure you. Where is this cottage, exactly?'

'Near the village of Dirleton. It bounds on to a place called Yellowcraigs.'

Fifty-six

'So Karen won't be in the office again, sir?'

'No, Sam, she's gone: she has four weeks' leave owing; add on a couple of public holidays and effectively, as of now, she's a civvy. You're going to be on your own in here for a while, but as soon as Karen's officially off the strength you'll move into her job and I'll pick someone to replace you. I'll invite applications for the vacancy.'

'Very good, sir. I'm sorry I didn't have a chance to wish her luck though. Say it for me, will you. Good luck to you, too, of course.'

The Head of CID smiled; 'As in "You'll need it", you mean? Tell her yourself. Have dinner with us on Friday. I'll book a table somewhere.'

Sammy Pye looked at his boss: there was something different about him, something very different. It wasn't simply his pleasure at the turn of events with Karen, that was self evident, but there was something else. He was quieter, less ebullient than the Detective Constable had ever seen him, and he exuded an air of . . . relief. He saw the healing lip and the fading bruises and he decided to ask no questions at all.

'Two things, sir,' he said. 'First, Spike Thomson from Radio Forth called. He said that Mr Skinner okayed you for his show and can you be there at half past two.'

'Jesus. No-one told me things had gone that far. I'll do it, though. What's the second thing?'

'Superintendent Pringle, sir. He's outside. He wants a word before the Divisional CID Heads' Monday gathering.'

'Show him in, then.'

Pye nodded and left, to be replaced seconds later by Dan Pringle, looking surprisingly bright-eyed for a Monday morning. 'What's this I hear?' he began. 'You and Karen?'

'Bloody office grapevine,' Martin grunted. But he smiled nonetheless. 'True though.'

'Good for you, Andy. She's a smashing girl.'

'Yeah. And I've come to my senses at last. Was that all you wanted to see me about?'

The Superintendent shook his head. 'No, no. I've been delving into the murky world of investment management, and I wanted to talk to you about it. I've been asking around town about this Paris Simons lot that the Bryant woman mentioned. It seems that they and Daybelge are the Hibs and Hearts of the money business.'

'Or the Montagues and Capulets?'

'What league do they play in? Naw, they're serious rivals; hate each other's guts and always have done. Paris Simons used to be kings of the midden, until Diddler Shearer founded Daybelge. He knocked them off the top of the pile and they hated him for it. Their senior partner's a bloke called Luke Heard. The original Paris and Simons went to the bone yard a hundred years back. Everyone seems to have liked the Diddler, but no-one's had a kind word to say to me about Heard.

'The Bank of Scotland held a piss-up for investment managers last Christmas in the New Club. Apparently the guy got drunk and took a swing at the wee fella. He was chucked out and told never to come back.

'Now, six months later, Shearer's battered to death, and Heard's firm stands to benefit to the tune of fuck alone knows how many millions. So just for a laugh, I asked Jack McGurk to check on all flights to Kuala Lumpur from Sunday and over the next couple of days, for a booking in Heard's name.

'They all came back blank, except for Cathay Pacific; they had nothing for the period Jack asked about, but they volunteered the information that they flew a Mr L. Heard to KL last Tuesday — three days before we identified Howard Shearer's body, and even before that e-fit appeared in the press.'

Fifty-seven

'Damn me: Bob Skinner! Susan! It's Bob Skinner.' He heard a shout from somewhere in the background. 'Susan sends her love, to Sarah as well. What can I do for you? You got some bigwig guests who'd like to play Witches Hill? No problem, if that's it.'

'No, it's nothing like that, Hector,' the DCC told the Marquis of Kinture. The policeman and the wheelchair-bound aristocrat had crossed paths a couple of years earlier, drawn together by crime, and a shared love of golf had cemented their friendship. 'Where the hell are you, by the way? You can never tell, when somebody's on a mobile.'

'We're in the Florida Keys,' the Peer replied. 'Fancied a spot of sea-fishing; got to find other pursuits now that the House of Lords is being put out of business. I'm strapped in a chair with a bloody great rod in my hand even as I speak. D'you fish, old chap?'

'Not me. Haven't got the patience. If I can't hit it, or kick it, then I don't want to play with it.'

Lord Kinture laughed. 'Spend a few years in a chariot like mine. You'll do anything for sport then.'

'Aye, I suppose so. Actually, I am off my feet at the moment; got a leg in plaster.'

'Ah, too bad. What happened to it?'

'It's a long story. Listen, to come to the point; we've got an investigation going on into the murder of an ex-copper named Alec Smith. One of my guys was up in Dundee this morning, interviewing a man who turned out to be your estate factor, and he discovered that Smith leased a cottage from you.'

Even across three thousand miles of ocean, the silence was loaded. Even bounced off a satellite, Skinner could hear the sudden exhalation. 'So someone's done for Mr Alec Smith, have they? About bloody time too. Not in my cottage was it?'

'No, in his own house.'

'How was he killed?'

'In an interesting variety of ways; he was tortured to death.'

'Appropriate,' said Hector Kinture, with undisguised pleasure in his voice.

'Hold on a minute,' Skinner exclaimed. 'If you hated Smith that much, why did you rent him one of your properties, and get involved in the deal personally?'

'Because the bloody man blackmailed me. I met him a few years back, when I had the Queen and Prince Philip at Bracklands and he was involved in the security. Shortly afterwards, he came to see me and told me that he was looking for a property; a safe house, he called it. Said that he'd seen the empty place near Yellowcraigs, that he'd found out I owned it and wanted to rent it from me.

'I told him to bugger off. The place had been promised to my head gardener at the big house as a retirement cottage; I was just about to start renovating it for him.' Kinture let out a half-cough, half-snort. 'The man, your ex-colleague, then produced a series of photographs of my brother-in-law. Don't want to say too much with Susan not far out of earshot; she doesn't know any of this.'

'It's all right; don't even mention his name. I know who he is. These photographs; male or female?'

'Male.'

'So you rented the place to Smith.'

'No choice.'

'You could have come to me. I could have squashed him like a fly.'

'I didn't know you then,' Kinture pointed out. 'So I did what he asked. He used a false name on the agreement; I expected him to welch on the rent, but he didn't. It was always paid on the dot. I couldn't take the chance, Bob; had to protect Susan and her family.'

'I understand that, man,' the policeman said. 'It's what you may have done to others in the process that's worrying me.'

'God forbid that I have, but frankly, Bob, the man intimidated me. Look, what can I do to help you now?'

'Simple. You can let my people enter that cottage without the need for a warrant. We think we have the keys.'

'You've got it. Do you want Gilbert McCart to be there?'

'Absolutely not.'

'Fine . . .' the Marquis hesitated. 'Bob; when you go in there, if you find anything, anything like . . . You will be discreet, won't you?'

Skinner let out a quiet, grim laugh. 'Don't worry, Hector,' he promised. 'In this one, discretion is the order of the day.'

Fifty-eight

'Y ou mean you don't plan your own programmes?' Andy Martin asked, gazing at a computer monitor screen in a small, second-floor office in the Forth Street radio headquarters.

'No way,' Spike Thomson replied with a dismissive grin. 'We have what we call music co-ordinators, two of them, who do all the programming for all the presenters. I'm one; although my show's on Forth AM now, I do all the programming for our FM station.'

'Christ, how much of your day does that take up?'

'Less than you think, Andy. We have our toys, you see. Watch.' He turned to the keyboard on his desk. 'We have software that does most of it for us. We load all of our play-list – that's all the music currently selected for airing – and the computer makes a random selection for each hour, with everything timed. Three tracks then a break, then another three and so on . . .'

He hit the Enter key and a programme schedule appeared on the screen.

'My skill is in knowing where the computer's wrong. Some artists just don't fit together. Look there, for example,' he pointed at the monitor. 'We're not going to have two rap tracks on the trot.'

'One on the trot's too much for me,' the detective chuckled.

'Ah, but you're a red-neck polisman . . . not that I disagree, mind you.' He pulled another title from the play list and substituted it for Puff Daddy. 'There're other things too,' he went on. 'The computer hasn't seen our research; it doesn't know that if you play three female artists in succession, your audience starts to switch off.' He saw Martin's surprise. 'Don't ask me why, but that is true. Doesn't matter who they are, either, and it doesn't work the other way around.'

Thomson made a few more adjustments, then said, 'Fine. That's tomorrow's breakfast show done. I'll print it out now, and Madge, our production assistant, will put it on the presenter's desk.'

He stood. 'Come on. We're on air in five minutes; we'd better get down to the studio.' He led the detective back down the stairs and past the entrance hall, to the basement nerve-centre of the building. As they walked, he explained the format of their on-air discussion. 'I'll play three music tracks at the top of the programme, past the news and traffic, go to commercials, then I'll introduce you.

'We'll talk about police work in general; the overall role of the force; about five minutes of that then I'll play another three tracks, more commercials, then back to discussion of the role of the CID. No live cases – I'll make that point on air – just general. How a typical investigation runs.

'Our discussion will split into three segments, and after about forty minutes, we'll be finished, and I'll cue you out.'

'Fine,' said Martin. 'Do I have to keep my mouth shut in there, other than when I'm speaking?'

'Hell no,' said Thomson. 'It's not like that any more. Nothing is as it was any more.' He stopped at a solid wooden door with a single small glass panel and punched in a code on a small keyboard.

'You should change the code. Three, one, four, two.'

The presenter looked at his guest, puzzled. 'How could you see? I had my hand over the panel.'

'First four digits of the decimal form of pi. Most common office-security code in the business.'

Spike gasped. 'Hey. I wonder if I can work that into the discussion?'

It was Andy's turn to gasp as they stepped into the Radio Forth studio. He looked around for turntables and CD players, but saw none. 'Where's the gear?' he asked, as his host waved farewell to the out-going presenter, and pulled a second chair up to the beechwood console in front of the yellow-covered microphone which hung from the ceiling. There was a production booth on the other side of a thick glass panel but it was empty. The full complement of the *Drive-Time* show was them, and a programme assistant. 'This is Audrey,' said Spike. Martin smiled at the woman across the console as he sat down.

A jingle sounded from the big speakers, followed by a woman's voice. 'I'm Lesley Davis and this is Forth News.'

The broadcaster pointed to a video-display screen, bigger than the computer screen in his office. It seemed to be an integral part of the console. 'That's it. All of it. This studio is state-of-the-art; everything's on digital audio tape now and the whole show, other than the live voices, are on that touch-sensitive screen.

'No more cueing up vinyl. Now, I just do this.' His fingers flashed in a complex demonstration of the screen's functions. As Martin looked he saw that it was all there; the whole programme. set out in different sections, all of it timed to the second. He watched as the news-segment indicator counted down to zero.

And in that instant the man beside him changed; the quiet, chatty figure turned into the broadcast version of Spike

Thomson; right out there and in the listener's face. 'Hi and welcome to *Drive-Time*, on Forth AM. Three hours of the music, news, conversation and traffic that means the most to east Central Scotland.

'A little later, I'll introduce today's special guest, the man in my hot-seat. But first . . .' He touched a corner of the screen, and the sounds of Gloria Estefan's brass section rang out.

He leaned back in his chair. 'That's us for nine minutes twenty, then ads. Relax. At least we can; I know of at least one FM station where they don't allow the presenters chairs. They like to keep them on their toes, literally. Seriously, though; you feeling comfortable?'

Martin nodded. 'I'm fine,' he said. 'I'm just gob-smacked by all this stuff.'

'I love it,' said Spike. 'I'm a real tech-head. This is like Toy Town for me.' On the desk a phone flashed, without ringing; he picked it up and spoke to the caller for several minutes. 'Okay, if that's your advice,' he said at last, 'sell the Royal Bank shares and buy Barclays.'

He hung up, with a quick glance at the screen. 'You saw the light as far as Rhian was concerned, I hear,' he murmured, casually.

'Yeah,' said Martin. 'She made me see a lot of things; I owe her that.'

'You're well shot of her, though. I didn't like to say at the time, but she's a man-eater. She tried for me, you know; I'm sleeping with her mother and she tried for me.'

'She and her sister will have had a bet about it. That's how it was with me. I should have seen it but I was thinking with my dick at the time.'

'Her sister?' Spike mused. 'Her big butch sister? You reckon?'

'Yup. You still keen on Juliet?'

'Oh sure. I've asked her to move in with me; she's thinking about it. Not the bloody parrot though,' he laughed. 'That stays.'

He looked at Martin. 'Rhian'll grow out of it one day,' he said. 'She's not a bad girl; just a bit screwed up over her father.'

'What, about him running off you mean?'

'That's what she told you. It's what Juliet told me too. 'S not true, though. Lesley Davis, the queen of our newsroom, spread the real story all around the office when she heard we were seeing each other; hell of a bloody gossip, Lesley, like all journos. She told the whole damn place that Juliet's husband committed suicide; it was hushed up at the time by the media, as these things often are.'

He held up a hand as the light on top of the console shone red.

'Okay!!!' Spike Thomson's alter ego reappeared like a genie from a bottle. 'Now, I promised you a special guest, and here he is . . .'

Fifty-nine

'... So you're saying, Andy, that we should forget all the drama that we see in the movies and on the telly? You're saying that real detective work is boring?'

Martin laughed easily. 'Not at all, Spike. CID is only boring to those who are bored by life itself. At the centre of a major criminal investigation lies a lot of hard work, gathering information, from scientific analysis of potential evidence found at crime scenes or, sometimes, revealed by post-mortem, to the picture of the event painted by witness statements and by wider canvassing through door-to-door interviews, or occasionally re-enactments to trigger the memories of people who might have seen something important without realising it.

'The skilled detective will sit and look at all this and build what amounts to a virtual-reality model of the crime. From that he or she – and these days, more and more women are filling senior CID posts – will draw conclusions and follow any signs which may lead to the perpetrator.

'Once everything has fallen into place, an arrest is made and we present a report to the Procurator Fiscal – whose agents we are under the Scots system – saying, "This is whodunit and this is our case against him."

'The public think of the term "forensic science" in a very

narrow sense. The skilled detective who looks analytically at all of the physical facts of an investigation, and determines what they say about truth or untruth, innocence or guilt – he or she is the true forensic scientist.'

'So what you're saying is, if you wanna be a detective, you have to have a mix of analytical skills and patience.'

'That's right. Although I mustn't miss out the magic ingredient.'

Spike Thomson seemed caught off guard. 'What's that?' he asked.

'Luck.'

'Nice one, Andy,' said Maggie Rose as she switched off the car radio. 'What he didn't say, though,' she murmured to her husband, in the passenger seat beside her, 'is that to get to the very top, you need to be a bloody good communicator as well – just like him.'

She swung their car off the Dirleton by-pass as she spoke, entering the village from the eastward side, then made another quick right turn, following the sign which read, 'Yellowcraigs 1' and showed a caravan symbol.

'Don't tell me that Alec Smith's safe house is in the middle of a bloody caravan site,' Mario exclaimed.

'I doubt it,' Maggie replied. 'There's a lot of land down there – a hell of a lot. Some of it's public but most of it's landed estate. The Kinture holding is relatively small, isolated between the sea and Eilbottle Forest.'

She drove along the narrow twisting road, until she came to a large parking area with only a few cars dotted about. As she turned into the entrance, an elderly attendant approached, only to back off at the sight of her police warrant card. She drew up as close as she could to the gate which led to Yellowcraigs beach, switched off and reached into the back seat for her briefcase.

'I've got a map of the area,' she said. 'Have you got the keys?'

'Of course. I'm a true forensic scientist; I wouldn't overlook something like that.'

She smiled. 'Don't take the piss out of the Head of CID; he might hear you.'

'I wouldn't be surprised. Tell you, Mags, I'll never underrate that man again.' He paused, as they walked down the widening path to the beach. 'Which reminds me. What did you think of this morning's sensation?'

'What are you talking about?'

'Ah, of course; you didn't go to the Divisional Heads' meeting this morning. Karen Neville's gone: resigned the force.'

'Why?'

'Because she and Andy are getting married. She's moved in with him already.'

'Bloody hell! I'd heard stories about them, but I never imagined . . . I mean, we all know Andy but . . . . Och, good luck to them both. They deserve it. Still . . . wow.'

'Aye, last week a sergeant; next month, our next Chief Constable's wife.'

'What? Andy? To succeed Proud Jimmy? Rather than . . .'

'Put money on it.'

'Time will tell. Here, do you think there's a message for us in Karen leaving the force?'

'When you're Head of CID and I'm a Divisional Commander – or the other way around – maybe, but not right now. The Boss has kept us a distance apart on purpose, from the very start.'

'Yet here we are on the same job,' she pointed out.

'On a very special job.'

'Very Special Branch, you mean.'

They stopped as the path which they were walking ran down to a curved golden beach. The island of Fidra lay only a few hundred yards offshore, a green hill rising steeply from the sea and surmounted by a white lighthouse. 'Picture postcard stuff,' said Mario. 'Where do we go from here?'

She pointed to her left. 'Eastwards, into that opening in the whins, as far as I can see. This is shown on the map as a Right of Way, until it hits the Kinture land, then it skirts round it. Come on.' She led the way forward along the narrow pathway, cut by ground-care workers through high, prickly gorse bushes; at once the seascape was obscured from their view, but they could still hear the slow, languorous sound of waves splashing on the shore.

They walked on for ten minutes, with the bushes thinning out gradually, and the tidal sounds becoming fainter. At last, the gorse to the north disappeared altogether, the path curved and was bounded by a waist-high fence made up of three strands of barbed wire. The land on the other side was forest, mature trees, with dark, threatening shadow beneath. Maggie stopped and looked at her map. 'A bit to go yet,' she murmured. 'We should see it soon.'

They carried on until at last they came to a small wicket gate in the fence. Beyond, a path ran through the wood to a clearing, where stood an old grey cottage. Mario put a hand on his wife's shoulder. 'If we get into that cottage and there's an old woman inside, chuck her in the oven and slam the door. I fancy a piece of gingerbread.'

'Don't joke; we might find worse than that.'

The gate opened easily; they stepped through and walked up the path towards the cottage. When they reached the front door Mario produced Alec Smith's keys from his pocket. He slid the

Chubb into a keyhole, the newer of two, and turned it, once, twice, then used the McLaren key on the second, brass-faced, lock.

They stepped inside. The cottage was gloomy, but there was no Hansel-and-Gretel feel about it. 'No-one's lived here for a long time,' said Maggie, shivering. 'A heat wave outside and yet in here it's freezing.' She saw a light switch beside the door and flicked it on. 'Electricity's working though.'

'Okay,' Mario muttered, opening a door on his right. 'No hide-and-seek games, Alec, please.'

His wish was answered at once as he stepped into the cottage's living-room-cum-kitchen. There in the centre of the floor stood a big, grey, cubic metal shape. He switched on the light and knelt beside it.

'Bugger it!' he called out at once. 'He didn't need to hide this thing. This is a Guardian safe; hand-built, top security, with a combination lock. Whatever the third key's for, it's not this.'

'Can we open it?'

'Johnny Ramensky couldn't have opened this in a hurry, Chief Inspector. I know all about this bastard; it's got a heat-resistant titanium-alloy outer casing over a lead lining, making it virtually explosive-proof. You get two shots at the combination; get it wrong twice and the locking mechanism freezes for good.'

'So how do we open it?'

'Unless Alec's left the combination somewhere, or unless we get very lucky, we're going to have to cut it open; and that'll take something hotter than the blowlamp that was used on ex-DCI Smith. We'll need to get the thing back to Fettes and work at it there. Can we get a heavy vehicle in here and the six guys it's going to take to lift this?'

'There is a vehicular access on the map, from a road that leads up to Dirleton, but it's overgrown. Mr McCart suggested that we come the way we did because it's easier.'

'It can't be that bad, because this thing was brought here. But if the road has grown over again since then we'll just have to bulldoze a way through it.' He sighed, in frustration. 'This is going to hold us back by a couple of days at least, you know; Alec Bloody Smith's done us again.'

'Maybe,' said Maggie, 'but he's told us something too. If he invested in this level of security, then he really did have something to protect.'

Sixty

'I've just spoken to Mitchell Laidlaw, out in KL,' said Skinner. He was sitting in his conservatory, holding Seonaid in the crook of his left arm and the phone in his right hand. The baby grinned up at him and gurgled; he made a point of spending personal time every day with each of his three children, the infant included.

He shifted awkwardly in his big upholstered cane chair. Somewhere inside its plaster, his lower left leg was developing an unreachable itch which threatened to drive him to screaming point.

'He and the Daybelge man have had two days of negotiations with the Golden Crescent people. The deal's still alive. The Malaysians have given them four weeks to brief their major clients; if they can hold most of them in, they'll complete, on adjusted terms.' He laughed. 'Mitch is like a dog with two cocks in a stand of trees. He loves to win and he's scored big out there.'

'But what about Paris Simons, sir?' asked Dan Pringle. 'What about the man Heard?'

'That's one reason why he's so pumped up and it's the reason why I'm calling you. The Malaysians told him that Luke Heard turned up unannounced in KL last week with his legal adviser . . . who just happens to be Mitch Laidlaw's biggest rival. He made a big pitch to replace Daybelge in the deal. He offered better terms and . . . he told them that Howard Shearer was about to be discredited.

'Mr Rezak, the CEO of Golden Crescent, said to Mitch that he heard him out, then threw him out. He told him that he had checked Shearer out thoroughly and that he would have to be dead to be discredited in his eyes. Only then, he said, would he consider Paris Simons, and even then any deal would be conditional upon Luke Heard leaving the firm.

'This didn't faze Heard one bit apparently. He said that the first stipulation was out of his hands, but that the second was no problem to him, given the sort of money under discussion. Rezak said, "In that case I pray for Mr Shearer's good health," and terminated the meeting.'

'Oh aye,' said the Superintendent, heavily.

'Indeed, Daniel, indeed. The timing of Heard's visit in itself looked odd, but add in the remark about the Diddler and it moves up a notch.'

'Should I get a DNA sample off him, d' you think, sir, to compare with the hairs in the shower in Coltbridge? He did offer violence to Shearer after all, at that party.'

'No point,' the DCC replied. 'Heard didn't kill the Diddler, not no way. I don't know the guy, but I've seen him around the New Club from time to time. He's got a withered left arm. Whoever swung that baseball bat did so with maximum force, gripping it with both hands. Luke Heard has to eat with his fork in his right hand, the other's so weak.

'No, Dan. Don't confront Heard; investigate him. Find out everything you can about him, and most importantly, who his known associates are. Everybody knows somebody, who knows somebody . . .

'Find out a bit more about the party incident too. Most probably my friend Andrew John was there; he's an AGM on the business side of the bank. Have a word with him and tell him I sent you.'

Skinner ended the call, then dialled the number of the Special Branch office. DC Alice Cowan answered, and put him through to Mario McGuire. 'What progress with that safe?' he asked, without preamble.

'Bloody nightmare, Boss,' McGuire grunted. 'The vehicle access to the cottage has about three years' worth of overgrowth on it. It'll take all day to clear that. I'm using Guardian Security people, all with top clearance, to collect the thing. I've also spoken to the Guardian division that made the bloody thing . . . and that was where I really got depressed.

'The safe was built to Alec's specifications, just after he joined the group. The way it's built, it's going to take about three days to cut through, if it comes to that. But this is the real sickener. Alec had a booby-trap device built into it; if it's ever opened by any means other than the combination lock, every piece of paper inside it will be incinerated.

'I asked Guardian to give me a specialist locksmith to get inside. They warned me that nobody can, but they promised to send someone along anyway.'

'Have you thought about recruiting your own specialist?' Skinner asked. 'Maybe there's someone in a jail somewhere, who could open it for a year or two's remission of sentence.'

'Yes, sir, I thought of that. But Guardian assured me that no-one's ever cracked one of these. They know where they all are and every one is still *virgo intacta*.'

'Fuck it,' the DCC whispered.

'That's my point, Boss. We can't. I've got the Guardian people

341

going through the detailed drawing of the safe right now, looking for a potential weakness, but they told me they'd be surprised and disappointed if they find any.

'The way things stand we will not get into that safe without Alec Smith's personal combination . . . and DCI Smith was not the man to leave it lying around for us to find. I'm pretty sure it was stored away in his head when he died. Stevie Steele's already asked the wife if she knew; but he never as much as told her what day of the week it was.'

'What about the usuals? First four letters of pi, wife's date of birth and so on?'

'Pick any two from a couple of dozen commonly used, sir. We've only got two shots at getting it right. After that the lock will freeze up and it'll be easier to get in and out of Chernobyl intact.'

'If it comes to it, Mario, you may have to take those two shots, and hope that the magic ingredient's on your side.'

He put the phone down and shifted the baby in his arms. 'Where's your mummy then?' he asked her, as he raised her, kicking and chortling above his head 'Cutting up cadavers? Or making our lunch? Or both?

'Ahh. There she is.' Through the open conservatory doors he saw Sarah, in white shirt and cut-away denim shorts, pluck James Andrew from the top of his brightly-coloured climbing frame. She turned towards him, to exchange one child for another, he guessed.

She was in the doorway, arms outstretched to take Seonaid, when the phone rang again. His burden gone, he picked it up, to hear Andy Martin's crisp, sombre voice.

'Morning, Bob. How's the stookey?'

'Itching like hell – which my wife tells me is probably a good sign.'

'For the sake of all concerned,' Martin grunted dryly, 'I thought I should bring you up to date on something. We've now completed a full trawl through DVLA and through all the manufacturers and importers of the sort of vehicle that hit you on Saturday. There haven't been that many supplied countrywide in black or very dark blue, with the tint of glass you describe, but there are some.

'Spike Thomson, for example, has a black Toyota Landcruiser with smoked glass windows . . .'

'Spike?' Skinner snapped. 'He's another Legend!'

'I knew you'd say that,' the Head of CID countered. 'Forget the Legends link, for God's sake, and forget Spike. When that car hit you he was broadcasting live to East Central Scotland, filling in for one of the weekend presenters who's on holiday. His vehicle also has a factory-fitted alarm and immobiliser system which makes it thief-proof.

'However, one other potential suspect car, a black Range Rover with glass to match, was reported stolen in Barnton on Sunday evening, after the owner and his wife got back from a weekend away in their other car, and was discovered this morning, junked in a small gorge up behind Nunraw. It's bashed to hell, but we're going all over the inside for prints and looking at the body work to see if we can find anything clinging to it; fibres from your jeans, for example.'

Skinner sighed. 'Okay,' he said heavily. 'Maybe it was someone with an unconnected grudge. Maybe Scotland did Alec, right enough. Maybe this man Luke Heard did hire someone to batter Diddler unrecognisable. Maybe my Legends theory is all balls.

'But I want you to do one thing for me, Andy. I heard you on radio yesterday, selling the concept of the detective as the true forensic scientist. Now I want you to prove it. I want you to gather together all the evidence in all three cases, including the attack on me, and I want you to examine it minutely.

'Strand by strand, boy, strand by strand . . . and see if you can tie just two of them together. If you can, the rest will fall into place just like that . . . a web, with a big and very poisonous spider right at the centre.'

Sixty-one

Dan Pringle's experience of bank managers had left him unimpressed; but Andrew John was different. For a start, he was a friend of Bob Skinner, and the Big Man did not surround himself with tedious or foolish people. But even more significantly than that, Pringle knew him of old.

More than thirty years before, the young Constable Pringle had occasionally drawn what were euphemistically known as crowd-control duties at Easter Road, home of Hibernian Football Club. He remembered the teenage wing-half who had forced his way into the side; one-footed but skilled, if not quite in the manner of Baxter or Puskas, a good passer of the ball and a solid tackler, and capable of bursting out of mid-field to change the course of a match.

Young Andrew John had flourished briefly in that sixties season, until visiting sides realised that he was at his most effective when Hibs were playing down their notorious slope, yet strangely anonymous and one-paced for the other half of the game. Word spread and he was marked accordingly.

The bubble had burst one winter day with the Hibees three-nil down to Falkirk before a sparse and unenthusiastic crowd, slogging uphill into cold sleety rain. Pringle had been there

345

when it happened, when the wag had stood up in the front row of the season-ticket area and shouted, as the struggling midfielder allowed a blue-shirted opponent to evade him, 'See you, son, you're deceptively slow!'

Breaking all the unwritten rules, and a couple that were written, the young player had stopped and glared up into the murky stand. His hopes of lasting stardom in senior football, of great days at Hampden Park and around the world, all ended in that moment.

A month later he had been sent back to the reserves and, eighteen months after that, he had quit the game to concentrate on his career in banking, where there were, in those days at least, no hecklers.

'I saw you play, you know,' Detective Superintendent Pringle told him across the desk in his St Andres Square office. 'See if you'd had two good feet—'

'I'd have finished playing at thirty-five,' the banker retorted, 'and have come to see a guy like me to beg him to lend me the money to buy a wee pub somewhere. Now if I was a young player today, I'd work at it until I had two feet – and I'd do hill running as part of my training.

'Everybody used to laugh at the teams that trained on sand dunes, you know.' He paused. 'Don't start me reminiscing, or we'll be here all day. What can I do for you? You said when you phoned that it was something to do with the Diddler.'

Pringle nodded. 'That's right; the Shearer investigation. It's come to my attention that there was an incident at a bank function for business customers last Christmas. The Deputy Chief Constable suggested that I should get in touch with you. He hoped you might be able to tell us something about it, or you might remember a colleague who saw it.'

Andrew John gave a short, gruff laugh. 'Hah, that's come out, has it? I should have known it would.

'I saw it myself, Superintendent. Very unpleasant it was, at the time. Afterwards, the Diddler asked me to say no more about it, so I've never discussed it with anyone, until now.

'The man Heard must have had a drink before he got there, or he must have been going at the champagne flat out, for the party hadn't been going for very long before he started niggling away at the Diddler. In company too, it was; completely out of order.' The banker looked down and shook his head. 'Very unpleasant.'

'What happened exactly? We were told that the man took a punch at Mr Shearer.'

'Eventually, but there were a lot of verbals before that. Heard went on and on, just chipping away. The wee man tried to ignore him; I even took him away to another group, but the guy followed us. Finally, the Diddler said something back to him, something mild by comparison . . . I think he joked that Paris Simons couldn't invest in a book of stamps without losing on the deal.

'That was all the excuse that Luke Heard needed; he dropped his glass and took a swing at the Diddler with his good arm.'

'Did he hit him?'

'No, no, he was well gone by then; he missed by a mile. The wee man saw it coming and ducked out of the way. I stepped in at that point, got hold of Heard and huckled him out the door. I told him that he wouldn't be welcome at another bank function until he apologised for his behaviour, both to the Diddler and to the Governor of the bank.

'All the top brass were all there, you know. They all saw it.'

'What did Heard say to Mr Shearer?'

John looked the policeman in the eye. 'He said, "I'll fucking kill you, you little bastard." His very words.'

Pringle remained deadpan. 'But before that?' he asked. 'Before it got to that stage. What sort of things did he say?'

'Ach, it was just unpleasant stuff. Bitterness, jealousy, nothing really; it wasn't just the Diddler he was niggling at. His partner, Johnston-White, he was there too.'

'Okay, but can you be more specific about what was actually said?'

'The gist of it was that Daybelge would do anything to get business. You could have taken the inference that they would lay on sexual favours of any sort for clients. At one point, he said that they were a bunch of faggots.'

'Do you know what was behind it? Where this hatred of Heard's came from?'

'It goes back to time immemorial, so the Diddler told me afterwards. He and Luke Heard were at university together; they were the two brightest people in their year, but the Diddler was brighter. Heard hates to lose at anything, so the problems started back then. There was quite a bit of animosity and, according to the Diddler, it got worse when he met Edith, because Heard had gone out with her first.

'It calmed down after they graduated, for they went their separate ways for a while. The Diddler went off to work with an investment house in London and Heard went straight into Paris Simons.

'Seven or eight years after that, Paris Simons decided to appoint a strategist, someone at partnership level responsible for long-term investment decisions. Heard assumed that he would get the job, but instead, the senior partner of the day went out and head-hunted the Diddler. Animosity turned to hatred then.

The Diddler told me that he could have had Heard blown out the door, but he didn't. It turned out to be a big mistake, for the guy formed a sort of rival cabal within the partnership; there were disputes and arguments over every major decision, even although the senior partner always came down on the Diddler's side.

'Then one day, said senior partner – his name was Rawlinson – dropped dead in the car park. The Diddler had enough votes on the board to get the job, but he knew that if he did, Heard and his clique would leave and set up their own firm. So he beat them to the punch. He left Paris Simons to them and founded Daybelge, taking a couple of partners and a few big clients with him.

'Six months later, the Stock Market crashed. Today, just about every fund manager under the sun will claim to have seen it coming and to have gone liquid in anticipation, but the Diddler was one of very, very few who actually did. When it happened, the investment trusts which he had set up were holding nothing but gilts and cash.

'With the market on the floor, he reinvested in blue-chip companies and sunrise industries. When the smoke cleared, Daybelge was far and away the biggest independent fund manager in Scotland, and probably the most respected in Britain.

'The Diddler may have been a rotten footballer, a real wee gossip and a fornicating little bugger, but as a fund manager he was a bloody genius. That was why he would have landed the Golden Crescent deal, no question.'

Pringle tugged at an end of his moustache. 'Aye,' he said, 'the Golden Crescent deal. I've heard about that.'

'I think that was what prompted the hostilities at the

Christmas party,' Andrew John suggested. 'It was only a rumour back then, but already the talk was that Daybelge was the top target.'

'Did Heard make any reference to it?'

The banker frowned. 'Come to think of it,' he began. 'I do remember him saying, at one point, "You look like the cat that's got all the fucking cream: but just you wait. It'll go sour on you before long." '

Sixty-two

Karen laughed. 'I don't know why I'm leaving the force,' she said. 'I might as well still be drawing the money, if you're going to bring the whole bloody office home with you every night.' She settled herself down beside Andy on the big living-room sofa, her legs tucked up under her. Before them, the coffee table was strewn with files, photographs and statements.

'Don't worry,' he promised her, with a grin. 'This is a one-off. The Big Man heard me say something pompous on radio yesterday and he's called my bluff.'

'I didn't think you were pompous!' she protested. 'I thought you sounded very sensible and completely committed. But what exactly have you been doing for the last hour or so, while I've been busying myself in the kitchen?'

'I've been reading the papers in the Alec Smith investigation, going back to the very start. Bob can't shake off the notion that there's a link between it and the Shearer murder, and the hit-and-run on him as well. He's asked me to confirm it or kill it off.'

'But I thought that Smith was a closed book, more or less.'

'As far as I'm concerned, it is. I'm just rereading it.'

'And what have you learned?'

'I've learned that Alec Smith liked his nuts . . .'

'Before they were burned off,' Karen murmured.

'Cashews, actually. I've learned that of all the people interviewed in North Berwick, not one had ever been inside Smith's house. I've learned that he was seen around walking his dog, but that at other times he let the animal run loose. I've learned that on the night he was killed, North Berwick was a ghost town; hardly anyone seems to have been out on the street. The pubs were full, though.'

'No suspicious sightings? No furtive bloke spotted carrying a Safeway bag with a wrench, a knife and a blowtorch in it?'

'No. One guy saw a figure in an anorak carrying a big parcel, but that was all.'

'An anorak? It was a warm night.'

Andy grinned. 'Makes no difference in North Berwick. Even on a mild night it can turn windy all of a sudden, and the haar can come in off the sea without warning.'

'So, to sum up, you've been wasting your time for the last hour?'

'Yeah,' he sighed. 'There's only one thing that struck me as slightly peculiar.'

'What was that?'

'Something from the post-mortem report, actually.' He leaned forward and picked it up from the coffee table. 'Sarah remarks that Smith was very fit and that judging by the musculature of his legs he must have taken a lot of physical exercise; walking, running or cycling, she suggests. Yet . . .' He paused.

'Yes?' Karen asked, eagerly.

'Yet Bob told me that Alec Smith gave up playing football with his Thursday night crowd because his right knee had packed up on him. Either he made a miracle recovery afterwards, or he was lying.

'If he was, it makes me wonder. Why did he really chuck it?'

'Maybe it occurred to him that a collection of middle-aged men kicking a ball around might look faintly silly.'

Andy laughed out loud. 'Don't you ever say that to Bob Skinner, or to Neil. It's their religion.' He tossed the report back on the table and stood up.

'You know what?' he began. 'I think I'll go to bed.'

She gave him a long, enticing look. 'Can I come too?'

He grinned down at her, on the sofa. 'That was the general idea,' he murmured.

Sixty-three

'Don't be crazy, Bob. No way will I cut that plaster off for you; I have to work in the Royal Infirmary. Granted, your leg is not broken, granted, you probably will be kicking footballs around in two to three weeks; but it's still possible that you could have damaged ligaments which could cause long-term problems if you take liberties with them. The orthopaedic guys said you must wear that for a week, and a week it is.'

'Sarah, come on. It's itching like . . .'

'No!' She looked at the plaster. 'I'll tell you what; it's loosened off a bit; I'll pour just a little baby oil into it. That might ease it.'

'Anything; I'll try anything.'

She took a bottle of Johnson's oil from her dressing table and soaked a piece of cotton wool, then rubbed it around his leg, above the plaster, as he sat on the edge of the bed. 'Ahh!!' he sighed as the balm made its way down. 'That's my girl.'

He lay back and settled down on the divan, leaving his plastered leg hanging over. 'I think I'll go into the office tomorrow,' he said. 'I'll get a car to pick me up.'

'And hobble around, putting weight on that leg?' she exclaimed. 'No, you will not.'

'God, you're a hard woman. I wonder if Alec Smith's wife was like you; maybe that's what made him such a morose bugger.'

She snorted. 'People like the late DCI Smith are not made: they're born. This may not be very scientific, but I do believe in human nature.' She took off her dressing gown and slipped, naked, into bed beside him. 'Take our younger son, for example; he's you in miniature, already.'

He smiled as she switched the light off. 'I wonder how the new one will turn out?'

'Ahh,' said Sarah. 'She'll be like her mother; a more placid and co-operative baby I have never seen. Let's hope that the next two are like her.'

'The next two?' he gasped. 'One, okay, but . . . It's tough, paying university fees out of a pension, and I'll be retiring by the time Seonaid's at that stage.'

'I'd sort of hoped you'd be retiring before then.'

Suddenly she was aware that he was sitting bolt upright in the dark. 'What is it?' she asked, anxiously.

'It's you. Something you said. Oh, you little cracker.'

He switched on the light once more and scrambled for his address book in the drawer of the bedside table. She watched as he flicked through the pages until he reached the 'Mc' section, then picked up the telephone and dialled.

'Mario,' he said at last. 'DCC here. Sorry if I woke you, but it'll be worth it. I've just remembered something Alec Smith said to me a long time back. I was quizzing him one day about SB security.

'I remember it now, as clear as day. He gave me a long look and he said, "The only way anyone'll ever crack my safe, sir, is if they know my mother's Co-op number". Alec's mother lived in Lochgelly, in Fife. She died four years ago. I wonder how long the Co-operative Society holds on to the records of departed members?'

Sixty-four

'What have you got for me, Jack?' Dan Pringle's heavy moustache bristled as he looked across at his sergeant.

McGurk laid a folder on the Superintendent's desk. 'Mr Luke Heard, sir. Age forty-four, senior partner of the firm of Paris Simons; married, wife's name Gwendoline, née MacDonald, one daughter aged seventeen and two sons, aged fourteen and twelve. Educated at George Watson's and Edinburgh University; the kids are all at Watson's too. He's a member of the New Club, Drumsheugh Baths Club, Edinburgh Sports Club, and the Merchant Company of Edinburgh.

'His salary at Paris Simons is one hundred and seventy thousand pounds per annum; in addition, as an equity partner he shares in profits. As well as his involvement with the firm, he holds non-executive directorships in a few firms in which he's invested. One's a software development house in Livingston, another's a design consultancy, and a third specialises in the disposal of clinical waste.

'He's also chairman of a company called Linton Heritable Trust; it's an investment vehicle based in Liechtenstein owned by a man called Dominic Jackson.

'Heard's last tax return declared total income of four hundred and ninety-one thousand pounds.'

'Fuckin' hell,' Pringle growled.

'Well put, sir. Yet he's not as wealthy as he should be. His pension's healthy but his house is still mortgaged, and looking at his bank accounts he isn't as cash rich as you'd expect. Our Mr Heard's a bit of a gambler; he goes to the casino out at Maybury quite a bit. He isn't a big loser, but he's consistently in the red.

'He told the manager there that his ambition was to be very rich and retired by the time he was fifty. If the Golden Crescent deal had gone through, that would have realised it for him.'

The Superintendent nodded. 'Aye, he must really have been pissed off with Shearer.' He frowned. 'This man Dominic Jackson; what do we know about him?'

A slow, slightly smug, grin spread over the Sergeant's face. 'That's where it gets really interesting, sir. I asked the police national computer that very same question, and it came up with only one answer. Dominic Jackson is an alias of one Leonard Plenderleith, currently resident in HM Prison, Shotts, serving three consecutive life sentences.'

Pringle seemed to sit bolt upright. 'Big Lennie Plenderleith! Tony Manson's minder!'

'Manson's heir, sir. When Terrible Tony was murdered, he left Plenderleith all his offshore cash; it's still there, untouchable, and it's growing. Heard visits him in Shotts every three months with investment reports.'

'For his sake, I hope they're good.'

'They are, sir. Big Lennie directs the investments himself; he's very conservative and he gets a good growth rate.'

'How did you find that out?'

'The Governor of Shotts told me; he and Plenderleith are on friendly terms.'

'What else did he tell you about him?'

'Quite a lot,' said McGurk. 'For a start, he said that he's bought a hell of a lot of equipment for the inmates. Not just pool tables and tellys but PCs with educational programmes. He's also set up a hardship fund, for inmates with family problems. He provides the money and the Governor deals with applications for assistance.

'In the nick, big Lennie is a god. After what he did for Tony Manson, he's held in a sort of awe, and even the hardest guys in there are terrified of him. Yet he rarely speaks to the other inmates, and when he does, it's usually to put a stop to potential trouble. If anyone has a grievance they can go to him and he'll raise it with the Governor, but he will not allow any nonsense. He's working towards the day, in ten years or so, maybe less, when the Parole Board comes to review his sentence, and he wants to be sure that when it does, no-one has a bad word to say about him.

'So he studies . . . he's on the verge of a PhD in criminology . . . he writes . . . his first novel's due out in two months . . . and he works out in the gym. The only people who ever visit him are Heard, his lawyer and his accountant . . . oh, and occasionally, DCC Skinner.'

'. . . who locked him up in the first place,' Pringle muttered. He looked at McGurk. 'Jack, are you trying to tell me that big Lennie could have had Howard Shearer killed as a favour to Heard?'

The tall Sergeant shook his head. 'From what I've been told, that's unlikely; Plenderleith's still a relatively young man, and he's far too clever to jeopardise his future by doing something like that. But maybe, maybe inadvertently, he mentioned a name to Heard during one of their meetings, a name from his past, who might be up to something like that.'

Quintin Jardine

'Maybe,' Pringle conceded. 'Do Heard's bank accounts show any unexplained cash payments to anyone?'

'They show cash withdrawals, sir, but he's a gambler, remember. If he did hire someone, he could have paid him out of winnings and we'd have a hell of a job proving it.'

'That's true. Tell me something Jack. Do you fancy Heard for this?'

'Who else have we got, sir?'

'True, but . . . If there's one thing I've learned in my thirty-something years in this job it's never to trust it if it's too fucking easy.

'So, son, you're going to have to do this the hard way for a while. Have you got that tail on Heard?'

McGurk nodded. 'Ray Wilding's watching him now.'

'Good. You get out there and join him. Follow the bugger to the toilet, even. Meantime I'd better speak to the Boss about his pal, big Lennie.'

360

Sixty-five

'**B**ig Bob,' muttered McGuire, fervently, to the empty room, 'you may be constitutionally incapable of keeping your hands off your officers' investigations, but every so often you do come up with a beauty.'

He cradled the phone, stood, and walked out of his office into the Special Branch room outside. Alec Smith's squat, grey, ugly safe stood in the middle of the floor. Maggie sat on the edge of a desk, making conversation with a middle-aged man in a brown suit, who had not been there when McGuire had left to make his telephone call.

'Mario,' she said. 'This is Mr Evans from Guardian Security; he's their top locksmith, so the company told me.'

The little man smiled in what was meant to be a self-deprecating way, but the Inspector knew that he was not about to disagree with the description. 'I do my best,' he said, lamely.

'Nothing else will do, Mr Evans,' McGuire boomed. 'Nothing else.' He looked at his wife and smiled. 'The Scottish Co-operative Wholesale Society came up trumps; the late Mrs Mary Eglinton Smith, of Morocco Lane, Lochgelly, was indeed a member, to the day she died . . . you might even say to the day the Co-op undertaker put her in the ground. Her membership number was five . . . three . . . six . . . four.' Maggie noted the four digits down as he spoke.

'There's nothing else for it, sir,' he said to the locksmith. 'We'll have to go with that as the combination. Can you open it for us?'

Mr Evans frowned. 'It's not just the numbers,' he said. 'This is a classic circular combination lock, not one of these shoddy keyboard jobs – you have to know the direction as well. Four digits, possibly in random order, either right or left, not necessarily alternately. Yes, that cuts the odds against guessing right down to around one hundred thousand to one.

'Forget all that stuff you've seen in films, too, where the safecracker uses a stethoscope to listen for clicks as the mechanism works. This lock is silent; when you key the first digit you have to hold it in position for five seconds before it engages, with the next it's six seconds, then seven, and finally eight.'

'Yes,' Mr Evans said, proudly. 'It's a clever little bugger.'

McGuire's face fell. 'So we're no further forward,' he muttered.

'In theory.' The little man beamed. 'But in practice . . . I built this thing and although I didn't tell my colleagues, I did include one little fail-safe, against the outside possibility of a situation such as this arising.'

'Like what?'

'I programme my own signature into the locking mechanism of every safe I build. It over-rides the owner's combination. Naturally, I have never breathed a word of this to a soul, not even within the group. If my small secret leaked out, I'd be a prime target for kidnap, wouldn't I?

'So as far as anyone outside this room is concerned, when you gave me Mr Smith's combination, we just got lucky.'

He turned, bent over the safe and twirled the dial of the lock for a little over a minute, then straightened up. With a soft hiss, sounding almost like a sigh, the door swung open.

'There.' His voice rang with pride. 'Behold! A ton and a half of useless metal; using the override knackers the lock completely.'

Maggie looked at him, eyes narrowed just a shade. 'Thank you, Mr Evans. You do realise that if anyone ever does succeed in cracking a Guardian safe, you're going to need a hell of a strong alibi?'

'No-one ever will, Chief Inspector. I believe I can promise you that.'

'We'll hold you to that,' said McGuire, with a grin, as he escorted the little locksmith to the door. DC Cowan was waiting outside. 'Show Mr Evans out, Alice, if you would. then come back and man, or woman, the phones. The DCI and I have some reading to do in my office, and we're not to be disturbed.'

As the general office door closed on the Constable and the visitor, he turned back to the safe; Maggie had already swung the door open fully. It was massive, but moved easily and noiselessly on well-lubricated hinges.

'Bingo!' she whispered. Given its bulk, it was surprisingly small on the inside; all that it contained was an Apple lap-top computer, complete with manuals, transformer, cable and plug, and a green metal strongbox. 'That spare key,' she said. 'Betcha that's what it's for.'

'Let's take these into my room and find out.'

He picked up the computer and the box, one in each hand and carried them into his office, laying them on his table. Maggie plugged in the transformer and attached it to the lap-top, then pulled up a chair and sat down. She released the catch and swung the screen into position, then pushed the start-up button.

As they waited for the Apple to boot up, Mario took out Alec Smith's key ring and slid the third key into the lock of the strongbox. It clicked open and he lifted the lid. 'Envelopes,' he muttered, as he stared at the contents. 'It's full of numbered envelopes.' He picked one up and looked inside. 'Photographs,' he told her, 'and negative strips. There are some computer disks here too.'

'Software, maybe; or copies of files.' Maggie smiled as the computer desktop appeared; the background pattern was an array of blue cats. 'Animal lover, eh,' she said. 'Let's see what's in here.' She double-clicked the hard-disk icon to reveal the machine's contents. 'Three folders; System, Applications and one that's called "John". John?' she wondered.

'Alec's son,' Mario whispered. 'The boy who died of AIDS.'

She opened the folder, to find a list of twenty-eight documents, twenty-seven of them titled with a number and one word. She looked at the first: 'Barnfather,' she read.

Her husband looked over her shoulder. 'I've only ever heard of one person of that name,' he said.

'Yes,' she agreed, 'and I've made his acquaintance. Not that he was aware of it at the time. He'd been dead for a couple of days.' She paused.

'Mario, I've got a feeling about this.' She opened the document and began to read.

'The subject is a senior Supreme Court judge whose proclivities have been rumoured around Edinburgh for many years.

'Barnfather was observed on several occasions cruising in Leith, striking up conversations with young men. (See photographic evidence) On more than one occasion the contacts accompanied him to his flat in Tevendale Street and remained there for several hours.

'Barnfather was also observed (See photographic evidence) frequenting an address in Cockburn Street, immediately above retail premises which operated as a homosexual gathering place. I attempted to have Drugs and Vice raid the premises, but was told that there were no grounds, since the premises were private and there was no evidence of soliciting nor of prostitution.'

She stopped and looked up at Mario, as he shuffled through the photographs. 'I make it seven shots,' he told her finally, 'each with the number one on the back, in accordance with the file number, of an old geezer chatting up what looks like the rough trade in Leith, or taking boys into a New Town flat. There are a couple of shots of him going into an entryway in what could be Cockburn Street and a blow-up of him shot through a window, presumably in the same place.

'What's the second document?'

Maggie turned back to the screen. 'Number two. Raeside. Jesus,' she hissed, 'this one's a Deputy Procurator Fiscal.'

Her husband picked up the envelope numbered two, and slid out the photographs inside. 'Is that right?' he exclaimed. 'He should be prosecuting himself in that case. Getting a blow-job off a bloke in a beach car park is definitely lewd and libidinous conduct in my book.'

He took another envelope at random and looked at its contents; then another; and another. 'They're all the same; Alec's been gathering information on gay men.'

'But not just a random selection. A judge, a Fiscal.' She scanned the files, picked one and clicked it open. 'Yes,' she murmured. 'Thought I recognised that name; this one's a Minister in the Scottish Parliament.'

'And that one,' she said, opening another document. 'Oh my! This one's a woman. The Chair of the Police Committee.'

'Mario, what are we going to do with this?'

In answer he picked up the phone and dialled Ruth McConnell's extension. 'Ruthie,' he asked. 'is the Boss in today?'

'No. He called to say that Sarah's making him stay at home for the rest of the week.'

'Okay.' He hung up and looked at his wife. 'That settles that. We're going to Gullane.'

Sixty-six

Jack McGurk snapped into wakefulness; he had been on the verge of dozing off as he leaned back in the passenger seat of the anonymous Vauxhall as he watched the building across Rothesay Terrace. He sighed, deeply; 'Ah, bloody hell, Ray,' he said, to the man behind the wheel, 'I hate this sort of duty. Sometimes I wonder if Dan Pringle's still blaming me for that crap my brother-in-law printed in the *News*.'

'Come on, Jack, you've still got your stripes, haven't you?' said DC Wilding. He grinned. 'No-one ever held that against you . . . at least not for long, anyway.'

'Maybe so, maybe so. Someone's got to do this, I know. It's just . . .'

'It's just that you thought that once you became a sergeant you could leave this sort of crap to poor bloody foot soldiers like me.'

McGurk laughed. 'Aye, I suppose so. Whereas all that's happened is that I get to sit on this side of the car, not in the driver's seat.' He glanced at his watch. 'Five to bloody one. Chances are they'll be having a boardroom lunch in there, and you and I'll be stuck here till fuckin' six o'clock or later.'

'Or maybe not,' said Wilding. 'Look.' McGurk followed the direction of his nod, and saw a man trotting briskly down the steps which led from the offices of Paris Simons. He seemed to move awkwardly, an impression created by his twisted, stunted left arm, undisguisable even by his expensively cut suit.

'Our man,' the Sergeant muttered. He made to open the car door, until his colleague laid a hand on his shoulder. 'Wait, Jack, wait.' As they watched, Luke Heard strode along the pavement and turned into an alleyway at the side of the building. 'There's a car park back there.'

'He can drive? With that arm?'

Wilding nodded. 'He's got an S-type Jag. Automatic, with adaptations, I suppose.'

The two detectives sat for a minute, watching, until a silver Jaguar with Heard at the wheel, appeared in the alleyway and turned left into the road, heading eastwards. The Constable slid the Vauxhall into gear and set off after him.

The fund manager took a right turn at the end of Rothesay Terrace, not noticing, apparently, the vehicle following. He headed downhill, and across Belford Bridge, the temporary resting place of Howard Shearer, then up Belford Road, until he turned into Ravelston Dykes.

'Where's he going, d'you think?' Wilding mused.

'Maybe he's off to the casino to lose another couple of grand. We'll see.' They tailed Heard down to Western Corner and then along the Corstorphine Road, out of the city. 'Aye,' McGurk muttered as they swept past Murrayfield Hospital, 'Looks like the tables right enough.'

The right turn took them completely by surprise. 'Fuck me, he's going into the zoo!' snapped Wilding. 'He'll twig if I follow him in there.'

'Pull into the filling station opposite,' the Sergeant ordered. 'We'll leg it.' His colleague did as he was told, swinging off the road and parking on the forecourt, well clear of the pumps, and flashing his warrant card at the attendant, before following McGurk across the road to the grey-walled zoo.

'Police,' the Sergeant barked at the girl on the admissions kiosk. 'Let us in, quick.'

Inside, they looked around, until Wilding spotted the sleek form of the Jaguar, brake-lights shining as it pulled into a car park beside a stone building. 'Look; the bastard's going for his lunch, Jack,' he gasped, breathlessly. 'There's a club out here, and he's probably a member. He must be, to be able to park there.'

'Let's just wait and see.'

The two detectives stood at the top of a rise, a hundred yards distant, watching Heard as he climbed out of his car. Before he closed the door he reached across to the passenger seat, picked up an object, and slipped it into his pocket. Then, instead of heading for the building he turned on his heel and strode out of the park, into the zoo itself.

'Going to throw buns to the elephants, d'you think?' murmured McGurk.

'Not in that direction. He's heading for the penguins; first place my kids make for when I bring them here.'

Edinburgh Zoo's penguins are its star attraction. At weekends or during holiday periods, their enclosure would have been surrounded by spectators, but on a midweek afternoon it was deserted, except for a tall girl in dungarees and green wellington boots; she was brushing the pathway around the pen. Heard walked straight up to her and stopped. She was as tall as him. As the detectives watched, maintaining a safe distance, she smiled and leaned forward as if to kiss him, but he swayed back.

'Now who the hell's she, I wonder?' the Sergeant whispered, under his breath.

'Bit on the side? Lucky him if she is.'

'He doesn't fancy it today, then; even from this far away, he does not look like a happy man.'

Their target stood stiffly, facing the girl. His voice was raised as he spoke to her, for fragments of incomprehensible sound seemed to drift across on the light breeze. She was in no way intimidated; instead she stared at him, eyes bright, lips moving in a retort. All at once, Luke Heard seemed to slump down into himself. He reached into his pocket, took out the packet which he had brought from the car, and shoved it roughly down the front of her overalls. Then he turned on his heel and walked away, back down the rise. McGurk and Wilding watched him, all the way back to the car park.

'What the fuck d'you think that was about?' the Constable exclaimed as they watched him slide back into the Jaguar.

'I don't know, Ray,' McGurk answered. 'But I think we should find out.'

'Will we brace the girl?'

'Not without checking with Dan Pringle; we don't want to blow our surveillance of Heard just yet. She works here. We can find out who she is, and talk to her any time we like.'

'I've just remembered who she is, Jack,' said Wilding, quietly. 'I recognise her from this distance, even if you don't; you and I took a statement from her the Saturday before last. She's the girl who spotted Howard Shearer in the Water of Leith.'

Sixty-seven

Skinner put down the telephone and stared out of the conservatory, across the wide Firth of Forth. There was something unsettling about Lennie Plenderleith; even when he spoke to the man by telephone, as he just had for the first time in his life.

Big Lennie, when he was Tony Manson's first lieutenant, had maimed or murdered God knew how many people; later, after his mentor's death he had taken revenge in savage and terminal fashion. He had even tried to kill Skinner himself.

And yet, in spite of it all, against all logic, he found himself liking the giant in Shotts Prison. 'Why?' he asked himself, yet inwardly he knew the answer. In his own way, Lennie understood the meaning of loyalty and obligation as well as anyone he knew and had practised them, even though it had led to his imprisonment for life.

Those were the virtues which Bob Skinner valued above all others and if, in Plenderleith's case, these were accompanied by awesome, pitiless violence when he perceived it to be necessary . . . the DCC knew that the same streak ran through him. They came from different backgrounds, they had taken different paths through life, yet as Skinner sat in his comfortable home, he wondered whether, had their circumstances been reversed, it might have been him who had ended up in a cell.

Forcing himself to shove the thought to one side, he picked up the phone again, dialled the Torphichen Place police office and asked for Detective Superintendent Pringle.

'Afternoon, sir,' said the veteran as he came on line. 'Did you get anything?'

'Yes, Dan, but nothing that's going to take you forward. I had the Governor bring Lennie to the phone and I asked him about his meetings with Luke Heard. He assured me that the two of them only ever talk business. Heard gives him a quarterly report detailing the performance of every investment in the trust portfolio; Lennie looks at it and makes a few off-the-cuff comments. Later, once he's had a chance to study it at leisure, he writes to him with more detailed instructions.

'There's never any small talk. The big fella told me that he doesn't like Heard; he thinks he's a nasty piece of goods. He only does business with him because the Diddler turned him down.'

'So Lennie had something against Shearer himself,' Pringle commented.

'Don't clutch at straws, Daniel. He understood Diddler's position and he still respects it.'

Pringle could not restrain himself. 'Do you believe all that, though? I mean, the man's a fuckin' murderer.'

Skinner chuckled. 'As someone once said, it doesn't make you a bad person. Seriously though; Lennie has never once told me a lie. Fact is, I doubt if he's ever told a lie in his life. Take it from me, he did not do Heard any favours, or drop him any hints, accidentally or otherwise.'

'Aye okay, sir,' the Superintendent conceded, wearily at first, until his voice changed. 'I suppose one bit of luck's all I can hope for in a day.'

'What d' you mean?'

'I just had a call from the diving team. They've found the Did– Mr Shearer's organiser thing in the river, just downstream from the house. No sign of the watch yet, though.'

'Bugger the watch! You give that lap-top to our technical people; with a bit of luck, there'll be retrievable data on it.'

'It's already on the way to them. I'll give you a call if we get a result.'

'Do that, but keep Andy informed first; everything goes through him.'

As he hung up, he glanced across at Martin, who was seated opposite. 'Did you get that?'

'Diddler's diary?'

'Possibly, unless it's goosed.'

'Our day for the high-tech, isn't it?'

'Seems to be. Go and get Maggie and Mario for me, will you? You understand why I didn't want them in the room while I spoke to Lennie? It would have been a breach of confidence, in a way, to have them listening in.'

'Sure.' Martin paused. 'Tell me something. Do you ever regret not just standing aside that night and letting him walk out of there?'

Bob shook his head. 'Never. Not for a second. Sod the guys that he did in; they were crooks and murderers. But he killed his wife, Andy; he cut her throat, and he had to pay for that.'

The Head of CID left the conservatory, returning quickly with Rose and McGuire at his heels. The Inspector was carrying Alec Smith's computer, while his wife held the strongbox full of photographs.

'Hi, folks,' said the DCC, pushing himself halfway up from his chair as they entered. 'Sorry to keep you waiting; I had something to take care of. We can get on with it now, though, in

peace and quiet too; Mark's at school, and Sarah's up at Edith
Shearer's with the other two.

'So what's the big mystery? What's this that Andy and I both
have to see?'

'Dynamite, Boss,' McGuire, the junior officer in the room,
answered. 'Sheer bloody dynamite. As DCI Rose told you on the
phone, the late Mrs Smith's Co-op number paid off. We got into
the safe, and we found this lot. Once we got into it, we realised
that you had to see it.'

'Okay,' said Skinner, 'let's have it then. How's the battery?'

'Fully charged. I switched it on as we were coming through.'
He handed the lap-top over, raising the screen as he did so.

The DCC looked at the small keyboard. 'Fiddly thing this.
Our Mark's the boy for these.'

'You wouldn't want him to see what's on there.'

'Let's have a look then.'

He looked at the listed folders and clicked open the one
marked, 'John'. He hit on the first name at once. 'Barnfather.
The old judge?' he asked, glancing up at McGuire, who nodded.
As he glanced down the list of names, one jumped out at him.
'Topham? Is that Marcia Topham, the Police Committee
woman?'

'The same,' Rose murmured.

He opened the first file, and read his way through it. As he
finished, the DCI handed him the first envelope of photographs;
he hissed with distaste as he looked through them, then handed
them to Martin and opened the next file. Slowly, carefully, and
silently, he read his way through all twenty-seven numbered files
and examined all twenty-seven envelopes.

The twenty-eighth file was headed, 'Report'. Skinner clicked
it open and gasped. 'Bloody hell! This is addressed to the Lord

President.' The document which showed on the computer screen was headed:

Private and Confidential.
Lord Murray of Overstoun, Lord President of the Court of Session.
Copy to: 'The Moderator, General Assembly of the Church of Scotland.'

The DCC read aloud:

'This report is written to draw to your attention a sinister network of individuals who exist in Scotland today, exercising a malign influence over our country's moral standards, and bringing to bear pressures which have the effect of undermining the principles upon which our society is based.

'Every person listed in this document is, or in the case of the late Lord Barnfather, was, an undeclared, practising homosexual. The evidence against them is clear and is presented in photographic form.

'They include, sir, two of your own colleagues, Senators of the College of Justice, five members of the Scottish Administration, including two of Cabinet rank, three Shadow Ministers, three Queen's Counsel holding public office, two high-ranking police officers, four senior civil servants, including one in the Lord Advocate's Department, two senior clergymen of the Church of Scotland and six prominent and influential figures in the Scottish financial and business community.

'The majority of these people, nineteen to be exact, are

married or co-habiting with heterosexual partners.

'The fact that sexually deviant people hold prominent positions represents a danger in itself, given that they are all still in the closet, and are therefore potentially subject to blackmail. However there is a greater danger and it is real and present.

'All of these people are linked by membership of a range of professional bodies, clubs and societies; many of them are known to each other as homosexuals, and there is strong evidence of collusion between them to achieve further sexual liberalisation in Scotland. There are also instances where it is apparent that criminal proceedings against homosexuals have been compromised because influence has been exercised improperly.

'Sir, this document is addressed to you as the senior figure in the Establishment, standing aloof from politics and at the head of the Scottish Legal system. It is my earnest hope that you will use your influence to ensure that these people are driven from office. I am not afraid to make this report public; my evidence is strong enough to withstand any action for defamation. However, I do not wish to cause a national scandal and I rely on you to ensure that this menace is rooted out.'

Skinner looked up and closed the lap-top. 'Jesus Christ!' he murmured. 'Old Alec must have been right round the twist.' He opened the computer again, but it had put itself to sleep. 'What was the date on the first of those files?' he asked Rose.

'About five years ago; the file on Lord Barnfather. It was compiled just after his son died.'

'Ahh, the poor guy. It must have hurt him incredibly for him to react like that. But he was so secretive; he just couldn't have been able to talk to him about it.'

He pressed a key to re-activate the lap-top and handed it to Martin. 'Look at some of the names on that list . . . especially number five.'

'No need,' said the Head of CID. 'I recognised him from the photographs. Assistant Chief Constable James Elder. Who'd have bloody thought it?'

'Not me, that's for sure.'

'So where does it take us?'

'In theory, it gives us twenty-six people with a reason to kill Alec. But in practice . . . I doubt if it takes us anywhere. There is a link to the Diddler, I'll grant you, but it's pretty tenuous; his partner, Ronald Johnston-White, is on the list.

'No, it doesn't help my pet theory, Andy, not a bit. Lawrence Scotland is still the man in the frame for Alec's killing. The guy Heard is still prime suspect for Diddler's murder. As for the attack on me; there's a small army of people would like to have done that; probably one of them did.'

'Do you think the report was ever actually submitted to Lord Murray, sir?' asked McGuire.

'No,' said the DCC. 'I'm certain that it wasn't. If that had been put into David's hands, the first thing he'd have done would have been to call me.'

'You don't think he might have called Sir John Govan?' Martin looked at Skinner, a suggestion in his eyes.

'Are you hinting that the First Minister's security adviser might have had Alec bumped off? If you are, you can forget it; I know the man. On the other hand, David Murray doesn't; he'd have called me, for sure.'

'So what are we going to do about this, if it doesn't impact on the murder investigation? Shouldn't we interview the people on the list, at least, just to eliminate them?'

'What? Interview a judge, two Scottish Cabinet Ministers, Marcia Topham and Jim Elder? To tell them all that they've been persecuted by a madman. I don't think so. There isn't a single piece of information here, or a single photograph, that could be used as evidence of a serious crime.

'Let me show you what I'm going to do with this lot. Mags, did you say something about copy disks?'

'Yes sir,' Rose replied. 'There are two.' She took them from the strongbox and handed them over.

Skinner reclaimed the computer from Martin, slid the two disks into the floppy drive, one after the other, and erased them. Finally, he selected the 'John' folder and dragged it to the wastebasket in the bottom corner of the screen.

'You sure?' asked the Head of CID quietly. 'What if one of them did kill Alec?'

'What if?' he murmured. 'I can live with it.' He pulled down a Command from the Apple menu and emptied the wastebasket, destroying Alec Smith's report for ever.

'Leave those photographs with me, Maggie,' he said. 'We're having a barbecue tonight.'

Sixty-eight

'So, what did you find out about the Lewis girl?' Dan Pringle asked.

'She's been working at the zoo full-time since she finished her Highers a few weeks back,' said McGurk. 'She was a pupil at Watson's. I did a quiet check-up there; she and Heard's daughter, Sophie, are best pals apparently.'

'Where's the Heard girl just now?'

'She's crewing a schooner around the Western Isles for her Duke of Edinburgh's Gold award.'

The Superintendent raised an eyebrow. 'She's doing what?'

'Crewing, sir.'

'Ahh. For a minute I thought you said something else. So do you reckon her pal's crewing her old man while she's away?'

'It's a thought, but it's barely relevant, is it?'

'Naw. Not a bit. But you know what I think? I think that Heard's been giving her one and now she's threatening to tell the girl Sophie and Mrs Heard. The way you described it, that could have been hush money he was handing her.'

'Still,' McGurk ventured. 'Do you think we should interview her, just to confirm it?'

'We've interviewed her already, son. A week last Saturday,

after she spotted Shearer floating under the Belford Bridge. You were there, remember. She was still shaking like a leaf, terrified; poor lass got a hell of a fright. Andy Martin told me that after we were done he had to get the MO to give her a sedative.

'If Heard's been banging her, she's of age, so it's no crime. If she's been blackmailing him, that is, but there's been no complaint. If there is, we'll investigate; until then, we leave her alone.'

'Fair enough, Boss. So we keep up the tail on Heard, then?'

'Until further notice.'

'Do you think we could get a tap on his phone?'

'Not a fucking chance. You do it the hard way.'

McGurk scowled. 'Great.'

The Superintendent chuckled. 'It's a hard old life, son. I'll give you some more bad news. The technical boys reported back on Shearer's electronic organiser. It's useless; it's been in the water too long. They can't get a bloody thing off it.

'Right. You get off and team up with Wilding again, so you can both follow Heard after he leaves work. And just in case you think I'm doing fuck-all on this investigation, I'm off up to Harry's Bar, in Randolph Place.

'I had another chat with the Bryant girl; she told me that Mr Shearer used to look in there sometimes, if he'd been working late.'

Sixty-nine

Martin swung the MGF into his driveway, smiling as he saw the raised garage door and Karen's car inside. 'We'll need to do something about that,' he chuckled to himself. 'The F-reg Nova lives outdoors.'

As he eased himself out of the sports car, a voice – a soft, familiar voice – called out behind him. 'How are you, Andy?' He had hoped to avoid the moment, but he knew in his heart that it was better faced sooner than later.

'Hello, Rhian,' he answered. 'I'm fine. How are you?'

'Okay.' He was relieved when she smiled. 'I can't help but notice, though, that you're a hell of a fast worker.'

He looked down, grinning himself. 'No. You're wrong there; it took me far too long to work out how I felt about Karen. I'd been taking her for granted, behaving towards her like an absolute shit. I wasn't much of a gentleman with you either; I'm sorry for that.'

'Don't be.' Her smile widened. 'I chased you like the strumpet I am. I'm sorry too, for letting you down like I did with Paul Blacklock.'

'Ahh, don't worry about that; I was no angel either.'

She gave him a long, meaningful look. 'I don't mean about fucking him; I mean about spilling the state secrets. That was a

381

really stupid thing to do and it compromised you. Look, don't feel guilty about me or anything; it was just a fling for both of us. You concentrate on being happy; I haven't spoken to your lady yet, but she looks terrific.'

He sighed with a sort of relief, as she turned towards her front door. 'Thanks, Rhian,' he told her. 'Just don't go calling yourself a strumpet again; not around me at any rate. Hey, Juliet's not mad with me is she?'

'Only because you didn't give her a seeing-to,' the girl laughed. 'No. Mum's full of herself just now. She's making noises about going to live with Spike and leaving this place to us. I don't know if I fancy being chaperone to my kid sister, though.' Her voice dropped until it became a confidential whisper. 'Between you and me, I fear she prefers girls to boys. She has this pal, Sophie Heard: I walked into her room one day and caught them doing something very naughty to each other. Tongues and things . . .

'A few weeks back, Margot got very mopey. Eventually she told me that Sophie's father had found out about them too; now he's sent her away to sea, or something, and told Margot to keep away from her when she gets back.' Rhian gave a mock sigh. 'Blood will out, I suppose. She always was Daddy's little girl.'

'How is your father these days?' he asked, casually. 'Do you ever see him?'

'No,' she replied, a little wistfully. 'He's living happily ever after.' She waved goodbye and stepped inside.

Andy scratched his chin as he walked into the garage, closing the door behind him and entering the house through the internal, fire-resistant door. Karen was waiting for him at the top of the stairs, in the living-room doorway, smiling broadly. He dropped his briefcase, took her in his arms and kissed her.

'D'you still love me then?' he asked, as they came up for air.

'Too bloody right. Guess what? I've got a teaching job. It's only a short-term contract, covering maternity leave for a girl in a school up in Oxgangs, but it's a foot in the door at least. I start after the holidays.'

'Good for you. In that case we'd better get down to planning the wedding: it'll have to be mid-July if we're going to spend a month on honeymoon like we discussed. That shouldn't clash with Bob's plans. He's taking the family to Spain for the last week in June and the first half of July.'

He picked up his briefcase once more and tossed it into the living room, before going upstairs to change. 'Have you got more work in there?' Karen asked as he reappeared, in jeans and a white tee-shirt.

'The latest statements and officer reports in the Shearer case: they're my reading for tonight. I'll chuck it in an hour or two though. Maybe we can catch a movie somewhere.'

'Deal. You get started, I'll whip up something exciting for supper.'

He opened his briefcase and took out the Shearer folder, homing straight in on the summary of Dan Pringle's interviews with Janine Bryant and Andrew John, and Skinner's note of his telephone conversation with Mitchell Laidlaw in Hong Kong. 'Oh yes, Mr Heard, you're well in the frame,' he murmured.

His eyebrows rose in surprise as he read Jack McGurk's report of the fund manager's lunch-time excursion, and his meeting with Margot Lewis at the zoo. Superintendent Pringle had added a note, recording his theory that a sexual relationship had existed between Heard and his daughter's friend, and that he had been forced to buy her silence.

Martin smiled as he read. 'Close, Dan,' he muttered, 'but no cigar. If Heard was paying Margot off, he was probably protecting his daughter.'

He had almost finished his reading when Karen reappeared from the kitchen, carrying a tray with a bowl of cold melon-and-ginger soup, setting them on two occasional tables which she had placed in front of the sofa.

'Well?' she asked, as he put the folder back in his briefcase and turned his attention to their meal. 'Any sign of the big breakthrough today?'

'Not much. We got into Alec Smith's safe and found, as far as any of us could see, no more than the sad ravings of an obsessed, lonely man.'

'No link between the two murders, then?'

'Other than Bob's football connection, you mean? No, none that I could see. There are a hell of a lot of threads in this investigation, love, but none of them appear to be inter-connected. It still looks as if that bastard Scotland killed Alec. As for the Diddler, on the face of it his arch-enemy Luke Heard is the main candidate but there's no evidence against him, not a scrap.'

They ate in silence for a while; when the soup was finished, they took the bowls back through to the kitchen and returned with plates of pasta, with a creamy *forestiere* sauce.

'You're no closer to an arrest with Shearer, then?' Karen asked, as they neared the end of their meal.

'No. The only positive thing that's happened today came from a chat Dan Pringle had with a barmaid in Harry's. She told him that she saw the Diddler on the Tuesday before he was killed. He came in on his own, then got into conversation with a girl. Eventually they left together, she thought she heard Shearer say something about the Bar Roma.

'The staff there were pretty vague, but Dan made them check their credit-card slips and receipts. They came up with an answer; one minestrone, one pasta starter, two Calzones, two cappuccinos and a litre of house red.'

She grinned. 'Any garlic bread?'

'Not that Dan mentions.'

'He must have scored, then. Fresh breath in the clinches and all that.'

'Whether he did or not, we need to talk to that girl. But we have no description, and the barmaid is sure she hasn't been in Harry's before or since that night.'

He forked up the last of his linguine, then leaned back on the sofa. 'Okay, enough shop. You want to go out? Anything you fancy seeing?'

She slid closer and laid her head on his shoulder. 'There's a new Miles Grayson movie on at the Odeon . . .' She paused. 'But to be honest, in the dark I prefer you to him.'

He laughed. 'Since you put it that way . . .'

'Oh, I do. You go and open a nice bottle of wine and we'll just have a quiet night in, talking and looking at the paintings.'

'Okay.'

He went back to the kitchen and chose a chunky Thomas Hardy Shiraz from the wine-rack. When he returned, Karen was standing, brow furrowed, looking intently at one of the pictures. It was a vivid oil of North Berwick beach, looking back from the sea.

'How long have you had this?' she asked.

'It's one of the newer ones: done by a local artist. I bought it in the Westgate Gallery. There should be a date on it.'

She peered at the bottom corner. 'Two years old. So that will be Alec Smith's house, there, at a time when he was actually living in it.'

'I suppose so.'

'In that case,' she murmured, pointing at a small, predominantly red, image which, as his gaze followed the direction of her finger, seemed to spring out from the painting as never before. 'What the hell's that?'

Seventy

The young Sergeant's face was split by a yawn, when the phone rang in his pocket. He answered it almost eagerly; anything to break the boredom of the stake-out. One day, Dan Pringle might forgive him for whatever it was he had done.

'McGurk,' he answered.

'DCS Martin, Jack. Where are you right now?'

'Outside Luke Heard's house, sir.' Unconsciously, he pulled himself up in his seat. Ray Wilding, beside him as usual, noticed his reaction and snapped awake himself.

'What's happening there?'

'Not a lot, Boss. A girl arrived about half-an-hour ago and let herself in with a key. I'm pretty sure it's the daughter.'

'Home is the sailor . . .' Martin murmured. 'Okay, Sergeant, I want you to stay there. Don't let Heard out of your sight. I may very well want to talk to him later.'

'Sir, we're due to be relieved by a couple of uniforms in an hour. Mr Pringle okayed it.'

'Don't make me repeat myself, Jack.'

'No, sir.' McGurk rolled his eyes at Wilding as he put the phone back in his pocket. 'Sounds like the DCS has lost patience. Thank Christ for it; so have I.'

*

Martin cradled the telephone and looked at Karen; he crossed his fingers and held them up. 'Honey, have you done a wash since you moved in?'

'Only a coloured one,' she replied. 'I couldn't work out the programme for a white wash on the machine; I was going to ask you tomorrow morning.'

'You beauty.' He turned and bolted downstairs, heading for the laundry room beside the garage.

When he returned a minute or so later, he was holding in his left hand a large white bin-bag, stuffed full. Without a word, he picked up the telephone directory and flicked through it until he found a single unique entry – there was no-one else of that name in the Edinburgh area. He memorised the address.

'Listen, I've got to go out. There's something I have to do and someone I have to see. If I'm wrong, I'll look like a bloody idiot. If I'm right, I'll have lived up to all that bullshit of mine on Radio Forth. I tell you, my love, there is one thing a detective should never take lightly and that's a Bob Skinner hunch.'

She stared at him, smiling in astonishment. 'Andy, what the hell is this about?'

He beamed back at her. 'You know, maybe we should rethink your resignation from the force,' he said, 'because you're playing a hell of a good game tonight.

'Don't wait up for me. I could be pretty late.'

Seventy-one

'How the hell did you get in here?' Spike Thomson's face was a picture of surprise as he turned in response to the tap on his shoulder to see Andy Martin standing before him.

'I showed my warrant card,' the detective replied.

'Even so, the doormen here have instructions to call the management if the police turn up, not to just let them in.'

'Ahh, but I can be persuasive, Spike.'

'I'll bet you can,' Thomson grinned, raising his voice still louder over a sudden surge in the volume of the thumping music. 'It's just as well you're plain clothes, though. Otherwise people would die in the crush, trying to get out of here.'

Martin frowned as he looked around the big, smoky, former warehouse, which had been transformed into House 31, Edinburgh's trendiest underground night-club. 'Why?' he asked, his voice raised above the din. 'Is there a drug problem here that we should know about?'

'If there was,' the disc jockey replied, 'I wouldn't be here. No, this place is very respectable; properly licensed for entertainment and drinks, fire-safety inspected, and everything else. We have our own undercover drugs police on patrol all the time. Any dealer caught here is always handed over to you boys, so they don't risk it.

389

'No, it's just that these punters like to think they're doing something daring when they come to an unconventional place like this, so they're conditioned to run at the first sight of a uniform.'

The policeman grinned. 'The whole world used to operate like that; not any more though. The good people run, the bad ones stand their ground and dare us. Here,' he observed. 'I noticed a "we", back there.'

'I have an interest in the place.'

'How big an interest?'

Spike Thomson leaned towards him, speaking in as close to a whisper as he could manage. 'One hundred per cent. Don't tell anyone, though. The bright young things might not like it if they found out that the operation was actually owned by a middle-aged, middle-of-the-road AM presenter. "Ma granny listens tae Forth AM." That's what one kid said to me one night, with scorn all over her face. No, the presenters here are all FM jocks; some from Forth, the odd one from further afield, and quite a few just trying to impress me, in the hope I can get them into radio somewhere . . . anywhere.

'What brings you here anyway?' he asked. 'You never said when you called me on my mobile.'

'I'll tell you, if you can find a place where I won't be telling the whole fucking world.'

'Sure. Come on through here.' Thomson led the way from his place beside the dee-jay's booth, moving quickly through the ranks of twisting, jumping sweating dancers, with the detective at his heels, until they came to a small door marked 'Private'. He nodded to the security man standing guard and stepped inside.

The room was sparsely furnished: a desk, two chairs and a table, on which sat a row of monitors, each showing a different part of House 31, and each linked to a video below, on the floor.

An elderly man sat behind the desk, counting cash into piles. 'Give us a minute, Uncle Bob,' said Spike.

Martin looked after the old man as he closed the door. 'He really your uncle?'

'Sure; my mother's brother. He's my book-keeper. It's great, because I can trust him not just with the cash, but to supervise the ticket sellers and keep an eye on the bar, too. If anyone was at it, he'd know.'

The detective nodded towards the neat bundles of money on the desk. 'What's that?'

'Tonight's takings at the door.'

'Jesus.'

'No, I'm not; but when He comes back, He's promised me that He'll make a personal appearance. Now, what can I do for you?'

Martin sat on the edge of the desk and gazed at him, evenly. He glanced at his watch; it showed a quarter to one. 'I've had a busy few hours, Spike. I began by reading a report into the suicide of one Dafyd Ogston Lewis. Then I interviewed two men, Ronald Johnston-White, of whom you've probably heard,' he looked quickly at Thomson as he mentioned the name and saw that his guess had been correct, 'and Luke Heard, of whom you probably haven't, although you may have come across his daughter, Sophie.'

'In the nicest possible way, you mean?'

He took out a small tape recorder, checked the battery and recording levels, and set it down beside him on the desk top. 'I doubt that, chum; I really do.' He switched it on. 'Anyway, now there are a few things I have to ask you about . . . starting with that bloody parrot.'

Seventy-two

Gazing at her as she stood there, holding the door open, he wondered whether Juliet Lewis had ever, in all of her life, looked even slightly dishevelled. She returned his gaze calmly, as if it was the middle of the evening, rather than the early hours of the morning and as if she was dressed for a night on the town, rather than standing there in a pink, silk, dressing gown.

She smiled at him; she actually smiled. 'Andy,' she exclaimed, with a hint of a laugh in her voice. 'Did you forget your keys? Did you ring the wrong bell?'

He shook his head. 'No, Juliet, no,' he replied. 'Every bloody bell I've rung tonight has come up trumps. I'm in the right place. Are the girls home?'

'Yes, but they're asleep. I wasn't; I don't, not much anyway, when Spike's not here.' She looked at him again, a gleam in her eye. 'What is this, anyway? Are you having second thoughts about dumping Rhian?'

'No,' he answered, roughly. 'It's the first thought I regret; the fact that I got involved with her in the first place, and wound up setting up my best friend.'

She frowned, taking in a long breath. 'I see. I don't think I like the tone this conversation's taking.'

'We'd better carry it on indoors, then.' He stepped past her uninvited, closed the door, then took her arm and eased her upstairs, in front of him, to her living room.

She turned towards him, without a word. He had known that he was right before ringing the doorbell, but it was almost unnerving to see the truth confirmed in the sudden iciness of her stare.

He walked across to the stand by the window and whipped off the white covering sheet. 'Hello, Juliet,' he said.

'Hello, Juliet! Hello, Juliet!' the bird echoed back. He threw the drape back over the cage and turned back to face the woman.

'You were crazy enough to tell me,' he exclaimed. 'Right at the very start. "His name's Hererro." Remember, you said you thought it was some South American reference. You know bloody well that it means "Blacksmith" in Spanish; only that should be two words, shouldn't it? Black Smith; black-hearted Alec!

'Why did you take it, for God's sake? You couldn't have thought that it would blurt out your name to the first copper to come through the door. The bird's a great mimic, but it's got no fucking memory. For sure, it would have made a lousy witness in a murder case.

'I know that you took the cage down from its hook to string Alec up there, but why did you take it with you afterwards?'

'To remind me of him!' Her sudden hiss chilled him even more than her eyes. 'I look at Hererro and I think of him, hanging up there. That beast tortured my husband to death; you cannot imagine how good it felt to do the same to him.'

He had known, of course. He had thought that he might have had difficulty making her confirm the truth, but she seemed eager to tell of it, to boast of it, even.

'Your husband topped himself, Juliet. In his garage, with a hose-pipe into the car.' He took a note from his pocket, and read:

> 'My darling
> 'I can't go on, living as I have done. I have deceived you. I have fallen in love with someone else; a very dear man with whom I have had a relationship for some months now. I can't keep this secret any longer, nor can I live with it.
> Tell the girls, I loved you all. Goodbye.
> Dafyd

'That was in the police file into your husband's suicide. It was an open-and-shut job; the Fiscal closed the case without a Fatal Accident Inquiry. And that note; that was all you knew at the time, wasn't it?'

She shook her head, violently, looking away from him. 'No. I knew about Dafyd's affair all along. I realised not long after I married him that he had this thing in him, and I feared that one day it would have to express itself. But that didn't stop me from loving him with all my heart. He was my whole life and, for most of the time, the girls and I were his. He would never have left us, and if he and Ronald hadn't been betrayed, I would have gone on turning a blind eye.'

'How did you know?'

'There were signs. He made love to me in different ways for one thing. There were vague trips to weekend conferences. Also, if your husband never wears aftershave but comes in smelling of someone else's, you tend to notice, and wonder.'

'Did you know who the man was?'

'Not at that time, no. I didn't want to know, for I bore him no malice, none at all; nor do I now. He was helping Dafyd be himself, and it didn't make him any less loving towards me; at least that's how I've always seen it.'

'But when Spike told you the whole truth, that made it all different, didn't it?'

'Oh yes,' she hissed once more. 'When he told me about that vicious, cruel, twisted man, and that miserable little weasel, Shearer, who betrayed Dafyd and Ronald . . . that made it very different.

'They killed him, between them; they put him through such mental torture. It was as if they had strapped him into that car and turned on the engine.' She paused. 'Does Spike know what I did?'

Martin made a slight, dismissive gesture. 'No. He never suspected a thing. Even now, I don't think he understands. But he did admit to me that he had told you what Howard Shearer – the Diddler, they called him – confessed to him, one night, with an extremely guilty conscience.

'He told me, as he had told you, that the Diddler was an inveterate gossip; he knew it, but couldn't help himself.

'That one Thursday night after a football gathering, he told Alec Smith that his partner, Ronald Johnston-White, was gay and was having an affair with a gynaecologist called Dafyd Lewis.

'That later, he learned from Johnston-White that Smith had a pathological hatred of homosexuals. That he had approached your husband and told him that he was not going to tolerate a – his words – queer gynaecologist, and that if he did not resign his hospital position and leave Edinburgh, some very nasty career-ending stories about him and Johnston-White and you, would appear in the tabloids.'

The policeman looked almost despairingly, into the woman's

iron-hard face. 'Diddler was totally conscience-stricken, you know, when he learned of the consequences of that single indiscreet remark to Smith. He had to confide in someone. He chose, from the Thursday night crowd, his oldest and closest friend, Spike Thomson.

'And four years on, Spike, poor bugger that he is, met you. When he realised who you were, he felt that he had to tell you the whole story.'

She nodded. 'Very good. Is that as far as you've got?'

He laughed, bitterly. 'Hell no; though I wish it was. No, Juliet, I've got all of it . . . although this next part is guesswork. I think you knew Alec Smith. Remember, you told me that you'd been out in the field, through your job? I think, that like all crazies, you dropped me a little hint there. Not as outrageous as the one with the parrot, but a hint nonetheless. I think that you met him then and that, when you needed to, you were able to find out where he had gone, after he left the force to pursue his own lunacy.

'Alec's phone records show that he had a call on the evening he died, from a public phone-box in Edinburgh. I think that call came from you, and that you made an appointment to see him on some pretext or other; job-related research, maybe.

'I think he let you in. Maybe he even did say, "Hello, Juliet". Maybe old Hererro there did mimic him. Maybe he turned to put the blue velvet drape – the one that we found left in the room – over his cage, and maybe that was when you shot him in the back with the tranquilliser gun which your kid had borrowed from the zoo.

'How much of that have I got right? he asked, conversationally.

'All of it,' she whispered, her eyes fixed on him. 'Clever boy.'

'I sure am, just a bit slow, that's all. Anyway, after that, the carnage began. You stripped him, tied him, taped over his gob, then strung him up like a beast for slaughter, all while he was still helpless from the shot. Then you went downstairs, selected a wrench from the cellar and one of Alec's two blowlamps – I don't understand why he bought two from B&Q on the same day, but he did – plus a knife from the kitchen, as your instruments of torture, and went to work.

'As a touch of flair, to show everyone how clever you were, you found his video camera and left us a horror movie of yourself at work.'

'Yes,' Juliet Lewis murmured. 'I only wish I'd been able to play it back.'

It made Martin shudder, just to look at her. 'You know,' he continued, 'I might have put you down as a poor sad woman who had been driven mad by what was done to her husband, but for one thing – the fact that you chose to involve Margot. I have to believe you knew she was going to kill the Diddler.' She frowned, a little surprised. 'I know it was her. I took a sample of Rhian's pubic hair from my laundry and had a comparison done with a hair we found on Shearer's body. It showed a close resemblance, a family resemblance.

'Yes, Juliet, involving the kid makes you a real nutter in my book.'

She seemed to flare at him. 'I did not involve her. Margot insisted; when I told her what Spike had told me, and that I planned to take revenge for her father. She insisted; I couldn't have stopped her if I'd tried. The tranquilliser gun was her idea. The plan for killing Shearer was hers. I didn't know she actually had sex with him, though.'

'Did you know what she did to Luke Heard?'

She looked at him, genuinely surprised. 'Who?'

'Sophie's father; her lover's father; he told me the story tonight. Luke found out about them, and tried to split them up. He was in way over his head, though. Margot knew from Sophie that Howard Shearer was Heard's Private Enemy Number One. She fed him an idea; she would pick up Shearer in his after-hours pub, lure him into a honey-trap, tie him up and take compromising pictures of the two of them together. He went for it; even agreed to pay her. So Margot did all that; only as you, and she if you say so, had planned, instead of taking bed-time snap-shots she cut some bits off him with the rose pruners, sliced him a bit more, then battered him to a jelly with his son's baseball bat.'

He laughed bitterly. 'Bloody obvious now. When Margot saw the body under the Belford Bridge. She didn't scream out of shock, but out of fright. She thought that it would have been long gone out to sea by then.' Her reaction told him that he had hit the mark again.

'You know, Heard shit himself when he came back from KL,' he continued, 'and found that Shearer was dead, not all over the *Sun* as he thought he would have been. He met Margot; we tailed him. She told him that from now on it would be business as usual for her and Sophie . . . or else . . . having already called the girl on her mobile and told her to jump her ship and come home.'

He nodded. 'Yeah. If you tell me that Margot insisted on being involved, I don't have any trouble believing you.' Then he paused.

'But as for Rhian . . . that really hurts. Why did she try to kill Bob Skinner? Did she insist too?'

Juliet's voice was almost a snarl. 'No. We did; Margot and I.

We told her that she had to play her part. We told her we'd kill you if she didn't.'

'It might not have been that easy,' he murmured. 'But why, for God's sake? Why kill Bob?'

The eyes flared again, wildly. 'Because he had to be the one behind it. Smith reported to him; he must have known. He must have given the go-ahead.'

'Ahh. You are so wrong, woman,' Martin shouted at her. 'Bob had no idea of what Smith was up to. Alec was as crazy as you. He was on a one-man crusade to avenge his son's death from AIDS. That's why he did what he did. If the Big Man had known about it, he'd have had him sectioned; put away in a Laughing Academy somewhere.

'Alec was so worried about Bob finding out that he made up a story about a knee injury, so he didn't have to face him at their Thursday night football get-together. Then, he was so intent on his campaign, he left the force, to pursue it full-time.

'Bob was completely in the dark about him.'

She gazed at him and decided to believe him. 'You say? Well, no matter, Rhian didn't kill him.'

'It isn't no matter to him, I promise you. It won't be no matter to Spike either, when he learns that she used his car. He told me that she drove him to the studio on Sunday, then picked him up afterwards.

'You've used that poor innocent guy, haven't you?'

'Only out of necessity; I really am very fond of him, you know. As was Rhian, of you.'

She sighed, with a hint of sadness. 'So, clever Andy. What happens now?'

Martin was about to tell her, when he heard a sound from behind. He turned and saw Margot, wild-eyed, a big kitchen knife clasped in both hands, running at him across the room. Adroitly, he avoided her lunge, and hit her a big, back-handed blow on the side of the head, sending her sprawling on the floor.

'Don't even think about getting up, girl,' he warned her. 'Don't even think about it.'

He looked back at Juliet. 'We'll pick you up in the morning,' he told her, 'when we're ready for you. Don't try to do a runner. You're all effectively under arrest now; the place is under surveillance, front and back.

'Margot's done; that's for sure. So's Rhian; we will find damage and fibres on Spike's car. You may doubt that, but our man Arthur Dorward will, if I know him.

'As for you? Yes, I think I have a strong enough circumstantial case against you. As for me? I'm going to grab a few hours well-earned rest. You have the same few hours to do some thinking . . . and packing. We'll be here for you early.'

He turned, trotted downstairs, and hurried back into his own house, to Karen. Back to sanity.

Seventy-three

It was just after three a.m. when he slipped silently into the moonlit bedroom. The window was open slightly and a draught of air was wafting the curtain gently, in and out, in and out, yet the room was still oppressively warm. Karen was sleeping on her back; she was naked, half-covered by a single sheet, having thrown or kicked the duvet to the floor.

As he undressed, he smiled at her, at the woman who had saved his life, and who had enriched it since with her unconditional love, bringing him a kind of tranquillity which he had never imagined before, yet for which, he knew now, he had been searching through all of his adult days.

He slipped under the sheet beside her, trying not to touch her, not to waken her. He felt a desperate need to look at her in the night light, to savour the statuesque lines of her body, to imprint the perfection of her profile in his mind for ever. And he needed something else too; he needed her once more as a shield, to force away the horrors of the last few hours, as long shots and far-out suppositions had turned into terrible, chilling certainty, as he had finally seized the separate strands of the multiple investigations and woven them into the blackest cloak of truth.

From somewhere in the sleeping Village outside came a muffled sound, as a car engine barked into life, then settled into a steady ticking-over throb. But nothing could have broken into his reverie as he lay there, imagining the life that he and Mrs Karen Martin would have together.

'Well?' she whispered softly. She had not moved, and he wondered for how long she had been awake. 'Do you look like a right bloody idiot?' She turned her face towards him on the pillow, smiling, gently. 'Or did you live up to the bullshit you fed Spike Thomson?'

She saw his grin, and through it to the trauma which lay behind it. 'Andy. . .' she said, sitting up, anxious now.

'Yeah,' he said, slowly, laying a hand on her thigh, his eyes softening, beginning to lose their haunted look. 'We are the true forensic scientist, you and I . . . We are, together at least, the great detective . . . We have, when we need it most, the magic ingredient . . .'

'You got a result, then?'

'Oh yes, I know who slaughtered Alec Smith, and I know who diddled the Diddler, and I know who tried to kill Bob . . . and I know why.'

She was wide awake now, intent. 'Well? Who?' she demanded.

His smile widened further. His eyes shone in the dark. 'The answer's downstairs,' he told her. 'In my briefcase, in our living room.

'Go on,' he challenged her, mischievously. 'Work it out for yourself.'

Epilogue

They were found next morning. Mother and daughters, in the back seat of the Vauxhall, in the garage, holding hands, their faces suffused and pink from the carbon monoxide asphyxia.

There was no note, or at least . . .

Dean Village Tragedy

by Paul Blacklock
Evening News City Reporter

'There was no note found,' reported Detective Chief Superintendent Andy Martin, the tragic trio's next-door neighbour, who raised the alarm and was first into the neat, terraced house, nestling beside the gentle Water of Leith.

Mr Martin refused to speculate on what might have prompted the Lewis family's triple suicide. 'They were very good friends,' he commented at the scene, deeply affected by his discovery.

'I know that Juliet never really got over the death of her husband,' said Forth AM presenter, Spike Thomson, a close friend of Mrs Lewis. 'I am devastated.'

There was no note.

Skinner's Rules

Quintin Jardine

As head of Edinburgh's CID, Detective Chief Superintendent Bob Skinner has seen it all. But the discovery of the savagely mutilated corpse of a young lawyer in a dark alleyway shocks the DCS and his team to the core. And when the lawyer's fiancée is found dead, Skinner realises he has a cold-blooded killer on his hands.

As he delves deeper, he begins to uncover a deep-rooted and intricate conspiracy at the heart of the city. Now, whatever the danger to himself, Skinner is determined that in Edinburgh, at least, folk will abide by his rules.

Praise for Quintin Jardine's novels:

'A triumph. I am first in the queue for the next one' *Scotland on Sunday*

'Perfect plotting and convincing characterisation' *The Times*

'Remarkably assured . . . a tour de force' *New York Times*

978 0 7553 5770 3

headline

Fatal Last Words

Quintin Jardine

It's August and the Edinburgh International Book Festival is in full swing. So it's a considerable embarrassment when one of Scotland's most successful crime writers is found dead in the author tent. Natural causes? Misfortune? Suicide? Or . . . ?

The victim's phone was tapped. Are the spooks involved? Or has mystery fiction become true crime? A second victim raises the question: have the authors become targets themselves?

The formidable DCC Bob Skinner doesn't need this new chapter in his life. He is going to have to dig deep to solve these crimes, even as his own world implodes and a famous friendship is shattered for ever . . .

Praise for Quintin Jardine's novels:

'Very engaging as well as ingenious, and the unravelling of the mystery is excellently done . . . Very enjoyable. *Fatal Last Words* will accompany many on their holidays and quite right too' Allan Massie, *Scotsman*

'Well constructed, fast paced, Jardine's narrative has many an ingenious twist and turn' *Observer*

978 0 7553 4885 5

headline

Inhuman Remains

Quintin Jardine

INTRODUCING SLEUTH PRIMAVERA BLACKSTONE
IN HER COMPELLING NEW SERIES

Her mind filled with thoughts of her dead ex-husband
Oz, Primavera Blackstone is settled in Spain with their
son Tom, when their peace is shattered by the arrival of
her formidable aunt.

All is not well in Auntie Adrienne's world; her roguish
son Frank is involved with a shady project, and is
missing. Prim flies to Seville to track him down, only to
find herself a fugitive, her life under threat, as her aunt
joins the missing persons list.

Pursued across Spain, struggling to keep herself alive,
yet determined to free Adrienne, Prim is at the centre of
a maelstrom of mystery, until the final startling solution
springs from the unlikeliest of sources.

The Blackstone legacy is in good hands, but will they,
and it, survive . . . ?

Praise for Quintin Jardine's novels:

'A triumph. I am first in the queue for the next one'
Scotland on Sunday

'Well constructed, fast-paced, Jardine's narrative has
many an ingenious twist and turn' *Observer*

978 0 7553 4899 2

headline